STILTSVILLE

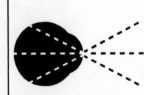

This Large Print Book carries the
Seal of Approval of N.A.V.H.

STILTSVILLE

SUSANNA DANIEL

WHEELER PUBLISHING
A part of Gale, Cengage Learning

Detroit • New York • San Francisco • New Haven, Conn • Waterville, Maine • London

GALE
CENGAGE Learning

Copyright © 2010 by Susanna Daniel.
Wheeler Publishing, a part of Gale, Cengage Learning.

ALL RIGHTS RESERVED
Wheeler Publishing Large Print Hardcover.
The text of this Large Print edition is unabridged.
Other aspects of the book may vary from the original edition.
Set in 16 pt. Plantin.

LIBRARY OF CONGRESS CATALOGING-IN-PUBLICATION DATA

Daniel, Susanna.
  Stiltsville / by Susanna Daniel.
    p. cm.
  ISBN-13: 978-1-4104-3384-8
  ISBN-10: 1-4104-3384-6
  1. Marriage—Fiction. 2. Families—Fiction. 3. Miami
(Fla.)—Fiction. 4. Large type books. I. Title.
PS3604.A5258S75 2011
813'.6—dc22   2010039792

Published in 2011 by arrangement with HarperCollins Publishers.

Printed in the United States of America
1 2 3 4 5 6 7 15 14 13 12 11

*for my mother
and for my father*

1969

On a Sunday morning in late July, at the end of my first-ever visit to Miami, I took a cab from my hotel to Snapper Creek marina to join a woman named Marse Heiger, whom I'd met the day before. When I stepped out of the cab, I saw Marse standing in the well of her little fishing boat, wearing denim knee shorts and a yellow sleeveless blouse, her stiff brown hair pinned under a bandanna. She waved and gestured for me to climb into the boat. She poured me a mug of coffee from an aluminum thermos and started the engine. "Ready?" she said.

We puttered out of the marina, under a bridge from which two black boys were fishing with what looked like homemade poles, down a winding canal flanked by mangroves. The knobby, twining roots rose from the water. I sat on a cushioned bench and Marse sat in a captain's chair at the helm.

She handed me a scarf and told me to tie back my hair, which I did. We passed an egret standing stock-still on a mangrove root, then emerged from the canal into the wide, open bay. The Miami shoreline stretched out in both directions. Marse picked up speed, and each time we came down on a wave, I gripped the corner of my bench.

I'd grown up in Decatur, Georgia, just outside Atlanta, and had been to the ocean only once, when I was eleven years old. My parents and I had spent a weekend on Saint Simons island, in a one-bedroom rental cottage three blocks from the beach. That weekend, I'd seen a dark fin from shore, but my father had said it was probably just a dolphin. And though I'd spent a few afternoons on lake pontoons with friends during college, never had I been out on the open water. From halfway across the bay I could see the low silhouette of downtown Miami, where Freedom Tower spiked above the blocky buildings. The bridge connecting the city to Key Biscayne looked like a stroke of watercolor. Above the wind and whine of the engine, Marse named Miami's parts for me, pointing: farthest southwest were the Everglades, then the twin nuclear reactors at Turkey Point — just built but not yet in operation — then Coral Gables and Coconut Grove, then downtown. To the east, the Cape Florida lighthouse squatted at the tip of Key Biscayne, signaling the edge of a continent.

We landed hard on each wave and the spray hit my face. Marse's boat — an eleven-foot Boston Whaler with a single outboard engine — was, in my estimation, little more than a dinghy. When we'd traveled fifteen minutes across the bay, Marse pointed ahead, away from shore. There was nothing there but sea and sky, but then a few matchbox shapes formed on the hazy horizon. They grew larger and I saw that they were houses, propped above the water on pilings. I counted fourteen of them. As we neared, I saw that some were painted, some were two stories high, some had boats moored at the docks, and some were shuttered and still. They stood on cement pillars, flanking a dark channel along the rim of the bay, as if guarding it from the open ocean. Marse slowed the boat as we entered the channel, and when we came to a red-painted house with white shutters, she shifted into neutral. A larger boat was tied to the dock, but there was no one around to greet us. Marse cut the engine and the world stilled. "Where are they?" she said. A

9

plastic owl perched atop a dock piling. An open bag of potato chips sat in a rocking chair on the upstairs porch.

"Guys?" called Marse. She stepped to the house's dock with the stern line. I took her cue and stepped up with the bowline. I imitated Marse's knot, a figure eight with an inward loop, and after the boat was secured, I heard shouting in the distance. I turned. Two men stood on the dock of a stilt house eighty yards east; they waved at us. One was dark-haired and held a duffel bag, and the other was fair-haired and wore bright orange swimming trunks. Marse waved back, and because the waving went on for several seconds, I raised my arm as well. As I did, the fair-haired boy dove off the dock into the water, then started to swim.

I'd taken the train from Atlanta two days earlier to attend the wedding of a college girlfriend. I'd met Marse at the reception, and we'd spent an hour chatting about Atlanta and Miami, and about the brides-maids' dresses and the best man's toast. Her given name was Marilyn, but Marse — rhymes with *arse,* as she put it — was a family nickname. From what little I knew of the city, I concluded that Marse was a true native daughter: she was darkly tan, with

10

premature lines around her eyes, and she dressed in a confident, sexy way that anywhere else would have seemed showy, but in Miami was unexceptional, even practical. She'd grown up in Coral Gables, in a Spanish-style bungalow with a wraparound porch and no air-conditioning, and had never considered moving out of South Florida. When she'd invited me to spend the day with her at a place called Stiltsville, I'd accepted readily. So that Sunday morning, I'd dressed in a pair of Bermuda shorts and my most becoming top — still plain compared with Marse's blouse — and called a taxi.

While we waited in rocking chairs on the upstairs porch for the boys to arrive, Marse filled me in. The dark-haired boy was Kyle, her older brother, and the fair-headed one was Dennis DuVal, whose parents owned the stilt house where we were sitting. Kyle and Dennis were in their last year of law school at the University of Miami; Marse was a year behind them. "You'll like Kyle," Marse said. "Girls tend to."

"And Dennis?"

"Dennis is mine. That's the plan, anyway."

She wore dark sunglasses and she'd pulled off her top to reveal two triangles of purple bikini. Her stomach was flat and tan, with

11

taut creases across the navel. The boys were yards from the dock, arms and legs lashing, sending up brief white wakes. "Does Kyle know I'm coming?" I said.

She nodded. "Don't worry, there's no pressure. You'll be gone tomorrow, anyway."

It was true: my train back to Atlanta left the following afternoon. In the time since I'd graduated from college, I'd dated a few colleagues from the bank where I worked as a teller. I was twenty-six years old, and though I'd come close, I'd never been in love. "What's your plan with Dennis?" I said.

She took lip balm from her pocket and applied it, then handed it to me. "There's this fund-raiser every year at Vizcaya," she said. She didn't explain what Vizcaya was but I already knew — it was a Renaissance-style villa on the bay in Coconut Grove, surrounded by elaborate formal gardens, open for tours and events. I'd visited Vizcaya the day before the wedding, sightseeing. I'd walked alone through the overdressed rooms, then stood on the limestone terrace and watched sailboats cross the bay. "Everyone dresses up and picnics on their good china and drinks champagne."

"You're going to ask him?" I said.

"I'm hoping he'll ask me."

"What if he doesn't?"

She frowned. "You're no fun." She stood and lifted one bare foot onto the porch railing, then folded over to touch nose to ankle. I was tall but Marse was taller, and her limbs were sleek and muscular. "Besides, that's why it's so great that you're here. You'll be my impartial third party. Just watch him, see how he acts."

"I'll do my best."

The boys reached the dock in a flurry of splashing and pulled themselves onto the transom of the big boat. The fair one — Dennis — took a towel from the console and dried his hair, and the other one — Kyle — hauled up a small duffel bag he'd strapped over one arm, then reached into a cooler and opened a can of beer. They resembled, in their unselfconscious mannerisms and the energetic timbre of their voices, overgrown children. Dennis called up, "Welcome!"

"Did you bring the burgers?" called Kyle.

Marse ignored him and smoothed her hair with both hands. "OK?" she said to me.

She wore no makeup and her hair was long, her body lean and tan. "You look great," I said, because she did. We went downstairs side by side. The boys stepped onto the dock and Marse greeted Dennis

13

with a quick embrace. His eyes were blue, his face was pink from exercise, and he'd grown a dusting of red beard since his last shave. He smiled at me. "Who are you?" he said.

"Frances Ellerby," I said. I shook Dennis's hand, then Kyle's. Of the two of them, Kyle was the looker. His eyebrows were thick and dark, his nose was sharp, and his teeth were white. He had a wide, confident smile and ropy muscles. Dennis's nose was crooked (from a boxing injury in college, I would learn), and his teeth were uneven (he'd resisted braces), and his legs were pale and skinny. "I hope Marse told you about our mission," Dennis said to me. His hair, drying in the sun, stuck up at odd angles. It was more red than blond, and it needed a cut. Freckles spotted his shoulders and earlobes. "Just because this is your first time," he said, "don't think we don't expect you to contribute."

"Damn straight," said Kyle. He opened the duffel bag he'd brought from the other stilt house, pulled out a machete, and removed its sheath; it glinted in the sunlight. They had swum to the other house, which Marse told me belonged to a family named the Becks, to borrow the weapon and also to prove which boy was the faster swimmer.

14

Kyle had won.

"What's the mission?" I said.

"I don't want anything to do with it," said Marse.

"She disapproves," said Kyle to me. He brandished the machete in the air, then brought it down over an invisible kill. "Take that," he said, "and that."

Dennis took the machete and set it down on the flat top of a piling. "Let's eat."

The boys cooked burgers on the grill on the upstairs porch while Marse and I fixed potato salad in the kitchen. "What do you think?" said Marse. We could see Kyle and Dennis through the kitchen window. They stood with spatulas in hand, swatting at mosquitoes.

"Of which one?"

She reached over and pinched my elbow. It was an intimate gesture, a gesture fitting old friends. It was Marse's style, I gathered, to rush into intimacy. I was flattered. "Come on," she said.

"He's cute," I said, and she frowned at me. "I can't tell yet. I need more to go on."

Marse put down the knife she was using to dice the potatoes. In her expression, I recognized a cautious optimism I'd felt many times. "I know he's not interested right now," she said. "But I don't see why he couldn't get interested."

She was pretty and strong. There was something dynamic about her, something vital. "I don't see why not," I said.

There was, explained Dennis and Kyle over lunch, an electric eel living in a submerged toilet bowl under the stilt house dock. "It's the meanest-looking creature you've ever seen," said Kyle, chewing his hamburger.

Dennis nodded. "It looks like a very old man. It looks like something that would yell at a kid for cutting through the yard."

I laughed. Marse crushed a peanut shell between her fingers and handed the nut to Dennis. "It's probably been there for years," she said.

"My father sank that bowl a year ago," he said, "and I've swum by it a hundred times without that thing poking out at me."

"Why did your father sink a toilet bowl?" I said.

"For the fish," said Dennis.

"But —" Marse started.

"Real fish," said Dennis. "Playful fish. And coral and plants and such. We replaced the downstairs toilet, and we wanted to see what would grow there."

"You have your answer," said Marse.

"It could hurt someone," said Kyle. "Shit,

16

it flashed its fangs at me, and I'm big. What about a kid? That thing could grab hold of a little arm."

"Ridiculous," said Marse. She handed me a peanut, then winked without letting the boys see. I admired the way she baited them.

Dennis stood up. There were crumbs on his lips. "I think it's time," he said, "for the skeptics to see for themselves."

Marse clapped. We followed Dennis downstairs, then lay on our stomachs on the dock, watching the rim of the toilet bowl skip beneath the water's surface. The water was the near-cloudy green of jade dishware, shrouding the seafloor. Marse jumped up and snatched the machete from the piling. "Dennis, you are not going to kill that animal."

Dennis faced her, smiling slyly, and I saw that he'd never intended, truly, to kill the eel. "We'll catch it," he said. "We'll give it a new home."

"Where?" said Marse.

"I thought we were going to kill it," said Kyle.

"We'll take it to Soldier's Key," said Dennis. "We'll find it a cozy little cave in the reef."

"We'll all be electrocuted," said Kyle.

Marse put down the machete and Kyle

17

reached for it. She snatched it up again. "No," she said, pointing a finger at him.

There were two nets on the premises — a flat one with holes the size of playing cards, which wouldn't hold the eel, and a round one attached to a pole, which was too small. Dennis decided to swim back to the Becks' house, where a cabin cruiser was docked, to return the machete and borrow a different net. He took off his shirt and shaded his eyes, searching the channel. It was empty. The only boats nearby were fastened to docks, rocking on their lines. It was early afternoon, the sun directly overhead. Westward down the channel, people stood in tight clusters on the dock of another house. Party noises — music, laughter — reached us in muted chirps. The whole world — the houses, the blue water, the still shoreline in the distance — swam in thick white light.

Dennis dove into the channel, sending up a stream of white bubbles. Kyle tossed him the duffel bag with the machete inside. We watched until he arrived at the neighboring house. He climbed up the transom of the cruiser, then stepped onto the dock. "I don't understand," said Kyle to Marse. "You used to rip the arms off your dolls."

"That's different," said Marse. She slipped out of her shorts and spread a towel. I took her cue and removed my shirt, revealing the top half of a navy one-piece. It was the only swimsuit I owned. Kyle went to the big boat and returned with sweaty cans of beer. I took a long swallow of mine, then unzipped my shorts and wiggled out of them, frowning at my pale legs. Wasted on the young: I didn't know how pretty I was, with my smooth skin and strong limbs. I had the habit of slumping to appear smaller and more feminine. Yet I admired the way women like Marse — she was almost as tall as Dennis, nearly six feet — seemed to relish their height. I lay down and put a palm on my stomach. The fabric was warm from the sunlight. "Here he comes," said Marse.

I sat up. Dennis, returning from the other house, carried a wad of netting above his head as he swam. He struggled to keep the net in one hand while taking clumsy strokes with the other. Every few strokes, a corner of the net dangled and he stopped to gather it up again. "Jesus," said Marse.

Kyle, who'd been lying with his face over the water, splashing at the eel, moved to stand beside us. His shadow darkened our towels. I scanned the channel, empty of boats. We were quiet. We were, I assumed, all imagining the same scenario: if the net came loose and Dennis found himself under it — what then? Could he keep his head above water without thrashing around? He could lie on his back, maybe, and breathe through a square in the net, and Kyle could swim out or Marse could take her boat.

Dennis inched closer. I kept glancing at the mouth of the channel, certain that a speedboat would come screaming down it, spreading white wake. Dennis's s stroke was sloppy. I didn't know him well enough to decide if he would have considered the danger of swimming with a net. Why didn't he drag the net behind him, or put it in the duffel bag? Maybe, I thought, he was one of the careless but lucky, as so many people are.

Kyle bounced on the balls of his feet, as if preparing to dive in. From where she was sitting beside him, Marse put a hand on his leg. "Don't," she said.

A corner of the net dropped behind Dennis's head; he kept swimming, oblivious. I took a breath and Marse looked at me. Kyle called out to Dennis and Dennis stopped swimming. Kyle gestured. "Pick it up," he shouted, and Dennis gathered up the net again, then resumed swimming. I could see the light lines of his legs through the water, the white bottoms of his feet. He reached the dock and tossed the net onto the wood.

20

Kyle kicked it aside and braced himself against a piling, then reached down to help Dennis climb out. I sat down beside Dennis on the dock. Kyle handed him a beer and he drank from it. My toes dipped below the waterline and, remembering the eel, I drew them up. "That was kind of dangerous," I said.

Dennis looked at me. Then he looked at the net, heaped in a puddle on the wood, and up the channel toward the Becks' stilt house. I saw the notion — the net dropping, his body flailing — enter his mind, but he shook his head. "I made it," he said. It wasn't bravado or machismo. He *was* one of those people, the careless but lucky. He always would be. "Do you want to see it?"

"The eel?" He nodded. Beside us, Marse's little boat rocked on the waves, its lines tautening and slackening. "Yes," I said.

Dennis jumped up and stepped onto the big boat — this was his father's boat, a twenty-one-foot Chris Craft Cavalier with a lapstrake hull — then returned with fins and masks and snorkels. "Marse?" he said, holding out the gear.

She sat up on her elbows and propped her sunglasses on her head. Dennis's eyes slid over her long body. She shook her head. "Fish freak me out."

Dennis handed me the mask and snorkel. "Try these," he said. I pulled the mask over my dry hair, and Dennis came forward to adjust the fit. I watched him through the binocular lenses, and when he was finished, he tugged it off. "All set," he said. "Get wet before you put it on." He laid his hands on my shoulders for a brief moment, then withdrew them. I looked down at the water, at the flash of porcelain beneath the surface. I curled my toes over the lip of the dock, then pushed off.

The water felt like soft warm fabric. Dennis crouched and I swam until I was underneath him, several feet from the toilet bowl. He handed me the mask and snorkel and I pulled them on and tested the suction. Water beaded on the lenses and slid off. I fitted the snorkel to my mouth and blew out, then let it dangle from its loop in the mask. Dennis slid onto his stomach, his face over the water. His shoulders, spotted with watery freckles, flexed as he gestured below. "It's pretty harmless, don't be afraid," he said. "Don't get too close, though, and don't — *do not* — put your hand inside the bowl."

I swallowed a mouthful of seawater and coughed. "Why would I put my hand inside the bowl?"

"Just swim on by, like you're minding your own business." There was the question of the eel's intelligence. I watched the bowl through the water, keeping my arms and legs clear. I would learn, months later, that electric eels can discharge as much as six hundred volts of electricity — enough to kill a horse. "Do you want me to get in?" said Dennis.

"Stay there," I said. I backed away from the dock, kicking, then turned and dove. Under the dock, the world was dim and calm. My body swayed with the current. I could see, but I couldn't see far. I did not know, then, that there was a difference between the tidal current that tugged at my legs and the surface current, wind-driven, that lifted my hair from my neck and dropped it again. The sandy seafloor sloped toward the house, textured with a thousand vulnerable peaks, the way dunes texture a beach. By nighttime the seafloor would be wholly re-arranged, each peak erased and re-formed in mirror image.

A school of needlefish, bright as new nickels, flashed by. I'd traveled several yards from the dock. Dennis stared down at me, his arms across his chest. I dove deep enough to fill my snorkel with water and kicked toward the toilet bowl. By the time it entered my range of vision, I could have reached out and touched it, and the eel did not uncoil or snap or even blink — it just nosed its bald head beyond the rim of its home, and watched as I kicked by.

I knifed one knee between my body and the dock, and levered myself up. "Well?" said Dennis.

"I saw it," I said, breathing hard.

From his towel, Kyle raised his head. "Dangerous son of a bitch," he said.

"I think you should leave it alone," I said.

Dennis seemed pleased. He nodded and handed me a towel. "From now on, no more swimming near the toilet bowl."

"Amen," said Marse.

In July in South Florida, the sunlight fusses and adjusts a hundred times over the course of the day. By mid-afternoon, hours from sunset, the blue of the sky was rich and dense, as if a dusting of powder had been wiped from its surface. Marse and I chatted on the porch for a while, but the conversation grew sluggish and she started filing her fingernails, so I took myself on a tour of the upstairs. Every so often, male voices filtered up through the floorboards: the boys were underneath the house, gathering lobsters from traps for dinner.

The main room of the stilt house was paneled with wood and stocked with old appliances and a shabby wicker sofa with turquoise vinyl cushions — it occurred to me that the cushions would likely float, if called upon. The kitchen and living area shared one open space, with two doors that opened onto the west and north porches. This design gave the house an inside-out quality, like the interior of a cabana or, I imagined, a yacht. A counter separated the kitchen from the rest of the living area, and trimming the edge of the countertop was a dingy decorative rope that sagged down an inch here and there. The windows had thick jalousie panes that operated on turn-screw cranks. On the coffee table was a stack of fishing and boating magazines, and above the sofa was a black-and-white photograph of a man — Dennis's father, I assumed — wearing white canvas pants and a captain's hat and holding a swordfish on a line. Beside the photograph was a hurricane tracking map, its tiny magnets (blue for watch, red for warning) huddled in one corner. Above the sink in the kitchen hung an enormous marlin with sparkling blue flanks and gray-green eyes. A short hallway off the living room led to a small bathroom and two dark bedrooms, one with two beds and a ratty dresser and the other with two bunk beds. All the beds were neatly made with a thin white blanket folded at the foot of each. I wondered how all the furnishings had come to be here, how the house itself had come to be.

There was a shower in the small upstairs bathroom, and a window that faced south, away from shore. There was a two-story rainwater tank just outside the back window, and beyond, the lumpy green bundle of an island a mile away: this was Soldier's Key. A toothbrush lay bristles-up on the window ledge. The mirror over the sink was tarnished and nicked, and in it my cheeks were raw with sunburn and my eyes were bright. Studying my reflection, I felt the queasy thrill of recognizing something unfamiliar in my own face.

I left the bathroom and went downstairs. Marse looked up when I passed but didn't say anything. The bottom story of the house was open on all sides, existing only to elevate the second floor away from the water — except for one corner where there was a tiny bathroom and a storage shed with a generator inside. I opened the door to the generator room and inhaled the briny air. Beside the machine, which was quiet, there were ceiling-high shelves piled with tools and old shoes and fishing gear. I closed the door and walked to the dock, then crouched and looked through the slats of the steps that led from the dock to the first floor. From there, I could see beneath the house to the space underneath, where Dennis and Kyle stood in knee-high water. Sea urchins and sand dollars dotted the beige seafloor. Stripes of sunlight streaked through cracks between the floorboards. Dennis held a net and water inked the hems of his shorts. He noticed me and gave a wave. He pointed at a dark creature crawling across the seafloor. "Dinner," he said. "You like lobster?"

"Yes," I said.

"We're going to feast." Droplets of sweat or seawater fell from his hair. He glanced at the scuttling lobster, then back at me. "We're almost done."

"Take your time," I said, then stepped up from the dock to the first floor. The water tower stood flush with the back of the house. I knocked on it to gauge the water level and it returned a booming, hollow sound. From below the house, Kyle called, "Come in!" and Dennis laughed. I looked around: the bottom story of the house was as bare as a picnic shelter at a park. The dock made a T with the first floor of the house, and alongside it the two boats rocked calmly on their lines, facing east, toward the Becks' stilt house and the wide ocean beyond. The second story was aproned on three sides by a veranda with a white wood railing, but there was no railing on the first floor. One could simply step off into the water.

There was, however, a shallow wooden ledge affixed to the exterior wall of the downstairs bathroom. It looked like the scaffolding used by painters working on high buildings — and I guessed that this was more or less what it was, used originally when the house was being built, then left behind. The ledge was about eighteen inches deep. To get to where I could stand on it, I had to take a wide step over a triangle of empty air between the bottom floor of the house and the ledge itself. It didn't occur to me until I put my foot down that the ledge might not hold. It did. Once I was standing on the ledge, though, I couldn't manage to turn around. I slid down the exterior wall until I was sitting on the ledge, then crossed my legs so Dennis and Kyle wouldn't see them dangling.

From seaward, the human eye can distinguish prominent shapes — the lighthouse or Freedom Tower or Turkey Point — at eight miles. To a person of my height stand-

28

ing above the waterline, the horizon is two and a half miles away: a stone's throw. Considering the blue expanse of ocean in my vision and the thousands of glassy wavelets and the fathoms of veiled blond seafloor, I would have thought I could see to Cuba. I felt tremendously calm. I felt caught in a swell of well-being. Maybe I was lulled by the waves and the sunlight, or maybe I believed that there were no stakes on vacation, and had abandoned my usual anxieties regarding the future, that unnavigable ocean. When I returned home, I knew, I would spend evenings on the front porch of my apartment house in Atlanta, where I'd lived and worked since graduating from college, chatting with my neighbors and slapping at mosquitoes. Soon the sunlight would weaken and blanch, and I would add a quilt to my bedspread and unpack the space heater. A smattering of my still-single college friends would get engaged or married, and I would swim through fits of loneliness like cold undercurrents. But that afternoon, on that clandestine ledge, I felt like a stowaway whose trip had begun. All I had to do was wait.

Splashing sounds came from beneath the house. "Where did it go?" said Kyle.

"I've got it," Dennis said.

With some effort, I swung my legs to one side and eased my stomach onto the bare, warm wood. I peered over the ledge until I could see beneath the house. Dennis was lowering a squirming lobster into a crate filled with other lobsters; their antennae lashed through the slats. Fish darted around the boys' legs. "Join your family," said Dennis to the lobster, and I pushed myself back into a sitting position.

The boys splashed through deeper water and hauled themselves onto the dock. "They're angry," said Dennis, and Kyle said, "Sweetens the meat." Their steps on the stairs were noisy and quick. I knew I should join them, but I felt fastened to that ledge, partly from inertia and partly from reluctance to try to stand in so tight a space. Below me, seven feet down, the sandy seafloor was covered by only a few feet of water: it would hurt if I fell, might even break a bone. Dennis called my name. I thought it would confuse him if I answered — where would it seem like my voice was coming from? — so I stood, carefully. Then I heard his steps on the stairs. "Frances!" His voice was gruff and resolute. It grew quieter as he moved down the dock, away from the house, then louder as he returned. "Frances!"

I closed my eyes. It was his concern, the

throaty pitch of it, that moved me to answer, even before I could manage to get myself off the ledge. "Here," I said. Then louder, "I'm here."

He appeared beside the water tower, leaning out beyond the back of the house. His mouth was tight. "What are you doing?"

"Nothing," I said. "Looking around."

He glanced south, toward Soldier's Key, then down at the water. "We wouldn't want to lose track of you out here."

"I wouldn't want that either."

The irritation slipped from his face. He looked around again, then stepped onto the ledge beside me. I edged over to give him room, and we stood with our backs to the wall, our arms at our sides. "Are you contemplating fate and the universe?" he said, not unkindly.

I smiled. I didn't want to seem overly serious. "I like it here."

"You're welcome anytime."

I wanted to say something about having felt like a different person all day, but I didn't know what I meant or how he would respond, so I stayed quiet. He said, "My father was boating back from Bimini once, and he ran out of gas right out there." He pointed. "He radioed the Coast Guard and told them he was ten miles northwest of the lighthouse, then his radio gave out. They didn't find him for hours. By the time they did, it was night. He asked what had taken them so long and they said they'd been searching for him on the north side of Miami Beach. Then they'd realized he'd given his position wrong — the lighthouse was ten miles northwest of him, not the other way around. I look out there and I think, how could he make that mistake?"

I followed his stare into the thick blue distance, bare of markers or guides. It would take an enormous act of faith, I thought, to trust the jittery needle of a compass. "I can see how a person might get confused," I said.

I don't think Dennis meant to kiss me. He was leaning in to hear me, and when I turned our noses and cheeks met and — this amazes me still — neither of us backed away. Our mouths were uncertain. We kissed without embracing. We kept our eyes open. We could feel even then that we were at the beginning of something, I think — something that might go on and on before it ended. After, we faced each other.

"We could go skiing, if you want, before dinner," he said. He reached toward my face. His fingers found my earlobe.

"I haven't skied since college, and then it

was in a lake."

"It'll come back to you."

I could feel the warmth from his body and I could smell his clean, sun-soaked smell.

"If we're going to go we should go," he said, "or we'll miss the daylight."

I nodded. He stepped from the ledge onto the bottom floor of the house, then reached for my hand and pulled me over the gap. I walked ahead of him up the stairs, and as we went he kept one hand on the small of my back, the gentlest suggestion of a rudder.

The sun was easing toward the horizon by the time we headed off. We took Dennis's father's boat because it was more powerful and because, Dennis said, the hull of Marse's boat was painted blue, which was bad luck. This was mariner lore: the sea might confuse the boat with itself and drag it down. I stood by while Marse affixed a towline and Dennis started the engine and Kyle handled the lines. The channel was dark and choppy and wide. Marse handed me a lumpy orange life vest and I tightened it at the chest and waist, but Dennis loosened it again. His knuckles brushed my stomach through the swimsuit. "It won't come off," he said, "but you don't want it too tight."

Our kiss rose in my gut. "I'm ready," I said, and because the lie was so obvious, we both laughed. He went to the console and put the boat in gear. I stumbled when the boat moved. When I regained my balance, I noticed Marse watching me.

We agreed that Kyle would ski first, then I would ski, then Marse. Kyle rose on skis as if from land, as if the baton were a sturdy hand. I recollected all I knew about water-skiing: Treat the water like a chair. Bend your knees. Let the towline pull you up. Lean back. Relax. Kyle skipped over the waves, and the boat rounded the mouth of the channel and returned, passing the stilt house, before he fell. I don't think he fell, actually — he threw his skis to the side and skidded, sending up white spray, then let go of the line. When we reached him, Marse asked if he wanted to go again, but he said he was wiped out. He climbed into the boat and took a beer from the cooler.

Dennis gathered the skis from the water — they were wooden, with a yellow stripe painted down the center of each. "Kyle will be your lookout," he said to me. "He won't take his eyes off you."

"I'm an ace lookout," said Kyle. He'd wrapped himself in a towel.

"Just don't leave me there," I said to

Dennis. "When I fall, come right back."

"I will," Dennis said.

I slid into the water, avoiding the stilled propellers. I struggled with each ski, then stretched my legs in front of me, drifting from the boat. The water cupped and jostled me; I tipped and righted. Dennis gave me a thumbs-up and I returned it awkwardly, and then the line spun out and I started to rise. Halfway up, I shifted and wobbled, and then I was hunched with my elbows over my knees. I straightened as much as I could without losing my balance. Kyle stood at the stern, watching me. Beneath my skis, the water whitened with friction and speed. The boat's wake, like the crease of an open book, stretched between the engine and my skis. We sped by one stilt house, then another. Kyle clapped for me and pumped a fist in the air. I tried to turn my grimace into a smile. Marse moved to stand beside Dennis, leaning toward him to be heard over the engine.

The sky was working up to dusk, the light so clear that I could make out the shoreline along Key Biscayne. Dennis's back was a landscape of swells and shadows. Marse had a hand on his arm. She was talking and he was nodding. I took one hand from the baton and sliced it through the air in front of my neck: I quit. Kyle turned to tell Dennis, and I let go. I skidded and started to sink. Dennis waited a few seconds before turning — maybe the channel was too narrow, or there was another boat — and as I waited, I closed my eyes and tasted the salt on my lips. There were dune-shaped ripples on every wave: ripples on waves on tidal swells. I felt like a very small piece of a very large puzzle.

The sound of the engine grew louder, then shifted as Dennis put the boat into neutral. I opened my eyes. Dennis leaned over the gunwale. He pulled my skis out of the water and reached for me. Marse was suited up by the time I was back in the boat. She dove in, and Dennis fed a ski into the water. I went to hand her the other one, but he stopped me. "She's going to slalom," he said.

"Wow," I said.

"You were good."

"I almost fell getting up."

"But you didn't."

"Let's go," said Marse. "Start out faster this time."

"You're her lookout," said Dennis to me.

She skied beautifully. The way her body responded to each wave, her rubbery maneuvers, reminded me of a child on a

36

trampoline. Her body held no resistance, no fear. We neared a stilt house and I alerted Dennis, but he just nodded and stayed the course. He was so intent that his jaw clenched and his eyes narrowed. I watched him for a moment, and when I looked back at Marse, she wasn't there. "Stop!" I said.

Dennis slowed the boat before looking around, which gave me a moment to search the water for Marse's orange life vest. I found her a ways back, in the dead center of the channel. Sit up, I thought. Show yourself. Dennis started his turn. "I'm sorry," I said. "I looked away."

"You can't look away," he said.

I pointed at Marse until he spotted her. Beyond her, a speedboat with a high red hull cruised toward us. "Hurry up," I said.

"I can't," said Dennis. "We'll fly right by her."

When we were close, Marse waved, rising from the water, and as she did, the red boat adjusted its course by a degree or two, and there were twenty yards of water between Marse and the red boat when it passed her. Dennis and the captain exchanged gestures of greeting. We were supposed to be flying a flag — I know this now — to convey to other boaters that we had a skier in the water. It was the kind of rule that most boaters ignored, which made me frantic: it's a terrific idea, that flag.

"Were you planning to leave me here?" said Marse. She spat water.

Dennis cut the engine. The boat's shadow swallowed Marse, and I noticed how dark it had become. Orange sunset soaked into the horizon. "Sorry about that," said Dennis.

Marse held up her ski and I pulled it into the boat. Dennis reached to give her a hand, but she was unfastening her life vest. "You go on," she said. "I'm going to swim."

The stilt house was about three hundred yards away. I had no idea how far a person could swim. "No way," said Dennis.

Marse handed the life vest up to me and, not thinking, I took it, but Dennis snatched it from me and threw it down to her. "It's getting dark," he said. "Get in the boat."

"Don't be such a bore," said Marse. She kicked away from us, leaving the life vest behind. Kyle pulled it out of the water. Dennis started the engine and maneuvered until we were puttering along beside her. Her stroke was fast and smooth. She raised her face from the water. "Go away," she shouted.

Kyle stood beside me at the gunwale. "Marse," he called, "I'm hungry. Get in the boat."

To Kyle, I said, "This is my fault."

"Not really," he said, but I saw in his expression that he didn't wholly trust me. Marse's stroke had started to falter. The tide was probably coming in, canceling her efforts. She could have swum all night just to keep the stilt house in sight.

"Dennis," I said. I thought he should have been doing something.

"She'll get tired," he said.

"She won't," said Kyle. When Marse tilted her head to breathe between strokes, her face was very red. Quietly, Kyle said to me, "Tell her you're sorry."

I cupped my hands around my mouth. "Marse," I called, "I'm a lousy lookout —"

"Not that," Kyle said.

I wondered if Kyle was particularly astute, or if I had been — if Dennis and I had been — particularly transparent. And I wondered how I'd gotten myself into this situation. Less than forty-eight hours from now, I thought, I'll be back in Atlanta, thinking that I kissed a boy I barely knew and hurt a girl who'd been nice to me. "Marse," I called again, "I'm going home tomorrow." She slowed, then treaded water. "I'm going home tomorrow," I said again, "but if you drown, I'll have to stick around."

The tactic was plain; it embarrassed us

both. "Big deal," she said.

"Get in the boat," said Dennis.

Marse looked away, toward Miami, then ahead at the stilt house, blue with evening. When finally she swam to the boat, her stroke had returned and her breathing was even. She sat at the prow without drying herself off, and Kyle sat beside her. They passed a beer back and forth and I watched them from the stern, holding my towel with both arms around my chest, clutching the solid, loyal edges of myself.

Dennis's father, Grady, had built his family's stilt house in 1945, when Dennis was just two years old. The idea came from a local fisherman named "Crawfish" Eddie Walker, who constructed a shack in shallow water in Biscayne Bay and became legendary for the fresh chowder he sold to passing boaters. Grady had friends who followed Eddie's lead. By the time Grady secured the funds and manpower to build his own shack, several more had sprouted, including a men's club called the Quarterdeck. By 1960, Stiltsville comprised twenty-seven shacks, but then the Quarterdeck burned in a fire and hurricane Donna leveled all but six of the other buildings. Many of the squatters, including Grady, rebuilt, and the new houses were cottage-style, larger and sturdier, designed to withstand all but the most devastating squall. Then in 1965, responding to complaints from Key Biscayne residents who claimed that Stiltsville ruined their ocean view, the state of Florida issued private leases for plots of submerged land. After hurricane Betsy hit that year, fourteen houses were left standing, and the state stopped issuing new leases and banned commercial ventures altogether. Grady was, by this point, Stiltsville's semi-official mayor — he kept the paperwork up-to-date and mediated grievances between stilt house owners and the state, or between owners and each other.

Dennis was twenty-six years old when I met him, same as me. He'd lived in Miami all his life, as I'd lived in the Atlanta area all of mine. After graduating from college, he'd worked for a sailing company that hauled tourists on sunset cruises. He'd lived briefly with a girl named Peggy on a yawl moored at Dinner Key marina, but she'd grown weary of the waterlogged life and moved to Boca Raton to become a travel agent. He'd missed her for a long time. He'd quit his job and spent six months in Spain with his high school friend Paul, touring and living on fried fish from street vendors. Then he'd returned to Miami to attend law school, and moved into a small apartment on Miami Beach. He liked school but wasn't crazy about the prospect of being a lawyer; he hoped an affection for law would come with the diploma. He knew Marse was after him and he liked her and considered having sex with her, but the thought of what would happen afterward made him feel unkind. He spent at least one weekend a month alone at the stilt house. On land, he studied in diners and took long drives at night, often ending up in the lounge of the Key Largo airport, where they served the best conch fritters in the state. Sometimes he thought about buying a house in Coconut Grove or Coral Gables — he couldn't imagine living anywhere except South Florida — but he made no promises to himself. He liked his small beachfront apartment. He kept his bicycle unchained on the balcony and walked barefoot to the corner store. Once a week, he paid an upstairs neighbor five dollars to give him an hour-long Spanish lesson.

That night at the stilt house, Kyle and I set the table for dinner while Marse changed clothes and Dennis used the boat radio to check the weather. The boats rocked against the dock; the blue-black water heaved

42

beneath the house. The lobsters' tails ticked against the steel insides of the giant cooking pot, slowing from desperate to resigned. I could taste and feel salt on my lips and skin. When we were finished, Kyle stared out the kitchen window toward land, where lights along the shoreline flashed like sequins.

"I'll be sorry to leave," I said.

He took a jug of water from the refrigerator. "You'll be back."

In the bedroom, Marse was leaning toward the mirror, applying lip gloss. When she saw me come in, she turned her back to me and put both hands behind her neck, holding the ends of a red halter-top. "Do me up?" she said. I took the fabric and tied a bow. The backs of my fingers brushed her neck. "Not quite so tight," she said. We looked at each other in the mirror. I admired the peaks of her collarbone, the hollows in her neck. The day before, at the wedding, her shoes had given her blisters — they were sling-backs, and new — so she'd taken them off and looped them around the strap of her purse so she wouldn't forget to take them home. "You could forget your shoes?" I'd asked, and she'd said, "It's been known to happen." She'd greeted the bride and groom in her stockings, standing tall and straight-backed.

"Marse —" I said.

"It doesn't matter." She shook her head and shrugged.

I retied the bow slowly, leaving a little slack. "You don't know me," I said, "but if you did, you'd know that this isn't like me."

She thought for a moment. "If you say so," she said. "I believe you."

It would have seemed ridiculous to say what I wanted to say at the time: that I hoped we could be friends. I said, "I appreciate that."

It seemed we were both making an enormous effort to act like grown-ups. She tugged at her halter to test the knot, then turned to face me. We both looked at her torso — the fabric was in place, everything covered. "How do I look?" she said.

"Lovely."

All at once, the room went dark and the generators stilled. She said, "He always does this for dinner. Saves propane."

Moonlight dove in through the windows, bluing the planes of her face. She led me into the main room, where the firelight from stout white candles made shadows on the walls. The room smelled strongly of garlic cooking in butter. Kyle and Dennis set down plates piled with lobster tails and filled cups with red wine. I watched their

44

faces in the candlelight. They were easy together, chatting and teasing. Marse joined in. Dennis pulled out a chair next to him, and when we were seated, I toasted the most beautiful scenery south of the Mason-Dixon, and Dennis toasted adventurous southern belles. The meeting of Styrofoam brims gave off a squeak. Wine sloshed onto the table and no one bothered to wipe it up. Dennis's knee brushed mine, then stayed there. Every so often I felt him looking at me. I cherished the sense of caged joy.

The lobster was so sweet I ate it plain. Kyle told a story about walking with a girl on the beach at night and slipping on a jellyfish. He'd cried real tears from the pain, and the girl had stopped returning his calls. Marse told a story about her first day working for a district judge — she'd been waiting for the judge to get off the telephone when he'd picked up a steno pad and written on it. He'd held it up for her to read: YOUR ZIPPER IS UNDONE, said the note. SORRY TO EMBARRASS YOU. We laughed so hard our eyes watered. During a lull, Dennis said, "The wind is up."

"Aye, captain," Kyle said.

"What does that mean?" I said.

Marse folded her long arms on the table.

45

"Dennis thinks a storm is coming," she said to me. I thought she winked, but it might have been the candlelight. "He's about to tell us we can't stay the night."

Dennis leaned back in his chair and wiped his mouth with a napkin. "I'll check the barometer after dinner."

"Either way," said Marse. "Just let me follow you in. I don't know the way at night."

It hadn't occurred to me that we might stay the night. I hadn't brought extra clothes. The boys went downstairs to check the barometer on the boat while Marse washed plates and I dried them. In the candlelight, without the thunder of the generators, the clatter of dishes punctuated the night. "Dennis is probably right about the storm," she said. "He has hunches about these things."

On land, one looks toward the ocean to predict whether a storm is coming. From the ocean, one looks to the horizon. But the sky through the window was black, the stars cloaked by cloud cover. I wondered what it would be like to ride out a storm at the stilt house. We would refasten the boat lines and shutter all the windows. The doors would rattle on their hinges, and surely the roof would leak. How much weather could the house withstand? This was a question that

46

would go unanswered for many years. We went downstairs and found the boys on the big boat, which lunged with every wave. "The barometer's falling," said Dennis.

Marse stepped onto the boat. "How fast?"

"Fast," said Dennis.

I stepped after Marse, but once I was standing in the boat, I didn't know where to go. Dennis and Kyle and Marse were spaced out around the deck; I stood awkwardly in the middle. "Come look," said Dennis, extending an arm. I followed him to the helm, and he positioned me in front of the steering wheel and stood behind me. If Marse and Kyle had been looking in our direction, they could have seen our necks and heads, but the console obscured our bodies. I put my hands on the metal wheel and jiggled it. It locked like a car's. Dennis reached over my shoulder and touched a circular instrument in a teak case. "The most important piece of weather equipment on a boat," he said. "A rise could mean strong winds or good weather. A drop means a storm." He moved his hand to my hip. Then it seemed he wasn't satisfied, and he pulled me against him, snaking his arm around my waist. "The quicker the drop, the bigger the storm." I layered my arm over his. I could feel the rush of my blood, my

47

beating heart. He spoke into my ear. "Come back with me. I'll take you home."

I turned to reply, but Kyle called out from the prow. "Let's go if we're going to go."

Dennis released me. "Pack up," he said loudly. "I'll close the house."

Marse's bag was upstairs, so we went to get it and I followed her from room to room, checking for forgotten items. Dennis and Kyle closed all the shutters and dragged the rocking chairs inside and locked the doors. Dennis pulled a gate across the stairs and secured it with a padlock. We gathered on the dock, and Marse stepped onto her boat and started the engine, and Kyle stepped onto Dennis's boat. To Marse, Dennis said, "Follow me to the second set of markers. You'll know the way from there."

"Got it," said Marse.

I hadn't realized we weren't all headed to the same marina. I felt a flush of resentment toward Dennis because he seemed to hold all the cards. He could come to Snapper Creek to find us, but we might be gone by then, or he could call Marse later to find out where I was staying. Or — what? He most likely would do nothing. He would drop off Kyle and drive home alone, wondering what might have happened. I started to say good-bye, but then I didn't. I untied the stern line and climbed into Marse's little boat. Dennis tossed aboard the bowline, watching me. We drifted from the dock.

In the dark, Dennis's body at the helm of the bigger boat was grainy and indistinct. We kept up with him for a while, trailing in his wake, but the water was choppy and soon it was difficult to distinguish wake from waves. I tried to keep an eye on his running lights, but I had to keep turning my head to avoid spray coming over the side of the boat, and eventually I lost track of him altogether. Marse shouted over the motor and the wind. "Shit," she said. "He's gone."

She pulled back on the throttle. The boat slowed, slapping hard against each wave. I lost my balance and grabbed the gunwale. Without stars, the night was black and suffocating. Not until we stopped could I even tell that it was raining. The fall was light but the drops were large and warm. Tropical storm, I thought. Hurricane. This toy boat, this floating saucer. I could barely make out the dark snake of shoreline. A minute later, in the thickening rain, it vanished entirely.

Marse went to the prow and searched the darkness, then returned to the helm. With her wet hair and clinging clothes, she seemed to have shrunk. I shouted over the

49

rain, "Tell me what to do."

She wiped her face. "Get up on the bow, hold on to the rail. Don't let go. Watch the water, make sure we stay in the channel."

"What happens if we leave the channel?"

"We could run aground. I don't want to be out here in a storm."

I thought I could see her shivering. "Go slow," I said.

At the prow, I crouched low and held on to the anchor chain with one hand and the metal rail with the other. The water was a roiling black tangle streaked with white and gray, and I couldn't judge its depth. Lightning flashed to the north. For an instant, I could see the whole Miami coastline, from the Everglades to Cape Florida, in one electric sweep. But then night fell again. Rain slid off my hair into my face. Every time I took my hand from the rail to wipe water from my eyes, the boat tipped and I stumbled. There was another flash of lightning, then another. I used the bright seconds to try to assess the depth of the water. The light silvered the slopes of the waves. "Frances!" called Marse. I couldn't turn toward her without losing my grip, so I looked up instead. Something ahead of us caught my eye: a red light. "Took you long enough," shouted Marse into the rain.

50

The red light approached, followed by the bright white of a boat's deck, nestled in the night like teeth in a dark mouth. I stepped down and made my way to Marse's side. Dennis's boat came closer, and then we could make out the captain himself, a solid figure with one hand on the throttle and one on the wheel. Kyle huddled under a raincoat at the stern.

Four weeks from that night, on a clear evening salted with stars, Marse would attend the Vizcaya gala in an enticing black cocktail dress, and Dennis would dance with her on the mansion's limestone deck while I watched from our picnic spot on the grass. The heels of their shoes would click against the stone, and over Marse's shoulder Dennis would meet my eye, and wink, and my heart would buoy. Dennis would say that love is like the electric eel, coiled wherever it happens to live, unflappable and ready to strike. We want to mess with it but we can't. On that stormy night, though, as the big boat drew nearer, I stood so close to Marse that the rain skated off us as if we were one person, and when we raised our arms to wave, Dennis could not distinguish my hand from hers.

1970

Six months after meeting Dennis, I stood over the kitchen sink in his parents' home, washing dishes. It was January. Beside me Dennis's mother, Gloria, smoked a cigarette. She held it more than she smoked it, and it burned away in her pale, thin hand. Although her mouth was closed, every few minutes her jaw worked, as if she were thinking aloud to herself. She tapped the ashes into the sink. This was the house where Dennis had been born and where he'd grown up. I'd been given the tour months earlier, including the room Dennis had occupied as a child, where neatly made twin beds lay under thin navy bedspreads and a University of Miami pennant hung on the wall.

Through the back window, I watched Dennis and his father, Grady, cross the lawn toward the canal that snaked along the back rim of the property. Dennis, slim in faded blue jeans, loped alongside his father in a way that drew attention to his joints. When they reached the short pier where Grady's boat was moored, Dennis reached across his torso to scratch under his shirtsleeve. Grady was doughy where Dennis was lean; for every step Dennis took, Grady took a step and a half. Grady's corkscrew sandy orange hair thinned at the crown of his skull; his gestures when he spoke were controlled and deliberate. Grady stood with his hands in his pockets, and after a few minutes — though they faced away from the house, I could tell they were talking by the way their heads moved — he stooped to wipe debris from the pier's planks with the flat of his hand. Dennis reached down and without bending touched his father's shoulder blade with his fingertips. When Grady stood again, Dennis's hand briefly rested at his father's waist.

Gloria whistled a long, low note and pulled a tea towel from her shoulder, where it had perched all afternoon. She dangled it over the sink and let it drop. "They're like women, aren't they?" she said. "The way they chatter."

I smiled politely. Gloria had given Dennis his slender frame and light eyes. She was two inches taller than I was, at least an inch taller than her husband. I glanced her way and caught her staring: the blunt tip of her nose was pink and her eyes were damp. Unlike my own mother's face, whose features were broad and suntanned and matted with freckles, Gloria's face was delicate and pale. Her chin came to a point. Earlier, she'd served coleslaw and chicken salad on the back deck, then filled our glasses with fruity rum punch and returned to the kitchen. In the months I'd known her, I'd learned that she rarely ate a meal during the daytime. She ate breakfast and might nibble on a salad at lunchtime, but eating an entire meal in the afternoon nauseated her. I'd also learned that she thought eating outdoors was distasteful, but agreed to it because she knew other people found it appealing. She took a nap every day and always had, even when Dennis and his younger sister Bette were children. "She just lay down in the playroom while we horsed around," Dennis had told me, "and a half hour later she got up again."

Gloria said, "If you were expecting a quiet house, you were mistaken. My men are talkers." She smiled weakly and turned away, and not for the first time I found myself unable to answer her. She had a dead-end way of conversing; no obvious next step presented itself. But as I watched her walk out of the room, then turned back to the window through which I could see Grady and Dennis standing together on the pier, separated from me by a wide expanse of un-mowed green lawn, two thoughts crystal-lized in my mind. One thought was that, in spite of the fact that she considered it in bad taste to travel hundreds of miles to visit a boy one barely knew, Gloria liked me. The second thought was that Dennis was plan-ning to propose marriage, and soon. This was the topic being discussed outside at that moment, under a sky dimmed by clouds. Dennis and Grady stood looking down into the well of Grady's lapstrake boat — still the most impressive boat I've ever seen, with its polished teak hull and gleaming brass railings — which rested in its slip, laced by bright white mooring lines. Then Dennis stepped toward the house and Grady fol-lowed, and as they walked Dennis kept his eyes on the kitchen window — on me — and Grady continued talking, his hands in his pockets. By the time they reached the swimming pool, brief droplets had erupted into a rare winter thunderstorm. I swiped two towels from the laundry room, then greeted them at the back door and ushered them inside.

■ ■ ■ ■

I'd been fired that week from my job at the bank. I'd missed so much work since meeting Dennis that the manager had called me into his office and asked me, not unkindly, to rearrange my priorities, which I'd promised I would. When I used the shared line in my apartment house to call Dennis and tell him I couldn't visit for a while, he'd said, "Just come one more time, this weekend." I suppose I knew then how it would go for us. Before I'd met Dennis, I'd liked my job well enough. I'd liked my small apartment and quiet neighbors and weekly dinners with friends and their husbands. I'd taken long walks on Sundays and spent weekend afternoons helping my mother in her garden. Some nights I opened a bottle of wine and cooked pasta for myself over a burner in the communal kitchen. But when I'd considered where my life was headed, I had not particularly liked the prospects. The men I dated did not woo me, the girls I knew who'd started families did not inspire me. My job, although wholly adequate, did not light anything akin to a fire in my gut. I was not yet sad, but I believed I was headed for sadness, and I blamed myself for having waited to be swept into a more thrilling life. For the first time, after meeting Dennis, I saw in my own future bright, unknowable possibilities. I'm a bit ashamed to have been a person without much agency in life, but I credit myself with knowing something special when I saw it.

In a period of six months, I'd visited Miami five times. I'd taken the train down twice, and three times Dennis had driven up to get me and stayed a night at the motel near my apartment house, then we had driven down to Miami together. During every visit, I saw Marse at least once or twice, for an afternoon shopping or on the boat. There are seven hundred miles of gray highway between Miami and Atlanta. The Sunshine State Parkway was barely a decade old, and it took more than twelve hours to drive each way. When I recall our courtship, I recall as much as anything else the landscape outside the windows of Dennis's station wagon: the asphalt of the turnpike and the drone of the headlights and the stuttering orange groves. I'd fallen in love in Dennis's car and under the fluorescent lights of truck stops. We'd spent so much of those six months in car seats that I knew his body as well seated as standing — the hard round caps of his knees, dimpled at the joint, and the bony elbows with which he jabbed me while shifting in his seat, unaware of his breadth.

Between visits, we'd had phone calls. The telephone I shared with the other tenants of my building sat on a wicker table in the hallway outside my room. The phone was butter-yellow in color, the handset heavy as a dumbbell, and when it rang the whole unit rattled as if mocking my heart, which lurched every time. He called most mornings before I left for work, and he would list for me everything he could see from his apartment balcony: two girls surfing, three men standing on the corner smoking cigars in the heat, an old woman wearing a housedress walking a poodle. Or he'd call in the evenings from the pay phone at the law library. "It's a hundred degrees in the shade here," he'd said once, "and everyone is studying without shirts on. Will you please tell me why I'm working so hard?" When Dennis spoke of school, he sounded drained.

"Even the girls?" I'd said. "No blouses?"

"Some."

"Cover your eyes."

"I'm wearing blinders, so I can see the books."

He called late at night sometimes, too, and

I dragged the telephone out to the porch so as not to disturb my neighbors. When we were together we spoke casually, about whatever happened to cross our minds, but on the phone he asked solemn, mining questions: What was my earliest memory? Did I prefer cats or dogs? Could I imagine myself living on a boat? What if it was a nice, big, clean boat? What was my favorite thing about my family? What was my favorite thing about him? Every thread of conversation stitched back to the topic of us.

I told him I remembered taking my father's cigarettes from the countertop in my parents' bathroom and bringing them to my nose — I liked the smell, even at age three. My mother found me and slapped my hand. Dennis remembered being carried on his grandfather's shoulders through orange groves down south. His grandfather — Grady's father — sang cowboy songs and whistled. Dennis remembered the smell of the fruit and the feel of the pomade in his grandfather's hair.

I said I preferred dogs, and Dennis said he did, too. I said, "I would live on a boat for six months, no longer." He said he would live on a boat for the rest of his life. "I'd like to fish for my dinner," he said. "I'd bake in the sun until my skin looked like leather." I told him that when I was a little girl, my father used to cook up reasons to take us for drives in the country, and my mother would let me wear some of her red lipstick, and my father would wave with one hand out the window at every car we passed. I told Dennis that I liked my father's sense of leisure.

"I like my father's patience," said Dennis. "He'll wait on the fish for hours. I don't have the heart for it." He said his father would come home from a day of fishing with small, exciting stories: He'd seen a barracuda jump across the surface of the water, its scales flashing in the sunlight. He'd felt a bump against the side of the boat, and looked down to see the domed back of a manatee. He'd seen a family of dolphins, the smallest no larger than his forearm. "My mother thinks he's a bit simple, I think," said Dennis, and I said, "He is simple." I knew very little of Grady other than what I'd been told. Dennis knew I meant it kindly.

Dennis told me that his sister, Bette, younger by three years, used to sleep in the backyard in the summer. He'd come downstairs in the morning and find his sister and mother sitting outside on Bette's sleeping bag in their pajamas, eating pancakes off Chinet.

"My favorite thing about you?" I said, thinking: You call me every day! You don't worry about what it costs. You kissed me mere hours after meeting me. "You're kind," I said.

"That's it?"

"I don't know you all that well."

"Yes, you do."

"You have great legs."

"I'm going to marry you."

I'd known a few men pretty well, and something I'd noticed about many of them was that for some reason they didn't like to give you what you want, whatever it happened to be — reassurance or approval or attention. This seemingly was not because they couldn't spare it, but because they wanted to teach you not to want it. But in my mind, people weren't needy or independent — they were a swirl of both. I wondered if these men thought they never needed. I knew they did, but then their needs were sated so fully and with such generosity by the women in their lives that they didn't recognize needing something in the first place. As I grew to know Dennis, it struck me that he was not one of these men. From the beginning, he did not withhold.

61

This, ultimately, was the answer to his question, though I could not have formulated it at the time.

It would be disingenuous to say, however, that I had no doubts about Dennis. Once he'd snapped at me when we'd been driving for hours and I'd taken too long to choose a radio station, and one night he'd bagged a dozen fireflies in the woods behind my apartment house and let them go in my darkened living room, as if this would charm rather than irritate me. More important, I wasn't certain I had the mettle to live in Miami, with its flash and heat and vanity. But still, Dennis seemed, from the start, inevitable. It hadn't taken long for me to succumb, but I'd faked it for a while. Sometimes I'd hemmed and hawed about taking time off work for another visit. But from the beginning, the sight of him yawning in the television's blue light, or running a fingertip across his eyebrow, or blowing on his coffee to cool it off, made me shiver with want for him.

Once when we were on the road, I woke up in the passenger seat and sat watching him while he drove, and it dawned on me that I could watch him for minutes before he noticed, because he was a man who lived inside his own head. I snapped my fingers and he looked over at me. "Awake?" he said. He reached into the backseat and rooted around. "Have an apple," he said. I ate what he gave me, and fell back to sleep.

After I lost my job, my mother drove me to the train station, drumming her short, strong fingernails on the steering wheel. Since I had nothing to return for, this particular visit to Miami would have no scheduled end date. I'd packed two large suitcases. "I'm going to play it by ear," I told her, and she raised her eyebrows at me. "I'd prefer you had a plan," she said, but she offered to drive me anyway. Her muddied canvas gardening gloves lay on the seat between us. When we arrived, she loaded me down with pimiento cheese sandwiches and a brown bag of peaches for Dennis's family. My mother was a tall, strong-backed woman with wide hips and a handsome face, and she spoke quietly and not often. She had been somewhat old-fashioned throughout my childhood and teenage years, but when my father moved out — I'd been in college at the time — she'd seemed to reorder her notions. She'd stopped going to church and started gardening. She'd let go of most of her old friends, one by one, and took up with a few single women, divorcees who drank and told bawdy jokes.

I would stop by her house, the house where I'd grown up, to find a group of them sitting in lawn chairs in the backyard, drinking Bloody Marys at noon. She'd stopped wearing makeup altogether — this might have meant something or nothing; I never understood it. The changes she made seemed to me like the ones a widow would make. She wasn't happy about the new arrangement, I would say, but she was willing to squeeze some advantages from it.

The girl who came to share my father's downtown apartment was named Luanne. Although she was young — twenty-seven years old when they met, compared with his forty-five — she had a child from a previous relationship who lived with Luanne's mother. When I called their apartment, she gave me a polite hello and handed the telephone to my father, and it seemed to me that she was keeping him close at her side at all times, though maybe the situation was reversed. When Dennis met them, he said he thought Luanne looked like a doll, and I shushed him. He said, "There's appeal, to some men, with that kind of woman." He swatted me playfully on the rear end. "But it's not for me." As a child I'd loved my father very much — he spoke enthusiastically about the physics of space flight and roller coasters, he liked to read about places he'd never been, he called in sick to work when I was five so he could finish building my tree house — but I never grew accustomed to thinking of him as the spoils in a battle between women.

My mother and I had more or less avoided the topic of what exactly I thought I was doing, disposing of my job and disrupting my life to visit a boy in Miami, of all places. But while we waited together on the train platform, she pursed her lips and turned to me. "Miami seems so . . ." she said, "I don't know. Far." She wasn't one to hold tight, but moving a plane ride away was another story. "It seems decadent."

"I guess maybe it is." I thought of the elaborate wedding I'd been to when I first visited, the giant water fountain a few blocks from the cathedral, the sprawling banyan trees lining the streets. I thought of the young girls I'd seen posing for photographs at the Spanish-style arches in Coral Gables, all gussied up for their *quinceañeras* in hoop skirts and capes. Atlanta was lovely — there were lacy white dogwood and redbud trees and dirt roads and orchards, and in the autumn the leaves turned and fell and were raked into colorful piles — but Atlanta was not decadent. "You'll like Dennis," I said.

"What will I like about him?"

"I don't know. Everything."

"Does he remind you of your father?"

I thought about this. "No."

"That's better," she said. She smoothed her chambray skirt and looked around, as if she'd forgotten something. My mother wore a ponytail every day of her life, even into her seventies. "Be nice to his mom, no matter what."

"I will be."

"Stay out of his bedroom."

"Mother."

"It won't be easy, but you'll be glad you did."

"Mother!"

She sighed. "Maybe I shouldn't be giving advice," she said, and then a whistle sounded, and the white light of my train appeared in the middle distance, as if gunning for me.

In the six months since we'd met, Dennis and I had not slept together. When I visited Miami, I stayed with his sister, Bette, who rented a two-room apartment above a shoe store on Main Highway in Coconut Grove. The apartment had a small cement deck that overlooked the street, and a screen door on squeaky hinges, and at night we could hear the traffic and the people on the street below. Bette had a couch with a creaky, shifting bamboo frame and flat square cushions printed with hibiscus blossoms — an uncomfortable place to sleep, made slightly less uncomfortable by layers of mildewy sleeping bags. She was tall like her brother and very thin, with white-blond hair and sharp, tan shoulders. She tended to slouch. She was not beautiful, exactly, but she had memorable, sharp features and lovely skin. She wore huarache sandals — I would wear them, too, after a year or so of being around her — and sleeveless shirts and culottes, and she carried a large crocheted handbag. She walked everywhere; she didn't have a car. After she'd graduated from high school, Grady and Gloria had offered her their old hatchback if she would go to college and stay in all four years; but she was an indifferent student and the most she'd been able to commit to was a couple of classes per semester. Three times a week after work she walked four miles to the University of Miami, then took the bus home. She took botany and biology and political science and comparative literature. She spoke German — she'd spent a year in Munich during high school, as an exchange student — and she could name every flower, bird, and tree in South Florida. She had never traveled north of North Carolina. She was at that time engaged to her high school sweetheart, Benjamin O'Dell. They'd been engaged for five years, since her senior year of high school, but they had yet to set a date.

Though Bette never said or did anything to make me feel unwelcome, I could tell by the way she lived that she was a private person, and probably didn't revel in having a regular houseguest. I had the sense that she could snap shut at any time, that any bridge to her could collapse. To make myself useful while staying with her, I cleaned the apartment and left sandwiches in the refrigerator for when she came home for lunch. The apartment was across the street from Bette's work. She was the groundskeeper for a private home called the Barnacle, which was owned by the family of the original owner, Commodore Ralph Middleton Monroe. Commodore Monroe had founded the first organization in the area — Biscayne Bay Yacht Club — in 1891, when Miami was little more than a fort. The Barnacle was nestled on the bay among ten acres of tropical hardwood hammock. No one lived there, but the family wanted someone on the property during the day, to make sure vagrants stayed out and the lawn was mowed and — most important — that the *Egret,* a schooner docked at the Barnacle's pier, was kept free of growth and rust. The *Egret* was Bette's main task, and the only one for which she truly was qualified — she had been sailing competitively since she was ten years old. There was a rumor that the family planned in the future to deed the Barnacle to the state and open the house for tours, and Bette hoped to continue to look after the *Egret* part-time and spend the rest of her time doing what she loved: scuba diving. Nights, she sometimes went into her room and closed the door, and I could hear music through the wall and the low tones of hushed speech as she talked on the phone. Two or three times, she'd stayed out all night — where, I didn't yet guess — and had come home at dawn, tiptoeing into the living room where I slept. Once, she'd made so much noise coming in that I couldn't reasonably pretend to sleep through it, and when I opened my eyes, I saw that she had dropped a large canvas bag filled with green and blue glass bottles. I helped her collect them — none broke — and the next day when I glanced into her bedroom from the kitchenette, I saw those bottles lined up on the windowsill, refracting the sunlight.

From time to time I kept Bette company

while she did her chores at the Barnacle. This is how I ended up lying on the Barnacle's pier one Tuesday afternoon during that last long visit, after losing my job in Atlanta. I'd been in Miami for almost four weeks straight. It was January, but still we wore swimsuits without covering up, and the heat on the wooden pier spread through my skin like a warm blanket. Dennis was at class. That morning, he'd stopped by the apartment after Bette went to work, and we'd necked on the couch until the cushions stuck to our skin. This is what I returned to, all day: the rushing, splitting-open feeling of touching Dennis, of being touched by him. My mother was right: it was not easy, staying out of his bedroom.

Bette wore a scarf over her hair and a neon orange bikini top and cutoffs with a red velvet patch on the thigh. She squinted while she polished the brass fittings of the *Egret*'s teak railing. I mistook the squinting for concentration — later I would learn that this was a side effect of her nearsightedness, which, in an uncharacteristic fit of vanity, she had not corrected with eyeglasses. "Those bottles," she said. "I've been dying to tell you."

I put aside the law journal I'd been reading, an article Dennis had published earlier that year. "Tell me," I said.

She squatted on the gunwale of the boat. I shaded my eyes to look up at her. She said, "I found them on a wreck. A shipwreck."

"Where?"

She pointed south across the bay. "Out there."

My first thought was that surely it was not legal to remove items from a shipwreck. "Can you get in trouble for that?" I said.

She laughed. "I don't imagine they're worth much. But they're beautiful. I found them in the forward cabin the other night. It took me two trips to get them all up."

"You dove at night?" It seemed impossible that on those nights when she'd been out until dawn, she'd been scuba diving. I'd seen Bette's boat — it was a seventeen-foot sailfish, a toddler of a boat. Surely it wasn't fitted with dive lights. This meant she'd been diving with someone else, from that person's boat.

"Don't worry," she said. "I go with a friend. It's safe."

I thought of Benjamin, a ruddy-faced bear of a man who spoke softly and had the habit, I'd witnessed, of lifting Bette over his shoulder until she battered him into letting her down. I stood up and stepped over the railing of the *Egret,* and maneuvered until I

71

was straddling the gunwale, facing her. "OK, tell me," I said. It was a little awkward, I admit. She hadn't ever invited this kind of gabfest, and I wasn't sure we were suited to it.

For whatever reason, though — she was excited, bursting — this was not a secret she wanted to keep. "I met this woman," she said, throwing me for a loop. "Her name is Jane. She's a professional salvor. You know what that is?" I shook my head. "She has an engineering degree or something, and she works with dive teams to raise shipwrecks. They have to do it without hurting anything, inside the wreck or outside it. It's very complicated work. Anyway, I met her at the club." The club was the Coconut Grove Sailing Club, where Bette taught sailing lessons on the weekends in exchange for a discount on her boat slip. "I'm teaching her to sail."

"And she's teaching you to — salve?"

"Salvage," she said. She looked off, as if remembering. "No, we just dive together. She knows the best spots. There's a wreck she's bringing up soon, and sometimes we just go there to hunt around, see what we see. It's an old hull freighter that sank on its way from Venezuela. Nothing valuable aboard, just trinkets. Memories."

I couldn't think of anything I'd ever done that was nearly as exciting as scuba diving in a sunken ship. "Does Dennis know?" I said.

"Of course not. Are you going to tell him?"

"Not if you'd rather I didn't."

"Jane said we should keep quiet about it. I guess the state wouldn't be too happy that she was diving the wreck before bringing it up."

"When are you going out next?" I said.

"Tonight, probably. I don't know why I told you."

"I'm glad you did." We sat quietly for a moment, and Bette returned to polishing the railing. "Are you ready to get married?" I said.

She dropped the polishing cloth onto the pier and stepped over the railing. "I guess not," she said. "Are you?"

"I don't know," I said. But I believed I was.

She dropped her shorts to the pier, pulled neon snorkeling gear from a bag, and put it on — first the flippers and then the mask. She held the snorkel in one hand and a flat metal tool — for shucking snails and barnacles off the boat's hull — in the other. "It's not as simple as it always seemed, is it?" she said. Her voice was nasal from the

73

mask, but she was unself-conscious. She walked to the end of the pier and turned her back to the water, then put her hand over her nose and mouth and stepped backward into the air. Once I'd heard her resurface and begin knocking around the hull, I relaxed. I felt we'd just had our first real — albeit stilted — conversation, and now could become friends. With no end to my visit in sight, this was fiercely important to me. To have a few friends in Miami — Marse and Bette, plus Dennis — felt like the start of a real collection, a treasure trove of my own.

That evening, rather than wait for Dennis to pick me up after work, I dressed in a linen sundress and walked half a mile to the bus stop, where I caught a bus to the University of Miami. There, I waited on a low cement wall under the wide canopy of a poinciana tree outside the law school until Dennis emerged, carrying a satchel in one hand and combing his hair with his fingers. I could not reconcile the disheveled student, sunburned nose and shaving nicks, with the suited lawyer he was working to become. Dennis saw me and waved, and as he walked toward me, in the moment between being alone and being with him, I experienced the sensation of being stunned by the instant.

The breath left my lungs. I looked at the boy coming toward me, who in my arms, by my side, seemed familiar, but in those baffling seconds revealed himself to be a stranger, essentially. It was like moving too quickly toward a painting, such that it distorts in proximity. Was this person my boyfriend? This lanky gait, this lazy posture, this wide smile? He reached me finally, and swept me into a hug that seemed to start before he was even beside me, and the moment of disorientation I'd experienced dissolved, the painting snapped back into perspective.

That evening, we made our way not to Bette's bamboo couch but to Dennis's apartment on Miami Beach. The pretext was that Dennis would cook us supper — a noodle dish he was fond of, a bachelor recipe with too much soy sauce — but I suppose during the long, windy ride down the palm-lined highway, I knew we had both signed up for something more, and I was nervous as we drove. We had both slept with other people: I with a boy in college, a close friend, just three times after we'd studied together and opened a bottle of wine, and Dennis with his ex, with whom he'd lived for three months.

Inside Dennis's apartment, it was quiet

and dark. He dropped his keys on the kitchen table and went to open the balcony doors. In blew a salty breeze that smelled of warm sand. He offered to make margaritas — this was a drink he knew I was fond of — and started rooting through the refrigerator. After a moment, he declared he was out of limes and would run to the market on the corner. He kissed me quickly and left. I went to the balcony and leaned against the metal railing. The sunset had started. Below, two Cuban men stood at the entrance to the café downstairs, talking animatedly in Spanish, and when they parted to let a third man by, I saw that the third man was Dennis, coming out of the building. He greeted the men and one of them raised a hand, and then Dennis walked a bit, tossing his keys into the air every few steps. He was happy. Any outsider could have seen it. He was happy because of me. After he went into the store on the corner — he called it the bodega — I watched the ocean, its rolling persistence, its calm fortitude. There were a few people still scattered along the beach. The sky was the color of bruised peaches, the sand bluish in the fading sunlight. Dennis emerged from the store with a brown bag under one arm. He came closer, then looked up and gestured toward the beach and the sunset. "Isn't it beautiful?" he called up to me. "Isn't it paradise?"

"Yes!" I called.

I cut the limes and he squeezed each half into a small glass pitcher. He dipped a finger in the juice and brought it to my lips. I tasted it and made a face, and he laughed. "We'll improve on it, I promise," he said. "There's nothing like fresh margaritas." As he spoke, I brought the knife down through a lime and felt it slice through my fingertip. I yelped and Dennis grabbed a dish towel from a drawer and pulled me into the bathroom, holding my bloody finger as we went. He sat me down on the toilet and rummaged through the medicine cabinet.

"It's not that bad," I said.

"It's a geyser," he said. He held my finger under the faucet while the cold water ran. Blood billowed and dissipated. "This is why I should never sharpen my knives," he said. "Clumsy female visitors, bleeding all over my kitchen." He smiled and I laughed. He toweled off my hand and spread a little ointment on my finger, then wrapped it in a small bandage. "Too tight?" I shook my head. He kissed my finger. "I don't like seeing you bleed, lady," he said. "I love you so much."

This was only the second or third time

the word had been said. I'd said it, too, of course, but he'd always said it first. I kissed him. After a few minutes, we went together into the bedroom, where the bed was unmade and discarded sneakers lay in front of the dresser. The sun was almost gone. Before we even lay down, I thought about afterward, when we would sip margaritas on the balcony. Dennis would be sweet. He would make the dinner he'd planned and rub my back and with every glance in my direction check subtly to see if I was happy. He didn't know I'd already done my reckoning. As we made our way to the bed, I had no doubts.

He started slow but that didn't last. Dennis made a joke about it having been a while, and I said it was like riding a bike, and he said not exactly, from what he recalled. Up to this point, we'd done some heavy petting on Bette's couch and in Dennis's car, but we had never been naked together. Still, his body was familiar to me, even the red hair between his legs and the warm, probing penis. What was most unfamiliar was my own body, the greediness of it, my eager response to his hands, his fingers. I was a me I'd never known before, a person who wanted baldly. Looking back, I realize that it was all relative, the sacrifices

78

I believed I was making, the risks I believed I was taking. Many people do much more for love than travel to another state and ignore their mother's advice. But you have to understand that to me, it was like falling with no net. It felt good, but it did not feel wise.

I returned to Bette's the next day, with Dennis, to change clothes. We found her sitting on the couch in the living room, smoking a joint with an ashtray balanced on her bare, bony knees. By this time, I'd seen Bette smoke several times and had even tried it with her twice — where Bette became calm and wide-eyed, I became silly and had difficulty finishing a sentence. For this reason, I'd decided marijuana was not, for me, a dignified option. The apartment smelled of bacon. "You're alive," she said. "Good to know."

"I should have called," I said. This was not something I'd even considered.

There was rustling in Bette's bedroom, and Benjamin emerged into the small open kitchen, wearing only slacks. "Want some bacon?"

He held out a plate, and Dennis stepped forward to take a piece. Benjamin cracked eggs into a bowl and whipped them with a

fork. I sat down next to Bette on the couch.
"Did you go back to the wreck?" I said
quietly, so only she heard.

She shook her head. "Jane backed out.
Something about her husband."

"That's too bad."

"I got excited over nothing. They're bringing it up next week."

"Won't there be another one?"

"We'll see," she said.

It was clear that something had changed.
Benjamin stepped into the living room from
the kitchen, holding a spatula. "Did you tell
her?" he said to Bette.

"Tell me what?"

"The first of April," he said. "Springtime."

"We set a date," said Bette. "My mother's
on her way over." As if realizing this fact for
the first time, she put out her joint and sat
up straight.

"Congratulations!" said Dennis. He shook
Benjamin's hand, then leaned down to kiss
Bette's cheek. She stretched to meet him,
but her eyes were dull, her mouth still. Her
cheeks were pink, probably from the marijuana.

"We don't have much time," said Benjamin. "Less time to get caught up in the
details, said this one." He gestured to Bette.

She squeezed my arm. "My mother is

80

making me shop for dresses. You have to come."

"Of course," I said, thinking that I wanted nothing less than to spend a day shopping with Dennis's mother. "Wash your face before she gets here," I said, and Bette nodded and got up, but Benjamin swung her into a bear hug and carried her into the bedroom. Her laughter was high and reluctant and his was baritone and booming. Dennis stepped out onto the little patio to try to fix the squeak in Bette's screen door, and I went to change my clothes and brush my hair in the apartment's small bathroom. When I joined him outside, Dennis said, "Good for them."

I wondered if this would change the timeline of our own engagement, then decided it didn't matter. "I guess I'm going shopping."

He took my hand. He was squatting and there was sweat along his brow and under his arms. We'd decided, during the ride from the beach, that I would stay at his apartment from that time forward. "I'll pick you up here, after. We'll go to Scotty's for fish, and then you can help me study for my exam."

"How do I do that?"

"Keep me from drinking too many margaritas."

"What about your mother?"

"My mother isn't invited."

"Be serious. What do I tell her?"

"Tell her about what?"

"About where I'm staying."

"Frances, my mother doesn't care."

"Of course she does."

"Well, she won't tell you if she does. And she won't ask." He stood up, and I heard his knees creak. We are not so young, I thought. Most people our age were married with children. He said, "Call me when you're all done with the ladies." Below us a car horn sounded, and we looked down over the porch railing to see Gloria in her shiny sedan, waving through the windshield. I called for Bette, and she came out looking freshly scrubbed, and we went downstairs together.

At a bridal shop on Miracle Mile — one in a row of them — Bette ended up in the dressing room with half a dozen gowns, sobbing while her mother snapped at the saleswoman to bring more options. Gloria tried in her own way to soothe Bette through the dressing room curtain. She told Bette it didn't matter what she wore, of course, she would look lovely, and all she was saying was that it would have been nice to have enough time to plan a *real* ceremony that would have some gravitas instead of rushing to throw a backyard barbecue. The saleswoman didn't seem surprised at this turn of events — apparently brides sobbing in dressing rooms were not uncommon — but she did align herself with Gloria. "April?" she said. "How do they expect you to find a caterer?" After half an hour of listening to Bette reject every dress handed to her, hearing her sobs turn to sniffles and back to sobs again, I opened the curtain and stepped into the room. Bette wore only a slip and a brassiere, and her face was a mess. The walls of the dressing room were cushioned with satiny white dresses on hangers. One of them was a simple silk gown, off the shoulder, with no lace or gems. I touched its hem. "I think this is rather pretty," I said.

"Then you should buy it," she said.

"Maybe I will," I said, ignoring her tone. I checked the price tag. The dress was $450. It all seemed a bit much all of a sudden, a bit quick. I could see how a person could become overwhelmed. I said, "Bette, do you have an idea of what you want?"

She seemed stymied by this question. "I guess not."

"Then you're not going to find it today," I said. "Get dressed."

She looked at me for a moment, then nodded and reached for her blouse.

Over time, I'd gotten a good idea of the role Bette and Benjamin's engagement had taken in the family — Grady teasingly called Benjamin "my son-in-law-to-be" or referred to their relationship as "timeless." Gloria fussed over Benjamin when he was around, and chastised Bette whenever she was glib or cross — Gloria was afraid, I assumed, that Benjamin might set off in the dead of night and never be heard from again. I had seen enough to know that this was not going to happen. When I'd met Benjamin over cocktails at Dennis's parents' house, I hadn't realized how long they'd been engaged and had asked him, stupidly, if he was looking forward to the wedding. He'd shrugged and looked sheepish. "I'm a regular guy," he said. "She knows that here." He touched his forehead. "As for here" — he touched his chest with a meaty hand — "I'm not sure." He seemed to me like the sort of person who might stroll headlong into his own broken heart.

While Bette dressed, I found Gloria on a love seat by the front store window, looking at the street. "This isn't going anywhere," I said.

"That is apparent," she said.

"She might be happier in something simpler. Something other than a gown."

"That's a good point, dear," she said. She was placating me. I sat down beside her, exhausted. I felt I should make some admission: I'm sleeping with your son. Or, I love your son. Or, your daughter doesn't seem to really want to marry Benjamin. She said, "You imagine certain ways of celebrating certain things. But your children have different ideas."

"It was very nice of you to take her shopping. I'm not sure she's ready yet."

"She'd better get ready."

"She will."

She stood and smoothed out her pants suit and walked to a row of dresses in the corner. She pulled a sleeveless beige shift from the bunch and held it up. "Now this, Bette would like. It looks like a burlap bag. Not for the wedding, of course, but maybe a luncheon." She took it back to the dressing room. After a few minutes Bette brought the dress to the counter and Gloria paid, and then we left the store for the bright afternoon.

I moved from Bette's apartment to Dennis's later that week. Bette sent me off with a joint rolled in a paper bag and a bottle of wine, and the way she repeatedly thanked me for cleaning and cooking convinced me, finally, that I'd been as much a pleasant diversion as a burden to her. I unpacked my suitcases into two of Dennis's dresser drawers, and we went shopping for groceries and bought a hanging plant for his balcony. In the mornings before he went to school, we ate breakfast and took walks on the beach. At least twice a week, I drove his car downtown to meet Marse for lunch or for drinks, or to pick up Bette from the sailing club and run errands or take her shopping. I'd never known anyone who'd lived with a boy before marriage. If Marse or Bette disapproved, or if Dennis's parents knew — we took pains to hide our situation — they didn't show it. Ultimately, I asked myself if I disapproved — and the answer was yes, but not so much that I was willing to change anything. Looking back, I'm proud of my otherwise traditional younger self.

The weeks passed in a sunny blur. On the weekends, we went to Stiltsville with Dennis's parents and Bette and Benjamin. The boys slept on the porch, Bette and I slept in the bunk beds, and Grady and Gloria slept in the big bedroom. Sometimes Marse came out in her Boston Whaler, and sometimes Bette took off in her sailboat in the morning and didn't return until evening. Gloria took naps in the hammock with an open book on her chest, and Grady took long walks on the wide sandbar that stretched between Dennis's house and the Becks' stilt house to the east — this area was called the flats. Sometimes I walked the flats with Grady and he pointed out starfish, sea worms, fire coral. One weekend, Marse insisted on teaching me to windsurf, so we took her boat to the Becks' house to borrow a windsurfer from Marcus Beck — merely a year later, Marcus's wife, Kathleen, would sponsor me and Marse for the Junior League — and within a couple of hours I managed to surf inelegantly across the flats on my own, my arms shaking and my knees bent. From the dock, Marse cheered me on.

Each week, new developments emerged in the planning of Bette's wedding. Gloria found a caterer, and she and Bette and I went to sample cakes at a bakery. We spent an hour taking bites from each sample and eventually chose a lemon cake with vanilla frosting. The following week, Bette and Benjamin arranged for the pastor from Grady and Gloria's church to perform the wedding. Then a week later Dennis was instructed to make sure his suit was ready and I was asked if I had a dress. Both Bette and

Gloria asked me this, on separate occasions, and I had the feeling they'd discussed the question beforehand: Does Frances have anything to wear? What if Frances shows up at the wedding in the same sundress she's worn every other day for two months? (I'd packed two large suitcases, but they were not nearly enough — I'd been in Miami three months at this point.) Marse and I went to Burdine's and spent an hour trying on clothes in the same dressing room, until the sales matron told us that our behavior — we were laughing and talking loudly — was disturbing the other customers, and we were asked to quiet down or leave. I ended up with an avocado-green shift and matching sandals from a consignment store, and Marse bought a wide-brimmed straw hat to wear with a white Easter suit she already owned. Instead of going back to Dennis's that night, we called him from a pay phone and had him meet us at Scotty's, and the three of us ended up going from one bar to the next, until at dawn we found ourselves at a tavern in Coconut Grove, sitting at a sticky wooden table in front of a dozen empty beer bottles.

I'd decided to stay in Miami through the wedding. The question of what would happen after was unresolved. I was out of money, of course. Dennis gave me some from time to time; he left twenty-dollar bills on the kitchen counter and joked that I was his courtesan, which I'd let him know I did not care for. I told myself that if Bette's wedding came and went and no plans had been formalized and still I didn't care to return to Atlanta, I would get a job and maybe even an apartment. Whether I would make these changes without a ring on my finger was not a question I allowed myself to consider.

But at this point I was so removed from my previous life that when I called home and my mother inquired about the future, I lied to her. I told her that I'd found a secretarial job at a bank, which I had not, and was looking for an apartment, which I wasn't. I told her that my supervisor's name was Millicent (she'd asked if I liked my supervisor, possibly because she suspected that I was fibbing, though I never knew for certain) and that Millicent was very strict. She asked if I could afford an apartment on my wages, and I said I was making almost twice what I'd been making in Atlanta. I told her I saved money by eating lunch in the bank's cafeteria and keeping half for my dinner. The cafeteria served a very nice meat loaf, I told her. I tried to avoid mentioning Dennis, as if my lies would reflect poorly on him. Every time I hung up the phone after having expanded my story in some way, I cried a little. I didn't recall ever having lied to my mother about anything more important than whether I was eating well or keeping my apartment clean. When my mother hinted that she thought I might be behaving irresponsibly — if only she'd known the truth — I rushed to reassure her. The fact that I lied to her so easily, with some regret but every intention of continuing, made me feel hardened and sad. When I told Dennis that I was lying to my mother, he took a breath and nodded, as if he understood the toll this exacted. This was the only pressure I ever put on him to move things along.

The weekend before the wedding, six of us — Dennis and I; Marse and her brother, Kyle; and Benjamin and Bette — packed into Dennis's station wagon and drove north on Highway 27 toward Lake Okeechobee, to Fisheating Creek. We stopped at Fisheating Creek Inn — a shack in the middle of a freshwater marsh, with a lunch menu that featured frogs' legs and alligator tail — and rented three canoes, then set off to a campground eight miles down the river. Dennis shared a canoe with Benjamin, Marse shared one with Kyle, and Bette and I canoed together. She sat in front and paddled distractedly. We took our time. The creek was wide and high for the season, and we portaged only twice during the trip. Fisheating Creek was flanked on both sides by bald cypress swamp and hardwood hammock dotted by oak trees and palm trees and ferns. Air plants clung messily to the trunks of the oaks; during the summer red and yellow flowers would sprout from their bellies. Along the edges of the water, between the knees of the knobby cypress roots, bloomed brilliant yellow flowers. "Butterweeds," Bette said, pointing. The flowers' bright faces were reflected in the black water. Bette pointed out an ibis, a hawk, an osprey. In the narrowest parts of the creek the forest encroached so heavily that the sunlight reached us in ribbons. Bette said that a century earlier, the creek had functioned as a highway to Lake Okeechobee, which supplied freshwater to all of Florida. She said that in the summer, thousands of swallowtail kites migrated to the creek to gorge themselves on water snakes and fish and rabbits, to prepare for the long flight back to South America. She told me to keep an eye out for panthers, black bears, burrowing owls, and of course alligators. It was like she was listing all that there was to fear around us, and as we passed I peered into the shadows of the swamp, alert for creatures that might strike or swoop. The first to appear was an alligator skulking among the cypress roots, its eyes hovering above the waterline. Once I'd seen one, I saw another, and before we'd gone a mile I'd seen too many to count on both hands, including babies as thin as snakes, sunning themselves on roots. The larger gators slunk into the water when we came close, and I tried not to think of them under the still black surface, swimming inches below my feet.

The others had already pitched the tents by the time Bette and I arrived at the campground, which was little more than a small island rising from the marsh, enough room for the canoes and tents and a picnic table and a few folding chairs. A tributary ran behind the mound of land, and a stand of cypress trees provided privacy that turned out to be irrelevant: we wouldn't see another human the entire weekend. Dennis used a machete to lop off the knobs of cypress roots that grew through the island's flattest parts, and the boys started a fire. We wore jackets over our swimsuits and cooked beans and hot dogs. We'd forgotten to bring bowls, so we ate out of mugs and cans, and once we'd settled in and darkness had fallen, the wildlife closed in around us. Owls made their strange humanlike calls, and every so often the muscular tail of an alligator splashed and a bullfrog croaked. "This place is creepy," said Marse, "but I can't seem to go a year without a visit." Her grandfather owned an old swamp house nearby, in Big Cypress — the government had been trying to buy him out since the preserve had been established twenty years earlier — and she told stories about using the outhouse and listening to panthers scavenging in the trash cans. During a lag in the conversation, I heard a grunt, and when I asked what it was, Bette answered, "Those are swamp pigs, rooting. They only come out at night." I could barely tell where the sounds were coming from, there were so many, and when finally Dennis and I crawled into our sleeping bags, I lay awake for an hour or more, listening.

In the morning, the men took off in two canoes to fish and Bette and Marse and I stayed behind. The river's glassy surface reflected the trees and tall grasses. Marse turned on a transistor radio and found a calypso station that barely came in. I had taken to wearing a swimsuit almost all the time, even when I wasn't planning on going in the water — this was something Marse and Bette did — and had even bought a new one, an orange-red halter with a zodiac pattern. Over the suit, I wore an old pair of Dennis's jeans that I'd cut across the thighs without hemming. I was tanner than I'd ever been and several pounds thinner, and had grown comfortable spending time outside in the sun, under a fishing hat Gloria had handed me at Stiltsville. We talked about Bette's wedding and Marse's love life — there was a guy from her office, a fling — and they asked me questions about Atlanta. No one asked when I was going home. No one ever asked.

It was South Floridian spring, which meant bright warm days and few mosquitoes, and nights as crisp as seventy degrees. We drank coffee until noon, then switched to cans of watery, ice-cold beer. After we'd been drinking for an hour or so, Bette wandered off to go to the bathroom, and Marse started cleaning up the campsite. I wanted her to sit down and relax with me, to enjoy the sunshine and the privacy and even the strange hollow calls of the wildlife around us. "We should do this again," I said to Marse.

"Sure."

"I mean it. We should make it an annual thing."

She looked at me strangely and started to speak, then stopped.

"What?" I said, but she didn't answer. I couldn't see any problem with what I'd said, but then it occurred to me: I'd taken to acting as if I was certain of my future in Miami, but at this point there was no ring on my finger. In Marse's mind, I might have been a placeholder in Dennis's life. "Marse," I said. "I'm not going anywhere."

"I know."

"This isn't a lark. I'm not . . ." I couldn't think of the right word. "An *affair.*"

"I know you're not." She took a breath. "I just wish we could forget what I told you when we met, about Dennis."

"Why?"

She stuffed beer cans into a trash bag. "It was really no big deal. Nothing would have come of it."

"I understand."

"I wasn't in love with him or anything."

I hadn't realized all that had gone unsaid between us. I wanted to say to her: I know what a crush is. And I know how difficult it is to look into your future and see nothing real, and how easy it is to conjure excitement out of thin air, just to have something

95

to keep you going. I said, "I behaved badly, I know." This was something it had taken me a while to admit to myself, though of course I didn't regret what I'd done. I said, "I was hoping you'd forgiven me."

There was a streak of mud across her forehead and another on her shorts. She wiped her brow with her forearm and pulled another beer from the cooler. She handed it to me. "I forgave you a long time ago." She sat down beside me. After a moment she said, "Maybe we'll do it again next year. But after that I'll be living in the south of France with my rich husband, and you two will be having babies and all that nonsense —"

Bette, returning from the trees, caught the tail end of Marse's sentence. "Not me," she said. "No babies."

"You don't think you'll have them?" said Marse, and Bette said, "No way."

Bette rummaged through her bag and Marse and I stood up to finish cleaning the campsite. After I'd filled a trash bag, I turned to say something to Bette — I don't recall what — and I noticed that she had a pair of silver scissors in one hand, and a good-sized chunk of her blond hair in the other hand. "What are you doing?" I said. She smiled, then closed the scissors. Marse and I gaped at her.

"You're crazy," said Marse. "Benjamin is going to kill you."

"Benny doesn't care about my hair."

"Your mother is going to kill you," I said.

"I don't care about my mother."

"Why are you doing this?" Marse said.

"Why not?" said Bette. "Do you have a mirror? I want to make sure it's even."

"I have one," I said. I went to my tent and fished a compact from my bag. When I returned, Marse caught my eye and shook her head. I handed the compact to Bette. "Much obliged," she said. She opened the compact and looked at the part of her head where the hair was gone, then tried to resume cutting while holding the mirror in one hand.

For a moment, Marse and I watched her snip awkwardly behind one ear. Then I sat down on the bench next to her. "Here," I said, taking the mirror. I held it up, but I couldn't get the angle right and she kept having to adjust it to keep sight of herself. I said, "Give me the scissors." She hesitated. "I know what I'm doing," I said. I'd cut my mother's hair twice a year for more than a decade. I handed her the mirror and she handed me the scissors. I sat behind her, facing her back.

"Holy Moses," said Marse.

My hands shook a little. "I can't believe I'm doing this."

"Let's not get sentimental," said Bette. "It's just a bit of *hair.*"

The scissors were sharp and cut easily. Her hair fell to the ground in feathery blond bits. I spent a long time making sure all the pieces were even before I stopped. Her new do was less than an inch in length, as short as a boy's. She looked in the mirror. "Much better," she said. She stood up and walked a few feet away, then turned around to pose like a model in a catalog, touching her head with both hands. "It's adorable, isn't it?"

"It is kind of adorable," I said.

"Hell of a job," said Marse to me.

"Let's go for a ride," said Bette.

We launched the last canoe and climbed in. Bette sat in front and Marse sat in back, which left me cross-legged in the well between them. As we made our way down the shadowy creek, I leaned against the yoke of the canoe and looked up at the cypress canopy, at the river of sky that flowed between the trees. It was like paddling down the nave of a cathedral. I closed my eyes. After a few minutes, I was jarred by a wild splashing and the tipping of the canoe to port and back to starboard, and when I opened my eyes Bette was standing at the bow, legs wide, wielding her paddle like a jousting stick against a large alligator a foot away. We had startled it — perhaps Bette had bumped it with her paddle when passing — and its top jaw was open and its teeth bared, its tail curled upward, and its strange pudgy claws spread wide against the marshy bank. Above it, Bette stood brandishing the paddle like a warrior and looking straight into its eyes. Marse gave a quick thrust and Bette pivoted as we passed, keeping the paddle inches from the gator's jaws. Once we were at a safe distance, she sat down. Slowly, the alligator lowered its jaw and settled deeper into the marsh. "Goddamn it!" said Marse. "What the hell happened?"

"We got too close," said Bette.

"Goddamn," said Marse again. I'd never been around a woman who swore as freely as Marse did. "That thing looked hungry."

"It might be hungry," said Bette, "but it doesn't want to eat us."

One might assume, given the prevalence of alligators in South Florida, that attacks on humans would be more common. Over the years, there was the occasional anomaly: once a gator chased down and mawed a young boy riding a bike down a boardwalk in Shark Valley, and once one found its way into a private swimming pool in Coral Gables and drowned a full-grown man. But for the most part, alligators eat fish and ducks. Despite their ability to outrun a human, they wait for their prey to come to them. Years after the incident at Fisheating Creek, I saw a photograph of an alligator being swallowed whole by a Burmese python (for some reason, many South Floridians come to own exotic nonnative animals, then release these animals into the wild when they become tiresome, and they multiply) and I remembered that day, when we were inches from an alligator's open jaw, and I felt sorry for it.

Down the creek, we met the boys head-on. Kyle held up a string of jewel-toned bass, and we turned and followed them back to the campsite. When the boys noticed Bette's hair, Kyle said, "Wow!" and Dennis said, "Can't we trust you girls to be left alone?" I thought I heard an undercurrent of irritation in his voice. I supposed he'd witnessed a lifetime of impetuous decisions on Bette's part.

"God, woman," said Benjamin, "you went ahead and did it, didn't you?"

I was relieved to know that the haircut had been discussed prior to that afternoon. I realized that Bette had brought the scissors for this purpose. When we were all standing on dry land, Benjamin touched Bette's head, laughing, then patted her butt affectionately. "You're something else," he said. He turned to me, because I was closest. "Isn't she something else?"

"Frances did it," said Marse.

Dennis said, "You cut her hair?"

"I have a little experience," I said. "I think it looks pretty good."

He looked at me as if he wasn't quite sure what to think. "You're not going to do that to yourself, are you?"

I put an arm around his waist. "You never know."

That night, Dennis taught me to gut a fish, and I helped him cook it and made potatoes in a skillet. The meal was as good as any I'd eaten in my life. We told the boys about our encounter with the alligator, and Dennis squeezed my knee and told me to be careful, and I caught Marse watching us in the firelight. Also in the firelight, I watched Bette bring a hand to her hair. Her gaze was deep and private. Though she and Benjamin were planning to wed in a few days, I knew in my bones that this would not happen.

We set the timer on Benjamin's camera and took a group photograph on our last morning at the campsite. Marse, Bette, and I sat cross-legged on the ground and the men stood above us. Dennis was behind me, Benjamin was behind Bette, and Kyle was behind Marse, waving at the camera. I wore a diamond-checked minidress, Marse wore a red Swiss dot jumpsuit, and Bette wore a crocheted halter top and long canvas shorts. The men were shirtless. All six of us were smiling so you could see our teeth. I love this photograph. All these years, I've loved it. And one day my daughter found it in a chest filled with other old photographs, and she framed it and propped it up on her bookcase, first in her dorm room and then in her home. Once I overheard her pointing it out to a friend: "These are my parents," she said. "This is my aunt Bette, and this is my mother's best friend Marse." In the way that old photos sometimes do, looking at it makes my heart ache a bit. But also I enjoy remembering my younger self this way: as an adventurer, as carefree. Mostly, I don't think I was these things, but I guess sometimes, in Miami, I could be.

On the morning of Bette's wedding, Dennis and I drove from South Beach to his parents' house with the windows down, trying to dry our hair by the time we arrived. We'd gotten up late, after making love in the warm patch of sun that came in through his bedroom window. Gloria had specifically asked me to be there early to help set up, and I'd promised we would be — in matters of timeliness and politesse, the woman is always held more accountable than the man — and I was panicked to think I would disappoint her. But when we arrived, Gloria was upstairs with Bette and the caterers had commandeered the kitchen and backyard. Flowers were already in vases on the tables, and a row of silver chafing dishes lined the buffet. A bartender was arranging liquor bottles on a table down by the water. Grady called up the lawn from the pier, waving, and Dennis squeezed my arm and took off down the green expanse, his hands in his suit pockets. When I turned toward the house, I saw Benjamin sitting in a chair on the back deck, facing the water. He didn't seem to notice me. I climbed the deck stairs, and when I stood right beside him he looked up, shading his eyes with one hand. "Hello there," he said.

"What are you doing out here?"

"Bad luck to see the bride, or some such. The pastor's late — car trouble."

"That's too bad."

"We were going to practice."

"Maybe you don't need to practice."

"Maybe." He reached over and opened his palm. In it was a plain gold band: Bette's wedding ring. "This is it."

He seemed to want me to take it, so I did. "Very pretty."

"It's what she wanted. All of this, even the dress, is what she wanted."

"The dress is lovely," I said. The dress Bette had chosen was actually a suit, a fluted skirt and fitted jacket made of creamy brocade. I'd seen it hanging on the back of a closet door at her apartment, and I'd complimented her taste. "I'm airing it out," she'd said, and I'd said, "Is it wet?" I was always confusing things she said, taking her literally. "It's soggy with starch," she'd said, and again I wasn't sure if she was speaking figuratively. It was an experience I would continue to have for as long as we knew each other.

"But it's strange," said Benjamin. "Don't you think it's strange? Don't you want more?"

"No," I said. I didn't think it was strange to not want gowns and diamonds and fancy parties on one's wedding day. I didn't think in itself this was alarming at all.

"Frances, I can afford a diamond. I want to buy my girl a diamond."

I shook my head. "I don't want a diamond."

He looked at me for a long moment, then forced a laugh. "Girls with heads on their shoulders — a mixed blessing." His hands twitched around each other in his lap. He was not nervous about marriage, of course: he was meant for marriage. He would be content in its warm headlock. But Benjamin knew, as I knew, that Bette was not made for marriage, and that if she didn't know it that afternoon, she would figure it out one day, perhaps in the grocery store while choosing a melon, or at the tennis courts on a sunny Saturday, or outside their child's school before the ringing of the final bell. He wiped his face. "Ignore me. Just jitters, I think. I'll make myself a drink." He walked off the deck and crossed the lawn to the bar. I watched him pour something into a glass and drink it and stand there alone, holding the table with one hand.

Inside, I knocked on Bette's old bedroom door, and Gloria's voice said, "Who's there?"

"It's Frances."

The door opened, and there stood Gloria in a brassiere and girdle and stockings. Behind her, Bette was lying on her bed fully dressed, complete with white patent leather

105

shoes, wearing more eye makeup than I'd ever seen her wear. Her short hair was blown dry and styled smartly. "Did the caterer find the wineglasses?" said Gloria.

Because I'd seen wineglasses on the bar outside, I said yes.

"Did they replace the wilted flowers?" she said.

"Yes," I said.

Bette sighed loudly at the ceiling.

"Is my husband still tinkering with his toy?" said Gloria.

"I think so," I said.

"What is Benjamin doing? Is he practicing his lines?"

I nodded. "He said the pastor's late."

"That pastor is always late," said Gloria. To Bette, she said, "I warned you."

"It doesn't matter," said Bette quietly.

Bette's old bedroom was large and bare, with beige walls and a light blue carpet that had seen heavy traffic. Her bed was high, with an antique wooden headboard, and each time she shifted it squeaked and knocked lightly against the wall. A car door slammed outside, and then another, and when I went to the window I saw that guests had begun to arrive. Grady was on the front porch, directing parking. He wore a blue seersucker suit with a red bow tie, and his hair was, as usual, uncombed.

Gloria joined me at the window. "The Tanners are here. And the Becks. And who is that? The Everests. People certainly are punctual, aren't they?"

She stepped to the closet and pulled a lavender suit from a dry cleaning bag. While she dressed, I leaned over Bette. She was staring at the ceiling and humming softly. "What's going on in your head?" I said.

I could see her deliberate between fibbing and telling the truth. "I'm just lying here, minutes before my wedding, thinking about diving."

"Just diving, or diving a wreck?"

She nodded. "There's one in the Keys, an albatross — that's a plane, not a boat. Jane asked me to go down this weekend."

"You're busy this weekend." In fact, Bette and Benjamin planned to take Grady's boat to Bimini for their honeymoon.

"Yes, I am." She blinked. "Mother, could you please leave?"

She said this as nicely as possible, but still Gloria, who was not yet zipped, was surprised. "I beg your pardon?" she said. I rushed to help her zip up. "Thank you, Frances. Dear, I will leave, but only because I want to check to make sure they didn't bungle the order of the buffet." She paused before leaving. "You look very pretty," she told Bette. "Refresh your lipstick. You have ten minutes."

When she'd left, Bette hopped off the bed and stood by the window, biting her nails. "We're serving cocktails first. That was Benny's idea," she said. "He said he wanted people to relax and enjoy themselves." She started to cry. When I stepped forward to console her — how I would do it, I didn't know, she wasn't a particularly consolable person — she raised a hand to stop me. "Don't. I deserve it. It's my fault."

"What's wrong?"

"Poor Benny."

"He wants you to be happy," I said, which was not quite the truth. He wanted her to be happy with him.

She stopped crying and stared through the window at the driveway. More car doors slammed. I stood next to her and watched as carload after carload of people — older people, mostly, Grady and Gloria's age — stepped out, holding their hats and smoothing down their skirts. "There are Benjamin's parents," said Bette. She waved ineffectually at the window pane. "Hi Maggie, hi Bud," she said softly. To me, she said, "They are such nice people. All of these people, all the people who are here, are really nice. It was kind of them to come." She turned toward me. "You should marry Dennis," she said. "You'll have a beautiful wedding. You'll look so pretty, and he'll look so handsome, and the way you two look together — the way you two look at each other — you should marry him." She glanced back out the window. "Will you?" she said.

"Yes," I said.

"Promise?" she said, and again I said, "Yes."

"My mother will be pleased. She likes you. I didn't tell her you cut my hair."

"I appreciate that."

She started to undress, shoes and stockings first. Then off came her skirt, then her jacket, and then she was standing there in just a camisole, shivering. I handed her a pair of blue jeans and a blouse from her closet. "Are you absolutely sure?" I said.

"I'm so sorry." She had her hand on the doorknob. "Will we still be friends?"

"Of course." I reached out to touch her shoulder, and though she was not fond of displays of affection, she turned and hugged my neck, hard, before stepping through the doorway and hurrying down the stairs.

I found Dennis on the back porch with a bottle of beer in his hand. "Is the girl ready yet?" he said. "My mother is restless."

Gloria was below us, on the patio by the pool, standing with a couple I'd never seen before. I caught her stare. Seeing my expression, she took a tentative step toward me, then stopped. She pointed at the back kitchen door. Dennis asked where I was going, but I didn't stop to answer him. She reached the kitchen before I did and closed the door behind us. Inside, two black women in white aprons were stacking dishes and wiping down the counter. "Could we have a minute?" said Gloria, and the women left the room. She took me by the shoulders. "What is it? What did she do?"

"Gloria, she's left."

"No!" She smacked the counter with the flat of her hand, wincing, then smacked it again. "That little brat," she said, but in the next moment her lip started to tremble. "Get Grady for me?"

I stepped out of the kitchen and signaled to Dennis. He came forward with long strides. "Get your father," I said. He started to step into the kitchen — he could see his mother bent over the counter — but I stopped him. "Hurry."

I led Gloria to the kitchen table and got a juice glass from the cupboard. I poured from a bottle of wine that was open in an ice bucket on the counter. She took several

110

long swallows, then started to cry. "I'm sorry I yelled at you," she said.

"That doesn't matter."

"I know it's not your fault."

It had not occurred to me, until that moment, that she might think this was my fault. How could it be? But the timing of events — my arrival on the scene, Bette's assent to setting a wedding date, our burgeoning friendship, and now this horror: I suppose it was possible my presence had stirred the brew of their lives, however subtly. Gloria finished her wine and handed me the glass. "More, please," she said, and I rushed to refill it. Grady came in the back door, Dennis behind him, and in a second Grady was kneeling beside his wife's chair, and she was in his arms, sobbing. "It's my fault," she kept saying. "That spoiled little girl."

Grady shushed her softly and said, "Sometimes things just go haywire."

Dennis pulled me to his side and we watched his parents. "Where is she?"

"She left. Someone needs to tell Benjamin."

"I'll do it," Dennis said. I stepped onto the back deck to give Gloria and Grady some privacy, and Dennis crossed the lawn toward the bar, where Benjamin stood with a small circle of friends. Dennis led him toward the house, and when they were far from other people, he put his arm around Benjamin's large shoulders and started talking. Benjamin stopped short, then put a hand over his face. When his hand came down I saw that he was not angry, not upset. He looked calm but weary, and he nodded and took several deep breaths. He even looked around a little, as if hoping to see her, then turned back to Dennis and shook his hand. Together they made their way back up to the house.

Back in the kitchen, there was some discussion of who should be the one to make the announcement. Benjamin volunteered, then Gloria, then Grady — it was as if they were fighting for the unpleasant task, attempting to revive the good manners one expects on a wedding day. But Gloria was a mess — it was clear she'd been crying — and Grady seemed unable to leave her side, even to refill her glass, which I was called on to do a third time. In the end, it was Dennis who stepped onto the back deck and tapped a spoon against a glass to get the crowd's attention. The rest of us huddled behind him. Fifty pairs of stylish couples and the odd single (including Marse, whom I'd spotted standing with Dennis's friend

Paul) peppered the lawn and the limestone patio, and in a moment all eyes were on Dennis. He held on to the wooden deck railing as he spoke. His voice shook. "Good afternoon," he said, then cleared his throat and raised his voice. "We are so pleased all of you could make it here today to celebrate with our family." He paused. It seemed, from his first sentence, that he was going to make a very different speech. "I love my sister," he said. "I know you love her, too. But let's face it, she's an odd duck. And that's part of what we love about her." There was some nervous chuckling. "We want you to stay and eat and enjoy the afternoon, please. But I'm sorry to say there is not going to be a wedding." A gentle gasp passed through the crowd. Benjamin's parents, who were standing by the swimming pool, clutched each other and his mother put her hand to her mouth. Dennis raised his glass. "To love and friendship," he said. "In all its forms."

Dennis and I left the backyard together and walked around the side of the house, out of view, and once we were alone, he bent and put his hands on his knees. "You did great," I said, and he said, "I thought I was going to vomit. I could kill Bette." But when he rose up again, he was smiling. "I

113

never said it would be dull, did I?" he said. I laughed, and then he started laughing. He took his keys from his pocket and pulled me toward the front of the house, then stopped: his car was buried several deep in the driveway. He took my hand and we weaved through the cars until we reached the far side of the driveway, and then we ducked under a ficus and emerged onto the neighbor's lawn.

"Should we leave your parents?" I said.

"They're fine. They'll host." He loosened his tie, and, not letting go of my hand, pulled me up to the neighbor's front door. When a man answered, Dennis said, "I'm sorry to bother you, Mr. Costakis, but I was wondering if I might borrow a car."

"Your sister's on the lam, is she?" said Mr. Costakis. I guessed that he'd been spying and had seen her flee from the house. He chewed tobacco and ran a hand through his slick gray hair. "I should drop by for some grub."

"Yes, it's all very amusing," said Dennis.

Mr. Costakis handed Dennis his keys. "Bring it back with a full tank," he said, then extended a hand to me. "I've heard about you. You've taken a bite of our boy's heart."

I blushed. "Nice to meet you."

We drove away then, and with the windows down I could hear the noise from Dennis's family's backyard, and from that distance it sounded no different from your average party, with glasses clinking and conversations humming. "Where are we going?" I said to Dennis.

"Wherever we want." He reached for my hand and brought it to his lips. He seemed content, driving through the early evening in a strange car. We took the highway north to Rickenbacker Causeway, then paid the toll and crossed onto Virginia Key, past the windsurfers off the narrow strip of beach, past the line of palm trees that shaded the sand, then over a second bridge onto Key Biscayne. We drove to the far tip of the key, then turned around and drove back. The sun was starting to set over downtown, and the buildings — the city seemed large to me then, though it would double in breadth and height and population during the time I lived there — reflected the pink-orange light. The water was dark blue, spitting whitecaps in the wind, and as we left the causeway behind I breathed deeply, inhaling the smell of the ocean. We wound down Bayshore Drive past Vizcaya, where we'd spent a magical night under the stars soon after meeting — it seemed a long time ago, even then — past Mercy Hospital, where almost every room had a bay view, past the coral rock houses of Coconut Grove and Biscayne Bay Yacht Club, where Dennis's parents were members and one day we would be, and past Scotty's and Dinner Key Marina and Dennis's old elementary school. I had learned my way around, but I didn't know how or when it had happened.

I suggested we head to the Hungry Sailor, a dark bar in downtown Coconut Grove where Marse and Bette and I had found ourselves many nights among a crowd of regulars, under walls ringed with colored Christmas lights. We parked, and Dennis led me up to the rooftop, where patio tables were scattered on tar matting overlooking Grand Avenue. Dennis ordered a round of margaritas and looked down on the crowded street. A rickshaw passed, carrying a tourist couple who hooted with laughter as the driver dipped and circled to entertain them. On the corner, a woman with a high Afro handed out fliers, and down the block a group of kids sat in a circle on a cement patio. Dennis took my hand and sighed. "Good Lord, my sister," he said. I saw that he cared enough about his sister not to care much about the ruined wedding.

The margaritas were tangy and cold. I let

my shoes drop and propped my feet on the low wall of the rooftop, and I held Dennis's hand. The sun went down, and it grew a little chilly. Dennis put his coat around my shoulders and ordered another round. It seemed we were celebrating after all. Dennis pointed below us, to a mannequin in the window of a lingerie shop across the street — but then I saw that she wasn't a mannequin at all. She was a live person, wearing red bikini underwear and a lacy pink robe, her legs tucked beneath her in a white wicker love seat, her chin propped on one hand. "What a job!" I said.

"Boring as hell," said Dennis.

"Some people love to be watched."

Dennis was looking at me. "When it's our turn, you won't run."

"No," I said. I knew that all I had to do was turn and meet his eyes. I knew that if I did this, he would sink to one knee and take off his college ring and slide it onto my finger, where it would feel as heavy as a stone. But maybe because we were living a stolen evening, an evening allotted for another activity entirely, or because my love for him raged so wildly that I felt it throbbing in my teeth and pressing against my lungs, I did nothing but sip my drink. After a while, the model's shift ended. She stood and stretched and tied her robe around her waist, yawned, and walked into the fluorescent innards of the store.

Looking back, it seems that the whole episode, from meeting Dennis to marrying him, went by in a blink. When Dennis did propose — kneeling, on the stilt house dock where we'd met — I believed my love for him was strong. Now, though, I know it was a blip, a farce. A thousand times, my love might have dampened instead of swelled. I had no idea then what would happen to my love, what nourishment it would receive, how mighty it would grow. I thought: I love him. And so, as if it were the only answer I could give, the only answer available to me, I said yes.

We married in Atlanta, in the Baptist church I'd attended as a child. I wore an empire-waist gown with lacy cap sleeves and satin Mary Janes with chunky heels. I was so stunningly, stupidly happy that I remember little outside of what is frozen in photographs: Dennis's grip over mine as we cut the three-tiered cake; my mother spreading my veil and my father pumping Dennis's hand; Grady extending his arm in a toast; me posing on the chapel steps with my mother on one side and Bette and Marse on the other. Back in Miami, Dennis's parents threw us a reception at their yacht club, and then Dennis and I spent a week in the Keys, hopping from island to island in his father's boat and camping on shallow beaches. One night we woke to the sight of hundreds of glowing anemones drifting by. In the morning, dozens had washed ashore and lay sickly at the foot of our tent. Dennis gave me a book of Wallace Stevens poems with certain pages dog-eared, and sometimes we read the poems to each other before falling asleep.

Dennis graduated from law school and passed the bar exam and was hired by a firm downtown. With inheritance from his grandmother, we bought our own home in Coral Gables, a three-bedroom ranch with a large backyard and a ponytail palm in one corner. We culled spare furniture from Dennis's parents' garage and secondhand stores, and hung paintings I'd made during college. Within the year I was pregnant. We had a little girl and named her Margo, ostensibly after Dennis's maternal grandmother but in truth because I loved the name: I thought it was earthy and wise and unmistakably South Floridian, a tropical name for reasons I couldn't explain. Margo was a fleshy, contemplative baby with Dennis's blue-green eyes and my pointy-tipped ears. My mother took the train down and stayed a month in our guest room, and during the day we took turns changing Margo and giving her long, warm baths. We sat on a blanket in the backyard and made plans for her future: my mother predicted she would be a stunning beauty, possibly a fashion model, and I predicted she would be a career woman with expensive handbags and a busy social calendar. We told her there had never been a sweeter baby. After my mother returned to Atlanta, it was, oddly, Grady who took time off to help me while Dennis was at work. He brought groceries and held the baby so I could shower, and stepped out to light a pipe when I opened my blouse to breast-feed. While I nursed Margo, she looked up at me as if she didn't quite know who I was, but she was willing to accept my love anyway, to give me the benefit of the doubt. When she was sleepy, she blinked in a slow-motion way that reminded me of a sloth I'd seen in a nature show on television. Instead of dividing, the focus I'd previously reserved for Dennis multiplied; in the early months of Margo's life I found myself stunned at my luck. I'd found a person to love, and together we'd made another person to love. It was simultaneously exactly what I'd wanted and more than I could have asked for myself.

When Dennis was home, we took long walks with Margo in her stroller, and on the weekends we put her in a life vest and went to the beach, or out on Grady's boat, or to Stiltsville, where I held tightly to her and stepped carefully, fearful of falling with her into the water. She clung to Dennis's chest as he walked the flats and giggled maniacally when he dunked her. She got sunburned and the pediatrician reminded me sternly about sunscreen — the only bottle we owned back then sat on a shelf in the downstairs stilt house bathroom, crusty at the neck and watery with time and disuse. She and I spent hours together in the hammock downstairs, napping and reading, sweaty locks of hair plastered to her forehead. She took her first teetering steps in the stilt house living room, from Dennis's lap to mine. After that, the stilt house became a kind of disaster area for a time, where I was called on to be ever-vigilant as she darted in each direction, small enough to fit through the porch railing or steps, clumsy enough to slip from the dock. Dennis and I had talked briefly about putting up netting or fencing, but with so many hazardous surfaces — the entire downstairs,

the wraparound porch, the T-shape dock —
it wasn't feasible. Instead, Dennis started
teaching her to swim when she was just ten
months old. When she was two, she spent
hours on his lap as he fished off the dock,
clapping each time he reeled in a fish. When
she was almost three, Marse bought her an
orange bikini with yellow polka dots and
she wore it every day of the summer, refusing every other garment in her closet. When
she was four, she and Bette put on elaborate
performances on the porch, wherein Margo
played a pirate or schoolteacher, and Bette
played a damsel in distress or an insubordi-
nate student, and by the end of the day they
were both sweating through their T-shirts
and glassy-eyed with exhaustion.

Those early years of Margo's life, of our
marriage, were uncomplicated to a degree
that I've never experienced again. But every
so often, during this period, I would find
Dennis sitting in front of a bottle of beer at
the kitchen table, or alone on the porch at
Stiltsville, and when I asked him what was
wrong he would say simply that he did not
like his job. I suppose if we had let it, this
could have become the ruling discontent in
our home. But he was not the kind of man
who took to moping, and for years this was
a back-burner issue, a low-grade nuisance.

We tried for a time to have a second child, and then when Margo was three I miscarried, and then eight months later I miscarried again, and then five months later, again. It was a terrible time. I felt as if our lives had been put on hold; the future darkened. It's incredible to realize that one can't have children simply by taking the usual steps. Doctors couldn't seem to help, and I might have become bitter in the face of this fact, as so many people do, but later in my life I would need to trust doctors, to be guided by them, so I am glad this wasn't the case. Then, some months after the third miscarriage, I chaperoned Margo's kindergarten class on a field trip to the Everglades, and we were walking in the early evening down a swampy path when our guide pointed to an owl perched on a high branch, and Margo's freckled face when she searched the sky for a glimpse of the creature was so open, so full of joy, that I decided (or I realized, I'm not sure which) I didn't need more children. Dennis had wanted a noisier household — this was difficult, knowing how he wanted it — but eventually he followed my lead. I concentrated on Margo, our marvel, and the sadness of losing the pregnancies ebbed over time, and I thanked God for her.

As for my new hometown, I'd fallen quickly and surely in love with it. I loved to drive through the dense neighborhoods with my car windows down and smell the rotting sweetness of a ripening mango tree. I loved to eavesdrop on the loud conversations of the ladies at the deli counter, ferreting out select phrases using the lazy Spanish I'd acquired over the years. I loved the lychees and star fruit that fell into my yard over the neighbor's fence, and I loved the bright bougainvillea that dropped its papery pink petals onto my lawn. I loved the rusty barges loaded with stolen bicycles that plodded down the Miami River and out to sea. I loved the half-dozen chilly February nights, all the windows in the house open and the fireplace going. I loved the limestone and the coral rock, the fountains and the ocean and the winding blue canals. I loved the giant banyans and the dense wet mangroves and the gumbo-limbo trees and the many-sized, many-shaped palms. I loved the pelicans and manatees and stone crabs and storms and even the thick, damp summers.

Miami is the only place in this country where Stiltsville could exist, and for a while I had the good fortune of spending time there.

I lived in Miami through scandals and

riots, through dozens of tropical storms and one devastating hurricane, through the Mariel boat lift and the cocaine cowboys. Outside Florida, I've never met anyone else who lived in Miami or cared to, or even anyone who is not somewhat surprised to hear that I lived there for half of my life. Perhaps what is still most surprising to me about Miami is that in spite of its lurid excesses and unreal beauty and unreal ugliness, it was possible for me, a girl from Georgia, to create a life there. Overall, an excellent life. A life I knew even as I was living it, I would miss when it came to an end.

1976

When Margo was five, we left her with Bette one summer weekend and took Marse and Dennis's old friend Paul, whom Marse had been dating on and off for a year, to Stilts-ville. The morning after we arrived, I was in the downstairs bathroom changing into a swimsuit when I heard an airplane's engine. The noise drew me into the sunlight on the dock and I watched as the plane — a Cessna with twin propellers and a red stripe down the fuselage — swept into the sky above our leg of the channel, then banked and circled over the Becks' stilt house to the northeast. Dennis was fixing breakfast while Marse and Paul dressed. Stiltsville was five miles from downtown Miami: from land, the plane would resemble a quiet mosquito, and the houses perched on stilts in the bay would dissolve in the blurring of waves and sky. But from where I stood, the plane's noise and proximity were overwhelming. It was seconds before I heard Dennis shouting over the sound. I turned to find him waving frantically from the upstairs porch for me to come inside.

I walked back up the dock, trying not to run, and up the stairs. Paul stood at the kitchen window holding binoculars to his face, and Marse stood beside him in her pajamas. Paul handed me the binoculars. "Looks like we have company," he said.

The Cessna's fuselage was pockmarked and the paint was faded and nicked. There was one man in the cockpit, but I couldn't make him out. "Drugs?" I said.

"What else?" said Paul.

"We don't know it's drugs," said Dennis.

"Who owns that house?" said Paul.

"The Becks," said Marse. "Marcus and Kathleen. They're hardly the type."

I thought of Kathleen Beck in her floral sundresses, and of the stork-shaped cookies she'd brought when Margo was born. Every so often I saw her in the parking lot of Margo's school, picking up her twin daughters. I'd thought she and Marcus had planned to be on the water that weekend, but they must have changed their minds.

A hatch door opened beside the cockpit. "Here we go," said Marse. We waited, and then a package dropped into the water ten yards off the Becks' dock. There was a small splash and the bright white package bobbed immediately to the surface. The Cessna circled once more and headed southeast, away from land.

We stepped onto the porch. There was little current, and any movement of the package was almost imperceptible. "What are we waiting for?" said Paul.

Dennis watched the package through the binoculars. It seemed to be heading toward the Becks' house; if so, it would slip under the dock, past the pilings, and out to sea. The whole process would take three hours, or five at the most. "Could be messy," said Dennis.

"We can't just leave it there," said Marse. "We should call the Coast Guard."

"Why would we do that?" said Paul.

I said, "Calling the Coast Guard isn't a bad idea."

"I'd rather not," said Dennis.

"Why?" I said.

He didn't look at me. "Because the registration on the boat is — well, it's lagging."

"I don't think they'll care about our boat registration, honey. Besides, the Coast Guard is federal."

"They could call the marine police."

Paul said, "How well do you know these

128

people, the Becks?"

"Fairly well," said Dennis.

"Kathleen's a Girl Scout troop leader," said Marse.

"Marcus plays the tuba, for goodness' sake," I said. "This has nothing to do with them."

Paul took the binoculars. "Someone could be in there," he said. We all looked at the Becks' stilt house, which was a smaller version of our own, painted white with blue shutters. "They could be waiting until dark to make the pickup."

It had become apparent that all the cloak-and-dagger talk was just that. But I was glad the men had found something to occupy them. Weekends at Stiltsville — our little island, our weekend oasis — tended to stretch out when we entertained guests. "Let's just keep an eye on it, see what happens," I said. "I'll finish breakfast."

"I smell adventure," said Paul.

"You always smell adventure," said Marse.

They were not a demonstrative couple; I'd rarely even seen them kiss. Dennis and I had set them up after years of having said we should; we'd had them over for dinner, and the following weekend they'd attended an office party at Marse's firm, and after the party — I knew this because Marse told me — they'd gone for a midnight cruise in her boat, and wound up having sex on the deck. For a time, Marse had been smitten. A month before the weekend at Stiltsville, though, she'd told me they were through — something about an argument at a wedding, where friends of his had not known who she was, or had mistaken her for someone else — but then he'd popped back into her life and their relationship had resumed. I didn't know the particulars. When it came to her love life, if nothing else, Marse was reluctant to give details. I could count on one hand the number of men she'd introduced me to. That's not including Dennis, of course.

When we'd arrived at the stilt house the day before, it had taken half an hour to dock. Our boat, which we'd bought after Dennis had been invited to join Grady's yacht club, was a nineteen-foot Mako with a single outboard engine and a center console — a boat for skiing and day trips, not serious seafaring — and the current kept fighting us off. I stood on the gunwale, knees buckling with the waves, prepared to jump to the dock — but every time we came close, Dennis shifted too soon into neutral and the tide pulled us away. The downtown skyline shimmered in the heat, supporting the sunset on its shoulders. Night advanced from the east. If we didn't dock soon, I thought, we'd have to open the house in the dark.

Marse climbed onto the gunwale beside me and stood there in her bikini, her hair wet with spray from the choppy ride. "I can make it," she said. "No offense, but I'm lighter than you."

I moved out of her way. "Be careful."

"Don't sweat it," she said, crouching. I was afraid she would slip off right then, while Dennis was bringing us around again. The dock was yards away, and the water in the channel was soupy with roiling sand and seaweed. I planted my feet. Dennis stood at the console, sweating and gritting his teeth, his too-long hair spiking into his eyes, and his beard — which he'd cultivated over the last year — dark with perspiration. He was a good captain. Over the years, we would upgrade to a twin-outboard sports fisherman, then to a thirty-six-foot Hatteras with a tuna tower. Now, though, in the midst of the docking fiasco, with only 175 horsepower at his disposal, Dennis was dejected. "This has never happened before, I swear," he called out. Marse laughed, and Paul slapped Dennis on the shoulder.

"Don't sweat it," said Paul. "We'll get there when we get there."

Paul was a pink-cheeked man, fleshier than Dennis but more muscular as well, with thick black hair that had started to recede. He and Dennis had sailed together during high school, and after graduating they'd spent six months together in Spain, traveling, and though this was a trip Dennis remembered fondly, they had not continued to be quite so close. I'd been around Paul many times, but almost always in a group setting — a dinner party, a luncheon at the yacht club, a day of boating with friends. He struck me as the type of man who believed himself more handsome and charming than he was.

Dennis gripped the throttle, his jaw sharp. The boat started toward the dock again. The engine sputtered as Dennis eased back on the throttle, then hummed as he shifted into neutral. I hoped our momentum would be strong enough to fight the tide until Marse had her chance.

She jumped earlier than I would have. Maybe my timing had been our problem all along. She landed on the dock with a slap and grabbed a piling for balance, then stood as we drifted away. "Here," I yelled, throwing her a line. She caught it awkwardly, hands splayed at knee level, then wedged a foot behind a piling and pulled us in. I felt her pride, her sense of strength. The men hooted and I clapped. When the boat reached the dock, Paul stepped off and took Marse in his arms. Over her shoulder, he winked at me.

I unlocked the gate and sent Marse to unlatch the bedroom shutters and crank open the windows while I lugged the rocking chairs onto the porch. Dennis started the generator and retied Marse's cleat knots, then lit the pilot lights on the refrigerator and stove — both of these ran on gas, and we used the generators as rarely as possible, for overhead lights — while I unloaded the groceries. On my last trip, Paul intercepted me at the bottom of the stairs. He took a bag from my arms and put it down. "You're bleeding," he said. He reached for my hand and held it between us. There was a shallow slice along the outside of my thumb, a ridge of blood. "You should get something on this," he said. "It might get infected."

"Yes, doctor," I said. I meant to tease, but he glanced up sharply. "It's nothing, really," I said. There was a bead of sweat or salt water on his nose. Already, the day's whiskers darkened his jaw. I wondered if he was the type of man who never shaved on weekends, if by Monday morning he would have a beard as thick as Dennis's.

Paul picked up my other hand, examined it, dropped it. "Hand me that, would you?" he said, motioning to a duffel bag at the foot of the stairs. I turned and bent down for it. Paul had a way — I'd felt it before — of making me feel like I had a stake in giving him what he wanted. "Get something on that cut within the hour," he said.

"Yes, sir," I said, and he turned away, as if I'd been keeping him.

After dinner, we sat in rocking chairs on the porch, our legs perched on the railing, eight feet pointing toward shore. The world had gone from blue to purple, and the only lights in the sky were the distant windows of downtown Miami and the stars. Dark water stretched in every direction. I said, "What does everyone want to do tomorrow?"

Dennis's hand was on my thigh. "I want to fish," he said, stroking my skin with his thumb.

"Me, too," said Marse. This surprised me. "And I want to swim."

I collected the empty beer cans and took them into the kitchen. While I was inside, I saw the others get up from their chairs and move to the porch railing. I heard Paul's laugh swell, and it was a wholehearted laugh, the laugh of someone relaxed. I felt the muscles in my neck and shoulders soften. Marse appeared in the doorway. "Frances!" she said. "We're jumping — get your suit."

"In the dark?" I left the beers on the counter and joined her. Dennis had a leg over the porch railing and held on to the roof with one hand. Next to him, Paul leaned out, scanning the water. Dennis swung his other leg over the rail and faced the water. "Here goes," he said. He jumped.

We'd never jumped at night before. I held my breath and searched the black water until a notch of moonlight glazed Dennis's wet hair. "Who's next?" he called.

Paul took off his shirt and turned to Marse. "You are," he said.

Marse was already wearing a suit, so she stepped out of her shorts and stepped over the railing. "Ready," she said. She stood on her tiptoes on the ledge, and then Paul edged away and she jumped. Mid-flight, it occurred to me to hope she didn't land on Dennis.

She didn't. Dennis cheered her and together they swam around the dock, talking in breathy fragments. The tone of their talk was open and friendly, lacking subtext. "Our turn," said Paul. He took off his shirt.

"Me first," I said. But I wasn't wearing my suit.

"I'll wait while you change."

"OK," I said. But I just stood there. The humidity pressed against the back of my neck. I unzipped my shorts and stepped out of them, tugging on the hem of my T-shirt.

"Indeed," said Paul, stepping aside. I climbed over the rail and watched Dennis and Marse as they rounded the dock. The wind lifted my T-shirt and brushed against my thighs. It occurred to me that afterward, I'd have to walk back upstairs with my shirt wet against my skin. But it was too late to change my mind. I jumped.

The water was warm. I swam under the dock to the ladder, where Marse sat on the lowest rung and Dennis held on with one hand. After cheering me, Dennis went back to talking with Marse about sharks in the bay. Marse was saying she'd seen tiger sharks and hammerheads, but Dennis said he had seen only nurse sharks. "It's the same as with anything else," he said. "They're more afraid of you."

Paul jumped and swam to us, then challenged Dennis to a race around the dock. They kicked away in a splash of elbows and ankles, dark heads bobbing. Marse sat down on the ladder, wrapping her arms around her knees.

"Do you want to get out?" I said.

"I don't know." She looked off. "You two usually sleep on the porch, right?"

The burden of hosting returned: Were there enough clean sheets? Would Dennis's snoring keep everyone awake? I said, "I usually do, but Dennis likes to sleep inside sometimes, when it's windy."

"I love sleeping outside."

"I can sleep inside with Dennis."

"Or we can all sleep on the porch."

The idea gave me pause. How widely apart would we space the mattresses? Would I be able to sleep with them beside us? If Marse had been with us alone, without Paul, I wouldn't have thought twice. There was practically nothing I wouldn't share with her. She'd been the one to first bring me to Stiltsville, after all — she'd introduced me to my husband. Over the years we'd shopped and cooked and exercised and boated together, and though she was not typically a person who fawned over children, when Margo was born she'd bought a slew of books and outfits and stuffed animals, and had come every weekend to hold the baby while I catnapped on the sofa. Margo called her Aunt Marse, and had believed until recently that Marse, like Bette, was a blood relation. Every few weeks Marse picked up Margo and strapped her into the backseat of her car, and they spent the entire afternoon together. When Margo came home, breathless with tales about their day, Marse smirked at me, as if reminding me that although I was the mother, she had license to buy the kid both ice cream and cotton candy in the same afternoon, then drop her off and drive away.

A few years earlier, we'd started a tradition of lending the stilt house to Marse's extended family for a long weekend every summer. We'd cautioned them about the electric eel beneath the dock, and a couple of years passed without incident, but then Marse's cousin Warren, a college student, had dove down with a machete and chopped off the eel's head. Marse, who hadn't known about Warren's plan, apologized to us, but Dennis told her very calmly that although she was like a sister to him and he expected her to continue to treat the stilt house as her own, her family was not welcome there again. To my surprise, he kept his word. The eel's severed head dried atop a piling for weeks, untouched by the pelicans that bothered our lobster traps, until I was sick of how angry it made Dennis and how lonely it seemed, perched there with its raisin eyes and bald head, and I knocked it into the water with the back of my hand. When I did this, Dennis closed his eyes for a moment, as if in eulogy.

There was a flurry of splashing. Paul and Dennis rounded the dock, heading toward us with their heads in the water. This had become, apparently, a serious race. Marse climbed the ladder and I followed. Marse called it. "Dennis had an arm's length on you, Paul."

"He's got practice," said Paul, breathing hard.

I went to get towels from the generator room, and when I returned they were standing on the dock, looking down at the water. Below — I didn't see anything at first, but then I caught the flip of a fin — was the smooth, pale body of a manta ray. It flickered across the surface and beneath the dock. We stepped across to watch it, but it dove and was gone. I wished Margo had been there to see it. I shivered with longing for her — how well was she sleeping, without me or Dennis to tuck her in? Would she have nightmares? Would she have fun?

The swim had worn us out, and after the clamor of bedtime — brushing teeth and changing clothes — Dennis turned off the generator, and the house lights faded and died. We towed four mattresses out to the eastern stretch of porch, four salt-damp pillows and four white sheets. Paul slept nearest the railing — Dennis warned him not to roll over during the night — and Marse slept beside him. Then me, then Dennis. There were no boats in the channel, no voices riding the waves from other stilt houses. The night closed in. I lay on my side, facing Dennis, and listened to his breathing and the rhythms of the water.

I woke from the feeling of a hand moving in slow circles across my hip. The rubbing stopped when I opened my eyes; Dennis stared at me. His hand moved to my waist, then he pulled me to him and kissed me. His teeth grazed mine and his fingers moved under the elastic of my underwear. My blood warmed. He rose to his knees and looked beyond me, at Marse and Paul, then put a finger to his lips and gestured for me to follow. The soles of our feet made sandpaper sounds against the weathered wood floor. He paused in front of the door to the living room, looked in, then continued walking, to the western porch, where the wind blew loudly. I watched the movement of his hair, raising up and flattening again.

140

He pressed me against the porch railing and slipped off my underwear, which I looped around one ankle. I held the railing and Dennis held my breasts. The wind blustered in my ears when I faced him, so I turned away, and gradually my attention shifted as well, and I watched the boat as Dennis moved inside me. There was a liquid compass the size of a man's fist on the boat console, and I imagined its needle jerking with every wave.

Dennis wanted my attention. Sometimes when he lost it, he let it go, and sometimes — this time included — he fought for it. He pulled out of me, keeping his hands against my hips. Then I was being pivoted, facing away from the house, with my hips squeezed against the porch railing and my torso pitched out over the water, holding on to the railing with both hands. He spread my legs with his knee and circled my waist with one arm, which was my cue, I felt, to let go.

That weekend, before leaving for Bette's, Margo had packed five stuffed animals and a smattering of bedtime books and every pair of shoes she owned — four, total. I didn't know how other only children coped with the long quiet hours, but Margo found ways to amuse herself — she put on performances for us, she tromped through the backyard, examining every stone and stick, and she sat coloring on the kitchen floor while I cooked or cleaned. She'd recently developed a habit of lining up her stuffed animals and talking to them as she puttered around her room. "Mimo," she would say to her stuffed monkey, "this is where the toys go when you're done with them. Nettie, this is where I keep my pajamas."

The only other time she'd stayed at Bette's overnight, she'd twirled so long on the swing in the backyard that her hair had tangled in the chains and Bette had been forced to cut her free. Her beautiful dark brown hair, chopped before I'd been ready — it had broken my heart. Margo was a somewhat serious little person and enjoyed the company of adults; Bette claimed to prefer conversing with her niece rather than with most of her friends. The plans for this weekend included visiting the Crandon Park Zoo — Margo had asked me to call her aunt ahead of time to make certain Mimo would be invited along — and swimming at Dennis's parents' pool, and baking cupcakes with Bette's lover, a pastry chef named Daphne. When we'd dropped her off, Bette and Daphne had been arguing. Dennis had taken Margo inside to unpack while Bette and I stood on the porch. "She's so stubborn," said Bette. She blew a thin stream of smoke and handed me the cigarette. I checked to see that Dennis was out of view, then took it.

"What's the problem with Daphne?"

"She has a bee in her bonnet about getting a cat. Imagine us, the lesbians and the cat. I can barely stand having people in my house, not to mention vermin."

"Cats aren't vermin," I said, though I more or less agreed about them — I'd never had any affection for them, but this was something I'd learned to keep to myself, since most people thought cats were just great. "Lots of people have perfectly clean cats."

"Plus, she keeps making these spicy Mediterranean desserts, and I don't have the heart to tell her, but Frances, they are not good."

I thought that probably Bette had told her, and more than once. "I try to imagine what Dennis puts up with."

"What?"

I took another drag on the cigarette. "You know, when I'm annoyed with him. I remind myself that there's plenty to annoy him, too."

"For once you might just commiserate."

"Sorry."

Across the street, at a bungalow even smaller than Bette's, a man walked to the street to check his mail. He had a life-size manatee mailbox, the kind with the manatee standing on its tail and holding the mail slot in its mouth. The man waved at us and walked inside again.

"That's guy's a poofter," said Bette.

"Bette!"

"I know I shouldn't talk, but my word — he sashays!"

I laughed in spite of myself. "Stop it."

She elbowed me gently. "Seriously, though, I'm thinking of kicking Daphne to the curb."

"Will you miss her? Will you miss anything about her?"

She thought for a moment. "Not the spicy desserts, that's for sure."

Daphne was the most recent in a string of girlfriends, the first of whom had been Bette's diving partner, Jane. I'd met Jane in person only once, years earlier; as it turned out, she'd been a decade older than Bette, and married. She had salt-and-pepper hair and a large, patrician nose, and her angular, rawboned body had reminded me of a waterbird. She hadn't smiled when she'd shaken my hand. After Bette had run out on her wedding, she'd seen a lot of Jane for a time, but then suddenly they didn't see each other at all. The second woman who had come to occupy Bette's attention was Delilah. She had crooked teeth and long, straight brown hair that might never have been cut. This relationship had ended for reasons I never knew, and it was not easy to recall the sequence of infatuations after that. Bette's circle of friends now encompassed, almost exclusively, a certain ilk of women: feminists and artists. As for Daphne, Margo liked her, and even Gloria and Grady invited her to dinners and holidays, and everyone loved her baking, but I had never sensed an uncontrollable affection between them.

Bette had left her job at the Barnacle shortly after Dennis and I married. With her part of the inheritance from their grandmother, she'd rented a storefront in downtown Coconut Grove and opened a dive shop. She'd started small, organizing day trips and classes, but within two years she'd moved into a larger space and had a staff of six. It had been more than five years since we'd camped together at Fisheating Creek, and still her hair was cut very short.

After Dennis came out of Bette's house — he was a little rattled at leaving Margo behind, I recall — we'd gotten into the car, and Margo had stood waving happily at us from the porch, clutching Mimo and leaning against her aunt's slender hip.

The package bobbed along while we ate breakfast, and every few minutes either Paul or Dennis walked to the window.

"Still there," Dennis said.

"No sign of the pickup," Paul said.

"Our detectives," said Marse, rolling her eyes. "I say, call the Coast Guard and be done with it."

"I agree," I said, and received a sharp look from Dennis.

I'd barely spoken to Paul during breakfast, but afterward, when I was washing the dishes, he came up behind me. Marse and Dennis were on the porch, drinking coffee and keeping an eye on the Becks' house. Paul took a plate from my hands and dried it with a dish towel. We continued for several minutes — me washing, him drying — without speaking. "Frances," he said after the last dish was in the cabinet. "I thought maybe we could walk the flats while they fish. I don't feel like fishing anyway, do you?"

"Not really." I should have known Paul would be interested in the flats — he owned a plant nursery down south. "Did you want to go now?"

"Why not? There's no wind, and the tide's out."

"Put on a T-shirt so you won't burn."

"Do I need shoes?"

I nodded. "There are some in the generator room. What size?"

"Eleven."

"I'll meet you down there."

On the porch, Marse was staring through binoculars at the shore, and Dennis was telling a story I'd heard half a dozen times. "Right about there," he said, guiding her binoculars. The buttons of his shirt were undone: Paul's influence, I surmised. "Just off Gables Estates — those gigantic houses with the fake columns and the sculptures in the yard, those ugly houses." Marse put down the binoculars and Dennis continued, "It just looked like a mannequin, to tell you the truth. That's what I thought — someone had lost a mannequin in the middle of the waterway. I was twelve years old. My mother went crazy when she saw. She started cursing like a trucker. I'd never heard her curse like that. Fucking Mafia, she yelled. Fucking no-good sons of bitches, fucking drug-dealing pieces of shit. You would've thought she knew the guy. My father covered her

147

mouth with his hand, and we drifted right by the body. I just stood there at the helm, watching it float by. It was a man, and he was twisted out of shape, like both arms were broken, and I could see one open eye, a bunch of bruises on his face. My father called the marine police, and they showed up in thirty minutes or so, and we went home. We had planned to go to the yacht club and get some sandwiches or something, but we just went home."

"Goddamn," said Marse. "My mother would have fainted on the spot."

I said, "Anyone interested in walking the flats?"

Marse shook her head. "Your husband and I are going to hunt and gather."

"You're sure?" I said. "There's no wind — it's clear as glass."

Dennis smiled. "Have fun," he said. He pulled my wrist to his lips and kissed it, then turned back to Marse.

In the generator room, under layers of old shoes — sneakers and flip-flops and even a pair of ballet slippers — I found a pair of navy deck shoes that had belonged to Dennis's father. I brought the deck shoes and a pair of sneakers to the dock. Paul slipped on the shoes, then jumped off the dock while I climbed down the swimming ladder, turning away from his splash. He dove, kicking, and did a handstand. When he emerged, he said, "This is fucking divine. How do you not come here every weekend of your lives?"

We moved from the deeper water beneath the docks onto the flats. "It takes a lot of work to leave civilization behind," I said. "And Margo isn't that strong a swimmer." Every weekend, Dennis practiced with her in his parents' swimming pool. She put her head down and made her way across the water, splashing erratically and coming up for air in mid-stroke, blustery and blinking. Dennis would tell her to focus on breathing for one lap, on her stroke for the next. When she tired, he perched her on his shoulders and told her he was her giant and the pool was her kingdom, and let her order him to take her to the steps, then back to the deep end, then back to the steps again.

The family who had owned the stilt house directly west of us, the Suttons, had recently moved to Orlando. This was the beginning of a period during which we were always learning of another family moving north. Often this had more to do with the changing demographics of the city, I suspected, than anything else. It had been almost fifteen years since the Bay of Pigs, and still

John F. Kennedy was the second-most-hated man in South Florida, after Fidel Castro. In the coming years a bumper sticker would gain popularity: WILL THE LAST AMERICAN TO LEAVE MIAMI PLEASE BRING THE FLAG?

The Suttons had transferred their land lease and sold their stilt house to a man whose name I never knew. Unlike every other Stiltsville occupant, he lived on the bay full-time, employing runners to bring food — and women — from Miami. We called him the hermit. Sometimes Dennis and I took binoculars to the kitchen window and watched the hermit's house, searching for clues about his lifestyle, about him. I wondered how he could afford to live on the water, what he did with his days. It was incredible to look over at his house — wood-shingled and squat, smaller than ours — and realize that a person was inside, but also that no boat was tied to the dock. Maybe he didn't worry about emergencies. Or maybe he assumed at all times that an emergency was coming, and was resigned to it.

Paul stopped walking and I almost bumped into him. I could see the pink of his skin through his wet T-shirt, the short hairs on the back of his neck. "Look," he said, pointing at the water. By his foot, a blue crab skittered across the sand, then slipped underneath a rock. He crouched and pointed again. "That's a vase sponge. They can get as big around as a barrel." The bright pink sponge was the shape of a bell. I squatted, burying a hand in the sand to keep my balance. "Watch it," said Paul, picking up my arm and steadying me against him. He pointed. "A fire worm. You'll sting for a week."

Of course I knew about fire worms — I'd walked the flats a dozen times with Grady or Bette, both of whom could name every sea creature in South Florida — but I hadn't noticed the one next to my foot. It was the deep waxy color of a red crayon. We could barely take a step without rubbing up against something living — sponges, sea urchins, coral, sand dollars. Beside the fire worm was a starfish, and beside that was a penny, which I picked up and dropped into the neckline of my swimsuit. I shifted away so Paul and I were not touching. He pointed to a green leathery lump the size and shape of a rolled-up pair of socks. "There — that's a sea squirt," he said. "Our direct ancestors, so they say."

He offered me his hand and I took it, but only until I'd stepped over a wide stretch of

151

coral. We walked for an hour. Paul spoke only to point out a creature or plant, and I spoke only to acknowledge him. The flats surrounded our stilt house on three sides, and I'd never before walked to their far edges, where the sea life petered out, the sandy spaces began to dominate, and the water deepened. When the waves started to push against my thighs, making my knees buckle, I turned back. The house looked doll-size and unadorned, its intricacies smudged by distance. The boat was not at the dock; Dennis and Marse must have gone fishing. They'd probably waved to tell us they were headed off, but we hadn't seen. Paul looked toward the Becks' house. "That goddamn package," he said.

It was still there. We wouldn't have seen it, bobbing along half-sunk, if we hadn't been looking for it. I took a few steps in that direction, watching for obstacles. The flats stretched right across to the Becks' house, and the distance was walkable as long as the tide was out. My heartbeat quickened. "Do you want to get it?" I said.

Paul shook his head. "I don't think it's a good idea."

I felt tricked. I'd been led into letting curiosity overcome me. "I'm going back."

"Don't," he said. "Let's talk."

For a moment, the sun-drenched flats seemed as sinister as a dark alley, and Paul as unpredictable as a stranger. "About what?" I said.

He shrugged. "Life, work, marriage."

"What about them?"

He picked up a sand dollar and studied its markings. "How long has it been for you two?"

"Almost six years."

"Happy years?"

I crossed my arms over my chest, but with the waves lapping my thighs and the breeze blowing my hair across my face, the posture felt ridiculous. "Yes," I said. I wondered if he was thinking of proposing to Marse. It had never occurred to me — not even once — that this might happen.

"Marse and me —" He took a breath. "Can I ask you a question? What do you think is the most important ingredient in a successful relationship?"

"I don't know," I said. I felt bullied and thrilled at the same time: was romance something Paul and I could examine together, as if from a distance? "I thought I knew when I got married," I said, "but now I don't."

I started toward the house, but he didn't follow, so I turned to face him. The sun was directly overhead and he shaded his eyes with one hand. "What did you think in the beginning?" he said.

The sandy ocean floor was warm and gluey under my feet. "I thought it was honesty, loyalty," I said, thinking: fidelity. It was a betrayal, talking this way.

"You don't think a little secrecy is good for the soul, the way a good scare is good for the heart?" He searched my face, but I made my expression blank. "I thought it was honesty, too," he said. "I also thought it was timing, like if the right woman had come along when I was twenty-three, I couldn't have held on until I was ready."

I knew he wanted me to ask, but I stayed quiet.

"You know what I think the secret is now?" he said.

"Money?" I said. "Riches?"

"No, but you're close." He picked up a stone and threw it — not the way one would throw a stone to make it skip, but as if he were throwing it away. He seemed serious in the way that children sometimes are, and I thought he was one of the most intense men I'd ever known. "The man has to love his job. Show me a man who loves his job, and I'll show you a happy home life."

I was relieved. "You love your job."

"Goddamn right I do. I spend my day with plants and people who take care of plants." He paused. "Dennis doesn't love his."

"Not always." I thought of Dennis's one-window office, his apathy toward litigation and resentment of office politics. He'd spoken many times of leaving law for teaching or consulting. Before Paul said what he said — about a happy career begetting a happy marriage — I'd thought only of the pay cut.

I started to walk toward the house, and Paul followed for a few minutes, then moved beside me and matched my strides. When the water was ankle-deep again and the sea life thick, we slowed down. The house was a solid, three-dimensional place now, with a line coiled on the eastern square of the dock and a book spread open on a chair on the porch. We waded into waist-deep water and I dove beneath the surface and swam toward the house in a burst. I pulled myself up the ladder, feeling the water slide off my skin into the sunlight. At the top, I turned to check on Paul, and found that he was right behind me, his face inches from my thigh. I twisted away, but his hand landed on my ankle. "Wait," he said.

I maneuvered out of his grip until I was

seated awkwardly on the dock, a puddle staining the wood around my body. Paul sat beside me and touched the hem of my T-shirt. "What is this?" he said. There was a bruise the size and color of a sea urchin on my hip; part of it peeked out of the edge of my swimsuit. I'd chosen my longest T-shirt to cover it. That morning, when I'd noticed the bruise, it occurred to me it might be a harbinger of something horrible, like leukemia, but then I realized where the bruise was from: the night before, with Dennis, against the porch railing. It hadn't felt so forceful at the time.

I pulled down my T-shirt. "I'm a klutz," I said. "It happened yesterday, at the marina."

Paul stared at me. "I heard you last night, you and Dennis."

I had no response, but he didn't seem to want one. There was a commotion in my peripheral vision.

"Holy shit," said Paul. We stood and ran to the far end of the dock. In the spot where we'd last seen the white package, there was a splash. Something sliced through the water's surface and submerged: a black fin. A second later, the water was empty and still.

"That was way too big for a nurse shark," said Paul.

"Just what we need in this channel," I said. "A great white on cocaine." At this, what had been pulling at us seemed to snap, and we laughed. Paul went to the boat to get another pair of binoculars, and I went upstairs to make lunch.

That night, we played poker in the living room after supper. It was Marse's idea — she said it would take her mind off her sunburn. We sat on couch cushions around the coffee table. We drank red wine and talked about Dennis and Marse's fishing trip — they'd caught three snappers and a grouper, all of which we grilled for supper — and about what Paul and I had seen. The morning's drama appeared to have reached its conclusion, and we were resigned to never knowing the contents of the package or its intended recipient. Marse suggested we tell the Coast Guard about the shark — wouldn't people want to know there was a large shark in the bay? — but Paul said maybe it wasn't as large as it seemed, and Dennis said it probably had gone straight back out to sea, where it came from. There was a lot of conjecture about what drug would most tempt a shark, and what kind of shark it most likely was, black tip or bull or lemon. I wondered if the incident should make me feel less safe in the water, but in the end, I felt it was just something that had happened and would not happen again. I was glad that we would all return to Miami with a story to tell.

We were so far from shore, so far from civilization. There was only the slap of the waves, so steady that the sound disappeared into the atmosphere the way cricket cries do in summertime, leaving human sounds to punctuate the night: laughter, jeers, the sliding of cards and change across the coffee table. Paul won fourteen dollars and I won eight. "What do you say we make a run for it?" said Paul. His eyebrows were thick and dark in the candlelight; the swells of his face cast shadows on the hollows.

"Don't mind him," said Marse, slapping his thigh. "Just say, 'Down, boy,' and he'll behave." She stood and yawned with her arms over her head. We all watched her; the moment expanded. "Bedtime," she said. I went to help her move the mattresses. When I came into the bedroom, she said, "Maybe we should split up for tonight. Would you mind if we slept on the porch? Or you two could sleep out there and we could take the master?"

Her tone was aloof. I said, "We'll take the big bedroom, and you take the porch. It's no problem."

"Good." She pulled a mattress from the bed and turned it on its side, then started to drag it across the linoleum toward the doorway. I was in her way, so I moved, and though she looked as if she could use some help, her manner suggested that she did not want any. At the door, she stopped and her shoulders sagged.

"Marse?"

She tipped the mattress over and it landed with a soft thump. "Paul can deal with this," she said. She left the room and I stood there alone, wanting to pick up the mattress but knowing I shouldn't. In the few years I'd known her, this was the second time I'd stood in that very room feeling as if I'd stolen something from her. I hadn't, of course — not really. Not the first time, with Dennis, and not now, with Paul, who I assumed flirted with all of his friends' wives. Nevertheless, I was astonished to find myself back in this situation. I thought, I'm not even the pretty one. This was not false modesty. In a room full of men, nine out of ten would have chosen Marse over me for a fling or more. She was thinner, with a more fashionable hairstyle and better clothes, and she was more self-confident. For whatever reason — and I don't deny that it might have been something I was doing, some competitiveness I didn't want to acknowledge — I'd attracted, twice, men she'd claimed as hers. And I knew that if I wasn't very, very careful, I would lose her over it. I might have lost her the first time, but she'd been gracious. The possibility of losing Marse — even then I knew that she could be my friend for life, this obstacle notwithstanding — was unthinkable to me.

I slept uneasily, and dreamed about playing poker. In the dream, I felt the queasy satisfaction of a person who wins by cheating, though I didn't know how I'd managed it. I collected my money — stacks of torn and faded green bills — and when I looked up to face my opponent, I saw that I'd been playing against a grown-up Margo. Her freckles had receded and her chin was sharp like Dennis's mother's; there was a beauty mark on her neck. I'd never before imagined so clearly what she might look like when she was older.

I woke Dennis by saying his name until he opened his eyes and looked at me, appearing not curious or irritated, but matter-of-fact, as if he'd been listening all along. I whispered, "Why didn't we bring her? We could have brought her."

"We needed some time alone," he said in

his gruff half-asleep voice, sounding unconvinced.

"We're not alone."

"We're with adults. It's different. We'll bring her next weekend." His face was no more than an inch from my own. He said, "Aren't you having a good time?"

I didn't want to say no, but to say yes would have been a lie. I understood that for whatever reason, I wasn't made for this kind of weekend, two couples on an island. I was too consumed by every little thing; it would've been impossible for me to enjoy myself. "It's gone well," I said, and felt Dennis relax. There would come a time, long after he and Paul were no longer friends, when I would tell Dennis that Paul had noticed my bruise. I would transform the story from what it was — discomforting but also thrilling — into just another anecdote. Did he watch us? Dennis would say. Or did he hear us from bed? Maybe he'd gotten up for a glass of water, I would say. Maybe he heard us sneaking back to bed and guessed where we'd been.

I never told Dennis what I believe happened, what I imagine when I recall the scene: Paul heard us rise from bed. He followed us. He stood in the kitchen window the entire time, watching us — watching me

161

— from the darkness.

We were standing on the dock, getting ready to head out to Soldier's Key for some snorkeling, when the Cessna returned. It was late morning, and we'd eaten breakfast and packed up in anticipation of leaving that afternoon. Dennis shushed us. "Listen," he said.

The low hum turned into a louder hum with a putter in it, and then the plane appeared in the blue sky. "Holy shit," said Paul.

Dennis didn't say anything. There was a fierce, protective quality in his expression. The plane started to circle.

"It won't drop anything with us standing right here," said Marse. "Will it?"

"No way," said Paul.

"I'll get the binoculars," I said, but Dennis caught my arm.

"Wait," he said, as if he knew that at that moment, after circling the Becks' house only two or three times, the plane would drop another rectangular white package. It did.

"Unbelievable," said Paul.

"Call the Coast Guard," I said to Dennis.

"I told you — the boat registration."

We looked at each other, and suddenly I

realized that I didn't have the whole story. Something inside me seized up and brought to surface a fear I would experience only a few times during our marriage: What if everything was not as it seemed? What if all the walls fell away and revealed a world turned upside down, inside out, defiant of everything I'd taken for granted? Before that moment, I would have said that Dennis had no secrets from me at all. The sound of the Cessna's engine faded as it headed, once again, out to sea. Dennis stepped onto the boat and I stepped after him, feeling it totter with my weight. Paul and Marse went inside.

"What?" I said, fighting the urge to cross my arms, to treat the moment like a stand-off. I reminded myself that Dennis was my husband, whom I loved.

He flipped a switch to let fuel into the carburetor. "It's no big deal," he said, "but there's a chance that if we call the Coast Guard, they might impound the boat."

"This boat?"

"Yes, Frances."

"Is it drugs?" I couldn't comprehend why it would be, but these were my natural associations: boat, Coast Guard, drugs.

"Baby, of course not."

We looked toward the Becks' house. The

wind was stronger and the bay choppier than the day before, and the white package was moving more quickly. I sat on the gunwale. "Why?"

He watched the compass on the console, the needle bobbing even though we were headed nowhere. "I didn't want to tell you because I knew you'd worry, and you wouldn't want to use the boat, and we'd have to cancel the weekend." I stared at him, my gut tight. He said, "I got a call from the police this week. Apparently, the guy who sold us the boat didn't own it."

We'd bought the boat from a man in Key Largo who'd just gotten divorced, who was, as he put it, liquidating his ass. I'd stood admiring the boat — our first! — while Dennis shook the man's hand. Dennis said, "Technically, it belonged to his wife's brother."

"But that has nothing to do with us," I said. "We didn't know that." He looked at me but didn't say anything. "You knew?" I said.

He shrugged. "I had a hunch."

"Oh my God."

"I just need to prove that I didn't know the guy before he sold me the boat."

"You didn't know him, did you?"

"I didn't know him. I didn't. But" — he

164

lowered his voice — "I knew something was wrong. He was too eager to sell, and the boat was too cheap. Really, Frances, think about it — we couldn't have afforded this boat. And I wanted it for us." Dennis had known colleagues to be disbarred for less. It was nothing I'd worried about before. In the past year, we'd built an addition on the back of the house, a high-ceilinged family room with a wall of sliding glass doors. We'd hired Kyle Heiger, Marse's brother, to be the contractor on the job, and though he'd done excellent work, the whole project had ended up costing more than we'd expected. Also that year, Dennis had been invited to join the Biscayne Bay Yacht Club, and though money was tight we didn't feel we could turn it down. This was the year, too, that we'd become partners in the stilt house, and so had begun the annual lease payments, the taxes, and the sharing of upkeep and repairs. It was, I knew, typical of many Miami families to live above their means, to hunker under a mounting precipice of debt, but I hadn't thought of us as the type.

"We should sell the boat," I said.

"Really, it's not that big a deal. I'm just not sure where the paperwork stands. It might be that technically, on paper only, we're driving a stolen boat."

"Are you concerned?" I said.

"No," said Dennis, coming to comfort me. "It's just a hassle, that's all." I turned away from him. Our boat wasn't ours — it was some guy's petty way of getting back at his wife, whom he had probably loved once, a long time ago. I stepped onto the dock and looked up at the stilt house. I felt cold and unsteady, as if I'd shed a more confident version of myself. I could already feel myself losing the version of me who'd wake to her husband's mid-night caress, the girl who'd have sex against a porch railing, arms flung over the water, as if submitting to the sea itself.

Beneath the Becks' dock, the white package continued its tortoise journey to sea. "Let's go get it," I said.

"Frances —"

I shouted for Paul and Marse, and they joined us on the dock. Marse read my face for signs of stress. I told them what I wanted. "Are you sure?" said Paul.

"If we don't do a little research," I said, "we'll never know."

"What if the pickup comes while we're there?" said Marse.

"It won't," said Paul.

Dennis climbed into the boat and started the engine. Paul untied the spring line and threw it into the well of the boat.

"It's the sharks or us," I said to Marse.

"Us," she said, stepping into the boat.

Paul handled the lines and we drifted from the dock. The channel was choppy and Dennis took it slow. I watched the horizon for planes and boats. My heart pounded. We coasted up to the package and Paul readied himself, an arm extended. The package seemed irrelevant now, a detail; Dennis's deceit loomed. The boat tipped as Paul leaned over the side. To Dennis, I said, "I'm nervous." Dennis looked at the package, then at me. He came to me and we looked around: the bay, the ocean, stilt houses in the distance, compact and still.

"We'll be OK," he said.

"Got it," said Paul. It was larger than I'd thought, and the plastic was light gray, not white, as it had seemed from a distance. It was tied like a gift with burlap string. "It's light," said Paul. He laughed. "It's way too light."

Paul brought the package to the bow and set it down. Dennis knelt across from him, and Marse and I watched over their shoulders. Dennis used a key to tear the plastic, then Paul spread the tear open with both hands. The plastic was thick; he had to put some muscle into it. When a portion of the

167

contents was visible, Marse said, with unconcealed disappointment, "Newspaper."

"What's inside?" I said.

"It's just a newspaper," said Paul. He widened the tear in the plastic and pulled out a crisp, neatly folded *New York Times.* "Sunday edition," he said.

"There's more," said Dennis.

Inside the package, bundled in the same gray plastic, was a smaller parcel. This one was tightly packed and lumpy. "Here we are," said Paul.

Dennis was tentative with the keys this time. He made a small tear in the corner of the parcel and widened the tear with his thumb. Paul hovered impatiently. Inside the widening hole, something silver reflected the sunlight, and I caught a whiff of the contents. Dennis stepped back to let Paul take over. What Paul revealed, after a few seconds of working at the package, was six or seven whole fish — bonitos, I believe. Silver scales came away on Paul's hands.

"Fish?" I said.

Dennis was delighted. "What the hell?" he said.

Marse picked up the *New York Times* and folded back the sections, one by one. In a crease of the classifieds, she found an envelope. Paul started to grab it but she stepped away from him. She read: " 'Marc and Kathleen — Another touch of civilization couldn't hurt. Hope the champagne didn't get too bubbly in flight. Crossed fingers that you catch something big with this bait. Any marlin yesterday? Happy anniversary, Mimi and Ronald.' "

"Holy shit," said Paul.

"Anniversary?" said Dennis.

We dumped the bait into the bay. Dennis started the engine and we headed back to the stilt house. Paul and Marse sat side by side on the gunwale, their legs dangling in the well of the boat. Within a few weeks, they would split up. I never had any reason to believe this had anything to do with me. She wouldn't know what had passed between me and Paul until many years later, long past the time when it would have made any difference. And although Dennis would see less and less of him, eventually Paul would burst back into all our lives and stay there, a surprising but permanent fixture. All around us, couples whose weddings we'd attended, whose unions we'd toasted, broke up: Kyle, who'd married a potter named Julia shortly after I'd moved to Miami, was first; then one of Dennis's law partners, with whom we'd become friends; then Benjamin O'Dell, Bette's ex-fiancé, who'd married a girl he'd met while traveling in England.

A month later, Dennis sorted out the paperwork with the boat, and we sold it and started saving for another. With the money from the sale, we paid off the addition on the house. Grady offered his boat when we wanted it, which meant more outings with Dennis's parents, which I didn't mind. Margo loved being with them — Grady carried her piggyback and never told her to keep her voice down, and Gloria kept sugary cereals on hand and let her try on her good jewelry. We kept our membership in the yacht club — Grady had gone to bat for us, and declining would have been humiliating — and for a long while we didn't take vacations or go to restaurants, and we put off sending Margo to summer camp. Whenever I grew frustrated with living lean during that time — and this would not be the last tight period during our life together — I reminded myself of the boat we'd never really owned, and thought of the choices we were making in opposition to the choices we could have been making, and I was relieved. It was so easy, I understood now, to take a wrong turn.

That afternoon, before returning to Miami,

Marse and Paul napped in the downstairs hammock and Dennis went into the big bedroom with a book. I finished packing our things and made light trips to the boat, prolonging the process to have something to do. There was a lot of garbage to tow in to shore. There was always, no matter what efforts we made, a lot of garbage. At one point when I came downstairs, Paul was alone in the hammock. "Where is Marse?" I said.

"I have no idea."

I put down the bag I was carrying and looked around. The downstairs bathroom door was open and she wasn't on the boat or the dock. I opened the door to the generator room, but there was only the loud motor and the many shelves of salt-crusted shoes. I went back to the hammock. Marse could certainly handle herself, but nevertheless I felt protective of her. "Really, where is she?"

"I really don't know." He had an arm under his head. The hammock swung leisurely.

"Get up."

"Why?"

"Go find your girlfriend."

He smiled. "She can take care of herself."

"I know she can, but I'd prefer to know

roughly where everyone is at any given time."

He gave a mock look of concern. "You think she drowned?" He was baiting me; of course he knew where she was. He sat up in the hammock and I stepped back. "I don't bite," he whispered. I heard Dennis talking upstairs, then Marse's laugh. Paul said, "I have no intention of hurting Marse, if that's what you're afraid of."

I took a breath. "That's exactly what I'm afraid of."

He was sitting down, but still I felt dwarfed by his intensity and charm and looks. "I can be discreet," he said. "I don't want to hurt Dennis either."

I didn't say anything.

"It's been a while," he said, "me wanting you."

"No," I said. "I'm sorry."

"You think you'll never do it, Frances?"

There was a warm wind coming from the north. I willed it to carry our words, and my memory of them, out to sea. "No," I said, "I'll never do it."

His voice was calm. "You will," he said. "One day you will, and you'll realize that what people say about it isn't true. You won't feel guilty, you'll just feel happy and horny and you'll think back and realize you could have done it with me."

He was broad and sexy. He would be good at sex, I guessed. He would put his heart into it. He would be generous and complimentary, would inspire an eagerness to please, a dismantling of inhibition. He would moan without checking himself. He was a man who loved plants, who worked for himself, who had great sex: I felt a brief flush of desire for him.

When I didn't say anything, he put his hands in his pockets and shrugged, then looked off. "That goddamn package," he said. He seemed truly to shift his attention. In the end, he turned away and walked upstairs, and I remained, overcome by sorrow for many reasons, not the least of which was this: I had a feeling that Paul was right about what he'd said. We were still at the start of a long road together, Dennis and me. The future was still so murky. For a long moment it seemed almost inevitable that our happiness would not last, could not last, and that at some point, after Margo left home or before, I would find myself in a similar situation, and this time I would want it badly enough to let it happen. And — this thought was incredibly sad to me — I might not even feel terribly ashamed. I might come to consider it just one episode in the life of the marriage, just another wave in the windy channel. Not a hurricane at all.

1982

On a Saturday evening in February of Margo's sixth-grade year, Dennis and I drove her to a slumber party in a gated community called CocoPlum, ten minutes from our house by car. The hostess was a girl named Trisha Weintraub, whom I'd met only once. Trisha was a year ahead of Margo in school. When we drove up, her mother, Judy, was sitting on the terracotta porch with her boyfriend, drinking white wine. Judy's boyfriend wore a loose linen shirt unbuttoned to his sternum, and Judy wore hammered gold earrings and an embroidered caftan. When I complimented her on the top, she told me she'd brought it back from Lima, where she'd been on retreat. Dennis asked the pertinent questions: How many girls were sleeping over? Was Trisha excited to be turning thirteen? (Margo was still only eleven.) Did Judy have our number, in case? Would any boys be dropping by? (He managed to slip this last one in jokingly; if I'd asked, I would have seemed uptight.) Judy didn't say anything about it, but I assumed that she'd heard Dennis was unemployed. All the ladies must have heard — it was exactly the kind of thing that got around.

Margo hopped from one foot to the other while the adults spoke, waiting to be released. When we ran out of small talk, I kissed my child good-bye. She thanked Judy for the invitation, and Judy cupped her chin and said, *"Qué linda."* It was a trend in certain circles, I'd noticed, to learn just enough Spanish to drop some into casual conversation, but not enough to have a discussion with the housekeeper. I handed Margo Trisha's birthday gift — a pricey blow-up pool float with a layer of reflective coating for even tanning — and she ducked through the oversize front door. I glimpsed Trisha and a marble staircase and heard a shriek from inside. Dennis and I said good-bye to Judy and her boyfriend and spent the following hours in a dark bar and grill on the Miami River, drinking beer and eating popcorn in lieu of ordering a meal.

At two a.m., Margo called and begged us to pick her up. We drove there in our bathrobes and found her waiting alone on

176

the dark porch, shivering in her denim jacket. She was barely coherent; we couldn't get anything out of her until she'd swallowed some water and — this was Dennis's idea — half an inch of whiskey. After she'd calmed down, she explained what had happened and told us very solemnly that she was never going back to school, then fell asleep against Dennis's shoulder on the living room sofa. He didn't move until light started to stream in through the blinds and Margo stirred.

What happened at the Weintraub home that night was the direct result of a meeting Dennis and I'd had eight months earlier, at the end of the previous school term, with Margo's fourth-grade teacher. Mr. Oxley was a lanky blond man with a thick white mustache and western-style blue jeans. He was older than most of the other teachers by a decade, and had the habit of winking at the close of a conversation. After Back to School night that year, Dennis had commented that Mr. Oxley had clammy hands, and Margo had said, "Mr. Oxley would never say that about you," and requested an apology on her teacher's behalf, which Dennis had provided. Mr. Oxley inspired in my daughter — and in her friends, from what I could tell — kindness and respect. His was a well-mannered class.

We met with Mr. Oxley in the fourth-grade classroom at Sunset Elementary, where Margo had been a student since kindergarten. Dennis and I sat in the front row of student desks. I fit snugly in mine, but Dennis's knees chafed the underside of his, and his elbows extended over each side. He fidgeted, knocking around. Behind him, cluttering the low shelves along one wall of the room, were two dozen models of Miami's proposed new public transportation system, the Metro Rail. The television news had been filled for months with sketches of the new system, which, upon completion four years later, would end up costing the city $215 million. Margo's model was wedged in the middle: cars fashioned from orange juice containers and tinfoil, pillars from balsa wood, and grass from sticky green felt. The project had taken us the lion's share of a weekend the month before. Blue ribbons — for participation — hung on sickly gold strings from most of the projects, including Margo's. The red-ribboned winner was partially obscured, but I could see that the railway was made from toothpicks. I started to care, but then all at once I didn't. While we'd worked on the model, a lock of Margo's brown hair had dipped into the jar of glue, and we'd ended up over the kitchen sink, giggling and soapy. This is where Dennis had found us when he'd arrived home from fishing. We'd thought his raccoon-eyed sunburn was unbearably funny, and he'd put on a Kenny Rogers record, moved the half-finished model off the breakfast table, and laid down newspaper so he could teach Margo how to gut a fish.

Mr. Oxley ushered a pair of boys out of the back of the room. When he'd called the house, I'd worried that Margo was in trouble for talking too much — this was the complaint we'd heard most often. On the contrary: it seemed he was suggesting that we consider promoting Margo to the sixth grade after the fourth, thereby allowing her to skip fifth grade entirely.

"Altogether?" said Dennis.

Mr. Oxley nodded. I could see that we amused him — because we were stuffed into the little desks, maybe, or because Dennis was there with me, a house-husband. I admit that I was proud of Margo. But Dennis, who years later when Margo applied to colleges would tell her to discriminate not by rankings but by how she was treated when visiting, was immune to this kind of smug satisfaction. He said, "Are other kids skipping?" and Mr. Oxley shook his head. Dennis looked at me. "She'll leave all her friends," he said.

She'll make new ones, I thought. At that moment, I could see Margo through the vertical blinds of the classroom: she was standing in the courtyard with her best friend, Carla, using her hands as puppets. One hand opened to talk, then shut as the other yammered on. I'd embroidered a red rose on the front pocket of Margo's jeans, and it wiggled as she moved.

"This is not a bad time for it, developmentally speaking. The skills in the sixth grade are advanced, yes, but it's not a complete departure from fifth-grade material," said Mr. Oxley. "We have a student who advances almost every year."

"Any serial killers in the bunch?" Dennis said.

Not knowing Dennis — not knowing that he was rarely entirely serious or entirely joking — Mr. Oxley was cautious. "Not that I know of," he said. Dennis threw up his hands, and his knees banged the underside of his desk. Mr. Oxley addressed me: "The concentration in the fifth-grade reading unit is comprehension — a skill Margo has evidently mastered."

"Mastered?" said Dennis.

Margo was, at that time, ten years old. When we browsed in the young adult shelves at the public library, Margo's choices, which Mr. Oxley went on to praise, mystified me. She was less interested in fourth-grade subjects — wizards and time machines and magical dolphins — than in broken homes and runaways and romance. But it became obvious as Mr. Oxley spoke that the suggestion of promoting Margo was not solely, or even mostly, based on academics. "There's also the matter of Margo's physical maturity," he said. "I'm a little concerned about her comfort level in the fifth-grade classroom." Dennis and I stared at him, slow to catch on. Mr. Oxley cleared his throat. "In other words, if you agree, this might be an opportunity to more closely match her physical development to that of her classmates."

Then I understood, before he'd explained to Dennis, who looked bewildered. Margo had been the tallest person in the fourth grade. Her height and, as Mr. Oxley put it, "advanced development" (meaning bra size, as far as I could figure, and maybe leg hair), distinguished her. It seems that in order to have had this conversation with a teacher, Margo must have been freakish, but photographs reassure me: she was taller than her friends, yes, but not excessively so. She wore oversize shirts and slouched, and she smiled a lot — people looked at her face.

"Holy hell," said Dennis. "Margo's too tall for the fifth grade?"

Outside, Margo finished her hand-puppet conversation and Carla cracked up. In the past year, Margo had become very talkative, almost nervously so, and very sensitive. She had started to put a lot of pressure on herself. Her dentist had fitted her with a retainer to use while sleeping so she didn't wear down her molars grinding her teeth. I checked on her sometimes in the night, and each time her eyelids fluttered a lot but she didn't seem to be grinding. When Dennis had mentioned the retainer to his mother, she'd recommended a psychotherapist. Sixth grade, I thought, could hurt her confidence. It could do damage. But the scales tipped when I considered that if she skipped the fifth grade, she would no longer be the most buxom girl in her class. Give her a classroom full of girls tossing their hair and applying lip gloss, I thought. Give her a few friends whose T-shirts reveal the lump of a bra strap on each shoulder.

Dennis knocked on my desk. "We have some parenting to do here."

Mr. Oxley smiled diplomatically. "It's not our decision, but it's possible Margo might feel more comfortable around classmates who are as far along as she is, physically speaking."

"I was just thinking the same thing," I said, and Dennis shot me a look.

Mr. Oxley said, "The older girls take health education classes. They spend a week learning about reproductive health and menstruation." His manner was that of a man who'd practiced not tripping over certain words. "Has Margo gotten her period?"

I wasn't easily flustered — with girlfriends, I could talk about PMS or sex or pregnancy — but in that classroom, beside the model Metro Rails, I floundered. "She —" I stammered. "Last summer, at sleepaway camp —"

Dennis started laughing. He knew the story: she'd had some spotting, so a counselor gave her a sanitary pad and explained how to use it, and Margo was so embarrassed that she'd pretended to be sick during swim time for three days. But the spotting went away as quickly as it had come, so the camp counselor explained about the hymen and said she'd probably torn it horseback riding. Margo had chronicled the

whole icky affair in a letter marked FOR
MOM'S EYES ONLY. When I got to the part
about horseback riding, I was so relieved
that I cried.

The real deal had arrived four months
later, in the bathroom before school. I'd
declared it a mental health day and we'd
fixed a picnic lunch and gone to Dennis's
parents' house to lie by the pool.

When he was done laughing, Dennis said,
"She's had it for a little while." He covered
my hand with his own. I felt bad for him,
crammed into the little desk. I felt grateful
for him.

"I can't say with certainty that this is the
best thing for your daughter," said Mr. Oxley. "We just want to make you aware that
promotion is an option."

I was sorry he wouldn't be Margo's sixth-
grade teacher, and her seventh-grade
teacher, and so on. He went on to discuss
Margo's math skills, which though adequate
had not developed at the rate of her reading
or her body. Tutoring was an option. During this part of the conversation, I day-
dreamed of stepping out of the classroom
to join my daughter in the sunlight.

Dennis had given notice in January of that
year, while we were still paying off Christ-

mas. On the evening of his last day of work, I'd found him in the backyard, sitting in one of the scooped rubber swings of Margo's jungle gym. It was raining lightly. His shoes and socks and necktie lay on the grass and his shirt was unbuttoned to the middle of his chest. His hair rose from his head at odd angles, as if he'd rubbed it around without smoothing it back into place. The sight of my husband disheveled was not rare, but the sight of him downhearted was. My impulse was to return to the house. I'm not proud of it, but there's something about weakness — even momentary weakness — that hardens my heart. Get up, I wanted to say. Occupy yourself. We're having fillet of sole for dinner. Dennis lifted his arms, palms out. A different man might have meant, Why me? But I knew that Dennis, who had never liked practicing law, not even right out of school, meant, What now? On the bright side, there were a dozen possibilities; on the downside, there were a dozen possibilities. We'd hoped Dennis would have a new job before the old one ended, but the search had taken longer than we'd anticipated, so we were poised to subsist on his year-end bonus and our meager savings, crossing our fingers. Dennis's mother had recommended that I take a position as a teller at the bank where his father worked. She'd made the recommendation even though she and I both knew she disapproved. I found the gesture touching. I hadn't held a job since moving to Miami.

I sat in the swing beside Dennis. Water soaked through the seat of my slacks. He said, "Babe, I have some concerns."

"I know you do."

He'd dug the sandpit himself. He'd carved away the grass and dry black dirt and shoveled in fifty gallons of glinting white sand. He'd secured each knuckle of the jungle gym with epoxy. Now, he wiped rain from his face and pushed against the ground to start swinging. I watched his back as he rose. The rain had soaked through the fabric of his button-down, and through it I could see the outline of his undershirt. When he drew back, I could see the round caps of his knees through his wet trousers, and the delicate bluish hollows of his pale ankles. As for his face, it wasn't grim exactly, but I could tell he was thinking hard and trying not to think, and that he was glad I was there, sitting next to him in the rain, and that he hoped I'd swing, so there wouldn't be any pressure to tell the story of the day. So I swung a little, but ended up circling above the pit, toeing the sand to keep out of

Dennis's way.

It had been a decade since he'd left the house for his first day of work as an attorney. I'd checked him for wrinkles and kissed him good-bye. "Are you nervous?" I'd said. He'd shaken his head. "A means to an end," he'd said, and rolled his eyes. Then he was off, and we'd fallen into a routine. And still sometimes when he came through the door at the end of the day, I saw him unshoulder his work and take on the life he meant to live. A different man could not have done it, that shrugging away of work cares, day after day. When women I knew complained about their overworked, overtired, overstressed husbands, I thought of energetic, unworried, distractible Dennis — Dennis, who would never fulfill his potential or win an award or retire early, Dennis the underachiever — and I understood that we were lucky. He was home by five almost every day, he never worked weekends, and sometimes he left the office in the afternoon and went to the marina to tinker with the boat engines — we now owned a twin-outboard sports fisherman — or came home to share a sandwich with me and water the alamanda bushes in the side yard, then re-tied his tie and returned to the office.

I couldn't think of a single job that Dennis

would truly love. And while I accepted the close boundaries of my own ambition, I was nonetheless a little unnerved by the same lack in my husband; I thought one of us should be setting an example. As I sat beside him, holding tight to the reins of the swing as he pumped away, I found myself warding off annoyance by recalling the things I appreciated about him: he loved to wake up early and go running, and as a result I never had to make the coffee. He spent money lavishly on things he enjoyed, like fishing equipment and gifts for me and Margo, and meagerly on things he didn't, like his own clothes and generic-brand deck shoes. He still wore his hair as long as he had worn it when I'd met him, so it hung half an inch over his ears.

Beyond the jungle gym, light from Margo's bedroom bled into the evening. She crossed the room and lingered out of view, then crossed again. Fourth grade was in full swing and sixth grade was still in the hazy long distance. I didn't know when her bedroom door had started being closed as much as it was open, or when I'd stopped knowing what she did when she was alone. I considered tiptoeing to the window and peering in, then watching as she danced alone to a cassette on the yellow shag rug, or as she dragged the telephone in from the hallway and shut its cord in the door hinges, or as she read a book with one hand in a bag of pretzels.

Dennis's swing rose as high as he could make it go. He tucked his legs under when he dropped so they wouldn't hit the ground, and then pumped them out when he rose. "It's not fucking long enough," he said. "We need one of these for adults."

"I don't think they make them," I said.

"Goddamn kid swings," he muttered, and then I'm not sure if he let go or if his hands slipped on the wet chains, but all of a sudden he was in the air and then on the ground, clutching his ankle. By the time I reached him, he was sobbing.

During the last week of fourth grade, Dennis and Margo and I sat down at the kitchen table for a family meeting. I'd cleaned up from dinner and Margo was freshly showered. Dennis had been scanning the classifieds and eating blackberries over the sink. When we were seated, Dennis clasped his hands. He started by explaining our meeting with Mr. Oxley to Margo, who interrupted to remind me that Elise Martinez, our neighbor for years until her family moved, had skipped second grade. She fidgeted until Dennis was finished. "But my friends," she said. She scratched at the table with a fingernail.

Dennis got up from the table and came back with a steno pad. He drew three rectangles and labeled them FOURTH GRADE, FIFTH GRADE, and SIXTH GRADE. Beside the rectangles, he drew a stick figure in a skirt and labeled it MARGO. Beside the figure, he drew a question mark. "The way I see it," he said, "we'll fill these boxes with pros and cons, and whichever has the most pros wins."

I said, "Fourth grade isn't an option."

"It's the standard by which all other grades are measured," Dennis said.

I said, "Mr. Oxley thinks you might be a little too mature for the fifth grade, sweetheart."

"Except he pronounces it *matoor*," said Dennis, and Margo giggled.

"I like Mr. Oxley," said Margo.

"Me too," I said.

"Me too," said Dennis, and in the fourth-grade box he wrote: MR. OXLEY.

"I don't think sixth-graders take art class," said Margo.

NO ART CLASS, wrote Dennis in the sixth-grade box.

I said, "They have health education in the

190

sixth grade," and Margo made a face. Dennis pointed out that she'd be in a different class from her friends, and Margo nodded solemnly. FRIENDS, wrote Dennis in the fifth-grade box. Margo pointed out that sixth-graders were allowed to take two elective classes per term. SHOP & HOME-EC, wrote Dennis, and she said she'd prefer to take gymnastics.

"Sixth-grade boys are cuter," she said, which came as a surprise. This was true, from what I'd observed. CUTE BOYS, wrote Dennis with difficulty. Margo said, "Graduation."

Dennis was always less reluctant than I to show ignorance. "Meaning what?" he said.

"There's no ceremony for the sixth-graders," said Margo.

There were plenty of times when I wasn't certain what Margo was talking about — music bands, for example, or slang, or comic book characters. For an instant, I thought this was one of those times, but then I remembered the most significant difference between fifth and sixth grades: although they were both located on the same campus, one was elementary school, and the other, as of a school board decision two years earlier, was middle school.

"You'll miss graduation," I said, and

Margo said, "Obviously."

Sunset School comprised two large buildings, one for kindergarten through fifth grade, and the other for grades six through eight. Grades nine through twelve, which didn't yet concern us, were located in a different place entirely. If Margo skipped the fifth grade, not only would she occupy a different desk in a different classroom — she'd cross into a new world order. This was not a minor distinction.

"They have lockers at middle school," I said.

LOCKERS, wrote Dennis.

"They have different teachers for every subject," said Margo.

DIFF. TEACHERS, Dennis wrote.

"They don't have to walk single file in the hall," said Margo.

Dennis wrote, NO SINGLE FILE. Then, in the fifth-grade box, he wrote, SINGLE FILE.

"I'll go," said Margo.

I marveled at her flexibility. "You don't have to," I said.

Dennis put down the pencil. "Why don't you sleep on it?"

Margo bit her lip. "No. It's OK." She put her arms around his neck. When she drew back, she hugged me, too, then picked up the steno pad with the boxes all filled in.

She tore off the top sheet and folded it as small and tight as a matchbook, then slipped it into her back pocket and wiped her nose with the back of her hand. "Can I have ice cream?" she said.

Two weeks later, Margo left in a van full of local kids for Camp Cherokee in southern Georgia, where she'd spent a month every summer since she was eight. In July, Dennis and I drove up to Atlanta to spend the weekend with my mother — we met my father and Luanne, whom we'd seen only occasionally over the years, for breakfast — and on the way home we visited Margo at camp on her birthday. We took her out for barbecue and she and Dennis went through ten packets of Wet Wipes each. Camp was only half over and already she was tan and hollow-cheeked, with a newly chipped molar. She explained that she'd been doing backward somersaults in the shallow part of the lake, one after the other without coming up for air, and then the back of her head had hit the metal swim ladder. She'd believed she'd been rolling in place, when really she'd been traveling. As soon as her head had hit, she'd felt something sharp roll over her tongue. She'd stood up and spat into her hand, then presented the shard to her counselor. I wondered why we hadn't been notified. Dennis sighed — thinking, I assume, of the dentist bill.

"On land," said Margo, "when I do a somersault, I roll about this far." She spread her arms. "But I thought that in water, I'd stay in place. Wouldn't you think I'd stay in place?"

"Like laundry in a machine," said Dennis, nodding.

Margo shrugged. "I guess not."

Usually when we drove up for her birthday — as we had done three summers running — Margo begged to stay at camp for another two-week session. We'd always refused. A month was already too much time without her, in my opinion, and Dennis always wanted to spend a week at Stiltsville as a family before school started. Not to mention that camp was expensive. But on the drive up, I'd told Dennis I thought we should let her stay this year. "What on earth for?" he'd said. "Are we feeling guilty?" I didn't answer. "I guess we are," he'd said.

I resisted the impulse to wipe a smear of barbecue from Margo's chin. "Aren't you going to ask to stay at camp?" I said.

She put a finger in her mouth and felt around. "Look," she said, pulling apart her lips. The broken tooth looked like the craggy face of a mountain.

194

"We'll get it fixed when you're home," I said.

"I don't want to stay this year," Margo said.

"Good," said Dennis.

"Why not?" I said.

Margo shrugged. Her shrug had become something of a default reaction, a prelude to the preteen years. She'd also assumed the habit of thinking before answering. "It's fun, but it's not that fun," she said. "You know?"

"Sure," said Dennis. "More Margo for us."

That night, in what must have been the crummiest motel room between Tallahassee and Panama City, I cried. Dennis was only moderately sympathetic — he'd long since dubbed our annual camp visit the Trail of Tears. He lay with his head propped on a stack of flat pillows, watching the weather report flashing on the television. "She's changed," I said.

Dennis nodded.

"She'll miss graduation," I said.

"Big deal."

"She would've received an award." Best Citizenship, I thought, or Best Spelling.

"Are we having second thoughts?"

"No," I said. I cried harder. "But she would've gotten a new dress, and I would've

195

fixed her hair."

"Frances —"

"And you would've taped the whole thing."

This got his attention. He'd purchased a video camera shortly before quitting his job. Since, he'd archived twenty-five hours of Margo practicing cartwheels in the backyard, and me reading a book on the sofa in my bifocals, and Margo running red-faced down a green stretch of soccer field, and me in one of his old polo shirts, fixing breakfast. When he trained the camera on Margo, she made faces. "Come on," Dennis would say, "be candid." Margo would lunge at the camera, fingers flexing. "Candid, candid, candid," she'd say in a monster voice. "Someday we'll look back," Dennis would say, reattaching the lens cap.

Dennis turned up the volume on the television. "She's all registered; she's ready."

"She needs new clothes," I said seriously.

His jaw tensed. "I'll borrow some cash." His parents had offered; we'd known it was only a matter of time.

"I'll take that bank job," I said.

"Shit," he said. On television, a local meteorologist stood in front of a red-and-yellow whorl: a tropical storm was brewing in the West Indies. Dennis said, "We can't keep her in a class where we know she isn't challenged."

"If only we didn't know," I said.

"Plus, the girl thing," he said. "Chests like mosquito bites — bad influence."

I stopped crying and laughed a little. I moved next to him and watched the grainy television. Hurricane season was under way, and this West Indian blip was its first noteworthy event. For months Dennis would follow weather events like elections. The meteorologist's chatter would function as the backdrop during every family meal. There had been only one real hurricane since I'd moved to Miami — David in 1979, which had torn several two-by-fours from the stilt house roof and half a dozen shingles from our house in Miami. Tropical storms brewed constantly from May to September, but they had so many ways of falling apart. They might diffuse over the continental reef or rub up against cold snaps and disperse like bubbles in tepid bathwater. Sometimes they just disappeared: angry radar spirals dissolved, and the screen went black. Dennis feared, as I did, that it was only a matter of time before another big one hit Stiltsville. He remembered Donna, Cleo, Betsy. If the worst happened — *when* the worst happened — I knew my little family would find itself unmoored. We would boat the bay and the Miami River, destinationless. Maybe we would anchor where our stilt house had stood and dive the spot like any wreck, searching for bed frames, shutters, shoes. We would feel loss and lost, and I would realize once again: This is what it means to be part of a family. There are no maps and the territory is continually changing. We are explorers, traveling in groups.

"Do you think she's changed?" I said.

"She's older," he said. "She's eleven now, for Christ's sake."

"She's become . . ." I couldn't think of the right word. The red swirl on the television flashed across the blue Atlantic. By the time it reached South Florida — if it even made it that far — it would be no more destructive than a rainstorm. "Reserved," I said.

He nodded.

"Take off your shirt," I said.

He thought I was getting frisky, but I'd spotted yellow on the fabric under the arm, and I was pretty strict on this issue, even when times were lean. I threw the shirt across the room, into a rusty metal trash can with the motel's logo printed on the side. Dennis shrugged, and all at once I saw where Margo had gotten the gesture. I felt a surge of fondness for this ability to discriminate between battles, large versus small. Then, because hotels and motels — anonymous, ghost-ridden, seedy — have always inspired me, we got frisky.

In the fourth grade, Margo had worn a pair of purple denim jeans that I loved. Like me, she was mostly legs, and her stomach puffed charmingly over her waistband. I might have admitted to Margo that I loved those purple jeans — I certainly never concealed my opinion of her more questionable preferences — but I never did. To me, those jeans represented the perfect balance of tomboy and girly girl. If the jeans had been black, it would have been another story.

The Saturday before sixth grade started, Margo and I had brunch with Marse — she had just broken up with a professional golfer whom Dennis and I had liked a lot, and who had given Margo a set of clubs and several lessons — and afterward, Margo and I went shopping for school clothes. I'd started work at the bank that week, and on Friday had received a check for the sum total of my earnings, which I planned to spend entirely on Margo's wardrobe. The purple jeans, I discovered that morning when she put them on, were fading through the knees, and soon would be too short at the ankles and too tight through the hips. I planned to find the perfect replacement. I believed new clothes put a spring in the step. Never, though, had the stakes been so high. For years, Margo had watched the big kids with longing and trepidation, and she was about to be catapulted into their world as if holding on to the end of a long, bendy pole. For sixth grade, Margo would need jeans in every color. She would need heart-shaped jewelry and brightly colored Duo-tangs and teen idol book covers. She would need armor.

"Do you know what the sixth-graders are wearing?" I asked Margo on the way to the mall.

"Sure," she said. I waited for her to elaborate, but she didn't, so I summoned from memory what I knew of middle school fashion. I'd parked in front of Sunset School every weekday afternoon for five years, waiting for Margo to emerge with Carla at her side, two droplets in a maelstrom. I'd studied the older kids as closely as the younger ones: many of the girls kissed each other's cheeks in greeting and valediction. They had good posture. They did not carry lunch boxes; instead, they slung backpacks over one shoulder, and each girl's backpack was a different color, as if they'd all drawn straws. The girls spent a lot of time sneaking glances at the boys, who slouched with their hands in their pockets and their legs apart, and whose clothes were too big and didn't match.

Margo led the way through the mall. We wound up in the juniors section of the department store, among clusters of paisley and polka-dot blouses, neon leggings, and plaid blouses and matching skirts. Margo took several pairs of pants, two skirts, and half a dozen blouses into the dressing room, and I sat on a stool in the corner as she pulled each item on and off. I returned the items to their hangers, checking the prices, alternately relieved and disappointed. In an hour, she'd chosen two pairs of jeans, one pair of black pants, and five blouses — *shirts,* she said — that looked more or less the same to me. I told her to choose three of the five, and she did. Before she put her old clothes on again, I said, "What will it be for the big day?"

I held the new clothes in my arms. She picked through them, then matched the black pants to a pink cotton blouse with red stripes. She stepped into the pants and buttoned them, then pulled on the blouse. Price tags dangled at her waist and upper arm. She stared into the mirror for a long time, and I kept my mouth shut. She would've gone through all her school years with the same kids, I thought, and now she'll go through the rest with an entirely different batch. Fourth grade had been a good year, a happy year. She'd learned that Mars has two moons, and that soap can be made from lard, and that Mount Kilimanjaro was formed by a volcano.

She pulled her hair from her face — we were waiting until just before school started to get it cut — and touched her earlobes. I knew what was coming. "Mom," she said.

I stood behind her. "Will you be the only one without them pierced?" I said, thinking: would it help?

"Not the only one," she said.

Dennis had always said we didn't have to worry about Margo becoming an actress — her expression always gave her away. In the dressing room, her face showed that she was highly alert, like an animal sensing a predator. She wasn't fearful, exactly — she was anxious, as if she knew in her bones that anything could happen. "I have one condition," I said.

She started hopping in place.

"You're not going to like it," I said. She stopped hopping. "New bras," I said. "Plus a fitting."

She considered her options, then reached for her old clothes. "Let's go."

As we wound through the store toward the lingerie department, I spotted a pair of jeans made of bright red velveteen. At most, she'd be able to wear them four or five weeks during the winter — but they were adorable. "What about these?" I said.

She eyed the pants and made me move out of the way. "Cool," she said, touching them, and moments later in the dressing room, admiring her long legs and little tummy in the mirror, I was unable to keep from admitting that I loved them, too.

For the bra fitting, a diminutive older woman prodded Margo onto a platform in front of a triptych of mirrors. To Margo, she said, "Arms up, dear," and Margo raised her arms while the rest of her body folded in. The woman looped a measuring tape around her torso and muttered a number. When she took the tape away, Margo tugged on her shirt and headed for the exit. If she'd been thirteen, she might have been glad to learn that she'd grown an inch in the rib cage, thereby earning the right to leave training bras behind forever.

"My turn," I said, stepping onto the platform. I tried to sound lighthearted. For

someone my age being fitted was like stepping onto a scale after years: who knows
what might have transpired? Margo sighed
and clutched a shopping bag to her chest.
The woman unwound her measuring tape.
"I thought I was a thirty-four C," I said,
"but it couldn't hurt to make sure."

When I saw myself reflected in the mirrors, my first thought was that I did not look
half bad. I'd lost weight over the past three
or four years. It was only about ten pounds,
but maybe the fashion of the times flattered
me, and maybe height was in style, because
my self-esteem was up. That was how I
thought of it, how I think of it still: a wave I
ride until it abates. I can divvy my life into
phases with regard to how I felt about my
looks at the time: good years, bad years,
so-so years; years of no makeup, years of no
jewelry, years of some of each. In good
years, I looked at myself in the mirror more
often and criticized my body parts — flabby
upper arms, too-wide hips — because in
those times, the problem areas seemed
discrete and fixable, as if all I needed was a
few lunges or a few laps in the pool.

But — and here is where I pat my parenting on the back — appearance was not a
fourth family member in my house, didn't
pull up a chair and sit with us at mealtimes,

peering at our plates. In this, I followed Dennis's lead: more handsome every year, ten pounds up or down depending on nothing more than whether the Dolphins had made it to the play-offs or how many times he had gone for a run. When he wasn't working, Dennis wore baggy blue jeans and deck shoes with no laces. He used his fingers for a comb, and when he saw himself in a mirror, he smiled. "Hey, man," he'd say to his reflection when he passed the full-length mirror that hung at the end of the hallway off our bedroom. "What's happening, dude?"

I'd hoped Margo might watch my fitting as I'd watched hers, making some meaningful connection between bra fittings and womanhood. Instead, she wandered into a corner of the room and stood in front of another mirror. She brought her hand to the top of her head and started patting, then brought the other hand to her stomach and started to rub in circles. Patting and rubbing, patting and rubbing. Inevitably, the motions became confused, and by the time my new bra size was announced — thirty-six B, to my surprise — she'd grown frustrated and turned away.

It hadn't occurred to me to confer with Dennis before negotiating with Margo on the matter of her ears. After the piercing was all done, I dabbed away the droplets of blood from the tiny gold studs she'd chosen, and thought she looked rather cute. At dinner that night, Dennis leaned over his meat loaf to push her hair from her face. "What the hell?" he said to me. "Did you know about this?"

"I forgot to tell you," I said. He'd spent the day at the marina and come home late, and we'd scheduled an after-dinner modeling session so Margo could show off her new outfits.

"It's OK, Dad," said Margo.

"I don't agree," he said.

"I'm in sixth grade now," she said.

I flinched. Dennis went back to eating, but it was clear that he was upset. Margo and I talked awkwardly about her soccer coach, who'd complimented her speed on the field and moved her from fullback to halfback, and about what she could do to welcome Carla home from Massachusetts, where her family had spent the summer. We decided to make a card and leave it in the mailbox for Carla to find when she arrived home. When I went to clear the plates, Dennis left the table without helping. The front door opened and closed. I pushed a glass of milk toward Margo and sent her to watch television in our room, and the phone rang.

It was Bette. "What's in that yam dish?" she said when I answered. "Rum?"

"Bourbon," I said.

"Can I make it with rum?"

"I suppose."

"You sound tired."

"Not really," I said, but then I found myself rubbing my eyes, as Margo had done when she was a little girl. I told Bette about our afternoon at the mall, the bra fitting and the ear piercing. "Dennis is brooding," I said.

"You worry too much," she said.

An hour later I circled our block, looking for Dennis. When I got back to the house, he was sitting on the front steps holding a can of beer. He must have rooted behind stacks of yogurts and sodas and vegetables to find the beer in the refrigerator; I hadn't even known we had any. Our stocks were thinning with each week that Dennis was unemployed. I seized over every purchase, every small distinction in price.

"I'm sorry," I said.

He didn't say anything.

"Please don't get gloomy," I said. "We're depending on you."

"I could've used a little warning."

"I was ambushed," I said.

"Self-mutilation, rite of passage. Shit."

"Oh, honey," I said. "I just want her to be happy."

He took several long draws from his beer and set it down with an empty clang. "It's not looking good out there, Frances," he said. "I feel like a slob."

It was mid-August. Dennis had been out of work for eight months. He'd been on five interviews: two with the University of Miami, two with consulting firms, and one with the parks department. He'd sent out many, many résumés. Friends and colleagues called regularly with news of an opening at this or that law firm, but Dennis always declined. Lately, though, it had sounded as if the possibility of returning to law was back on the table. I wasn't sure which I feared more: Dennis not finding a job as our funds dribbled to nothing, or Dennis taking a job he wouldn't like. "You're not a slob," I said.

"I feel useless."

"You're definitely not useless."

"I feel —"

"This is the hard part, Dennis. We knew this was going to be hard."

"I know. I'm sorry."

I shrugged. "I don't mind it so much."

This was true. I'd carved out a little place for myself at the bank, and had been promoted from teller to loan processor, for a higher hourly wage. The people were friendly and the work was easy. I'd always planned to go back to work someday, and now I had done it. "It's going to be fine," I said. But reassurance was rarely my responsibility, and it sounded forced. I tried again: "It's going to be *fine*." If he couldn't believe it, I wasn't sure I could.

"I was thinking something."

"What?"

"Used to be," he said, "she had twelve years of school, total, before we sent her off."

I inhaled sharply. How could I not have considered this? We'd robbed ourselves of an entire year of Margo. "I've been thinking maybe fifth grade was the best year that never happened."

"Right," he said. From inside I heard Margo calling for me.

"Come see what she got," I said to Dennis.

"I saw plenty," he said, but he rose anyway, and stretched up on the balls of his feet, pointing his long arms toward the sky, and when he came down again he put one arm around me, and we went inside. The next week, I drove Margo to the front entrance of Sunset School, where Carla was waiting for her. They stood on the sidewalk, admiring each other's outfits — Margo had worn the red velveteen pants, despite the muggy weather — and then Carla walked in one direction, and Margo walked in the other.

Dennis and I were late for parent-teacher night because Marse and Margo and I had spent the afternoon on Marse's boat and lost track of time. Dennis and I snapped at each other in the car, and I was flustered upon arriving at the school gates, where a student handed us name tags and a schedule. According to the schedule, our evening would follow the design of our daughter's day: ten minutes in each of her classes. I studied the schedule as we walked toward her homeroom, then looked across the courtyard at the elementary school building. There, our other selves headed to the fifth-grade classroom, where we would have drunk coffee from Styrofoam cups and chatted with parents whose faces were familiar but whose names we'd forgotten. The fifth-grade teacher would have taken me by the elbow and told me that Margo was doing marvelously, that she had many dear friends, and that her scores were top-notch. We would have popped our heads into the fourth-grade classroom and waved hello to Mr. Oxley. Margo might have felt the same nostalgia. In the month since school had started she'd been spending a lot of time on her schoolwork and in the backyard on a blanket with sunscreen and a book. From what I gathered, she had not made new friends.

Dennis was bored by the time the homeroom bell clanged. He slouched like a kid in his chair. Margo's English teacher was a handsome, dimpled young man named Mr. Lopez, and her social studies teacher, Mrs. Gonzalez, wore tinted glasses and chunky brass bracelets that clattered when she moved. Mrs. Gonzalez's class was starting a unit on the Constitution; she explained that every student would be required to write a report about an article or an amendment. "Finally, something useful," said Dennis as we shuffled with the other parents to Margo's science class. Our group finished back in homeroom for refreshments, and Dennis and I stood in the corner while the other parents shook the teacher's hand and filed out. Margo's homeroom teacher was Mrs. Madansky, a short bony woman with spiky yellow hair. "Can we leave?" said Dennis to me. Cookie crumbs dotted his lips and he licked them off.

"In a minute."

"Did you see that Lopez guy's earring?"

"Don't be provincial."

Finally, Mrs. Madansky headed our way with an outstretched hand. "Margo's parents," she said. "I was hoping we'd get a chance to chat."

"So were we," said Dennis, and his forward-leaning stance gave him away: he thought Mrs. Madansky was a dish. His taste was, in my opinion, rather banal.

She gestured to an empty circle of desks and we sat down. The group was thinning out; a few people touched her shoulder to say quick good-byes. "First," she said, "I think you should know that I've been keeping an eye on Margo from the start of the year."

"And?" said Dennis.

She pinched her lips in concentration, as if choosing her words. "She's doing well. But so far my impression is that she — well, she's high-strung, if you know what I mean."

"Sure," said Dennis.

"I don't know what you mean," I said.

Mrs. Madansky met my eye, and I felt a shudder of enmity. I know her best, I wanted to say whenever a teacher chose an adjective for Margo. I'd heard *garrulous, precocious, outgoing, sensitive, mature,* and

— this from her second-grade teacher, whom I did not care for — *prideful. Presumptuous,* I wanted to say in response. *Demanding, obtuse, restrictive.* I was not a mother who believed her daughter was flawless — on the contrary, I thought Margo sparkled with faults, bubbled with imperfections. She talked too loudly and too much; she was stubborn, unpredictable, and moody. She had personality.

"If I may ask," said Mrs. Madansky. "What time does Margo get to bed at night?"

"Eight-thirty or nine," said Dennis.

"Does she fall asleep easily?"

"Not always," said Dennis. "I've been having trouble sleeping, and sometimes she sits up with me."

This was news to me.

Mrs. Madansky said, "How often?"

"Twice a week, maybe three times. It's a phase."

I said, "Has she been sleeping in class?"

"No, no," said Mrs. Madansky. "She's very alert. Too alert. She raises her hand every time a question is asked." She took a breath. "Even when she doesn't know the answer."

"She's eager," I said. "She's proving herself."

Mrs. Madansky cocked her head. "She's tense," she said. "And getting more so. I'm recommending that she spend an hour a week with the school counselor, Mr. Callahan."

"But she's trying to fit in," Dennis said.

I agreed, absolutely. It would take a dozen shopping excursions, I thought, to fix that smear on her reputation: school counselors were not cool.

"She can meet with him during her elective period," said Mrs. Madansky. "We can be discreet."

"We'll think about it," I said.

"Margo is probably reluctant to worry you," she continued in her calm, teacherly tone. She looked at Dennis as she said it, but the comment pierced me.

On the way home, on the verge of anger fueled mostly by pride, I asked Dennis why he hadn't told me about Margo's sleeplessness. "I'm sorry," he said. "I figured you'd stop sleeping, too. We'd wander the house at all hours, a family of ghosts."

Carla's parents had skipped parent-teacher night, and Margo had eaten dinner at their house, so we stopped to pick her up on the way home. While she gathered her things, Carla's mother, Sylvia, stooped to speak to us through the car window. "I've

214

been meaning to ask you," she said. "How did you manage to get Margo into the sixth grade?"

Dennis looked as weary as I felt. "It's a long story," he said.

"We have some news," Sylvia said. "We're moving to Massachusetts."

"Oh, no," I said. Weeks earlier, their house had been burglarized and Margo had told us that Carla's parents thought Miami was becoming too dangerous. Margo had wanted to know if this was true. "We have an alarm system," Dennis had told her. He didn't mention that we rarely used it. "You don't have to worry."

"We close in December," said Sylvia. "Do you want to tell Margo?"

Dennis nodded and started the car as Margo scooted into the backseat. Sylvia backed away, waving.

"Did you meet Mr. Lopez?" said Margo to me.

"Cute!" I said.

"Take a number," said Margo.

That week I called the school to give permission for Margo to meet with the school counselor. Margo stomped to her room when we told her, but within two weeks — looking back it seemed she sloughed off old traits and grew new ones overnight — she was saying, "Mr. Callahan says I'm a fast learner," and, "Mr. Callahan didn't like social studies and history when he was in sixth grade, but he liked English. I'm the opposite."

"You don't like English?" I said.

She shrugged. "History's better."

When Dennis and I were in bed, I said, "I think the counselor thing is working out."

He turned to me. "There's something you don't know," he said seriously. I braced myself. "Mr. Callahan," he said, "is cute."

Now that I knew about Margo's insomnia, I often woke in the middle of the night to find that Dennis was not in bed. Some nights I crept silently to the end of the hallway until I heard the murmur of the television or the scrape of a chair on the kitchen tile. I stood in the dark in my nightgown, my heart beating fast and loud, my breath cloudy on the hallway mirror. From what I could tell, Dennis did most of the talking. Margo — if she slept at all it was early, beginning at bedtime and stretching to one or two a.m. — interrupted in brief fragments. Compared with Dennis's gruff murmur, her voice was high and uncertain, a threadbare sound. She sounded, in the drowsy fog of early morning, as if she'd wilted and faded, and I

216

ached to think we'd caused that change. But Dennis was a dedicated comic, and every so often Margo's laugh rose, and my heart unclenched. Most mornings, I found two glasses, empty but for a film of milk, in the kitchen sink.

Despite all the signs — the sleeplessness, the difficulty concentrating, and several unusually aggressive plays on the soccer field, one of which caused her to sit out the rest of the game — it was a surprise when, weeks later, Margo admitted (first to Bette while spending the night at her house, then to Mr. Callahan in one of their sessions, then to Dennis in the early morning hours, then to me in the car) that she did not like school. She did not like haughty Mrs. Madansky (my word), or the snotty girls in her class (her word). Mr. Lopez was OK, but he picked on her. Bette told her, unhelpfully, that her teachers sounded narrowminded, and Dennis told her she seemed overly concerned with whether or not her teachers liked her. "Of course I want them to like me," she said, her voice shaking, and Dennis had no response. He was a person who truly didn't care about that kind of thing; it was marvelous, certainly, but also mystifying.

Margo decided she'd chosen the wrong elective — French — so she switched to Spanish, but she'd missed too much to catch up. To make matters worse, Florida was experiencing one of the coldest winters in history, and Margo owned only old sweaters and ski coats — too small and out of fashion. I took her shopping, but she said nothing was right. She ended up sobbing in the dressing room and we left empty-handed. I had trouble understanding the nature of her anxiety — mostly social, mostly academic, or equally both? Did she have no friends at all, or did she dislike the few friends she'd made? Once or twice a week someone named Beverly called the house and Margo chatted with her on the kitchen telephone, but Margo spent the rest of her free time with Carla, whose days in Miami were numbered. The girls did home-work together at our dining room table, their dissimilar textbooks faced off like war-ring factions.

"They think I'm a snob," Margo told me when I prodded her about her social life. Her voice was unsteady. We were curled up together on the living room sofa under a blanket. Margo was wearing a pair of Den-nis's ski socks and my long underwear. Dennis sat on the floor, polishing his good shoes for no reason: he hadn't had an interview in two weeks. There was a chill in the air that we couldn't cut without lighting a fire or turning on the heater, but we were out of wood, and every time I wandered near the heater controls, Dennis perked up and said, "Really? It's not so bad. Put on some socks."

"Who thinks you're a snob?" I said.

She took a moment to answer. "This girl laughed at me in social studies."

"Why?"

"I had something on my notebook. She saw it and told Melanie."

"What was on your notebook?"

"Just a drawing, Mom."

"What kind of drawing?"

"A stupid rainbow. They think I'm a baby."

"A baby and a snob?"

She nodded, sniffling.

"Define your terms," said Dennis. "What's a snob?"

Her lip quivered and she wiped away a tear. It occurred to me that this was all very adult, this choking on tears, this swallowing of sorrow. "A snob is someone who thinks she's better than everyone else," she said.

"That's not you," said Dennis.

Margo hiccuped. "I don't think it is."

I said, "Why do you think they think that?"

219

"They won't talk to me. They talk about me."

I said, "What else do they say?"

"Who cares?" said Dennis. He stopped polishing. "Trust me, you're not a snob. I've known snobs, and they're nothing like you."

"I don't know what to do," she said.

"Screw them," he said.

"Dennis," I said.

"Margo, school is your job. You get up in the morning, you go, you get your work done. I know this Spanish thing is messing you up, so I say focus on that. Once you've got it licked, concentrate on something else. It's like I always tell your mother — you can't worry about everything at the same time."

Margo nodded and her tears stopped, but I could feel her shivering in the warm space between our bodies.

The temperature continued to drop. A low frond from the king palm in our backyard shriveled and crashed to the ground. Margo spent an hour in the yard, crunching the grass under her boots. I borrowed electric blankets from Dennis's parents and ordered a purple parka from a catalog for Margo. Every day, I wore Dennis's flannel fishing jacket over my normal clothes. One weeknight, Marse came over with firewood and ingredients for s'mores and we sat in chairs in front of the fireplace with our sticks out. "It's OK if it burns a little," Marse told Margo. "Sometimes that's the best part." Marse told stories about her awkward years. Once, she'd told a friend she liked a boy, and that friend had spread it all around school. Once she'd gotten her period while wearing white pants, and had to walk home in the middle of the day to change. The episodes hadn't been particularly mortifying, but I think the stories made Margo feel better.

One night I woke to Dennis's hand on my shoulder, his soft voice saying my name. He and Margo stood beside the bed in sweaters and blue jeans. "We made coffee," said Margo.

The windows were black. "What's going on?" I said.

Her voice was excited. "Dad has a surprise for us."

I dressed and poured coffee into a thermos, then mixed hot chocolate for Margo and put muffins into a paper bag. We loaded into the front seat of the car, with Margo in the middle. It was two o'clock in the morning. Dennis headed north on the highway and drove for an hour, then took the Okefenokee exit and headed east. Margo rested her head on his shoulder. Orange groves stuttered by on both sides, dusty with moonlight. Every half mile or so, a bright light flashed through the trees. Dennis pulled onto the shoulder of the road and turned off the engine. The headlights died. "Listen," he said. I heard the flutter of citrus bugs and the croak of cicadas, wind in the thick black groves. Then there was a popping sound in the distance.

"What was that?" I said.

Dennis stepped out of the car and crossed the road. "Come on," he said, then vanished down a dark seam between the trees.

The air in the grove smelled of ripe and rotten fruit. Fallen oranges pocked the ground and tree branches scattered the moonlight. Dennis's figure ahead of us was shadowy and nebulous. Another muted pop sounded, then another. The noises resembled shots from miniature guns. Margo and I hustled to keep up, but Dennis moved fast; I tracked the sound of his movement. My pulse quickened. It was a school night — was my husband nuts?

"Turn left," called Dennis. He was at least twenty yards off. We crossed into the next row of trees and a light appeared ahead. "Still with me?" he said. His voice and the light came from the same place.

"This is freaky, Dad," called Margo. She sounded happy.

As we neared the light, I saw that it came from a flood lamp attached to a picker nestled in the high branches of a tree. In the basket of the picker was a man holding a bucket of oranges in one hand. Dennis had taken off his sweater and held it in front of him.

"I forgot to bring a bag," said Dennis as we caught up. In the scope of the lamplight it looked like daytime. The man above us wore a red plaid jacket and heavy leather gloves. Dennis called up to him. "Got a few to spare?"

"Who's catching?" called the man in the picker.

My arms rose, palms cupped. The man tossed an orange and I caught it, then placed it in Dennis's sweater. I worried briefly about stretching the fabric, but then the man threw another orange, then another. When we'd collected half a dozen, Dennis knotted the sweater sleeves and slung the bundle over one shoulder. I took off my own sweater and Margo stepped up. "Here," she called. I watched her in the grainy light, the lines and angles of her. She took a little hop every time she reached for a falling orange. Her hair swung. Her expression shifted from intent to ecstatic. The load in my arms grew heavy. From deeper in the grove, another shot rang out. "What is that?" I asked Dennis.

"Had enough?" said the man in the picker.

"Thank you kindly," called Dennis, and the man waved. To Margo, Dennis said, "That sound is the fruit — it's bursting."

"The oranges are breaking?" she said.

"They have to," said Dennis. "It's too cold for them."

We walked a little, shivering in cold air, and Dennis explained that the man in the picker was spraying the oranges with water. The water would freeze on the peels and the reaction would release the tiniest germ of heat, enough to keep some of the fruit alive. Dennis led us back to the road, and on the way I listened for bursting oranges and peered through the grove to spot other flood lamps, other pickers. The sound came every minute or so, always from a different direction, and I glimpsed half a dozen more lights. The grove was a galaxy, the flood lamps and explosions stars and celestial events. My family steered through space, linked, until we reached the highway. To Dennis, I said, "How did you know?" He smiled at me but didn't answer. He seemed to regard fatherhood and husbandhood the way a magician regards magic: the delight is in the mystery. His father had probably brought him to beg for free oranges the last time the crops froze. By the time Margo became an adult, there would be fences to keep us out.

We put the oranges in the car trunk. I figured I would make marmalade and no one would eat it. I would make orange-chocolate-chip cookies and Margo would say she preferred the regular kind. It didn't matter. On the way home, Margo's cheeks were pink in the brightening light. She chatted for a while about the orange groves, then grew quiet. After a long silence, she said, "When Carla moves, I won't have a best friend."

"You'll make a new one," I said. "Or two or four."

"Mighty Margo," said Dennis. "Many people will love you."

This time she cried almost without sound. We'd made a mistake in pushing her ahead — of this, I was certain. I'd let pride influence me. Shamefully, though, I felt a little grateful for the mistake, because my daughter needed me, and I knew she wouldn't need me in the same way for much longer. Still, I couldn't shake the image of Margo sitting in Mrs. Madansky's class, raising her hand again and again.

In mid-December of that year — Margo had been a sixth-grader for three months — a dozen Dade County police officers chased down and fatally beat a thirty-three-year-old black insurance agent named Arthur McDuffie. They said McDuffie had rolled through a red light on his motorcycle while giving a cop the finger, and that he'd kicked one of the officers, who in turn cracked McDuffie's skull open — these were the prosecutor's words — *like an egg.*

Mrs. Madansky sent home a typed letter addressed to all sixth-grade parents. *"Dear Mom and Dad,"* read the note, *"your son/ daughter's class will study Current Events this term. Students are required to bring a news article to class every Monday/Wednesday or Tuesday/Thursday."* On our copy, the second pair of days was circled in red pen. *"Please supervise your child's choices to make sure they are appropriate. Parents have expressed concern that certain local events might cause students to become upset."*

At the dinner table, over lasagna, Dennis tore up the note and tossed it theatrically over one shoulder. "Your teacher is an idiot," he said to Margo.

"Dennis!" I said. "She's being cautious."

"She's being a coward." To Margo, he said, "Something horrible happened and people are going to remember it for a long time."

"The police killed a black man," she said.

"Right," said Dennis, "and now people have to face the fact that Miami isn't so much a melting pot as, I don't know . . ."

"Potpourri," I said.

"Why did they kill him?" said Margo.

"We don't know exactly why," said Dennis. "But people feel so strongly about Mr. McDuffie's death that a judge moved the trial all the way to Tampa."

"What will happen to the police officers?" said Margo.

I said, "They'll be punished."

"In Tampa?" Dennis said to me. His jaw tightened. "No, they won't."

After dinner, Dennis spread a newspaper on our bed and pored over it, trying to find an article for Margo to take to school. There was no use telling him this was her assignment. "Here's one," he said. He called for Margo and a minute later she appeared, wearing a Dolphins jersey and white ankle socks. Dennis tore out the article and Margo read it while I got ready for bed. When she'd gone back to her room, I asked him what they'd chosen.

"That fisherman who drowned in his nets," he said.

I stared at him. "How is that any better?"

"She's going to show the kids how to signal an airplane from water."

"You're using Margo to teach Mrs. Madansky a lesson."

"Which one was Mrs. Madansky?" said Dennis. He walked to the full-length mirror that hung from the back of the closet door. "I look older."

Dennis had become very focused. He either went on an interview or made phone calls every afternoon. Marse had begged him to interview with her firm, but he'd declined. I'd taken on more hours at the bank. We owed his parents so much money I thought we'd never be able to pay it back.

"You look tired, not older," I said.

"Same difference," he said, borrowing an expression from Margo.

He came to bed and laid his head on my thigh. I took off my bifocals. Dennis worried sporadically, in consuming fits, while I worried consistently at a moderate intensity, so it was rare for a new concern to spiral me into full-blown panic. I thought of his advice to Margo about school. "List the things you're most anxious about," I said, "and we'll cross off the last two."

228

He paused. "I'm nervous about the possibility of homelessness and poverty."

"Ours, though? Not generally."

"Ours, yes."

"What else?"

"I'm worried that I won't find a job —"

"You'll find a job."

"Assuming I do, there's no guarantee I'll like it any better than the last one." This was true. "And I'm concerned that our daughter doesn't have any friends."

Truthfully, in those moments, Dennis did look older. "Anything else?"

"I don't know." He didn't speak for a long moment. "I wonder if maybe Miami isn't the best place for us."

I sat up, knocking away his head.

"You've never thought about moving?" he said.

"Of course I have." In fact, I'd thought of it a few times in recent years, as Miami had started to change. I'd noticed that on the bay there were more large flashy power-boats, and on land there were more luxury cars and new houses with security gates and surveillance systems — and I'd heard on the news that there were now more banks per capita in Miami than anywhere else in the country, and more cash in those banks than anywhere else. These seemed signs of something ominous. The summer before, in broad daylight, men in an armored van had pulled up to a liquor store at Dadeland mall and shot up the place, and since then, one could scarcely turn on the the news without hearing about the cocaine cowboys. More than once I'd heard the joke that in Miami one could always find work as a tail gunner on a bread truck. But although we saw the changes happening around us, they barely affected my family. We were insulated by where we lived and the circles we moved in. To this day, I've never seen cocaine in real life.

"It's last on the list," I said. "Cross it off."

"Let's talk about it," said Dennis.

"We can talk about it, but we're not going to do it," I said. "Cross it off. You take the job thing, and I'll worry about Margo. If you get tired, we can switch."

Margo and I also negotiated over the next month. It was an unspoken negotiation. She'd taken Dennis's advice, and Dennis had taken mine, and they seemed to be trudging along with their respective duties — the sixth grade, the job search — without sliding into despair. Meanwhile, I was experiencing a surge of energy: I prepared lavish breakfasts and hemmed old skirts to a more fashionable length. I devoured novels while Dennis made phone calls or Margo studied. I engineered inexpensive weekend activities: the zoo, the science museum, the beach. When I picked Margo up from school, she walked from the gate to my car without speaking to anyone. Weekends, she helped out behind the counter at Bette's dive shop. We went out on the boat with Grady and Gloria, and Margo sat chewing bubble gum at the stern, flipping through magazines. Marse took her shopping at the outlet mall in Boca Raton, and she came home with a pair of designer sunglasses and sneakers with silver laces. Gloria told her that adjusting to change takes time, and Bette told her that very often other people stink. Soccer season was finished, and Carla's family had moved away.

Our negotiation was this: if she could avoid becoming terribly unhappy, and she continued talking to Mr. Callahan once a week, then I would not nag her about school and friends and whether her life was improving.

One afternoon, she came to the car after school with Trisha Weintraub in tow. She introduced us and said that Trisha needed a ride, and they climbed into the backseat. I started the car and pulled out of the lot without knowing where I was going. Trisha wore tight blue jeans and a sweatshirt with a wide neck that revealed a flesh-colored bra strap. She usually rode home with her best friend Melanie's mom, she explained, but that day Melanie had left school early with the flu. Trisha directed me through the gates of CocoPlum to the stucco house with the terra-cotta porch. "See ya," she said to Margo as she scooted out of the car. "Don't forget to ask." She slammed the door.

I waited to drive away until Trisha was inside. I tried to meet Margo's eyes in the rearview mirror, but she was studying her fingernails. "Ask what?" I said.

"Trisha's birthday is Saturday. She's having a sleepover."

"You can go. What time does it start?"

She shrugged, so I asked about the school day, and then she chatted a little about the softball unit in gym class. We arrived home, and together we walked into the house and found Dennis standing in the kitchen in his boxer shorts, drinking milk from the carton. "Enough," I said. "You need to find a job." I was mostly joking.

"Done," he said, spreading his arms. "I start Monday."

He'd been hired by a small firm that

specialized in immigration and admiralty law. It was law, yes, and there was less money in it than in other areas of practice, but it was a close-knit and casual office, and he believed he could be happy there. Over the years, this would prove true.

We celebrated by going out to an Italian restaurant on Miracle Mile. "Patience is a virtue," said Dennis, raising his glass. "Right, Margo?"

"I was invited to a sleepover," she said uncertainly.

"Well done!" said Dennis. We toasted.

That Saturday afternoon, Margo came into the living room, where Dennis was watching basketball and I was reading the newspaper. "Mom," she said. She gestured for me to get up. I put down the paper and followed her to her bedroom.

"All packed?" I said.

It had been almost a year since Margo had attended a sleepover. She looked miserable. She slumped on her bed, her hands wedged between her knees. Through my mind flashed a memory of her standing on the sidewalk outside Mr. Oxley's classroom, looking confident and charming, and my gut clenched. "I have a problem," she said.

I tried to sound capable and maternal. "Let's try and solve it."

She looked around the room, avoiding my eyes. I knelt in front of her. "What's wrong?"

Her arms looped around my neck and her head found my shoulder. I felt the hard chill of an earring on my skin. "Trisha shaves her legs," she said. "And so does Melanie, but she won't be there tonight because she's still sick. Beverly Jovanovich does, too, and Sonia Rodriguez."

This had always been a cross-the-bridge-when-we-come-to-it issue, and here we were. It seemed as if Margo had just turned eleven — though she'd really turned eleven six months earlier — but her classmates were twelve and thirteen. She'd skipped a year of school, of development, of everything. Fourth grade was simultaneously one year and two grades in the past. For the purposes of this conversation, Margo wasn't eleven at all. The math was confounding.

"Once you start," I said, "you never get to stop." After a certain point, I wanted to tell her, your whole life will be like this — more or less the same forever, the same sadnesses and joys returning again and again. But Margo did not need to know that her mother had difficulty distinguishing between the trivial and the all-encompassing, that a person could so easily sidestep from shaving to despair.

Margo's eyes were clear, her face still and serious. "I know," she said, and in that moment I believed she did.

"Not today," I said, and though she scowled, I suspected she was relieved. "Wear pants and take your pj's — no one will know."

"When?"

"When you turn twelve," I said. I almost said, "When you're home from camp," but I remembered that Margo wasn't returning to summer camp. She was going to take tennis lessons at the Youth Center instead, then she and I would drive up and spend a week in Georgia with my mother, who wanted to teach Margo to knit and take her strawberry picking, and then in August we were planning a road trip to Washington, D.C. Dennis wanted Margo to see the Capitol.

"A birthday present?"

"Sure thing," I said, thinking, Just you wait. The stubble burn, the red bumps, the never-ending chore. "I wanted to tell you something."

Her arms dropped. "What?"

I spoke carefully. "One reason your father and I believed you should move ahead a year was because you're more mature than most girls your age. Physically, I mean."

She avoided my eyes. "OK."

"So even though I don't want you to start shaving your legs so young, I'm happy that your new friends are so mature, because I think you probably feel more comfortable with them."

"Dad told me all that."

"He did?"

She turned toward the closet. She dressed in the red velveteen pants and a white top, and then we called for Dennis and grabbed Trisha's gift from the dining room table and got into the car. Dennis hummed along with the radio as we drove, and Margo's voice piped up from the backseat to join his. "Bye-bye Miss American Pie," she sang, at first softly and then louder. "Drove my Chevy to the levee but the levee was dry . . ." By the time we reached the Weintraub house, Margo was singing high and strong, like someone excited about what the world had to offer.

There were boys, of course. Judy and her boyfriend took a bottle of wine into the master suite and closed the door, and the girls — eleven of them, enough for an entire soccer team — called the boys on the phone to give the all-clear. They met in an empty lot three doors down and stood shoulder to shoulder so the boys could kiss them one by one, snaking down the line. There was a boy there who was not cool, and had been invited only because he was older and had a history of sneaking the car keys from his father without being caught. This boy, Devon, had acne and bad breath and when he reached Margo in the line, Trisha pushed Margo from behind and Devon grabbed her breasts and when she twisted free the girls called her a prude and Trisha said she should never have invited her, but she'd wanted someone for Devon since he'd offered to drive the boys. After a while the boys wandered off. The girls were worried about getting into trouble if Judy found out they'd left the house, so they went back to Trisha's bedroom. The room had a sitting area with a fluffy white area rug and a private bathroom with lavender walls and white trim. The girls changed into pajamas and laid out their sleeping bags — Margo's was blaze-orange and thick as a mattress, a relic from our family's early camping days — and talked about the boys. And then some of the boys were back, throwing stones at Trisha's window. Trisha went to the window and hushed them, then whispered in another girl's ear. The girl giggled and whispered to another girl, who whispered to another. When the whispering reached

Margo, she was horrified to learn the plan: they were going to line up at the picture window in the living room and moon the boys on the count of three. She trudged out to the living room with the pack, and for the second time that night they all lined up, facing away from the window. Trisha counted to three but after Margo pulled down her pants, she looked up to discover that no other girl had gone through with it, and instead they were shrieking and pointing at her. She heard muffled male laughter, too, punctuated by catcalls and swear words. Back in the lavender bathroom, she tried to hold it together before sneaking out to call us from the telephone in the kitchen.

Margo spent Sunday in her room and refused to eat. I called Judy Weintraub, who said that she would have a long talk with her daughter about sneaking out. I was too exhausted to ask for more. I called Bette and asked her to come over. "I'll be there in a jiff," she said, and I said, "What would we do without you?" She brought cookies and went into Margo's room with glasses of milk. I knew Bette would advise Margo in ways I couldn't; she would call the girls nasty names and brainstorm pranks. Her advice would be irresponsible — retribution, humiliation, that sort of thing — but her wicked outrage would make Margo feel better, and while she talked she would wink in a way that told Margo she wasn't completely serious. When Bette came out of Margo's bedroom, closing the door softly behind her, we convened in the kitchen and she poured two glasses of wine. "Those little devils," she said. "Did you do that kind of thing at her age?"

"I was too shy to do things like that."

"I was just like this Trisha. I was horrible, and then at some point I had no friends."

"I don't believe you," I said.

She smiled. "I would have eaten you for breakfast. You poor thing."

I started to cry, and she put an arm around me and we drank more wine. After she left, I debated for a long time about calling the home of Beverly Jovanovich, whom Margo had mentioned during her retelling of the events and who, according to Margo, had told Trisha to lay off when it was clear she had my daughter in her sights. I decided it could hardly make things worse. "I want to thank you for standing up for Margo last night," I said to her when she came to the phone.

"OK," said Beverly.

"What's it going to be like tomorrow?"

"Trisha was pretty mad she left," Beverly said. I started to tell her what I thought about that, but held my tongue. "I think it's kind of hard for Margo," she said. "Sixth grade is tough."

"I'm starting to realize that."

"Seventh is way better," she said. I had to believe her. There was no other option.

Monday morning Dennis hemmed and hawed about calling in sick on his first day at the new job — he'd seized on the idea of taking Margo to Stiltsville to help her feel better — but I forced him out of the house. He told Margo he loved her through her locked bedroom door. Before getting into his car he said to me, "If we did the wrong thing, why not just put her back where she belongs?"

"Because she doesn't belong there anymore," I told him.

After he left I stood outside Margo's room for a long time, weighing the options. I looked at my watch and calculated that homeroom was already over. I called my supervisor at the bank and asked him to find someone to cover for me for the rest of the week. I called Sunset School and asked firmly to speak to the principal, who listened to my story and promised that he would ask sixth- and seventh-grade teachers to do their best to check this kind of bullying behavior, as he put it. I called Mr. Callahan, the school counselor, and he recommended increasing Margo's sessions to twice a week. He also recommended, strongly, that I bring her to school right away. I called Dennis's mother and left a message asking if we could come for dinner that week; we hadn't seen her and Grady in a while and I thought it would be good for Margo, and for me. I knocked on Margo's door and told her to get dressed for school. "If you can do this," I said through the door, "you can do anything." When she came out, her eyes were red and her face was still. She didn't argue. In the car I handed her a tube of lip gloss and she put it on compliantly. I touched her hair before she opened the car door. "This sucks," she said.

"No swearing," I said. "It does suck. It sucks very badly."

She hesitated, one foot on the ground outside. The school was imposing and inanimate, as if arrested in time. There was no one outside, no movement beyond the frosted windows. Then after a minute, a man emerged from the school office, folding a piece of paper. He walked to his car and got in. A woman crossed the courtyard toward the gym. Margo adjusted her backpack and stepped out of the car and closed the door behind her, waving quickly, then walked toward the school without looking back.

The good news was that since they were not in the same classes, Margo didn't see Trisha that day until the last class let out and she was pulling books from her locker, at which point, she reported, Trisha walked up, called her a snitch, and kept walking. As Margo left school, Beverly came up and said she liked her sneakers and they walked the rest of the way to the parking lot, where I was waiting in the same spot I'd taken that morning, as if I'd never left.

That night we tie-dyed T-shirts for ourselves and for Carla, who had called to tell Margo she hated her new school in Massachusetts. This made Margo feel better — though not, as she put it, in a mean way — and the next morning we drove back to school and Margo took a deep breath and got out of the car again. We did this again the next day and the next. I took Margo to the hardware store and let her choose a paint color for her bedroom — she chose scarlet — and the three of us moved everything out of the room, painted the walls and let them dry, then moved everything back.

While we painted, Dennis tried to explain to Margo what maritime law was all about, and she asked questions and told him she was happy he was happy. That Saturday Margo went to a movie with Beverly, and soon after that she started smiling again. I woke up in the middle of the night several times, but every time Dennis was asleep beside me, and Margo was asleep in her bed.

We'd been unlucky and now it seemed we might become lucky again. Sometimes I think the guiding principles of good parenting are luck and circumstance. And sometimes when I'm feeling pompous I think there is no such thing as luck, that Margo's strength comes from our steerage. The night she fled Trisha Weintraub's house, I'd told her while she cried that no one should have the power to make her feel bad or ugly or embarrassed, that she was the one to decide who could hurt her feelings and who could not. I was just filling the air, of course; she knew well enough that this wasn't true. I hoped, however, that at some point she'd learn what is true: that although we like to believe we are our own little islands, capable of protecting ourselves as well as sheltering and welcoming others, this is never really the case. Still, we must behave as if it is, and hope that we can withstand the wills of other people more often than we cannot.

In mid-May of that year — a month before the end of sixth grade — an all-white jury in the McDuffie case acquitted the accused officers of all thirteen counts after less than three hours of deliberation. Riots broke out in three Miami neighborhoods — black neighborhoods — immediately after the verdict was read. From Stiltsville, we could see smoke rising over the city, and when we got home, South Bayshore was a ghost town. Dennis took the long way to work to avoid the rioting, and when he was home he walked around the house checking the locks on the doors. Although we lived only a five-minute drive from some of the violence, we were shielded from it. Two miles from our house, at a stoplight in a rougher part of Coconut Grove, a white man was dragged from his car and beaten. Governor Graham summoned 3,500 National Guard troops to Miami. Fifteen people were killed, hundreds were injured. Our television stayed on all the time, tuned in to the frequent news alerts. On the third day of rioting, with the troops in place, along with a curfew and a ban on liquor and gun sales, the violence started to abate. On television, the cameras focused on dark empty storefronts with broken windows, on alleys where small fires still burned. Journalists shoved microphones in the faces of crying black women who shook their heads in disbelief. The federal government declared Miami a disaster area and allotted funds for rebuilding.

Shortly after the trial verdict, Margo spent the night at the Jovanovich house, and when she got home, she said, "Beverly's dad says those people are just destroying their own neighborhoods," and Dennis said, "Margo, we don't say *those people* in this house. If you want to talk about black people" — a few years later he would adopt the term *African-Americans* — "then say *black people*. And they're angry. This isn't a conspiracy, it's a riot. This is what rioting is."

A few days later, Dennis and I took Margo and Beverly out on the boat to see Christo's *Surrounded Islands* in Biscayne Bay. The day was bright and blue, and the girls chatted at the stern about a classmate's new haircut and what to wear to so-and-so's birthday party. Having crossed off his job search, Dennis and I had agreed to talk, at some point, about the possibility of leaving Miami. It had seemed that the riots would make this talk more urgent, but they hadn't. To Dennis, this was what parenting was about: teaching our daughter how to think about these events. If we moved somewhere smaller, somewhere less messy — what would Margo learn?

Dennis cruised along the shoreline past the mouth of the Miami River, then slowed to a putter. The girls and I sat at the prow, holding on to the boat railing. The *Surrounded Islands* were replicated in the lenses of their sunglasses. It had taken dozens of workers and 2,200 feet of woven polypropylene fabric for the artist to transform eleven small islands in Biscayne Bay into enormous pink flowers. Each tuft of island, as dense with green mangroves as a paintbrush with bristles, wore a wide pink wreath, a horizontal tutu. The *Miami Herald* had run a full-color photo: from above, the islands looked like giant hibiscus blossoms floating in a vast green pool.

From fifty yards away — there were patrol boats milling to make sure we didn't get too close, like guards in an art museum — I could make out the weave in the pink fabric, water puddling in grooves. The pink undulated and shimmered in the sunlight, fading and brightening. It was like nothing I'd ever imagined. Like so much of Miami, the islands were vain, gaudy, and glorious — and in this way they belonged there, undeniably, and I hoped unrealistically that their pink skirts would stay fastened forever.

It was safe to say Dennis and I were not looking through the same lens. "Slap plastic around some land and call it art," he said, but he lifted the video camera anyway.

While he filmed, Margo stared from behind her sunglasses. She'd chopped her purple jeans into shorts, but she wouldn't let me hem them; fringe dangled past her knees. "Why did they put this here?" she said.

"Here in Miami, or here in the bay?" said Dennis, training the camera on her.

She covered her face and spoke through her fingers. "Here in Miami."

Dennis shrugged. "Who knows why artists do what they do?" he said. "I have only one request of you, dear — never marry an artist. That goes for you, too, Beverly. Just as easy to fall in love with a rich man as a poor one." He trailed off, lacking conviction. He spoke in a radio voice. "On this day," he said, "May seventeenth, nineteen eighty-two, this ordinary American family discovered a scientific phenomenon no human has ever witnessed: flowers as big as yachts."

He went on, amusing himself and the girls. Maybe the mutant flora had resulted

247

from a spill at Turkey Point, he speculated. Maybe they were spaceships, said Margo, transporting aliens who ate humans for fuel. Beverly laughed. Margo agreed to be interviewed on camera. She used her fist for a microphone. "I'd like to thank my best friend, Carla," she said. Her hair curved against her face. "If she hadn't sacrificed her life to the aliens, scientists might never have discovered the location of the mother ship."

Why Miami? I thought. Because anywhere else, the islands would have seemed garish and bizarre, and Christo would've seemed like a loon. Because a century ago, swampland enveloped this shoreline, before developers drained it and built a city from the bog. Because our piece of Florida was invented, not discovered. Like the *Surrounded Islands,* Miami was at once impossible and inspired, like a magic trick practiced for hours, performed in seconds.

The following year, Bette would teach Margo to sail and she would join the Coconut Grove Sailing Club's junior division and start to bring home trophies. She would get braces and keep them on for two years. For years, her closest friend would be Beverly, followed by a few kids from the club with whom she traveled to regattas on weekends.

Shortly after she turned fifteen she would spend a weekend in Sarasota with her sailing club, and her first boyfriend, Dax Medina, would kiss her behind the Days Inn.

We circled one island and moved on to the next. The process was like negotiating a labyrinth — only a segment was visible from any given perspective. "Take us farther out," I said to Dennis. "I want to see them all at once."

"Aye, aye," he said. He eased forward on the throttle and turned us away from shore, and soon the islands spread out in a disorderly line. I stepped up onto the gunwale and rose on my tiptoes, but still the dark water all but swallowed the pink. We would've needed an airplane to view the project as a whole; we would've needed a mountaintop. Instead, we patched the project together in our minds, like pieces in a colossal, unmanageable puzzle.

1990

When the Biltmore Hotel in Coral Gables underwent renovations, Margo was one of several high school volunteers who ended up on scaffolding along the tower, applying a coat of the hotel's signature terra-cotta color. Her photograph appeared in the "Neighbors" section of the *Miami Herald:* a black-and-white close-up of my daughter wearing a rolled bandanna on her forehead, a paint streak along one cheek. Three years later, I visited the Biltmore to use a guest pass given to me by Dennis's parents, who were members of the golf club. I spent an hour swimming in the pool where Esther Williams had performed, backstroking past the soaring colonnades, and in the locker room afterward, I noticed a flyer tacked on a bulletin board amid news of support groups and housecleaning services. The flyer advertised the Biltmore tennis center's newest team, the Top Forties. I knew immediately, though there were no other clues, that the title meant the team was composed of people who had reached middle age. I was forty-seven years old, and alert to the attendant afflictions: empty-nest syndrome loomed, midlife crisis itched, menopause dogged. Though I had not played tennis with any regularity since high school, I knew before I'd finished getting dressed that I would join the team. I crossed the parking lot and climbed the tennis center's exterior staircase, walked through the lounge past a row of windows overlooking the courts, and knocked on a door marked OFFICE. On the other side of the door was a tall, dark-haired man in tennis whites. His name was Jack. So began the summer of 1990 — the summer of tennis.

After I handed over a check for $200, which committed me to the team for one twelve-week season, I left the tennis center and stood on the sidewalk outside the fence that enclosed the courts. The air smelled of gardenias and was filled with the hollow popping sound of balls hitting rackets, and I was suddenly, overwhelmingly satisfied with myself. Not until I arrived home and was unloading groceries from the car did I remember that the following Saturday — the day of the team's first practice — was already consumed by one principal activity, an activity to which I'd given surprisingly little consideration: this was the day when we would pack up the station wagon, drive north for six hours, and drop off my daughter at her new college.

After returning from the Biltmore, I went to the garage to look for my old tennis racket, and it was there that Dennis found me half an hour later, elbow-deep in a box marked ATLANTA, a porcelain-faced doll in one hand and my old wooden Wilson in the other. He gave me a look but didn't ask any questions. "Is she all packed?" he said.

"I doubt it." I turned off the garage light and followed Dennis back into the kitchen. He was just in from work, slightly sweaty; I could smell the dry cleaning of his suit. That evening, Dennis's parents were throwing a farewell barbecue for Margo, and as usual it would be a struggle not to arrive late. I took my old racket down the hallway and knocked on Margo's door. "We're leaving in half an hour," I called. There was no answer. I knocked again and opened the door. Margo stood on the far side of her bed, sorting through a heap of clothes and shoes. She was tan and freckled from a month spent fishing with Dennis in the early mornings, and from driving our car around with the sunroof open. She looked up. "I heard you," she said. She gestured toward the pile on the bed. "I have no system."

Why hadn't I made certain she was packed before now? "I'll help you tonight, after the party."

She pointed at the racket in my hand. "What's that?"

"Nothing. A tennis racket. There's a team at the Biltmore."

She looked dubious. I hadn't been one for joining teams in her lifetime. "Is Marse joining, too?"

It hadn't occurred to me to rally Marse, but I didn't think it would be her cup of tea. She'd started teaching aerobics at her health club. I'd gone to a few classes and left exhausted, with a bruised ego. "No, just me," I said.

"Nobody uses wooden rackets anymore, Mom."

It always surprised me when my daughter seemed to think I noticed nothing. "I know that," I said, "but this is what I have." I picked up a pair of old gym shorts from the pile on her bed. They were printed with the insignia of her high school. "I don't think you'll need these," I said. "Or this." I picked up a straw hat she had not worn in years. I separated the gym shorts and the straw hat and a fringed leather jacket from the heap.

"I guess not," she said.

"You need to get dressed."

"I am dressed." She moved out from behind the bed so I could see her. She wore a long patchwork skirt that she'd bought in Coconut Grove, a white peasant top, and a wide leather belt. "Should I take this?" She held up a stuffed dolphin she'd had since childhood. I remembered buying it for her at the Seaquarium gift shop. "Or this?" She pulled a Miami Hurricanes baseball cap from the pile; Dennis had given it to her the first time he'd taken her to a baseball game. I looked at the faintly dirty cap, which evoked a whole afternoon's memory, and I wondered which was preferable: clinging sentimentally to the unending stream of items that flow through our lives, or letting them go as if they had no relationship to memory, no status.

"Don't take them," I said.

"What if I want them?"

"Then I'll send them."

"You won't throw things out? I think you're going to throw things out."

"I promise," I said. I made a mental note: do not throw things out.

In my bedroom, I pulled on a sundress

and briefly worried that Dennis's mother would think we had not dressed up enough. When I was ready, I found Dennis and Margo in the living room. Margo was in Dennis's arms, crying. "What's going on?" I said.

Over Margo's shoulder, Dennis said, "She's sad."

Margo said something into Dennis's shirt, which was not yet buttoned. His hair was wet and uncombed. "What?" I said.

"I don't want to go," she repeated.

"Margo, your grandmother's worked hard. She's invited all her friends —"

"No!" she said. "I don't want to move away." She cried harder.

It was a situation we alone seemed to face. Margo had graduated from high school two years earlier, and at that time all her friends had been itching to get away. And maybe if she'd been accepted at one of her top choices — Chapel Hill or University of Virginia — Margo would have been itching as well. She'd applied to six colleges, and her school counselor had seemed to think that with one or two she was reaching, but the others were within the realm of possibility. "You never know," the counselor had told me. "Margo is very bright, yes, but her grades are not stellar. In that situation they'll be looking for something extra." She'd left unsaid the fact that there was no obvious something extra. Margo had been a reporter on the newspaper staff and in the chorus of a few school plays, but she hadn't really committed herself to anything. She'd floated from activity to activity, competent but uninspired. When she'd given up competitive sailing, she'd said it was because the regattas monopolized all her weekends. When would she get to Stiltsville? she'd said. Dennis had been proud.

We'd taken a road trip in the spring of her junior year. We packed a cooler and three small suitcases and looped through the dreary, damp eastern seaboard. We hit the Carolina schools, then the University of Virginia, then the D.C. schools, then the Boston schools. On the way back we spent a night with my mother, then stopped in Hilton Head, where Dennis played a very expensive round of golf. We sidetracked to the camp where Margo had gone for three summers. The grounds were closed. The air was cool and smelled of wet clay and spruce. We stepped over a chain that crossed the main camp road, and Margo led us to a cluster of one-room wooden cabins with rickety screen doors. We stepped inside the cabin where Margo had been assigned her last year of camp, when she was eleven years old. The room was claustrophobic. The bunks had no mattresses — they were in storage for the season — and there was a sink in one corner with rust stains in its bowl. Margo walked to one of the top bunks. "This was mine," she said, and I pictured her there, writing letters on the stationery we'd sent with her, her hair wet from swim time. We'd left the cabin and wandered through the campgrounds, past the locked dining hall and the still waterfront, until we were spotted by a groundskeeper, who asked us kindly to leave.

As it turned out, Margo had been accepted only at the University of Miami, her safety option, and had continued to live at home because of the school's high cost. Beverly Jovanovich had gone to Swarthmore, and Margo's on-again, off-again boyfriend, Peter Sanchez, a tall boy who wore tortoiseshell eyeglasses and had excellent manners, had gone to Davidson. For two years we'd encouraged Margo to transfer so that she could move away, too, but when the time came she'd lacked the heart to repeat the entire application process, so she'd applied only to the University of Florida. She'd been excited, at first — she'd talked about decorating her dorm room and eating in the dining hall. But in time her excitement had morphed into anxiety. Then she'd been informed by the school that before starting her junior year, she needed to take a summer class to satisfy a math requirement. So not only was she now moving away — which I simultaneously wanted for her and did not want at all — but she was leaving at the start of the summer instead of at the end. What did it matter, though, really? Those extra weekends together, luxuriating in free time with Margo, would have been merely a stall, and soon enough we would have found ourselves in the same position we were in now: packing her up, driving her away.

"Margo," I said, pulling her from Dennis to face me. "This is a whole new ball game. New people, new classes. You'll like the dorms. No mother hovering all the time."

Margo scowled. Was this an adult, I thought, prepared to go off and live on her own?

"Your mother's right," said Dennis. "Free at last."

"I guess," she said. I wondered how often, over the course of her life, she would desire something only to feel ambivalent once she got it. I thought of a young woman in Margo's high school class, a girl with grades worthy of the Ivy League, who had gone to the University of Florida because her father had given her the choice between an out-of-state education and a new convertible. Somehow, a reporter for Florida Public Radio had gotten wind of the story and the parents had agreed to be interviewed on the air. Callers had phoned in to rail against the family's values and praise the benefits of an excellent education. The father had said — very reasonably, I thought — that one does not have to be a plane ride away from one's family to read books.

"The thing about going away for college," I said to Margo, "is that you can start over, be whoever you want to be."

"Who else would she want to be?" said Dennis.

"I just mean you can make new friends without all the history mucking it up."

Margo nodded solemnly. The sixth grade had left wounds — she was a skittish friend, slow to bond. Over the years she'd let go of early friendships just when I'd sensed that they were growing, as if afraid of what might happen next. And she'd never become preoccupied with romance or heartbreak or drama the way other girls had. Her only boyfriend in high school had been Peter — every so often, during her junior and senior years, he had come to the house after school and stayed for dinner, or picked her up on a Saturday morning for a day at the beach. For a few days he'd be in her conversation or plans. But then weeks later I'd realize I hadn't seen him and he hadn't called. It had been three years since Margo had asked me to take her to get birth control pills — a task I'd completed with surprisingly few tears — and since that time Peter was the only boy who had come to the house alone, without a group. I used to try to get her to talk about him, but she would just say banal, complimentary things like "He's a very kind person" or "It's not serious, but he's a good friend." From what I could tell, this was true: he was a nice person. When he'd left for Davidson, Margo had seemed genuinely happy for him and not at all possessive. There had been no pretense that I could surmise that they would not date other people while he was away. But during her two years at the University of Miami, Margo had made few new friends and hadn't dated at all.

"We need to get a move on," I said. Margo's eyes were pink and swollen. Dennis looked as if he'd forgotten where we needed to be. "Wash your face," I said to Margo. I kissed her warm forehead before she left

260

the room.

"I hope we did the right thing, encouraging her to transfer," said Dennis.

"I was just thinking that." The Oriental rug beneath our feet was threadbare and faded; we'd bought it new on vacation in Asheville a decade earlier. I told Dennis about the tennis team. "But it starts Saturday morning," I said, "so I'd like to go before we get on the road."

Dennis held tight to the belief that road trips begin before dawn. Practice started at eight a.m.; I promised we would be on the road by eleven. He nodded and rubbed his face. Margo returned, wearing fresh makeup — a little too much, considering Gloria's distaste for young ladies with painted faces, but I stayed quiet. "Kiddo," said Dennis, "your mother has something to do Saturday morning, so we're going to leave a little later."

"Good," said Margo.

"We can spend tomorrow night at Stiltsville. We'll swing home in the morning and pick up Mom and get on the road."

I was reminded of one reason I didn't take up activities: because then I missed things. "As long as you're packed," I said.

"I shouldn't take so much anyway," she said.

"I thought the last time at Stiltsville was the last time," I said. We'd skied and Dennis and Margo had fished off the dock. It had been five years since the state of Florida had declared Biscayne Bay a national monument and began pushing for an end to private ownership of the stilt houses. Marcus Beck, a trial lawyer, had negotiated a deal guaranteeing that current residents could keep our houses until the year 1999 — after that, Stiltsville would belong to the state. Since the decision, we'd gone out every possible weekend.

"There's no last time," said Dennis.

We'd never had a graduation party for Margo — at the time, she had been so glum about her plans that a party had seemed inappropriate — so when they heard she was transferring, Grady and Gloria had seized on the idea of throwing a farewell party. The theme of the barbecue — BON VOYAGE — was printed grandly on a banner that hung over the backyard patio. Gloria had staked tiki torches around the pool; they smelled powerfully of citronella. Grady had made rum punch, and Gloria ladled it into crystal goblets. The party was for their close friends, mainly, and a few of ours. My mother had wanted to come but had planned a cruise with friends the same weekend, so she'd called Margo to schedule a time when she could visit during the fall semester and take her out for a proper meal, as she put it. Grady and Gloria's friends were spry, seemingly unhindered by age, and they wore expensive clothes; the ladies looked as if they'd just come from getting their hair set. They were warm and doted on Margo and seemed genuinely interested in her plans for the future, which left me wondering if they'd never met a grandchild before.

Gloria had specified on the invitation — which had a drawing of a girl at the prow of a cruise ship, waving to shore — that gifts would not be welcome, but Margo had a few checks thrust into her hand anyway; and Gloria's bridge partner, Eleanor Everest, presented her with a small brass-handled hammer with a bow around its neck. "It's seven tools in one," she said, demonstrating how the handle unscrewed to reveal a screwdriver, which in turn unscrewed to reveal a smaller screwdriver, and so on. "My granddaughters are very handy," she said. I could see Margo wondering when she would ever use such a thing, but I could also see that this gift would remain among my daughter's possessions for many years.

Marse gave Margo an expensive portable radio for her dorm room and a gift certificate to a hair salon in Gainesville. Bette gave her a large woven floor pillow, and Bette's girlfriend Suzanne, a real estate agent who spent part of the evening smoking marijuana around the side of the house, gave her a Dr. Seuss book. Bette promised to visit Margo that semester, to take her off campus to do some shopping, and Marse hugged her and told her not to party too hard, but not to neglect to party at all. Then Marse and Bette and I took the gifts into the kitchen and stood watching from inside. Bette took off her large dangling earrings and Marse stepped out of her heels. Their faces were reflected in the kitchen windows, superimposed over the backyard. Marse, who had recently taken up with a boat salesman named Ted, wore a string of expensive-looking pearls. Bette's hair was whiter and shorter than ever, a silver swim cap. She'd never colored it. I'd begun highlighting mine when I'd turned forty. One morning I'd been backing out of the driveway, and when I'd looked in the rearview mirror I'd seen one unmistakable silver strand rising above the rest. I'd turned off the ignition and gone inside to call my salon.

"How are you handling all this?" said

Marse to me.

"I'm completely unprepared," I said.

"Better buck up," said Bette. "I hear it gets worse before it gets better."

Later, Grady gave a toast thanking everyone for coming and telling Margo how proud he was. "You are thoughtful and smart and gracious," he said, choking up. "And we love you." When his speech was through, he and I stood watching the party from the far side of the swimming pool. Margo was across the water from us, making conversation with a woman from Grady and Gloria's church. Her dark wavy hair reached past her shoulders and she bit her bottom lip in concentration, as she had a habit of doing. She'd been asked a dozen times what she planned to major in, and each time the answer was different: political science and history, then political science and art history, then art history and biology. I'd even heard her say that she wanted to take dance classes.

"Ah, the nest," Grady said, clinking my glass with his beer can.

"Empty," I said.

In the torchlight I saw, as I often did, the shadow of Dennis in Grady's curly mop of hair, mostly gray now, and the scattering of freckles across his nose. I hadn't allowed myself to think much beyond the coming weekend, when Dennis and I would leave Margo in Gainesville. I hadn't thought about returning to an empty house. Two years earlier, I'd left my position at the bank for a part-time job as the bookkeeper at a small medical practice in downtown Coral Gables — I thought now that maybe I would take on more hours, keep busier.

Grady said, "Of course Bette stayed home, but she wasn't around much. Dennis was off in the dorms and came home on the weekends. It was quiet. We didn't know quite what to do with ourselves. Gloria started with the bridge club then, and she's still at it. I started fishing more."

"Dennis has been running a lot," I said. He'd been getting up before dawn, then returning to make a big breakfast before heading to work. He'd done this two or three times a week for six months.

"Go with him," said Grady. "You might like it."

I'd gone twice, and both times I'd felt a little sick from the early hour, and Dennis had to slow down when I cramped. "I joined a tennis team," I said.

"Now that's something," said Grady. He put an arm around my shoulders. "My granddaughter is moving away from home.

I'm an old man."

"You are not," I said. He was sixty-eight that year, but he looked much younger in the red-gold light of the tiki torches. His hair was thick and tousled, and his face was flushed.

Gloria came up behind us and slipped an arm around Grady's waist, then took a long drag from her cigarette and blew a thin line of smoke over the pool. "My lovely," said Grady.

"Isn't this a success?" said Gloria. "Margo's charming."

"We were just discussing the empty nest," said Grady.

"You should travel," said Gloria. "Go on an archaeological dig in Egypt. They teach you everything you need to know."

In twenty years, Grady and Gloria had never seemed to understand that their means were not our means: we could not afford to travel, at least not to Egypt. To say this aloud would have ruined their vision of us, not to mention the conversation.

Across the swimming pool, Margo had started what seemed to be a serious conversation with Ed Everest, Eleanor's husband. Margo was using her hands to make a point, and he was nodding and asking questions. The torchlight accentuated her planes and contours — her fit upper arms, her collarbone and jawline, the dark waves of her hair. I had no idea what my daughter would have to discuss with Ed Everest, who was the pastor at Grady and Gloria's church, but Margo had a way with adults and always had, even when she was a little girl and had sat quietly with clear, wise eyes at our dinner parties, answering questions in complete sentences and offering to help me clear the plates. I suppose as an only child she'd had little choice in the matter. After a moment, Ed laughed heartily, and Margo put out her hand to shake, and the success of the interaction, the maturity of it, struck a chord in me, and I felt a little dizzy.

That night, Margo took my car to meet girlfriends, and at three a.m. I awoke to the still house, my heart pounding. I was certain that when I opened the door to her bedroom I would see an empty bed, but I was wrong: Margo was sleeping heavily with an arm across her forehead. She'd done more packing after getting home: there was a row of three suitcases just inside the room, facing the door like eager dogs waiting for it to open.

Dennis woke Margo early the next morning, and after an hour they departed with only a large tote of food and a change of clothes each. I went through the house straightening up, and in Margo's room I made the bed — she would not sleep there again before we left — and cleaned her little bathroom. I took her suitcases to the car, then returned for two boxes of books she'd packed up that morning. I stood a long time in her closet, then spotted four shoeboxes on the highest shelf: all were filled with paper confetti, which Dennis and Margo and I had made when Margo was fourteen. Dennis had come home with half a dozen reams of multicolored office paper his firm was going to throw out — I have no idea why; perhaps it had been ordered mistakenly — and Margo had decided that instead of wasting it we should make confetti, which one day we would use to celebrate something. The next day, Dennis had brought home three-hole-punch gizmos, and after dinner every night that week we'd sat at the breakfast table and made confetti. One shoebox was filled with pastel pink and green confetti, another with yellow and orange, another with baby blue and red, and another with all the colors, which Margo had called tutti-frutti. When I removed the lids from the boxes, several pieces floated up and onto Margo's bedspread. I got a large freezer bag and filled it with the tutti-frutti, then returned the boxes to their shelf and swept up the leftover confetti with my hand.

Later I drove to the department store and bought Margo a red bathrobe and matching slippers. I was struck with a momentary sense of regret that I had not thought of this earlier, so I might have had the bathrobe monogrammed. I added matching towels and left, having spent more than I should have. On the way home, I stopped at a sporting goods store in South Miami and looked at tennis rackets. I didn't care about the aluminum or the lighter weight, but it seemed to me that an oversize head was a wonderful idea. A salesman told me it improved play by enlarging the so-called sweet spot. I left with only a can of tennis balls and that evening, after leaving the new bathrobe and slippers on Margo's bed, I popped open the can, letting loose a cloud of thick canned air that smelled of spray paint and rubber, and I took my old wooden racket outside to hit against the garage door. It was a clear, quiet evening. Fireflies darted around the gardenias in the side yard, and the air smelled of key limes and barbecue. The next-door neighbors waved as they went out, and then the street was empty. I aimed for the flat parts of the garage door and tried to avoid the beveled paneling, which skewed the ball in the wrong direction and sent me running after it. After a while I managed to hit many more than I missed. I was sweating and felt a blister starting to form on my palm. I kept it up until the ball was difficult to discern in the blue evening, and when I stepped up onto the porch I was surprised to find myself winded and my legs aching a little, as they did after Dennis and I swam laps around the stilt house.

I was early for the first practice. I asked in the pro shop and was directed to a court on the far end of the property. Jack stood at the baseline, serving one ball after another over the net. Each hit the opposite fence with a heavy thud. I stood watching his form — the light toss, the full range of his swing, the powerful follow-through. His legs were long and thick. If I'd been trying to receive those serves, I thought, they would have knocked the racket right out of my hand.

I stood on the sideline, under a gazebo between the courts, until he noticed me. "Frances, right?" he said. He motioned to my racket in my hand. "That's a relic."

I smiled and nodded, a little flattered that he had remembered my name. A man and two women — twins — came through the gate onto the court. Jack marked down their names on a clipboard and asked the man — Rodrigo — to collect the balls on the court using a red wire hopper. Rodrigo jogged off and one of the twins put out her hand for me to shake. Her name was Twyla. Another woman came through the gate and approached the gazebo — she had short gray hair and prominent cheekbones, and she was familiar to me but I couldn't place her — and within ten minutes there were two dozen players assembled around Jack in the gazebo. I shook a few hands but there were too many people. I wondered if the group would thin out as the weeks passed.

Jack explained how the team would work: he would pair us up to get a sense of our game, then at the next practice he'd assign us a practice partner. Each practice would start with half an hour of hitting, then continue with drills for an hour and a half. "I encourage you to stay afterward to play matches," he said, "and it's mandatory — this is not negotiable — to play at least one full match per week." He looked down at his clipboard, then up at me. "Frances," he said. "Beginner, right?"

"Definitely," I said.

"You two" — he pointed at Twyla — "take court three. Show me what you've got."

We walked together across one court and onto another. "I'm not much for taking orders," said Twyla.

"He's just being coachy," I said.

"Take it easy on me," she said. We separated at the net and when I turned around, Twyla said, "Ready?" and I nodded. She bounced the ball once, then hit it far over my head. I raised a ball to signal that I would start the next one. I dropped it and hit it and was pleased to see it sail elegantly away from me, and bounce a few yards in front of her. She swung at it and missed. It went like this for another fifteen minutes — she served out and either missed mine or hit them into the net. It was humid and bright; my sunglasses kept sliding down my nose, and after only a few minutes my racket started to feel heavy. I began to run for Twyla's balls even when they were going out. I caught them in midair and swung hard to get them all the way back to her baseline — this at least kept the ball in play for a moment more. Soon Jack blew his whistle from our sideline, and Twyla looked over at him mid-swing, and missed the ball. "You," he said to her, "court four. Swap with Jane."

She trudged off and Jack walked over to me. "You need more of a challenge," he said. "Jane might be out of your league, but she'll bring out your best."

"I'm not sure about all this," I said.

Jack smiled. There was a tiny chip in his front tooth, and it looked like he hadn't shaved that morning. The hair on his arms was thick and dark. "You have a lot of power but not a lot of control," he said. "Let's see your serve."

I stepped to the baseline and pointed my feet the way I remembered I should, then tossed the ball and slammed it into the net.

"Don't chase your toss," he said, then came up behind me and positioned my arm. I tossed several times without swinging, and then when I served the ball went long. He said, "We're just taking stock here, don't worry."

Jane — this was the woman I knew from somewhere — jogged over in white shorts and a pink polo. She tapped the net with her racket and moved into position. "Ready?" she said, and before I could respond, she jackhammered a serve over the net. It flew past me.

"Good luck," said Jack as he moved off the court.

I did my best to return Jane's shots but

they were streamlined and swift. After hitting against her for fifteen minutes, I was demoralized, but then we ran drills as a group and I managed well enough. By the end of the practice I was sweating through my shirt. Still, there was something calming about the tennis center itself, about simply passing a couple of hours on the groomed clay courts, leaving marks in the clay with each lunge and turn. Over the mesh-lined fences rose the tops of wide banyan trees along the golf course, like gentle monsters keeping watch. I simply wasn't used to spending time outside other than at Stiltsville. I had missed it.

When I got home, Dennis and Margo were on the front steps, drinking orange juice out of the carton. They looked windblown and relaxed. "How was it?" said Margo.

"Like riding a bike," I said as I went up the steps past them.

Margo's things took up the trunk and half the backseat, and she wanted to drive, so I spent the trip wedged in back beside a portable television and a box of framed photos. Margo turned the air conditioner on high, but it was a tiny trickle in the heat. The turnpike offered a bleached, changeless journey unbroken into parts. Almost every billboard we passed advertised a men's club called Café Risqué. I'd heard somewhere of girls stripping to put themselves through college and wondered how many university students worked there. "Margo," I said. I tapped her shoulder until she turned to face me. "If you need money, just ask us. We'll give it to you. Don't strip for it."

This was very amusing to both Dennis and Margo, and once they started laughing they couldn't stop, so I settled back in my seat, thinking: they don't realize what can happen. I had the feeling that very soon there would be a tear in the fabric of my life, an enormous divide. On one side would be the time I moved through and things I did and the people I saw, and on the other side would be a great expanse of black time where Margo lived her life, and she and I would move parallel to each other like cars in different lanes, allowing only passing glimpses. I had to remind myself that, strangely enough, this was the way it was meant to go. They grow up, they move away.

It was still hot but the sun had waned as we navigated through campus to the dated, boxy Rawlings Hall, where Margo would live for the summer semester with a room-mate assigned by the university. We parked and Dennis and Margo headed toward an entrance, but I stayed behind. There were two other cars in the drive, both open with boxes and bags inside. When Dennis and Margo came out of the building, blinking in the sunlight, Dennis handed me paperwork. "Room 105," he said. "First floor — only one flight of stairs."

"No elevator?" I said.

"No elevator, no air-conditioning."

"That's not possible," I said. My blouse stuck to my back.

Dennis and Margo exchanged a look. "We will not melt," said Margo.

Her room was divided symmetrically, and the two sides looked like before-and-after photos: one side was bare, with a thin mattress on a metal bed frame and an empty desk and gaping dark closet. The other side looked as if it had been staged for a photo shoot: the bed was covered with a pink plaid duvet and white dust ruffle — it hadn't occurred to me to buy Margo a dust ruffle — and there was a neat stack of glossy textbooks on the desk. I opened a box and started to unpack, and Dennis and Margo shuffled out to get another batch of things from the car. Margo's new twin-size comforter, a gift from Gloria, was sky blue with white clouds on it. I made the bed with great precision, thinking it might be a long time before Margo had neatly pressed sheets again. If this is all I do, I'll do it right, I thought. Dennis and Margo came back and left again, and I dug through the boxes until I found a bright red-and-pink tapestry Margo had packed; I spread it over the desk and placed a notebook on top of it. I put a handful of pens in a ceramic mug with the logo of Margo's old camp on it. I unrolled Margo's SAVE THE MANATEES poster and when she came back upstairs asked her where she wanted it.

She gestured toward the bare wall above the desk and looked around, at the neatly made bed and the colorful desk. "I like that," she said quietly.

I taped the corners of the poster to the wall. "Does this look straight?" I said, but when I looked over my shoulder she was looking away, at the other side of the room, the anonymous side, and she didn't answer.

Dennis lay on the bed while we futzed. Margo lined up her shoes — sneakers and flip-flops, primarily — at the bottom of her closet. There was a knock at Margo's door, and when I turned around, there stood a boy about Margo's height, completely bald, with large blue eyes and a wide, expressive mouth. He wore a T-shirt covered with streaks of paint. "Margo, is it?" he said, reaching out to shake her hand. He introduced himself as Joshua, her resident adviser. He explained where his room was located and invited Margo to call on him if she needed anything.

"Alopecia," said Dennis after Joshua had left.

"I think that's just the style," I said.

"No, that's alopecia, I can tell," said Dennis, and Margo shushed us.

Dennis had gotten the name of a fish place just outside town, so we got back into the car to go for dinner. This was something he did — he tracked down hole-in-the-wall restaurants and planned ahead to visit them when traveling, and sometimes he bought their T-shirts. Afterward, when we dropped Margo off at her dorm, the light was on in her room, and the next day at breakfast, she told us about her roommate, Diana. Diana was from Chipley, a town in the Panhandle that I'd never heard of. Since Diana hadn't brought a stereo and Margo hadn't brought a hair dryer, they'd agreed to share. I could tell by Margo's description that they wouldn't be friends but they would get along. After breakfast we crossed a main quad dotted with date palms and bicycle racks and half-clothed girls tanning on blankets, and we toured the gym, which was humid and busy with kids who seemed, for the most part, very serious about the business of getting fit. Outside, there was an empty track. I mentioned that I hoped Margo would run in this bright, public spot instead of along back streets.

"Mother, you worry too much," she said.

"That's true, babe," said Dennis.

We continued on to the student union, a clean, chilly place peppered with egglike orange chairs and recycling bins. We were stalled by an enthusiastic young man at the summer orientation table; he gave Margo a packet and led her through it piece by piece. When she told him she was a transfer student, he rushed her away to get a student ID, and Dennis and I sat down in the orange chairs. Lack of enthusiasm for sports was not, I gathered, common at the University of Florida. Everywhere I turned I saw a cartoonish orange alligator emblazoned on a T-shirt, a sign, a duffel bag. Dennis read from a brochure, then looked at me. "This is the ninth-largest school in the country," he said.

"She'll be swallowed whole," I said.

Margo returned and we left the air-conditioning to wander through campus. Gainesville, I realized with difficulty, would become Margo's home, filled with places she liked to go hiking and neighborhoods she preferred over other neighborhoods. We walked her up to her room and lingered at the door. Diana was out. Dennis kept it light. "You can still hightail it home with us, pronto," he said. "We'll flatten that bald boy if he tries to stop us." Margo laughed and remained, for that moment, clear-eyed.

"Wait here," I said, and slipped past them into the room. I fished in my purse for the freezer bag of confetti and sprinkled a bit on Margo's bedspread, and a little more on her desk. Then I stepped out and told her I was proud of her and hugged her good-bye. I kept my tears in the back of my throat, and on the long drive home Dennis and I tried to make conversation, but it didn't come. The car felt so empty that when we spoke I almost expected to hear an echo.

After we returned from Gainesville, I fell into a routine of driving over to the Biltmore most evenings after supper to hit against the backboard. This was in addition to twice-weekly practices and a match every other weekend. To my surprise, I did not find reasons not to go to practice — in fact, I stayed late more often than not to hit with other members of the team. Also to my surprise, I quickly became a better player. The games I played took on an air of serious competition — I was truly heartened when I won, truly disheartened when I was defeated. I lost ten pounds. My legs took on a firmer shape, and all that time outdoors gave me a deep tan, with sock lines. Every so often when I missed a shot that I should have made, I cursed under my breath. "Easy," Jack would say. "Next time, Frances."

Another player who took the team seriously was Jane. After only a few practices in, as I watched her lunge for a shot near the net and grimace when she didn't make it, I realized how I knew her. She had aged, and her hair was shorter with more prominent streaks of gray, but Jane was Bette's ex-girlfriend — her first girlfriend, the one with whom she had gone diving all those years before. Jane had been married then, but now she wore no wedding ring. She wore almost no jewelry at all, only small gold posts in her ears. There was something distinguished about her features, something noble. I could see, vaguely, what had attracted Bette.

"You'll never guess who plays tennis with me," I said to Dennis one evening when we were getting ready for bed. But when I told him, he didn't remember Jane. At that time, Suzanne was living in Bette's house in Coconut Grove. They'd found an abandoned black lab puppy and were devoted to him; every night they took him for a three-mile walk. Bette had sold her dive shop to a franchise and spent her days sailing or tending her backyard. When Dennis and I visited, they served curry and good wine. They listened to folk music I knew I'd like if only I knew more about it. They had season tickets to the opera. Suzanne was a real estate agent and drove a Porsche and wore fine, draping tunics and wide-legged pants. They spoke German together — Suzanne's father had been in the service and her family had lived briefly in Hamburg — and Bette had taught Suzanne to scuba-dive.

Jane tended to outplay the rest of the team, along with Rodrigo. His wife, Twyla, was one of three women on the team who knew each other socially, all of whom were a little on the bawdy side and very pretty in the blond, well-coiffed way of many Coral Gables women. They wore tennis skirts with grosgrain ribbon waistbands and matching tops. One morning they passed me on the stairs as I went up to the lounge for an iced tea — I knew they liked to congregate there after practice, usually with mimosas — and

Twyla said, "Oops, it's the teacher's pet," and sidestepped to let me pass.

"Ha," I said. "Hardly."

Jack was sitting in a leather club chair by the windows; I sat next to him with my iced tea. "You're hustling out there," he said. He clicked his glass against mine. It wasn't the first time he'd let me know I was doing well. That morning, in fact, I'd gotten several points off Jane, though she'd mentioned afterward that she'd been up late with her sick cat. Jack gestured toward my racket. "You need an upgrade," he said. "It's time, Frances."

I'd mentioned to Dennis that I needed a new racket, and he'd told me to go ahead and buy one, for goodness' sake — he didn't like it when I pinched pennies — but I'd been holding off. Jack took my racket and pressed his palm against the strings. Physically, there was much about him that reminded me of Dennis: the scattered gray in his hair, the freckles on his arms, the light-colored eyes. But Jack was larger in size, broader and taller, and his hair was black. His eyes were a little close-set. He crossed his legs when he sat down, which was a move with just enough femininity to enhance his masculinity. When he did this — as when he put his hand flat against my back while I was serving, or when he stood at the sidelines with his sunglasses on and his clipboard against his chest, watching me and interjecting a coaching point every so often — I felt a distinct longing.

"I know," I said to Jack, and took my racket back.

"Tell you what," he said. "Why don't you try out a few? See what you like, and I'll buy it here with my discount."

My face got hot. "I can't let you do that."

"Don't be so sensitive, Frances."

I was caught off guard. It was an intimate thing to say, and his tone was disarming. I thought of my clothes — there was nothing wrong with them, nothing shoddy. In fact, my clean white tennis skirts were both new, and I'd been wearing the diamond earrings Dennis had given me on our fifteenth anniversary, because they stayed out of the way and looked sporty when I had my hair pulled back. I thought also of my car, which was in good shape, the better of our two. "Of course you're right," I said, gathering my things to leave. Jack stood, too, and we walked out together.

"Well," I said as we walked. "What do you recommend?"

"You should try out a few, see what suits you."

285

"They'll let me do that?"

"They have to. Everyone's different. Spend some time with each. Don't forget to show your left shoulder on your forehand."

"I'll try to get to it this week," I said.

"Why don't I go with you?"

We reached my car and I opened the door. "I'll be fine," I said. "Really, I'll get a new racket. I promise." I slid into the driver's seat, and when I did my skirt pulled high on my thighs — thighs that had, along with my waistline, tightened a bit in the past weeks. He stood in the door with his hand on the hood. I caught a whiff of his scent — sweaty but clean, with a ghost of the cologne he'd applied that morning. "Frances —"

"No, you're absolutely right," I said. It had been years since I'd blushed, and now it seemed I couldn't stop. I looked at my watch without registering the time.

"You don't want company? I'm a professional."

I shook my head. "I'll figure it out."

He shut my door and leaned down to talk through the window. "I know I'm pushy," he said.

"You are pushy," I said. "I needed a push."

He stepped away, and I sat still for a moment. In my peripheral vision Jack walked across the parking lot toward the tennis

286

center, and his figure diminishing in the distance had the power of a person standing squarely in my vision, staring me straight on. That night after dinner, I brought three rented rackets back to the Biltmore to hit against the backboard, and within half an hour had decided which one I would buy.

Margo came home for July Fourth weekend, and we went to Stiltsville to watch the fireworks over the skyline. From the porch we could see several small pockets of them sweeping from downtown to the Everglades. When Dennis stepped inside for a moment, Margo turned to me. "I have a request," she said. In the reflection of her eyes, tiny blooms of red and white light burst and fell. Her hair was damp and kinky from the saltwater and she smelled of coconut oil.

Her request was this: when the fall semester started, she wanted to move out of the dorms and into an apartment complex off campus. "It's only a couple of blocks away," she said. "It's practically student housing — they pair you up if you don't have a room-mate."

"What's the rent?" I said.

"It's about the same."

Dennis returned to the porch and sat in the rocking chair between me and Margo.

"Margo wants to live off campus," I said.

"What's this?" he said.

"It's not so different from the dorms," she said. "Except I'd have a kitchen and no adviser."

"How is Joshua?" I said.

"He's fine." She touched her cheek. "I went out with him."

"Alopecia?" said Dennis.

"Yes, Dad. We saw a play. His friend was in it."

"Are you going to see him again?" I said.

"No."

It was clear to me that this was disappointing.

"Why not?" said Dennis. "Is it because of his hair?"

"Of course not," she said. "I think he's cute."

"Then why not?"

Margo started to speak, then stopped. The bursting of the fireworks reached us in waves, a second after their lights had started to fade. "Because he doesn't like me," she said.

Dennis waved a hand. "Other fish. Where did this apartment idea come from?"

I assumed the two topics were at least loosely linked, but Dennis didn't need to know that.

"I know some people who live there," she said.

"You wouldn't need a car?" said Dennis.

Margo shook her head. "Tons of people do it. Especially upperclassmen. There's not enough room in the dorms for everyone."

"But it's only your first year away from home," I said. "Can't this wait?"

Margo ignored me and explained the costs: the rent was a little more expensive, but she wouldn't have to buy the university's meal plan, which would make up the difference.

"You'll cook?" said Dennis.

"Sure," said Margo. She had never cooked much, but I didn't see any reason why she couldn't start.

"We'll think about it," said Dennis. "And sweetheart, don't worry about the boy."

Kathleen Beck's twin daughters attended the University of Florida. I had the notion that I might call Kathleen — whose husband, Marcus, had recently left her for his high school sweetheart — and ask her if she'd heard anything about living off campus, or about the apartments where Margo wanted to live. Margo went inside to brush her teeth and Dennis and I ferried the mattresses from the bunk room to the porch, and while I was tucking the sheets under the corners, fighting a bit with the rising wind, Dennis said, "I'm not inclined to go along on this one."

I remember it so clearly, with an ache in my gut: he was not inclined. And because I was the mother, I felt the nudge to fill in for her. I said, "The dorms don't really seem to suit her."

"Who knows what suits her?" he said. He was exasperated. No matter what we provided for Margo, it seemed, there was always something more she wanted. Kathleen Beck would be no help: her daughters were willowy, complacent things. He said, "It just seems like I'm constantly having to shift my expectations."

"Parenthood," I said. "If you don't want her to do it, then she won't."

"It's fine," he said. "If you think it's fine, it's fine."

"I think it's probably fine," I said, and when Margo returned to the porch, I shuffled away to the mattress nearest the outside railing and Dennis went inside to sleep in the big bedroom. The water beneath us slapped against the pilings. I asked Margo to remind me of the name of the apartment building where she wanted to live. She answered: Williamsburg Village Apartments. I remember thinking that this was a bland, nondescript name that I would likely forget. Moreover, I did forget, and a month later when she moved in (without us, with the assistance of a friend who owned a truck) I asked for the name again. And every time I forwarded mail or addressed an envelope for Dennis, who had a habit of cutting out newspaper articles and sending them to her with a greeting scribbled along one side, I had to work to recall it.

Jack noticed my new racket as soon as I stepped onto the court. I was late, and he was already running a volley drill. He paused only a second when I arrived, time enough to nod at me as I pulled my new racket out of its cover. I got in the back of the line, behind Jane.

"New racket?" she said. "It's about time."

I felt bold. Maybe it was the bright day, the breeze that had returned after going missing, or the image I'd caught of myself that morning in the hall mirror, my strong tanned arms and legs, my pretty face. How had I forgotten, for so long, that I was attractive? "You know, Jane," I said as we shuffled forward in line, "I know you."

She frowned. "How is Bette?"

This threw me. "She's wonderful."

"She always worshipped you."

"We worship each other." She was next in line, and started to bounce a little on the balls of her feet, shifting her weight from side to side. You certainly take yourself seriously, I thought. "How's your husband?" I said.

"I'm divorced," she said. "How's yours?"

I didn't have time to answer. It was her turn to hit, but instead of rushing up for the volley as the exercise required, she hit high and long, and then it was my turn. After practice, Jack and I headed toward the parking lot together, and as we walked he reached over and took my new racket from my hand and in the same motion handed me his racket. The back of his arm brushed briefly against my stomach, but he didn't apologize or smile awkwardly like a person without a certain level of intimacy would, and when we reached my car he handed my racket back. "Good choice," he said.

It was a week later that Jack and I had lunch together. He'd been frustrated that day — several players had not shown up, and the heat was stifling, making us sluggish — and afterward I'd offered to buy him a soda, and he'd said, "I'm hungry. Are you hungry?" It was Wednesday and Dennis was at work. We went in his car to a Cuban restaurant in Little Havana and ate beans and rice and eggs with hot sauce and drank *café con leche.* On the court, I was easy and even flirtatious with him, but when we were alone together, I was self-conscious. "I'll tell you what," he said. "Coaching teenagers is a lot easier."

"Whose idea was it?" I said. "The team, I mean."

He pointed to himself and rolled his eyes. "I'd had a few clients who'd asked about it, so I thought it might get a good response."

"It did."

"Sure, but it's waning now. Their hearts aren't in it."

"Mine is."

"I know."

I blushed a little and looked away, out the window toward the midday traffic, the pedestrians with their grocery bags and trailing toddlers. We talked about our spouses. He'd met his through a friend; she didn't play tennis. I told him that I'd met Dennis on a visit to Miami, that I'd never before thought of moving here. He told me he'd grown up in the Keys, on Islamorada, and had moved to Miami after a run on the pro tour.

"Did you go to one of those schools where

the bus drives on the beach?" I said.

"I walked to school," he said. "And you're not the first person to ask me that."

He picked up the check, and when we were back in the hot car, he said, "I'm free the rest of the day. I was thinking of going to the beach."

"It's a perfect day for it," I said.

"Come with me?" he said.

Of course my first instinct was to decline, but at that moment I couldn't think of anything I'd rather do. I directed him to my house and he waited in the car while I ran inside. Dennis had shut the curtains to keep out the heat during the day, and the house was still and shrouded. I put on my bathing suit and a cotton skirt and flip-flops, then put some sodas in a small cooler. I grabbed a magazine and sunscreen and towels and threw it all into a bag.

"Nice house," said Jack when I stepped back into the car. It was nice enough, certainly — a good-size ranch with creamy yellow stucco and a terra-cotta roof, not the nicest on the block but holding its own. We drove to Key Biscayne with the windows down. Along Virginia Key, windsurfers dipped and meandered just offshore. "I used to know how to windsurf," I said. "Once upon a time." Years before, after

Marse taught me, I'd windsurfed every so often, to jog between stilt houses or take a quick run down the channel, but it had never become second nature and eventually I'd given it up.

"You should get back to it," he said. "You have good balance."

This was something Jack did — he made pronouncements about a person, like he'd been studying up. "Maybe I will," I said.

The beach was not crowded. I looked away while Jack wrapped a towel around his waist and changed into his swim trunks, then we headed toward the sand. There was a Cuban family having a picnic and some surfers doing very little with the meager waves. We laid our towels on the sand and Jack took off his shirt. He went straight to the water while I applied sunscreen, but then after a few minutes the heat found my lungs and hair, and I went to join him. When I was waist-deep my nipples hardened from the chill of the water, and out of embarrassment I dove under, and came up near Jack.

"I love Miami," he said. "Paradise."

"You sound like my husband."

"Smart man."

We swam out another twenty yards, to a shoal where we could sit in the low water and look back at the beach. The Cuban family started packing up, and the surfers paddled south, away from the point. "It's amazing how rarely I actually come to the beach," I said. It had been a year, maybe more. When Margo had been a little girl, once a week we'd bring sandwiches and sit on an old blanket and maybe Dennis would go for a swim or we'd all wade around in the surf, then head back home at sunset.

"Do you work?" he said.

"Part-time." I was still considering increasing my hours. The fact that I was at the beach on a Wednesday afternoon seemed a good argument for it. I asked Jack what his wife did for a living, and he said she was the creative director at the science museum. "I haven't been there in ages," I said. I'd chaperoned a field trip when Margo was in second grade, then again when she was in seventh. I remembered Margo's silhouette fading from the shadow wall. I remembered a cyclone-shaped drain where she had sent a penny spinning and spinning until it dropped. "You don't have kids?" I said.

"Never did," he said.

"My daughter will be a junior at UF in the fall. She transferred there. It's her first time away from home."

"Big adjustment," he said.

We were reclining in the shallow water, propped up on our elbows. The exposed part of my bathing suit dried quickly in the sunlight; the mix of cool and hot was delicious. I felt magnetic and aroused — not by Jack exactly, or by Jack only, but by the heat on my suit and the smell of the air and sand, by Jack's strong legs and the dark hair that covered them, and by my own body, even. There was no question I was attracted to Jack, and I knew in that moment that he was equally attracted to me — there was a pull between us. But all at once it was too much. I knew that if I waited another long moment he would touch me. Alarms in my head sounded distantly, then grew louder. Without thinking, I scooted to the deeper water. "I'm going in," I said. He moved forward as if to reach for me, but I turned away and started to swim, then dove through the water until the beach rose up and I could stand.

In the Biltmore parking lot, Jack kept the car running while I gathered my things. "Next time we'll try windsurfing," he said, and I said, "Sure." As I climbed into my car, my hands trembled, and I had the thought that there was a great doorway opening to me, with all kinds of pleasure waiting on the far side. I wondered if I had either the necessary courage or the necessary foolishness to pass through.

That weekend Dennis and I drove down south and picked blueberries and blackberries, but it was late in the season and they were good only for preserves. We shared a milk shake in the car on the way back and stopped at a nursery owned by Dennis's old friend Paul, but Paul wasn't there and we didn't buy anything. I rolled down my window even though Dennis had turned on the air conditioner. He followed my lead and rolled his down, too. We passed fields dotted with migrant workers, and roadside stands advertising key limes and tomatoes. "You're not here," he said to me. "Where are you?" At home, he watched football while I jarred preserves, and when I was done I put five tightly sealed containers in the cupboard. That night I led him to the bedroom and had sex with him, my eyes closed.

One Friday night in early August we went to Bette's for dinner. She and Suzanne served seared tuna and sake, and after dinner we lay on lounge chairs in the backyard, watching the kidney-shaped swimming pool. Bette had bought the house when she'd sold her business. It was a one-story bungalow nestled in a wooded part of the Grove, with a carport and heavily textured stucco walls painted earthy colors — taupe in the kitchen, butterscotch in the living room — and the rugs were all kilim. "Bette," I said to her when Dennis and Suzanne were engaged in conversation. "You'll never guess who's on my tennis team."

She smirked. "I can't believe you're playing tennis," she said. "You're so suburban."

"I know, but guess."

"You said I'd never guess it."

"You won't."

"I'll just take one guess, then." The pool bubbled quietly. Dennis and Suzanne were discussing real estate, and Suzanne was saying that South Beach was *exploding.* "Jane Brevard," said Bette.

I looked at her. She wore an ankle-length batik sundress and gold chain earrings. "How did you know?"

"I'm clairvoyant."

"Seriously."

"I ran into her the other day at the dry cleaner. I see her every so often, around."

I lowered my voice. "You see her?"

"Oh, Frances. For a while there she was dating my friend Tina. You know Tina, with the art."

"I can't stand her," I said.

"Tina?"

"No."

"Jane? Really? She was saying what a good player you've become."

This surprised me. "She's the best on the team."

"She said that, too."

Dennis and Suzanne were arguing lightly about property taxes, whether the cap was good for Miami in the long run. I felt a little sleepy from the sake and the food. Bette said, "Jane said you're pretty tight with the instructor."

Bette's face was a mask. "I wouldn't say we're tight, no," I said. "He's a good coach."

"And handsome, Jane says."

I didn't answer. She got up to refill our drinks. Suzanne was speaking intently to Dennis — "There's more money in Florida real estate right now than in tourism and citrus combined," she was saying — and over her shoulder Dennis looked at me. His eyes lingered for a moment and I felt a small stirring inside, and then thought of that day at the beach with Jack. I lay back on the lounge chair and thought again of what might have happened if I had not swum away. This was my new private pastime. Dennis and I had been having the best sex we'd had in a decade. This alone, if not something else, would give me away, I thought. And then I felt a rush of gratitude for myself, for the me who'd backed away at the beach, for the me who'd made the right choice.

Bette returned and handed me a glass. "You know what I've always liked about you and Dennis?"

"We bring dessert," I said.

"You stay up late. All these couples we know, they're in bed by nine."

It was after midnight. A car alarm was going off nearby. Bette and Suzanne's dog had come outside and was standing in the water on the top step of the swimming pool, looking around warily like a self-conscious woman in a bathing suit.

Before we left, Bette handed me a poinsettia in a copper pot. "Someone gave it to me," she said. "I thought of you."

It was compact, its flowers immature but bright. "I'm not sure I have a place for it."

"You'll find one. Be strong, woman."

In the car, Dennis said, "What was that about? Being strong?"

"Your sister is strange," I said. "Drive carefully. You've been drinking."

I balanced the plant between my knees. I didn't want it, and I knew I would eventually let it die. Bette knew it, too — I realized

301

this in a rush — and that's why she'd given it to me. She'd seen the flow of plants through my household over the past two decades. It was easier for her to give it to me, which she knew meant certain death, than to keep it and watch it die on her own. If she'd kept it, she would have rescued it from near-death out of guilt, then let it subside, then rescued it again. This could go on for years. "Stop the car for a second," I said to Dennis.

He pulled over. We were at the corner of LeJeune and Barbarossa, in front of Merrie Christmas park, which I knew had once been a rock quarry. It now was a grassy basin filled with craggy banyans and a jungle gym. As a little girl Margo had swung from the vines. I took the plant, walked into the dark park, and placed it in the middle of a picnic table. I wanted to write a note — TAKE ME — but I didn't have a pen or paper.

"That seems ungracious," said Dennis when I got back into the car.

"Maybe," I said. "But it's exactly what she would do if she were me."

Margo came home for a week before the start of the fall semester. She was settled into her apartment by this time — she'd been assigned a roommate, Janelle, whose boyfriend more or less lived with them, which concerned me — and we'd planned to spend some time shopping for kitchen necessities. As soon as she got off the bus, she said she needed to find a pay phone. She'd left the oven on, she told me, or thought she might have. Janelle's boyfriend answered and she asked him to check. We waited. It was a muggy night, starry and bright with moonlight. She'd gained some weight since July Fourth weekend; her face was rounder, her jeans tight against her stomach. She caught me staring. "Stop looking at me, Mom," she said. "So I put on a few pounds, so what?"

"So what, indeed?" I tried to sound breezy.

Margo spoke into the phone. "God, I thought so. Why do I always do that?"

"You really left it on?" I said. My breath caught. Would my daughter burn down her building?

She hung up. "I made toast this morning," she said to me. "I left the broiler on."

I hadn't known Margo to use the word *broiler.* "Sweetheart, you have to be careful," I said.

She threw up her hands and walked off toward the car. We'd been together ten minutes and already we were bouncing off

303

each other like we did sometimes. "Are you hungry?" I said, and she said, "Starving."

We went to a Mexican restaurant in downtown Coconut Grove, an area that at this hour was busy and frenetic. I paid to park and took her arm as we walked down Grand Avenue, past a pair of unwashed teenagers playing guitars on the sidewalk, then past a man wearing a JESUS SAVES sandwich board. At the restaurant, we slid into a corner booth and Margo dove into the tortilla chips and salsa. I ordered a margarita on the rocks and Margo said, "The same" and the waitress wrote it down without even looking at her.

"Well!" I said when we were alone.

"It's OK, right?" she said. "I mean, I can drink."

"I guess I don't see why not."

I avoided the chips and ordered my enchilada with no sour cream. "Are you on a diet?" said Margo.

"Sort of."

"I mean, you look good."

"It's the tennis."

"I'll come watch tomorrow," she said.

It hadn't occurred to me to bring Margo to practice — would she even enjoy it? "That would be wonderful," I said.

That night I checked the oven before going to bed, then in the middle of the night woke with the thought of Margo burning down her apartment, and couldn't get back to sleep. In the morning I found her and Dennis in the kitchen, drinking coffee. The newspaper covered the breakfast table. "We were talking about heading down south," said Dennis, "maybe taking a ride on an airboat."

I felt a rush of relief that Margo wouldn't be coming to practice with me. "Sure," I said. "When will you be home? Should I make dinner?"

Dennis looked at me strangely. "You don't want to come?"

"Of course I do. But I have practice."

"You can miss one, can't you?"

I felt my jaw clench. It wasn't an unreasonable request, I told myself. I was probably the only one who had never missed. "I'd rather not."

"We'll come with you to practice, then we'll all go," said Margo.

"Sounds good," I said. I asked Margo where this idea — the Everglades, the airboat ride — had come from.

"I was thinking about it the other day," she said. "I remembered that place down Tamiami Trail, with the frogs' legs."

"You wouldn't eat them last time we

went," I said.

"I'll eat them now."

At the club, Margo and Dennis followed me to the gazebo between the courts. Jane and Rodrigo were hitting and Jack was sitting in the shade with a cup of coffee, his visor pulled low on his forehead. He stood up as we approached. "Visitors!" he said. He put out his hand to Dennis, and I introduced them.

"Is my mom going pro?" said Margo.

"She's on her way. The new racket helps."

Margo had admired my racket in the car. She'd commented on the scratches and dings it had accumulated — I'd noticed this, too, and felt the pride of ownership that comes with using something hard.

"Mind if we stick around?" said Dennis.

"It's OK with me if it's OK with Frances," said Jack. "We're going to work on ground strokes," he said. "Frances? Want to fill that hopper?" Jack touched my elbow briefly, a gesture of familiarity. I saw Dennis notice the gesture, and wondered if Jack had done it on purpose. I took the hopper two courts away to pick up tennis balls. Jack had probably been working on his serve before practice started. I'd caught him at it half a dozen times by now, and each time had watched his strength and control during the toss and follow-through, the power of his body. From across the courts I could hear the cadence of Jack's and Dennis's voices — and every so often Margo's — but I couldn't hear their words. The men stood facing my direction, both with their arms crossed against their chests. Margo sat Indian-style in a chair. When I returned to the gazebo, the hopper full, Dennis was saying, "I saw him play once," and Jack said, "Yeah?"

"The man is a tree," said Dennis.

Jack laughed. "He's a big boy."

"Who?" I said.

They looked at me. "Boris Becker," said Jack. He took the hopper. "Was that 'eighty-six?" he said to Dennis.

"I believe so," said Dennis.

Dennis didn't care about professional tennis. Years earlier, Margo had worked as a ball girl at a tournament on Key Biscayne, and Dennis had enjoyed watching her sprint across the court for the ball, then snap into position at the edge of the net. When he'd clapped, he'd clapped because she had made a good ball-girl move, like managing three balls at once while Jimmy Connors barked at her to get him a different one.

Jack lined us up at the baseline for a drill: we each took a turn hitting three rapid-fire shots. I'd never hit the third shot before, but this morning I did. Jack called "That a girl!" and then it was the next player's turn. I couldn't resist glancing over toward the gazebo where Dennis and Margo both sat watching from behind sunglasses. Dennis gave me a thumbs-up and Margo waved, and I felt ebullient.

After an hour of drills, I was paired with Jane — we were expected to play at least one set at the end of each practice — and as we walked together to a court several down from where Dennis and Margo still sat, looking a little bored by this point, Jane said, "Your daughter is lovely."

"How nice of you to say so," I said.

"She's in college?"

I explained about her transferring to the University of Florida and the summer class she'd taken, how she would be a regular student there in the fall. The fall, as it were, started in a week. Summer was almost finished. As for the tennis team, there were only four weeks left, but I was leaning toward rejoining. During the year the teams traveled and played in tournaments against other country club teams: Delray Beach, Bal Harbor, South Miami, and as far north as Naples, West Palm Beach, even Sarasota.

"I went to UF," she said. "Where's she living?"

We'd reached the court and were standing at the net. She was balancing a ball on her racket strings, bouncing it evenly.

"Off campus," I said.

She cocked her head at me. "For her first year there?"

"Are you ready?" I said.

She turned toward her baseline. "Right, not my business."

I regretted immediately the tone I'd taken. "It's just that there are so many little battles," I said.

She nodded. "Want to serve?"

She won the set 6–4, and when we finished I found Dennis and Margo in the lounge — they'd wandered away mid-game — drinking iced teas at a table in a corner.

"We can see you from here," said Margo. "You lost?"

"I never get more than a few games off her," I said.

"Your coach said to tell him before you leave," Margo said. I thought I noticed a look on Dennis's face — slightly peeved — but it vanished. I looked around — Jack wasn't in the lounge, though he might have ducked into his little office. "I'm going to clean up," I said. "Give me fifteen minutes."

I showered quickly in the ladies' locker room. Despite my loss to Jane, I felt a sense of calm pleasure. It was a feeling that often came after exercise, a feeling that I existed in a bubble of peace and leisure, and there was much good ahead. In the hallway outside the locker room, I ran into Jack. From where we stood, all that was visible of the lounge was one side of the bar, where the bartender sat on a stool reading a book. I could not see Dennis and Margo, who were presumably still seated in the far corner of the room.

Jack had changed from his whites into a navy polo shirt, open at the collar. He was a man I could imagine wearing a gold chain, though on most men I found jewelry unseemly. "Nice work," he said.

"I only won four games," I said.

"You're getting there."

He had a way of staring that glued me in place. "You're interested in the Thursday night team, right?" he said.

"Probably. I'd like to play some doubles." The Thursday night team, I knew, assigned doubles partners, and then the players split time between doubles and singles. Every team played on Saturdays, too, but each was known by the evening when they met during the week. There was a Tuesday night team, which was for little old ladies — this was Jack's assessment — and a Friday night team, which was more or less composed of young moms.

"It's a good choice for you," he said.

I took a small step to my right, the start of a move to end the conversation, but he shifted almost imperceptibly to his left, and though he wasn't blocking me by any stretch, I paused. I said, "We're off to the Everglades. Margo wants to try frogs' legs."

He nodded distractedly. Then he did something that I thought — even in the moment I thought this — was incautious and at the same time uncertain: he reached up and brushed a lock of hair from my shoulder, and then his hand trailed down my arm, and with a look that was both sad and very sexy, he stepped away, through the door of the men's locker room. There, standing several feet behind where Jack had been, was Margo. Our eyes met. She spoke immediately, which was good because for a split second I feared neither of us would speak. She said, "Are you ready?" and I smiled my most easygoing smile — that smile was, in the end, one of the most duplicitous acts of my marriage — and said, "Yes! This is going to be fun."

We took an airboat ride through the

swamps of Coopertown, population eight, and stopped to watch a family of alligators sunning in the shallows. Water lapped quietly at the tin edges of the boat — it was a flat-bottomed, lightweight vessel with a cage over the propeller, which I knew was standard at least in part because Dennis's great-grandfather, Grady's grandfather, had fallen into the blades of an early model and died from his injuries. I had the thought that even though all the gators were at the moment uniformly still and silent, they could burst into frantic, terrifying motion at any moment. And then all at once, the largest one did just that — his tail whipped first, then his gigantic jaw, and he scurried not toward us but away, into the sawgrass. I gripped Dennis when it happened, and Margo gripped me, and we clung to each other, laughing uneasily, as the two smaller alligators followed their leader. Back on land, we shared a basket of frogs' legs and chatted with the mayor of Coopertown, a salty man in his seventies who wore a silver alligator ring and a trucker cap, and who owned both the airboat company and the café.

If Margo was suspicious, she didn't say anything, and I convinced myself that what she'd witnessed was nothing a person would find inappropriate. Jack had been blocking me from view, and she might not have been able to see when he'd touched my arm. The rest of Margo's visit was easy and relaxing. Except that when I drove her to the bus station — this was her preference, though I'd offered to drive her all the way back to school — I gave her a brief lecture about locking up at night and not bringing strange men back to her apartment, and ended with, "I don't want you to be scared, sweetheart, but I want you to be safe," and she'd responded by saying, "I want you to be safe, too, Mom," and then kissed me quickly on the lips — it was something we did sometimes, on special occasions — and stepped out of the car.

Jack followed me to my car after practice the following week. I knew he was behind me, but I didn't turn around. In the lounge, we'd both gotten drinks to go at the same time, and I'd gone into the ladies' room to brush my hair and apply lip gloss, and when I'd come out, Jack was standing on the exterior stairs with Rodrigo. I'd walked by, and our eyes had met, and I'd known he would follow me. At my car, I looked back at him.

He kept his voice low. "Want to go windsurfing?"

I scanned the parking lot — there was no one close by. "We could just watch," I said. I followed him to his car and he opened the passenger door for me. That day at practice he'd stood at the sidelines while I'd served, and every time I'd sliced one perfectly over the net he'd clapped or said, "Nice one," or — this was the thing that made my stomach pitch — "Good girl." With each serve I'd felt myself getting brighter and hotter, as if channeling a great energy into each toss and hit, until he was called over to another court. My serves had grown messy and uneven then, and I'd had to sit down.

We drove through Coconut Grove toward Key Biscayne. We passed my first residence in Florida: the apartment over Main Highway, where I'd lived with Bette before marrying Dennis. I knew I jeopardized my marriage by even being in Jack's little sports car, both of us in tennis clothes, his knee next to my knee, his forearm next to mine. I'd spent hours thinking about what it would be like to really touch him, to run my hand over his chest or along his arm. But I didn't believe that until that day I'd done anything Dennis should have known about.

We passed the giant moving billboard for

the Seaquarium, its circling mechanical shark like a restless zombie, and Jack handed a dollar to a woman in the tollbooth. Then as we started again on our way, the blue bay stretching out on either side of the causeway, I moved my hand just an inch, and the back of my fingers met Jack's arm. He glanced quickly at me and shifted gears, then touched my knee with his fingertips, then shifted again. My heartbeat quickened. We pulled into the long asphalt strip of parking lot that ran parallel to Virginia Key beach. Before Jack turned off the ignition I knew that I'd made only part of a decision and could still change direction. I thought that another woman's fantasy of Jack might involve candlelight and music, whereas mine involved tongues and fingers and a certain roughness I wasn't used to. We looked at each other quickly before getting out of the car. Jack's jaw was set — he was nervous, I realized. This was discomforting; if something was going to happen, it had to happen because he made it happen. He opened the trunk and pulled out the towel he'd brought on our last trip to the beach. In my memory the sunlight that day had been clear and white, whereas on this day the light was golden and thick. The two beaches were very different: Bill Baggs Park, where we'd

315

gone the first time, was wide and white-sanded, clean. The slender strip of sand where we stood now was wet and dark, laced with seaweed. Rickenbacker Causeway, where cars raced to and from Key Biscayne, was a stone's throw.

Jack closed the trunk and we took off our shoes and moved toward the water until our feet were wet. The windsurfers were all there, as if they'd come beforehand to set up. They wore brightly colored shorts and their hair dripped onto their shoulders. They were all men. They were muscular and confident, even when they fell, even when climbing back onto the board and lifting the sail out of the water. Jack walked away from the shoreline toward a short, fat date palm. He spread out the towel. I followed him, and we sat down with a foot of space between us. The view of the windsurfers, the breeze, the warm air — it was all lulling. I hugged my knees, then rested back on my elbows. My ankles were pale; my toenails were painted light pink. Jack got up and went to his car and came back with a sweatshirt and another towel, and he balled up the sweatshirt and handed it to me, so I could use it as a pillow. When he sat down again he was closer to me. We lay back. The traffic was only twenty yards away, but I felt invisible to the passing cars and to the men windsurfing, who were absorbed utterly by the task of staying afloat. I felt Jack's body next to mine, parallel, untouching, and I closed my eyes and concentrated on the heat between us. It felt like a blanket, but like a blanket when it's being pulled slowly off of one's body, the slither against the skin. Jack's forearm lay over his eyes. "Are you sleepy?" I said softly.

He looked at me, at my eyes and forehead and lips. "Yes. Are you?"

I nodded. My mouth was open. My body was still but pushed to the limits of stillness — I was poised on the edge of moving, toward him or away from him, I wasn't sure. He, too, was on the verge of moving, I could sense, but we stayed still and I closed my eyes again, waiting for either his mouth on me, or his hands on my body, or for nothing at all. He might have been waiting, too. We ended up dozing on the sand, and as I half-slept I felt the shade of the palm fronds moving over my body, back and forth in the breeze like a hand.

We slept for just under an hour. When I woke, Jack was sitting up with his legs crossed, facing the water. I touched his back and smiled when he turned around. A look briefly appeared on his face — a cross

317

between fear and desire. I was hot, sweating along my brow and behind my knees. I got up and walked to the surf while Jack shook out the towel and folded it up and put it back in his car, along with the sweatshirt and towel we'd used as pillows.

"My body feels like Jell-O," I said when he joined me at the shoreline.

"You'll be sore tomorrow," he said. He was referring to practice that day, to the dozens of serves and volleys.

"I can feel it starting already," I said.

All of a sudden he'd moved behind me and pressed himself against my back, his mouth in the hair at my neck. His hands pulled against my hips. I felt off balance, like I might fall, but he was solid on his feet and held my weight. He hardened against my back. His breath on my neck came in bursts, like he'd been running. He made a sound like a soft grunt and his hand slipped under the front of my shirt and pressed against my stomach. I put my hand over his and his breathing in my ear slowed. I felt his mouth and nose move against my neck, his hot breath. Then he moved away. By the time I turned around he was walking back up the beach toward the car. He stopped at the door on the driver's side and looked back at me, and I followed, still catching my breath. He got in, and I got in, and for a moment we sat there, not saying anything. "I'm sorry," he said.

I wanted to say, I'm not. But then I thought that if I wasn't now, I would be. "Don't be," I said.

"You do something to me."

"We do it to each other," I said, and I knew that by saying it aloud we'd cut the taut line that ran between us, and it would fall.

Marse's brother, Kyle, married his second wife in late August in the Church of the Little Flower, down the street from the Biltmore Hotel, and the reception was held in the Biltmore's main ballroom. Kyle had been there the day Dennis and I had met, and we'd hired Kyle's contracting firm when we'd built the addition on the house, and so I suppose he'd felt obligated to invite us even though we hadn't seen each other socially in years. Or maybe Marse, who was in the wedding party, added our names so she would have someone to dish with.

Bette called while I was getting dressed for the wedding, and I answered the kitchen phone in my panty hose while fishing with one hand through my purse for lipstick. "Suzanne wants to move," Bette said. I pictured her rolling her eyes, her tight-lipped grimace. "She thinks the house is too small. She wants a garage, for crying out loud."

I loved her house, which is what I told her. "But if Suzanne's not happy there . . . ," I said.

"She's concerned about the investment." She exhaled loudly. "She says we need to put our money where it can grow."

"It is growing."

"She said something about closet space."

"Well, she has a point there."

"And she says she's tired of Miami."

I put down my purse. "What does that mean? Where does she want to go?"

"I shouldn't have told you. I knew you'd panic."

"I'm not panicking," I said. She'd never mentioned moving away before, not even once. It had never occurred to me that this was even possible.

She said, "Maybe what I need is a new girlfriend," but she didn't sound convinced.

"I'm sorry," I said.

"I guess I have a decision to make," she said before hanging up. "I hate that."

Later that night, I found myself huddled with Marse on a divan in the corner of the Biltmore ballroom, a plate of hors d'oeuvres between us. Marse was telling me about the bride, a management consultant with very fresh-looking breasts and heavy white-blond bangs. "She's not quite as young as she looks," she said. "Kyle was drunk at the rehearsal. He was saying all sorts of crap. He said women our age are bitter, so he steers clear. He said he hoped she didn't get bitter. I told him it was inevitable."

"We're bitter?"

"I am, he said. Single women my age are. You get to a certain point, he said."

"Men shouldn't use that word."

"No, they shouldn't. I didn't mention that there's a word for men his age who live in condos and buy black leather furniture."

"Loser?" I said, and she nodded. Kyle wasn't exactly a loser, but he had grown untidy with age; his hair was unkempt, and he didn't put much thought into his wardrobe. But he'd made some money and drove a very silly car — something sporty and expensive, which I assumed younger women liked. His first wife, Julia, was a potter with a studio in Coconut Grove. Over the years I'd bought several of her pieces as gifts. She was at the wedding, too, and from where Marse and I were sitting, I could see her having what seemed to be an engrossing conversation with a man I didn't recognize.

She wore a light peach tunic and pearly white slacks. "Julia looks great," I said.

"Kyle said she couldn't be happier for him." Marse pulled at the top of her dress, smoothing it out. "I'm too old to be a bridesmaid. I'm too old to have other people pick out my clothes." She wore a garnet-colored, strapless organza dress with a sheer, cream-colored slip that showed at the hem, and a ribbon of the same color around the waist. I thought the outfit was pretty, but it didn't agree with Marse, who was more comfortable in a fitted suit or a short tailored dress.

"I'll take it," I said.

"Done."

"It might even fit me now," I said.

"You look good. I've been meaning to mention it."

I was wearing a dress I'd bought more than a year earlier but had never worn, because it had never fit right. It was a black-and-white plaid taffeta sheath with a low neckline. It hit just below my knees. Truth be told, I didn't think it was dressy enough for a wedding, but I'd wanted to wear it — it finally looked good on me, after all — so I'd added patent leather pumps and jangly crystal earrings and swept my hair up. "It's the tennis," I said.

I knew it was hard on Marse, going to wedding after wedding, year after year. At some point the weddings had tapered off — when we were about thirty, I suppose — but a decade later the divorces had started, and then the second marriages. In the meantime, Marse had dated a dozen handsome, emotionally unavailable men. I didn't think she wanted to get married per se, but she wanted something. "What's happening with that guy?" I said, thinking of Ted, the boat salesman.

"Nothing. Over."

"Do you want to get some air?"

"Lord, yes."

I scanned the room for Dennis and saw that he was talking to Julia. I caught his eye and waved as we went out. At some point since the brief wedding service, it had started to rain. We stood under an awning in front of the hotel among guests who had come outside to have the valet get their cars. "Don't we all look handsome," mumbled Marse. She turned to me. "You've been absent lately. Is it possible you're playing that much tennis?"

"I know. I don't know what it is." In the past week, I'd baked two loaves of bread and taken a nap every day. I'd been to the grocery store three times and painted two

323

bookshelves that had been in the guest room since we'd moved into the house. They had been white, and now they were yellow. It was a modest change, but it made me happy — if not because they now matched the wallpaper, then because painting them had been on my list for so long and now was done. I hadn't been to practice since the day at the beach with Jack, but I'd planned to return the following Wednesday and pretend nothing had ever happened.

"I thought with Margo gone you'd be a pain in my neck. How is she?"

"Fine. Apparently starting a new semester involves a lot of parties," I said. "She's enrolled in a class called Harbingers of Evil in Postmodern Literature. I keep meaning to ask for a copy of the syllabus. I could be one of those mothers who reads along with her child's class." A woman left the hotel and stepped into a black Lincoln, turning to wave as she did. I waved back. "Is that Eleanor Everest?" I said to Marse.

"Oh, God, I know — they botched her face-lift." One of Eleanor's cheeks drooped considerably, and the eyelid on the same side drooped as well, as if she'd been stuck with something and deflated. "She's going to that guy in Naples to fix it, but they can't get her in for six months. You'd think this would qualify as an emergency."

"How did you hear all this?"

She waved a hand. "Around." Marse's social life had always been a bit of a mystery to me. When she was with me, when she picked me up in her Wrangler and we ran out to Dadeland mall or she came over with a movie (usually a movie she'd seen and wanted me to see), or we took her boat to Stiltsville to watch the sunset, then came back to my house to make dinner — during these times, she referred to the activities that comprised her week, often mentioning people I knew casually or men she'd dated and broken up with before I'd even heard about it. Mostly, though, she remained close with people I considered acquaintances, women from our days in the Junior League, people whose families her family had known for decades. In so many ways, Miami was a small town.

Did I think Marse had made a mistake, staying single? Did she?

When Marcus Beck had first left Kathleen, Marse and I had gone to Kathleen's new condo for dinner, and Marse had asked her more or less the same question. "Do you miss him?" she'd said, and before I could stammer a protest — Marcus had left *her,* after twenty years together — Marse cut me off. "Let her answer," she'd said, and Kathleen had nodded. "I wouldn't say I miss him, because that would be pathetic," she'd said. Truth be told, I hadn't ever respected Kathleen much. She wore Laura Ashley dresses even though she was gaining on fifty, and her twin girls were sweet without seeming to mean it, and they'd been dorm roommates in college, an arrangement that I thought reflected poor parenting. But at this moment, sitting at Kathleen's country French dining table, drinking the bold red wine Marse had brought, I'd been impressed. "I will say that I don't like being alone," Kathleen had said. "That's all. I don't like it." She'd looked at Marse, who was shaking her head silently, and suddenly both of them looked older to me. They looked tired. "It sucks, doesn't it?" said Marse to Kathleen. She looked at me, and then Kathleen looked at me. "We hate you," said Marse, and Kathleen laughed lightly for a long time, and it had occurred to me that Marse had been faking it — maybe she wasn't tired of being alone, and instead was trying to give an old friend someone to lean on. Marse wanted Kathleen to think they had much in common, but Kathleen was a housewife who was suddenly not a wife and not living in her house

— she was a fish out of water, whereas Marse's life made sense. Marse had a successful career, a busy social life, and a stream of romantic prospects. It wasn't the same thing at all. Kathleen would be more lonely now precisely because she'd once had a husband and a home, not in spite of that.

I said to Marse, "Margo is living in an apartment, did I tell you that?" The rain was coming harder now, spattering the tops of my feet and ankles. Marse and I huddled closer together.

"Why would she want to do that?"

"I think it might have something to do with a boy."

"A man," said Marse. "She's in college. They're men, and she's a woman. That's what they want to be called, anyway."

"I don't think quite yet," I said.

"You're not ready."

"I suppose not."

"Who does she live with?"

At that moment, under the canopy outside the Biltmore's stately main entrance, I could not recall her roommate's name. "A girl from Tampa," I said. "And I guess the girl's boyfriend is pretty much a third roommate."

"Have you met them?"

As a matter of fact, Margo and I had made plans that afternoon for me to come up for

327

a weekend in October. "Not yet, but I will. Next month."

"Do you know anything about this man?" said Marse.

"You're interrogating me," I said. "Margo is fine. She was paired with a roommate and she says they're very compatible. Janelle — that's the girl's name. Margo gets along with the boyfriend. The apartment is right off campus — lots of kids do it, I guess. It's common." Even as I spoke, I felt uneasy — it had struck me as overly mature, this live-in boyfriend situation, but I'd told Dennis that I felt comforted knowing a boy would be around.

The wind was picking up, blowing around the royal palms that rimmed the Biltmore's circular drive. Marse said, "I still think of her as thirteen years old, that brace face. Let's get a drink. We'll toast her independence."

We'd had a couple of drinks each already. The bar inside the reception was serving wine, beer, and several flavors of daiquiris, which Marse had noted said a lot about the bride, and possibly about the promise of everlasting happiness. Marse didn't want to go back to the party, so she headed to the hotel bar while I stopped in at the reception to tell Dennis where I'd be. I found him in a corner with Julia, standing close and laughing. His daiquiri was peach, hers was strawberry. Before I left them alone again, I said, "I won't be our ride home," and Dennis raised his glass and said, "We can take a cab."

The hotel bar was walnut-paneled and dim, with burgundy chairs grouped around low glass tables. Marse ordered us whiskey sours, which was her drink of choice, and one I enjoyed when we were together but never once without her. "Julia is flirting with Dennis," I said when I sat down.

"Ha!" said Marse. "Good for her."

"Good for him," I said. "She's very pretty."

"Kyle told me he was disappointed when I RSVP'd for one. That's the word he used — he was *disappointed.*"

"Is he trying to prove that he can make a person bitter?"

"Apparently." She drank a piece of ice, then spat it back into the glass. "Hey," she said, "let's swap outfits."

We took our drinks into the powder room, which had an anteroom with chaise lounges and a wall-sized mirror, and she unzipped me, then pulled her dress over her head, revealing her lean torso and sheer, nude-colored bra. I could see the outline of her dark nipples through the fabric. I stepped out of my dress. On Marse, the bridesmaid dress had been floaty and flowing, but no matter how much thinner I'd become, I was still a good deal larger than she was, and though it zipped without a problem, it was not floaty. Where on her it had been a sort of princess dress, like something you'd find on a young girl's doll, precious and not sexy, on me it was — well, it was *showy*. We faced the mirror. The neckline of my dress — the one Marse now wore — was low, but there was plenty of room inside it, whereas Marse's dress fit snugly around my chest, lifting and cupping my breasts and deepening my cleavage. Marse and I both stared into the mirror at my chest; the cleavage was lovely, a style I could see adopting in the future, should my figure remain more or less the same, but I was still wearing a bra and the black straps showed. Marse helped me unhook it, then stuffed it into my purse. "There," she said, "you're in the wedding party. You owe me two hundred bucks for the inflatable kayak I gave them."

When we returned to the bar, the bartender gave no sign of noticing that we'd swapped outfits, but he did glance briefly at my cleavage, I noticed, and seemed if not impressed then at least not appalled. Marse was ordering another round when I heard a deep voice from behind us. "Well, well."

Marse and I both turned. Jack stood there with a wiry, gray-haired man who was familiar to me from the tennis club — another pro. "Who's this?" said Marse, not rudely but with an air of not caring about the answer to the question — an air I assumed was affected.

"Marse, this is my tennis instructor, Jack. Jack, this is my dear friend Marse." I gripped Jack's outstretched hand. We shook hands in the way that you do with old friends, where you don't pump so much as just hold tightly. Jack introduced his companion as Adam. They were both wearing navy button-down shirts with the hotel's insignia on the pocket. "Are you working?" I said, motioning to the insignia.

"More or less. There was a dinner for the board." He gestured upstairs, where the dining room overlooked the lobby, and I wondered if he'd seen me and Marse cross the lobby, and if that was what had drawn him downstairs. He said, "We thought we'd stop for a beer before heading out."

"We were given drink tickets," said Adam.

"Drink tickets?" said Marse.

"It's a bribe," said Jack. He sat on the stool next to mine. "They're afraid we won't come, or if we do, we won't schmooze. Ten-

331

nis is this club's cash cow."

"What about golf?" I said.

"Golfers," said Adam, rolling his eyes. He sat on the far side of Marse.

"What are you drinking?" said Jack.

"Whiskey sour," said Marse.

"How is it?"

"Delicious," said Marse.

I tipped back so Marse and Jack could see each other. "So Marse," said Jack, "how's that spelled?" Marse spelled it for him. "What do you do, Marse?" he said, and she told him, and for a moment they spoke about a man they both knew — a partner at her firm — and when Adam joined the conversation, Jack turned back to me. "I have a confession," he said. "I knew you were in here. I saw you from upstairs. But I believe you were wearing that." He pointed discreetly to Marse. "Very nice, either way."

"Thank you," I said, and I realized from the way I said it — encouragingly — that I was fairly drunk. In the mirror behind the bar, I could see the entrance to the room and most of its occupants: if Dennis arrived, I would be prepared.

"You shouldn't stay away," Jack said. "You don't need to do that." He spoke softly, but I was aware of Marse sitting beside me, her uncanny ability to read my mind, and I

thought of the first day we met, at Stiltsville, when she'd known even before I had
that I'd won Dennis and she'd lost him. I
turned toward her, to try to pull her into
the conversation, but she wasn't there.
She'd stepped a few feet away and was
intent on the television behind the bar.
Adam was standing, too, chatting with
another man who had come in. The bartender was watching the television, and he
had — I realized this without having registered it at the time — turned up the volume
a moment earlier. I had the thought that
maybe Marse was going to flirt with the
bartender, and that Adam was occupied,
and Dennis was with Julia, many steps away.
"I'm sorry," I said. "I'll be there Wednesday,
I promise."

"Let's not trash your tennis career over
one afternoon at the beach."

"No, of course. Of course not."

"I've missed you," he said.

"Frances?" said Marse. There was an edgy
timbre in her voice, a shiver of hardness. I
turned toward her, and she crooked her
finger. "Come here," she said.

"Excuse me," I said to Jack. Had our flirting been so obvious, so terrible, that I was
being scolded? When I reached her, Marse
said, "Watch this," and put her hands on

my shoulders to turn me toward the television. On the screen was a newswoman in a yellow blazer with large gold buttons, and behind her was a white front door in a low brick building cordoned off by yellow police tape. There were officers milling around, and in the corner of the screen, an ambulance with its back doors open.

Did I recognize the building, in that instant? In the bottom third of the screen was the story ticker: GAINESVILLE STUDENTS SLAIN, it read, and then: TWO DEAD AT WILLIAMSBURG VILLAGE APARTMENTS.

I had no trouble placing the building's name. The newswoman was saying, *"We're reporting that the victims were both women in their late teens or early twenties, students at the university, where the fall semester is currently under way. The bodies were discovered this afternoon at four p.m., after one of the girls' mothers reported that she had not heard from her daughter. The killer appears to have entered through the apartment's sliding glass doorway."*

"Dennis?" I said to Marse.

"Your friend's getting him," she said.

"When did I talk to her?" I said.

"I don't know, but I'm sure she's safe."

"You're sure?" I said.

"Yes."

Dennis rushed into the bar with Jack as the newswoman closed her segment, saying, *"For now, Gainesville students are being cautioned by police to stay alert, travel in pairs, and lock their doors."*

"Give me the phone," said Dennis to the bartender, and after some maneuvering, the bartender was unable to pull the phone away from its spot beside the cash register, so Dennis went around the bar. He started dialing, then stopped and looked at me. "Is it 5269 or 6952?" he said, then without waiting for an answer turned back and finished dialing. Marse and I watched him. After a long moment, he spoke into the phone. "Call your parents," he said urgently, then put the phone down and reached across the bar for my hands. "Just the machine," he said. "She's not in, that's all." My chest was tight. "We're going home — we'll be there in ten minutes — and she'll have left a message. If I know Margo, she's already on a bus."

I nodded. Home seemed a long way away.

"I'll walk out with you," said Marse. She collected my purse and took my arm, and the three of us headed together toward the parking lot. Only later did I consider that I hadn't said good-bye to Jack, and that I owed him a word of gratitude: not only did he retrieve my husband when I needed him, but he also must have paid for our drinks.

Today, with cell phones and the Internet, the whole event would have unraveled differently. But then, the only people I knew who had cell phones were a secretary at Dennis's firm whose husband was rumored to be a member of the Cuban mafia, and a doctor I knew from my office, who preferred it to a beeper in case of emergencies. We knew several people who had car phones, and indeed our next car would have one, but at the time we did not, and so we drove in silence, Dennis squeezing my knee. As I'd watched the newscast at the bar, my mind had been cloudy with panic, my vision had narrowed, and I'd had difficulty viewing the screen as a whole — instead I'd seen the ambulance in the corner, then the words on the screen, then the newswoman in her yellow jacket. But in the car, looking out at the clear bright night, I grew calm. Not this, I prayed. This is not going to happen to me. To someone else, this is happening, but it is not happening to me. One thing I felt, beyond the fear and frenzy, was love: for my daughter, for my husband. When we turned into our driveway, I said, "If there's no message, we'll call the Gainesville police, and if we can't get through, we'll get back in the car. We can be there in six hours."

Dennis paused. "We'll check the machine," he repeated. "Then we'll call the police. Then we'll drive." We were people who needed a plan, and he seemed to consider this a good one. But when we rushed into the kitchen, I saw the red light on the answering machine blinking, and I cried out in relief. He hit the play button, and then there was a woman's voice — but it wasn't Margo, it was Gloria, and she said something about a picnic at the beach before Dennis hit the delete button, and the machine sounded a long beep. And then — finally, like wheels touching down after a turbulent flight — it was Margo, saying, "Are you there? You're going to see the news. I'm all right." She paused. "Those girls — they lived right next door to me." There was the soft, wailing sound of my daughter crying, and I started to cry, too. Dennis replayed the message and we listened again. He dialed her number, frowned, and handed the phone to me. I got the tail end of a recorded message, and then it repeated: *All circuits are busy, please try your call again.*

"The world is trying to get through," he

said. "Those poor girls."

"Their poor parents."

He pulled off his tie, and we moved together to the living room and sat on the sofa. After a long time, he said, "Frances, why was Jack at the wedding?"

I closed my eyes. It seemed ridiculous to talk about this now, but I didn't have the energy to refuse. "He wasn't. He was upstairs, having dinner."

"Were you with him? At the bar, I mean?"

"No." Then I said, "No more than you were with Julia at the reception." This seemed a nod toward a confession, and it was the only admission I would ever make.

"Will you see him when you switch to this new team?"

"No." This wasn't exactly true — he would be around, even if he wasn't my coach — but I knew I would not join another team at the Biltmore. I would play somewhere else, if I kept playing at all.

"Thank God for that," he said. "I don't think of myself as a jealous guy . . ."

I took his hand, and pulled his palm toward my mouth, then kissed the warm soft space at the base of his thumb — this was something I did when I wanted to express my love, though I knew it wasn't a gesture he particularly understood. "I love you," I said, and the tears came again, along with the specific feeling of being at the end of something long and difficult, like a marathon, or in this case short and difficult, like a sprint, or both.

Dennis was partially correct: Margo had gone to the bus station, but after waiting an hour and a half had been unable to get out of town, even though Greyhound had added two buses to its southbound service. We continued trying in vain to get through to her, and finally, at midnight, she called. Dennis was watching the news in bed and I was in the bathroom, staring at myself in the vanity mirror. "Are you coming home?" said Dennis when he answered the phone. I rushed to the kitchen to pick up the other line.

"Mom? Isn't it horrible?" she said. "A policeman threw up on my doorstep."

"Lord," I said.

Dennis groaned. "Don't think about that, sweetheart."

She explained the situation at the bus station. "I'm not at the apartment anymore. I'm at the dorms, with friends. There are five of us sleeping in one room. We're on campus. We're safe."

Gainesville seemed a very small town. In my mind the place was dominated by the presence of a roaming monster, like the flashing red dot on a radar screen, blinking closer to its target. He could be a student, I thought. He could be one of the students Margo was with right now.

"I'm coming to get you," said Dennis. Over the line I heard a dresser drawer in our bedroom opening.

"Daddy?" said Margo. "I'm going to stay. The semester's just starting, and I don't want to miss anything. I won't be able to catch up."

"I don't think that matters, sweetheart," I said. "Aren't other people leaving?"

"Some," she said. She sounded stern when she spoke again, even though her voice was shaking. "I think I'm going to stay. I'll be safe. I promise."

Dennis breathed into the phone. I said, "We won't sleep until he's caught."

She was crying again. "They lived in One-Thirteen," she said. "I live in One-Twelve."

"I know, sweetheart," said Dennis. Again he insisted that she come home, and again she refused. Then, after giving her caution-ary tips — don't walk alone, don't go out at night, lock the doors, and for Christ's sake, lock the windows — and after getting the phone number of the dorm room where she was staying and repeating it twice back to her, he reluctantly said good-bye.

The following morning we woke to learn that the Gainesville police had found another body, a student named Christa Hoyt. She was found in her apartment, two miles from Williamsburg Village. Again, the killer had pried his way in through a sliding glass door. (From this time on in my life, I've disliked sliding glass doors, and have wondered if the tragedy would have occurred without them. I'd let my daughter live on the first floor of an apartment complex, never thinking to ask whether there was a solid barrier between her and the outside world. The Williamsburg Village Apartments had a swimming pool — of course there were sliding glass doors.) The reports said only that Christa's body had been mutilated; we learned later of the rapes, the decapitation, the gruesome poses. Gainesville officials urged students to be careful, to not go out at night, and to stay in groups whenever possible. All the murders had happened during the daylight, in the victims' homes, but still this was the advice given. A press conference followed: the president of the University of Florida, John Lombardi, answered questions about precautions being taken. They'd added thirty more campus police (again, I thought: but this killer could be a member of the campus police!) and were opening up unused dorm rooms to students living off campus who wanted the extra protection.

It hit me, as I sat in bed watching television: this was not even a danger I'd thought to fear. The notion that I had let this happen, that my daughter had been asleep while on the other side of her wall two girls were raped and murdered, sent me into a panic. I reached for the phone and the piece of paper with the number Margo had given us, but the line was busy again, that goddamned automated message. Dennis wrapped his arms around me. One of the many things I felt at the time was anger — at myself for letting her move off campus in the first place, and at both of us for letting her stay in Gainesville while this killer continued to choose new victims. Of course I understood that living next door to a murder is not a fate equal to the murders themselves; I'd never felt a stronger sense of gratitude. But I knew that this experience — her proximity, her unbelievable luck — would haunt Margo. The knowledge that this might have happened to her would change her life. This was not the carefree college experience we'd wanted for our daughter. "It's my fault," I said to Dennis, because I'd approved of her moving off campus, and he said, "It's not your fault." But I'll always remember the tone of his voice as he said it — weary, guilty, and impatient — because in that moment, if not after, I think Dennis might have agreed.

We heard from Margo again that afternoon. She'd moved with friends into a vacant dormitory suite, which meant she now had her own bed. We continued to insist she come home — Dennis packed a bag in anticipation that she would finally relent and he could go get her — but she was determined to stay. It was as if she had seized on staying as the only way to get through it all intact. She reminded us that she was twenty years old. Twenty! How old this seemed to her, and how young it seemed to me. The next morning Dennis left for work as if it were a normal day, though I stayed home. I got dressed and straightened the house, but left the television news on in the bedroom and the living room, and whenever the coverage shifted to the murders, I sat down and watched, and it was many minutes before I could return to my feet. I called Margo in the morning, then twice in the afternoon, then Dennis and I called together when he got home from work. "It's like a ghost town," said Margo when we finally reached her. The university continued to remain open — President Lombardi explained to the press that many students couldn't reach their homes, and the university was better equipped to ensure student safety by continuing business as usual. We watched the news together that night: stores were selling out of Mace; Southern Bell was begging people not to call Gainesville unless absolutely necessary; pizza joints were losing money because of a rumor that the killer might be a delivery man; gun shops were reporting record sales; hardware stores had run out of deadbolts and door chains.

And the following morning, August 28, there were two more victims, which brought the total to five murders within seventy-two hours. This time, the killer had varied the profile. One victim was a petite twenty-three-year-old brunette named Tracy Paules, but the other was her male roommate, Manny Taboada. Manny was — these details were included in the reports — six feet, two inches, 200 pounds, and a former football player. Again, the killer had entered through a sliding glass door by jimmying it with some kind of tool. These killings had happened in the middle of the night, when

Tracy and Manny had been sleeping. When I reached Margo on the phone, Dennis grabbed his packed bag and headed to the kitchen to get on the other line. "Don't let her talk you out of it," he said to me, and I nodded. But again she repeated what she'd been saying: that she was safe on campus, that she was with people all the time, even at night, and that she knew the university was forgiving tuition for anyone who needed to leave Gainesville — this is when Dennis picked up the other line — but she really didn't think it was necessary, and besides she really liked her American history class. Her professor wore a tunic and took off his shoes when he came into the classroom. "Don't let him sell you any baloney about the 'good' war," said Dennis, who had always had, in my estimation, an enviable talent for switching focus. "If he does, ask him about the internment camps."

Before she hung up, Margo reassured us again. "They gave us whistles. If I get in trouble, I just blow on it and someone appears in the blink of an eye."

"They gave you whistles?" I said, thinking of the tools this killer had: a knife, obviously, and duct tape, and cleaning products of some kind — there were reports that all the bodies had been cleaned up before being staged for discovery. And of course he had something unnameable and unknowable, something Margo and Dennis and I could not understand: a force. I found it amusing and terrifying, this fact: the university had issued my daughter a whistle.

Dennis reluctantly unpacked his suitcase. In the face of Margo's determination not to let us rescue her, I realized that the transition we'd been so worried about had come to pass. She really had left home.

Despite the fact that a man had been killed, I was reassured by the roster of Margo's bunk mates. In one suite, there were two rooms and three kids sleeping in each room — the housing division had hastily made space and provided cots — and four of the six kids were young men. Normally, I would've been appalled to learn that the university was allowing my daughter to room with boys, but in these circumstances, I think the administration showed an admirable willingness to depart from tradition. They did what they had to do. We can go on about the benefits of equal rights, but when a killer is loose, you want a man — or men, plural — looking out for your daughter.

Several times when we called Margo's suite we reached a young man named Stuart, whose name we'd never heard before. "Margo kicked ass on her biology assignment," he would say to me. Or, "Yesterday we rode out to Hampton Lake for a swim." By the third time we'd talked, I'd developed the sense that this boy and my daughter were close, in no small part because of the speed with which she reached the phone whenever he passed it to her — physically at least, geographically, they were together. Once, Dennis asked him bluntly how tall he was, and Stuart said, "I'm not tall, but I'm fast and strong. You don't need to worry about your daughter. We're taking good care of her. We're taking care of each other." This was something I'd seen stressed in televised interviews with the university's director of psychological services — students relying on each other not only for safety but for comfort. Dennis choked up when Stuart said good-bye. He wanted to be the man protecting his daughter.

A day passed with no news — no leads on the killer, no new victims — and then another day passed, and then it had been a week. Five thousand students had left campus. There was a lot of nonsense in the Gainesville student paper, the *Alligator* — Margo sent us a copy — linking the murders to Ted Bundy, who had been executed a year earlier. (The theory went: Bundy was born on November 24 and executed on August 24 at the age of forty-two; the Gainesville murders started on August 24 and happened in a neighborhood off State Road 24; the second murder was on SW 24th Avenue, and so on.) I ran into Kathleen Beck at the grocery store — her twins had come home and were enrolling in classes at the University of Miami so they wouldn't fall behind. Kathleen seemed confounded when I told her Margo was still in Gainesville, so I rushed to reassure her. "She's not off campus anymore," I said. "She's in a dorm with a bunch of kids — half of them are boys."

"Boys?" said Kathleen. "She lives in an *apartment?*"

"Not anymore," I said, but then I ran out of patience with Kathleen, and said goodbye. That evening, Gloria called — she'd called daily since the murders — and after I'd reassured her that yes, Margo was still insisting on staying on campus, and still being very cautious, Gloria said, "You know, with all the hubbub I'd forgotten what I wanted to ask you."

"Yes?" I was putting away groceries, leaving out ingredients for a stew. I had a bag of black beans in my hand.

"Eleanor Everest said she saw you the other day at the beach with a man." I put down the beans. The tone in Gloria's voice was one I'd never heard from her before: not accusing exactly, but stumped and oddly intimate, as if she were saying: *Come on, you can tell me.* "Someone with dark hair," she said. "She didn't recognize him."

I didn't say anything. I suppose I was deciding whether to lie, or how much.

"Was that you?" she said. "Are you not working anymore?"

"Actually, it was me," I said. My voice was loud and unsteady. "I'm still working — I'm working more, in fact, as of this week — but I've been playing tennis at the Biltmore this summer" — Gloria knew this — "and after practice one day a few of us went to the beach. It was just so hot . . ."

"Who was the man?" said Gloria.

"My coach, Jack." And then it occurred to me that the best lie was a stretching of the truth. Don't deny, embellish. "There were — let's see — four of us? Plus Jack. The women are wild about him, but he's married — and so are they, to be honest." I used a gossiping tone, as if I were as interested in the tidbit as she might be. "We've gone to lunch together a few times, several of us girls, and that day someone — I don't remember who — invited Jack along. We ended up at the beach." The story was fine, depending on when exactly I'd been spotted by Eleanor Everest: was it while we were standing at the car, closest to the road — this was most likely, I thought — or in the brief moment when we'd stood together at the shoreline, where we would have been recognizable only by people on the sand? I didn't recall there being anyone close by. A betrayal of Dennis was a betrayal of others, of Gloria and Grady and Bette, and even Marse. I felt a little sick, lying to my mother-in-law. I felt lesser for it, and I suppose I was.

"Eleanor said you were picnicking — I thought maybe Dennis had played hooky. Maybe you should do that sometime, kidnap him from his office in the middle of the afternoon. That would be pretty, wouldn't it? Take slacks for him so he doesn't ruin his suit, and a nice fruit salad."

"That would be nice," I said. "It's a great idea." It was something I vowed to do, in that moment — sweep by his office in the middle of the day and abscond with him to the beach — and also in that moment, as Gloria said something about how they used to go to Key Biscayne as a family when the

350

children were young, I heard Dennis's key in the door, and I said, "Gloria, I'm sorry, I hate to interrupt, but Dennis is home and I just have to —"

"Go on, dear," she said. "I just wanted to check on you."

"Love you," I said. I said it only every so often.

"You, too," she said.

Dennis appeared in the kitchen doorway. His hair was wet, and I could see through the window that it had started to rain. He wiped his cheek with one hand and asked me about my day. I took his briefcase and set it down on the kitchen table, and although I really wanted to apologize for betraying him — never again, I would say, I don't know what I was thinking — I couldn't do that, not exactly. So instead, I said, "Do you want to fool around?" and he nodded and we went together down the hallway, past Margo's room and the guest room that so long before I'd wanted to turn into a nursery. We went into the bedroom with its outdated furniture and the alarm clock that didn't work very well but we'd never replaced and the clothes on the bed that I'd folded but not put away. And while we took off our clothes, I turned away from him, so he wouldn't see that I was keeping myself from crying.

That week I joined a tennis team at the YWCA. I was matched with a doubles partner named Carolyn Baumgartner, who became a friend. Shortly afterward, I ran into Jane Brevard at the grocery store and told her about the team, and then she joined, too, and every couple of weeks she and I had lunch together after practice. She asked once if I knew that Jack wasn't coaching at the Biltmore anymore — she might have been checking to see if we were in touch — but she didn't say where he'd gone and though I wanted to, I didn't ask. Carolyn and I won more than we lost, and though a few of the pounds I'd dropped crept back, tennis continued to be part of my life. Sometimes while I played I imagined Jack standing on the sidelines, watching me from behind sunglasses, calling out pointers: Don't chase your toss! Show your shoulder on your forehand! In September, Dennis and Margo ran together in the Conch Classic 5K in Key West, and Dennis placed third in his age group. I'd had no idea, but that summer, while I'd been improving my tennis, Dennis had become a serious runner.

The Gainesville hysteria dissolved. No more bodies were found. The police arrested a disturbed teenager, but then let him go because he had an alibi. It would be a year before they charged the real killer, a Louisiana native named Danny Rolling; even then he would be arrested first for robbery, and only afterward would confess to the murders. Apartment 113 at Williamsburg Village would become a model apartment, the one management showed to prospective renters. Security alarms would be installed and extra locks added to the sliding glass doors throughout the complex. I know this because I called the management office to ask.

Margo changed dorm rooms again, this time with Janelle, who had by that time broken up with her boyfriend. She pledged Alpha Chi Omega but by the end of the semester went inactive. She brought three girlfriends home on break, and we took them all out to Stiltsville. She continued to live on campus. That year, Gloria and Grady decided to downsize, and they bought a condo and gave us their house — just gave it to us, no strings attached, nothing to pay but the property taxes. Then when we sold our home — our first home, where we'd raised Margo — we made enough to pay off Margo's student loans and have a little left over for savings. When Gloria and Grady handed over the keys to their house, along with the paperwork transferring ownership, Gloria said to me, "You don't get sentimental, now. You make it your own." I stripped the wallpaper from every room. Bette, who at this point had sold her own house and was preparing to move away with Suzanne, helped me paint: butter yellow for the kitchen, chalky blue for the living room, deep red for the dining room. Still, in the months after we moved in, the house felt stolen — from Gloria, who'd left the linen closet smelling of cedar, and from Grady, whose tools still filled black silhouettes along the pegboard walls of the garage.

Eventually, their ghosts faded. Dennis let our lease expire at the marina, and we moved the boat to the slip behind the house. One night just after we'd moved in, while there were still unpacked boxes on the kitchen table, Dennis dragged me outside in my pajamas, and we opened a bottle of champagne and sat on the boat drinking it out of paper cups, looking up the lawn at the house, which was lighted and still. I half expected to see a figure moving past a window — someone like me but not exactly me, someone who lived among us quietly and didn't notice much when we came and went, but was always there lurking when we were gone.

I saw Jack again one time, a year later. I was waiting to board an airplane to Atlanta, for my father's funeral. Jack was with his thin, red-haired wife at the gate opposite mine, and when their plane was called, I watched as they stood and gathered their things, and Jack put out a hand so his wife could walk ahead of him. And then maybe he felt me watching him, because he turned and looked at me, and after a moment he waved a half-wave, like he wasn't certain he should, and I smiled without waving, and he turned away. I miss you, I thought — these were the words that came to mind: I miss you. Even as I wondered how it was possible, I knew it was true.

1992

Dennis stood beside the swimming pool in bathing trunks and goggles, snapping on a pair of bright yellow kitchen gloves. It was August 25, the morning after the hurricane, and we'd spent hours tramping through the debris that littered our property. Mr. Costakis's royal palm stretched across our backyard, the deck sagged with split planks, and the swimming pool churned with foliage. Our street was impassable, crowded with shredded trees and a felled telephone pole, and the canal at the back of the house teemed with window shutters, patio furniture, palm fronds: little rafts escaping for the sea. Among the unsinkable, our boat listed against its battered pier, crowded but unharmed. We'd lengthened the mooring lines and padded the hull with fenders, imagining a storm that would lift the boat aboveground, then recede in a breath.

Upstairs, Margo and her new husband,

Stuart, slept in her childhood bed. They were living with us that month, house-hunting in lieu of honeymooning.

Miami was still and cloudless, cruelly hot. Dennis and I had assumed, wrongly, that the electricity would return within days. I'd lived in South Florida for more than twenty years, and never had I faced August without air-conditioning; the prospect sent me into a mute panic. I was in menopause, prone to hot flashes. The hurricane, the tattered lawn, the leaky bedroom ceiling — these I could handle. But the heat and humidity coated the little woes like soot: it was all too much.

Maybe it was my heavy breathing as we crossed the lawn, or my profuse sweating — in any event, Dennis declared that we would skim the swimming pool first, so I would have a place to keep cool. He jumped into the deep end, then emerged with a bullfrog the size of a football squirming in his gloved hands. I shrieked. He ran down to the canal and tossed it in. When he returned, I lifted the camera — we'd brought it out to document the mess for the insurance company — and he posed, hands on hips and feet apart. "I am Captain Amphibian," he said. "Rescuer of frogs." His wet hair, the singed color of red clay roads after rain, lay flat against his forehead.

I skimmed the pool while Dennis fished out a few more frogs, and when the water was clear, I dove in. Dennis raked the yard, making piles, and the sodden leaves I'd trimmed dried in the sunlight, releasing a mulchy smell into the air. Dennis was just rearranging the junk, I thought. He was just moving it around, as Margo had done long ago with the vegetables on her dinner plate. He found a flattened soccer ball in the rose garden out front, and a windshield, scratched but not broken, in the bougainvillea. He found a whistle on a red shoestring, which he looped around his neck. Next door, Mr. Costakis whipped at shrubbery with a machete. I could see sunlight strike the blade between the tilting trunks of gumbo-limbo trees. Every so often a helicopter roared overhead, but otherwise, save for the whipping sound and Dennis's raking, the world was quiet. There were no passing cars, no ringing telephones, no boats humming down the canal.

Dennis leaned against the rake and rubbed his neck. "I'd help," I said, "but there's a risk of self-combustion."

"Stay in the pool."

"I wish it were just a layer," I said. "I wish we could just vacuum it all up." I made a

358

sucking sound, gesturing largely.

"I was thinking of forest fires," said Dennis. "The way they nourish the soil. By April, we could have plants we didn't know we had."

"I want our old plants," I said.

"No pouting." He blew his whistle. I saluted.

There was, looming but unspoken, the matter of Stiltsville. Days earlier, when the National Hurricane Center had issued a storm watch for Dade County, I'd imagined the stilt house without its roof, the dock splintered — after all, the house had survived Agnes and Betsy and Hugo. When the watch became a warning, though, people started to gather provisions — batteries and flashlights and bottled water and canned goods — and I pictured the stilt house caved in on itself like a sunken cake. Then the storm arrived, and Dennis and I watched the wind bend our melaleuca trees until their branches brushed the ground, and I knew there would be nothing left.

A marine patrol cruiser made its way through the canal, sending the floating rubble into fits. The boat fenders rubbed against the pier. Dennis raised a hand and the patrolman waved back. There would be more of these good-natured greetings in the coming weeks. Overnight, Miami drivers would become uncharacteristically civilized, waiting patiently at stop signs and even signaling for others to go first. We would learn about a woman, a friend of Gloria's, who volunteered to direct traffic for hours each day at an intersection near her house. Neighbors we'd never met would call out across the street or canal. We would exchange best wishes with strangers.

When hurricane season was still a distant and nebulous concern, faint breezes in the doldrums, Margo had called to tell us she was engaged to be married. She was twenty-one years old, in her last year at college. I answered the phone; a commotion in the background told me she wasn't alone. "Mom?" she said. "Don't cry."

"You're engaged to whom?" Beside me, Dennis dropped his newspaper. Margo had mentioned Stuart from time to time, but her references to him had been so casual, so incidental to our conversations — as in "Stuart and I went for barbecue and my car broke down and I changed the tire by myself!" or "I can't talk long because Stuart is here unclogging my sink" — that I'd formed the idea they were not serious. When I'd visited her at school, we'd gone out to eat with a few of her girlfriends, but no boyfriend had been in evidence.

"Come meet him," said Margo, her voice ringing with delight. It was this tone of voice that sent a shiver of excitement — joy, even — through my alarm. "Come tonight," she said.

Dennis took the phone without asking for it. There was no telling how he would react; sometimes he took emergencies in stride, like when Margo was sixteen and woke us in the night to say she'd crashed Dennis's car into a bridge down the street, and Dennis cleaned blood from her forehead and took her to the hospital. Since then, whenever we'd passed the scene of the accident, Dennis had made the same joke: "I think I see pieces of my headlights in that bush over there. Yep, there's my back fender in the gutter." A year later, though, when Margo had talked me into taking her to the gynecologist for birth control, he'd avoided her for two days.

Dennis snapped his fingers at me and covered the mouthpiece. "Do we know this person?" he whispered. I made a gesture with my hand: *sort of.* Into the phone, he said, "What do you mean?" The insect-like sound of Margo's voice came through the telephone receiver, and I stood up to pace.

"Sweetheart, it's too late for us to get on the road." He waited. I knew that my daughter's voice had taken on a whine, a tone used exclusively with her father, a plea for approval. "Of course we're happy for you," said Dennis. "Sometimes it takes us time to digest. Haven't we always come through?"

We drove to Gainesville the following morning. I watched the orange groves through the window, parting and seaming, and chewed my fingernails. "Stop that," said Dennis, pulling my hand from my mouth. "This is not some stranger we're talking about here. This is our daughter."

"She's impetuous," I said. "She's romantic." In fact, I'd never before thought she was either of these things.

"Those sins," said Dennis.

They were sitting on the front steps of Margo's apartment building when we arrived. Through the windshield, I watched the boy stand to greet us: he was short — Margo's height — and sinewy, with a mop of dark hair that swept across his forehead and crowded his eyebrows, making him seem pensive and fierce. Margo hugged my neck and Stuart shook my hand. "The mysterious man and the concerned parents meet at long last," he said, then forced a

362

chuckle. He was muscular and his voice was deep, which together with the height and haircut gave his appearance a confused quality, manly and boyish at once, like a cartoon superhero.

"Let's get out of the heat," said Dennis.

Margo linked her arm through mine and led me inside. We sat in her living room, drinking mango juice blended fresh by Stuart, and Dennis and I interviewed the man who might — we still considered it a remote possibility — become part of our family. The juice was warm and oversweet. He was twenty-four, originally from Sarasota, and worked as a general contractor. He'd accepted a job with a builder in Miami — there was always something being built in Miami, malls or offices or condos, either on the outskirts of the ever-expanding city limits, or over razed buildings in the city center — which meant that Margo could continue with her plans to start a master's degree program at the University of Miami the following fall. The degree would be in, of all things, modern dance. She'd stumbled on a passion for dance at the University of Florida, and had mentioned several times, proudly, that she would be the only person in her graduate program without at least five years of technical training. This made me feel inadequate, as if I hadn't recognized the talent she had hidden away. Instead, I'd pushed ballet classes (not the same, she emphasized), sailing club, piano lessons, swim team, academics. It was like spinning a large wheel and hoping it would stop in exactly the right place. Dancing? How could we have known?

While the men talked — Dennis asked questions, and when the conversation paused, he took a sip of juice and started again — I studied Stuart's body language. He sat straight-backed on the edge of the sofa cushion, rubbing his hands together, as if preparing to spring into action. I waited for him to leap away, and also waited to recognize something — anything — that might coax from inside me some seed of goodwill. Margo sat cross-legged, listening to Stuart and glancing at me. My skin surged with the early tingles of a hot flash. I stood up, interrupting the conversation. "I feel a nap coming on," I said.

"Why don't we plan to meet for dinner?" said Dennis.

"Absolutely," said Stuart. I would come to recognize such expressions of certainty as one of his idiosyncrasies. "No problem," he would say in the following weeks, when I called Margo and he answered and we tangled ourselves into awkward chitchat. "Definitely."

Dennis and I spent the afternoon in our motel room, and I sobbed while he comforted me with one arm and flipped television channels with the other. "Big deal," he said. "We know plenty of divorce lawyers. There's Donald Tanner, and that Nordic guy — what's his name — from the yacht club."

"One has hopes for one's only daughter."

"He could be worse," said Dennis. "Think of him as a grab bag — there's a chance, at least, for a wonderful surprise."

Dennis liked Stuart, despite me and despite himself. He liked the boy's high-keyed energy, and he liked the idea of welcoming another person into our little family. I'd liked this idea, too, in the abstract, but I had never considered that it might happen so soon. When Margo and Stuart entered the restaurant that night — she in a dress and he in a sport coat — I forced a smile. We ordered wine.

"I was thinking it should be a small ceremony, just close friends," Margo said. "I'd like to have it in the backyard."

She was pretty in her sundress, tan shoulders and dark hair and freckled nose. She'd lost some weight in her face since last I'd seen her, which was — it hurt me to think it — four months before, at spring break, when I'd picked her up on the way to Atlanta and we'd spent a week with my mother. We'd hiked every morning and spent afternoons swimming at Anna Ruby Falls; she and my mother had worn straw hats and bathing suits, and I'd packed tuna fish sandwiches and cold dill pickles for lunch. Margo had brought my mother a copy of a novel she was reading for class — I'd read it years before, and declined to repeat the experience — and in the late afternoons they had reclined on opposite sofas, each reading and piping up every few minutes with a comment. After dinner, they'd discussed the novel at the kitchen table while I cleaned up. Margo had mentioned Stuart once or twice during the trip, I recalled, but only in her casual way. You are too young, I thought. "When?" I said.

"August," she said. Hurricane season. Her eyes searched my face. "We can put up a tent in case it rains, and I'd like Marse to be a bridesmaid, if she wouldn't mind." Behind her, a family sat around a table like ours. The father lifted a forkful of pasta, the teenage boy chewed ice from his soda, and the mother cut her steak. A quiet diorama. It seemed to me that my family's stress must have been evident, each gesture insincere and jolting.

"That all sounds fine," I said to her. Then I had a thought. "Margo," I said a bit loudly, "you're not pregnant?"

"No!" said Margo.

"No way," said Stuart.

Dennis took my hand. "That's good to hear," he said. He raised his glass. "Look, we trust our Margo," he said. "I won't lie, young man, we wish we'd met you earlier. But we look forward to getting to know you."

I raised my glass and took a long sip. This was my husband telling me that there would be no more self-pity. It was time for support.

Margo and Stuart stayed in Gainesville after graduation — we drove up for the ceremony, and I sniffled while Dennis snapped photos of Margo onstage in her gown — and the summer that followed was busy with week-end visits and wedding-themed phone conversations. I grew used to Stuart, if not quite fond of him, and felt alternately exhilarated and saddened by the situation. They moved home the first week of August and we held the wedding at the house, the air conditioner on high and the lawn be-decked in ribbon and sunflowers. Bette flew home from Santa Fe, where she and Suzanne had bought an adobe bungalow behind a strip mall, and she and Marse came over early to help me dress. Marse wore a sleeveless red floral dress with a sweetheart neckline, and her chest was rosy from the heat. Bette wore a lavender suit that I thought aged her; I guessed that it had been selected by Suzanne, who preferred a more conservative look. Dennis was already downstairs, dressed and waiting for guests, and Margo was in her own bedroom with Beverly Jovanovich, who was her maid of honor. Marse insisted on plucking my eyebrows — it was something she'd wanted to do for a decade, but I'd never relented until now — and Bette brought up a bottle of white wine from the kitchen.

My bedroom door was closed, but still Marse lowered her voice to speak. She said, "Am I the only one who thinks this is a little old-fashioned? She's practically a teenager."

"Marrying young is back in fashion," said Bette. I was reminded of the day years earlier when she had prepared to wed in the same backyard.

"That Stuart is handsome," said Marse.

"In a way, I suppose," said Bette.

"He's a flirt. Margo will have to keep an eye on him," said Marse.

They both looked at me, waiting for a reaction. "I hadn't noticed," I said, though I had. Just that morning a young girl had arrived with the florist's crew, and he'd pulled a daisy from a bouquet to give her, he said, as a tip. He'd done this right in front of me, which told me that there was nothing beneath the gesture, no murky undercurrent.

"You could stop her," said Marse to me.

"I could not," I said.

"Well, I could," she said.

"No one's stopping her," said Bette.

Marse studied my brow. "You're done," she said. She handed me a tube of lipstick and turned to Bette. "How's life in the desert?"

"It's just fine," said Bette. "Come for a visit. We have a very nice guest room." She topped off her own glass, then Marse's and mine. In the time since she'd moved, this was as much as she'd revealed to any of us: Santa Fe was fine, the house was fine, Suzanne was fine. It had been rough for Suzanne to break into the real estate business, but things had been picking up. They took long walks in the dry heat with their dog. I scrutinized each conversation for some hint that she might move back but didn't find one. She did not seem overjoyed with her new life, but she did seem settled.

"Do you miss home?" I said to her.

She squinted, as if considering the question. "You know what I don't miss? Dating."

"I can imagine," said Marse.

"Do you miss us?" I said.

"What a silly question," Bette said. For a moment no one spoke and I wondered, ever so briefly, if it was silly at all. Then she said, "It's like I moved away from my heart," and I had to turn away.

When I'd composed myself, I stood up and started toward the door — it was time to lend Margo a hand — but then I turned back. My two friends looked at me, Bette in her suit and Marse in her low-cut dress. Their faces were as familiar to me as my own. I said, "Maybe it will be just fine."

"It just might be," said Bette.

"She has good role models," said Marse. "It makes a difference."

"Thank you for saying that," I said.

That evening, I accepted the good wishes of our friends with a bright smile, and was surprised to feel a swell of optimism as Margo said her vows. Of course I hoped for her sake that the marriage would last, but I also hoped something more personal — more selfish, I should say: that Margo would come, through marriage, to understand Dennis and me in ways she never had before. I hoped Margo would learn that the cement of a marriage never really dries, and she would apply that understanding to her parents, and value the work we'd done to survive.

The city of Coral Gables had closed the canal to private traffic — we'd found neon notices stuck to the front door and the boat console — so we'd resigned ourselves to not knowing the fate of Stiltsville until the canal cleared or the telephones worked. Several times a day, helicopters beat overhead and a marine patrol boat cruised by the house, dragging a net glutted with debris.

"They're looking for something," said Dennis about the marine patrol. We were in the backyard, taking an ax to Mr. Costakis's royal palm. Dennis was clumsy with the ax; he had a hard time hitting the same spot twice.

"They're cleaning up," I said.

The cruiser puttered away. "No," he said. "They're searching."

"For what?"

"What else?" said Dennis. "A person."

This seemed unlikely to me. I took the ax from Dennis and hoisted it over my shoulder. "Here comes that dark side of yours," I said. I brought down the ax.

"I'm tired," said Dennis. His shoulders sagged and his face was red. He sat down suddenly — or did he fall? I replay it in my mind, the slow bend of his knees, the arm reaching out.

"What's wrong?" I said.

"Nothing. Just the heat."

I crouched beside him, surrounded by a dozen chunks of royal palm. "This is not our job," I said, meaning Mr. Costakis's tree.

"That doesn't matter." He stared at his shoes, then looked up at the canal. "If the stilt house is gone, I don't want to rebuild."

"Why not?"

"All that work, just for a few more years — doesn't it make you tired?"

"Are we getting old?"

"No way." He stood. "Spring chicks." But his steps toward the swimming pool were sluggish and wooden.

Businesses were closed, including Dennis's firm. Grady and Gloria had fled to Vero Beach to stay with friends. There had been looting — we saw footage on the portable television — and a curfew was in effect for all of Dade County. We stayed home, playing cards and taking walks and living off food we'd stockpiled: deli meat and eggs and fruit and bottled water, all nestled in squat white coolers. Every day, the National Guard passed through our neighborhood, heading south. We raised hands to them as they passed. Down in Homestead, the Red Cross built a tent city for the newly homeless. Our neighborhood felt to me like an island refuge — like Stiltsville, in a way — isolated from a continent of disaster and disaster relief. Our block buzzed with people working in their yards, grateful that their troubles were limited to landscaping, broken windows, a few irksome leaks. Marse stopped by once or twice when she could manage it. She lived in a condo on Biscayne Boulevard downtown, and in her neighborhood the phones were working and the roads had been cleared, but the lobby of her building had been transformed into a command station for the National Guard. Every morning, she spent an hour helping them field calls.

A marine patrolman knocked on the back door a week after the hurricane. It was early, and Margo and Stuart were asleep. The patrolman apologized for disturbing us and said he was opening the canal to traffic. Dennis invited him in. "Did you find anything?" he said.

"Still looking," said the man.

I could tell by the way they spoke that they'd met. Probably out back, when Dennis was working in the yard. They shook hands and Dennis closed the door.

"What was that about?" I said.

Dennis looked at me.

"What?" I said.

"Let's take the boat out now. Let's get it over with."

"Is that what you want?" I said.

Dennis stared out the window, then nodded. "I'll get the kids," he said.

I stood in the hallway as Dennis knocked on Margo's bedroom door. "Rise and shine," he said loudly. In the kitchen, with the patrolman, I hadn't been shy about my prebreakfast ensemble — one of Dennis's old button-downs and slippers — but in the hallway, I felt exposed. Around Margo alone, I'd always been casual. Too casual, perhaps — she was constantly telling me to button the next higher button or tighten the cord on my bathrobe. I wanted to dash to my dresser and pull on a pair of shorts, but Margo's bed creaked and feet slapped the floor, and the door opened. There stood Stuart, rubbing his face. "Morning," he said, a throaty croak.

Behind him, Margo shifted under the bedsheets, revealing the pale underside of her upper arm. Dennis faced away from the doorway. "Swimsuits," he said.

"Pardon?" said Stuart.

It was a game Dennis and Margo played: she had to guess a destination from a list of clues. Margo usually resisted playing, but it was the kind of game in which one automatically participates; even as she declined to answer aloud, her mind took guesses. In a sleepy voice, she said, "Where are we going?"

"Swimsuits and towels," said Dennis.

Stuart went to a duffel bag and pulled out a pair of blue swim trunks. "Swimsuit, check," he said to Dennis. To me, he said, "Towels?"

"In the laundry room," I said.

"Towels in the laundry room," said Stuart. "Check."

Margo stirred until we could see her face. "Just tell us where we're going," she said.

We looked at her — me over Dennis's shoulder and Dennis over Stuart's and Stuart over his own. I felt a chill pass through my husband as he realized she was naked beneath the sheets. It is one thing to hide from one's child the indignities of middle age, the sagging and emissions and diminished libido and hot flashes. But for a parent to witness a grown child's sexuality — how were we meant to respond? Dennis kept his eyes on Stuart. "Sunscreen," he said.

Stuart turned and scanned the room, then took a bottle of lotion from the dresser. "Sunscreen, check," he said. It was just right, this playing-along. But I confess that every time I felt myself warm to Stuart, the impulse fled as soon as I recognized it.

"The beach," guessed Margo.

"You're warm," Dennis said.

"What else?" said Stuart.

"Sunglasses," Dennis said. "Snorkeling gear."

Margo sat up, clutching the sheet to her chest, and Dennis shifted backward. "The boat?" she said. Her hair was a mess. She was lovely. "Really?"

"We leave in fifteen minutes," said Dennis.

We shut ourselves inside our bedroom. I took off my shirt, feeling the muggy air on my breasts. Dennis stepped into shorts and eased his hands into the pockets. He was lean and tan from a summer of half days at the office, afternoons spent jogging or boating. Before the wedding, we'd spent a long weekend at Stiltsville, and he'd worked out an exercise routine in which we swam laps around the house in the morning, then stretched and did sit-ups on the dock in the evening. He liked activity and goals — this was the same man who used to swim to the Becks' house and back when he could have used the boat — whereas I was content to lie in the hammock on the porch, reading or watching the sky darken over the skyline. "This is strange," he said.

I thought of Stiltsville, likely gone, and Margo, married. "I know," I said. "I can hardly think."

He looked at me. "What? I'm talking about this." He motioned to his chest. He wore a Hawaiian shirt with the buttons undone.

"What is it?" I said, but then I saw: he was trying to button his shirt, but the fingers of his left hand trembled. "Oh, baby," I said. "Let me." I buttoned his shirt and pressed myself to his chest. His heart beat against my forehead. "It will be OK."

The boat engines sputtered and smoked when they started. I handled the lines, and Stuart and Margo perched at the bow, their legs dangling over the water. Our wake lapped at the low stone walls that edged the waterway, where an occasional heron stood blinking at us, unperturbed. We cleared the mouth of the canal and the bay unfurled. Normally, Dennis would accelerate beyond the channel markers, but today he down-shifted into neutral and we stood facing the miniature boxes that dotted the horizon. Our stilt house had stood seventh from the right. We counted under our breath: one, two, three houses remained, all west of where ours had been. The house was gone. From a distance, the breach seemed neat and deliberate, as if God had plucked our stilt house from its stem. I could only imagine how violent the destruction had been, and ached to think of it as I'd ached to think of Margo being teased or scratched when she was a child. Warm, wet winds ricocheting through our kitchen, living room, bedrooms. Floors buckling and mirrors fracturing into shards.

Dennis brought down a palm on the console, sounding a hollow thud. "God-damn it," he said.

"Dad?" Margo started toward him, but he held out a hand.

"Sit down," he said. "We're moving." He shifted the boat into gear. I held on to my visor and turned away from Stiltsville, then watched the shore recede. To the east, the Cape Florida lighthouse stood at the tip of Key Biscayne, the sole structure on a beach darkened with debris. I imagined pieces of our stilt house stranded there — shutters or dock planks or even the hurricane tracking map that had hung in the kitchen, its little red and blue magnets scattered across the bay floor.

The boat slowed as we entered the channel. We passed one of the remaining stilt houses and waved to a man who stood on a ladder on the dock, boarding up a window. He raised one arm, a lonesome hello. Two other houses were missing dock planks and sections of roof. We passed slowly by, wayfarers through a ghost town.

Dennis had steered his way to that plot of watery land a thousand times. He could have done it blind. When he cut the engines, the boat drifted to a stop in front of four pilings that rose, slanting, from the water, no dock between them and no house behind. Dennis looped the bowline around a piling and I stood beside him at the starboard gunwale, staring into the sunlit water. I could see a few girders and joists embedded in the sand and some planks of wood, and that was about it.

Eighty yards east, where the Becks' house had stood, there was a dock but no house. To the west, our hermit neighbor's house had vanished entirely. My mind rested on the hermit: Where had he gone? Had someone entreated him inland? Dennis leaned over the gunwale and knocked on a piling. He turned to Margo. "Your grandfather built that house," he said. His voice shook. "These pilings are buried fifteen feet into the bedrock." He pushed against one and the boat carried us away, then jerked on its line.

When Margo was six, she'd sneaked down the stilt house stairs and slipped off the dock. Dennis had heard her cry out and jumped from the porch into the water, then swam frantically until she was in his arms. I wondered if she remembered. Once she was old enough to drive the boat, she'd spent time at the stilt house without Dennis and me; probably it was those days she remembered instead, friends and boys and sunshine. "I'm getting in the water," said Margo. She retrieved a snorkel and mask for herself and one of each for Dennis, but when she handed them over, he just put them down. I felt his sadness blanketing my own, and it was difficult to breathe.

"There's nothing to look at down there." To me, he said, "What's for lunch?"

"Egg salad sandwiches," I said.

"How do we know until we look?" said Margo. She stepped onto the bow and untied the drawstring of her shorts, then kicked the shorts to the deck. She stood in her turquoise two-piece, our colorful and curvaceous bowsprit, then stepped over the railing and dove into the water.

"You should go," I said to Dennis.

"I'm hungry."

"Me, too," said Stuart.

"Eat later," I said. "Go."

Margo swam beyond the pilings and over the scattered debris. Her snorkel branched into the air and her rump crested the surface; she kicked her pale heels. I handed Dennis the mask and he put it on and sat on the transom, the snorkel dangling.

"What are you waiting for?" I said.

He shrugged.

I thought of him teaching Margo to ski, to ride a bike. "Want me to push you?"

"Not really."

Stuart spoke up. "Want me to go with you?"

"Sure," Dennis said.

There was a mask for Stuart but no snorkel. The men sat side by side on the gunwale, then counted to three and pushed off. I opened a diet soda and watched them swim. Margo and Dennis kept their heads down as they kicked around, but Stuart kept righting himself to breathe. Once when he came up for air, he called out, "Frances."

I looked up. "What?"

He lifted a hand and waved. "Come in."

I shook my head.

"Why not?"

"I'm fixing lunch," I yelled, though I was finished.

"Spooky down here," he called, then lowered his face to the water. I didn't want to go in — someone needed to stay on the boat, near the life preservers — but I gleaned a certain satisfaction from the invitation. I lay on the gunwale, a boat fender my pillow. The sky was vast and blue, and the site felt lonely and remote. It was a treasure, this sense of isolation. How would we achieve it, if we didn't rebuild? Many of our friends had bought cabins in the Carolinas, but we didn't have the money for that, and it wasn't the same. Over the years, Grady and Gloria had used the house less and less, and rarely stayed overnight; the decision about what to do now would be up to us.

Dennis hauled himself onto the transom, arms shaking with exertion. I brought him a towel and we sat at the stern, eating halves of the same sandwich. "I think we should rebuild," I said.

He looked at me. "We've got ten percent of what we'd need here, at the most." He stared down the channel, toward the houses that remained. "Let's let it go. Can we let go?"

It would be only five years before our lease ran out, permanently, no matter what we did. And Dennis had never seemed so certain to me, or so weary, so I didn't argue. Margo and Stuart climbed aboard, and after we were done eating, we made our way back down the empty channel.

Stuart came downstairs one morning while I was drinking my coffee at the kitchen counter. He said, "Margo would sleep until noon if I let her," and I said, "Since she was a teenager." He filled a mug from the carafe and stirred in creamer. The spoon clinked against the sides of the mug. Dennis was in the backyard, shoveling my rose plants — dead, every one of them — into a wheelbarrow. When he bent at the waist, I could see the faint, ridged trail of his spinal column under his T-shirt. Come here, I wanted to say. I wanted to say it all the time, whenever he was more than a room's width away from me. Come here, sit down.

"Is Dennis OK?" said Stuart. "He seems tired."

"He is. We all are."

Stuart nodded. "The house on the water meant a lot to him. To you, too, I imagine."

"Memories," I said. I thought of telling him that when Margo was ten she'd spent an entire weekend lying in the stilt house hammock, reading *The Grapes of Wrath* from start to finish. Then, during a storm that had rattled the shutters and left foamy puddles on the porch, she'd written her book report at the kitchen table. Years later, she and Beverly had spent the afternoon slinging water balloons at a sailboat from the upstairs porch. You should have seen it, I wanted to say to Stuart, how the balloon punched the sail — *thwack* — leaving a wrinkle that filled with breeze, causing the boat to heel. You should have seen how the balloon slipped down the fabric and burst on the deck, and the captain hollered and the girls ducked into the house, leaving Dennis to gesture apologies. You should have been around a few years later, I wanted to tell him, when Margo and Dennis took up studying survival tactics. They'd quote to each other from camping manuals and field guides: *"You can tell a manta ray from two sharks swimming side by side because the ray's fins will submerge at the same time,"* she'd read to him. Then, he'd read to her. *"To survive one must overcome the need for comfort and maintain the will to live."* Once, she and Dennis had spent an entire evening on the stilt house porch discussing what to do when lost at sea, how to tell which fish are poisonous and how to catch and kill the ones that aren't, how to bail the boat and check the wind.

Oh, let her tell him, I thought.

The night before, in bed, Dennis had remarked that Stuart seemed more self-confident than most short men. The comment struck me as both sensitive and callous — Dennis was tall, and so it seemed indelicate of him to comment on another man's stature — and I wondered if Dennis was as good a sport as he seemed. We spoke regularly but obliquely of Stuart, the way we would come to speak of the hurricane: by listing each feature, struggling toward perspective. It continued to unsettle me that my daughter had become engaged to a man I'd never met. Did Margo not consider my opinion worth gathering? My mother had met Dennis during our courtship; I hadn't asked for her blessing, exactly, but I had given her the opportunity to speak her mind. I worried not only that Margo did not want to hear what I had to say on the subject, but that she simply didn't care. This wasn't Stuart's fault, of course, but it felt like it was.

Dennis took the wheelbarrow around the

side of the house, and when he returned it was empty. Stuart dumped the remainder of his coffee into the sink and went outside to help.

That night, we lay on top of the sheets, craving breeze, listening to the crickets call up through the window screens, and I remembered that there was something Dennis had forgotten to tell me. "That policeman," I said, "in the kitchen — what was that all about?"

He sat up and looked at the wall of our bedroom, where moonlight sliced by palm fronds interrupted the darkness. "Oh, Frances," he said. "The Kleins' oldest son — he's missing. No one's seen him since the day of the hurricane."

The Kleins lived in the house across the canal. We'd been invited to a barbecue when we'd first moved in, but had scarcely said more than a few words to them since. Every so often we were in our backyard while they were in theirs, and we all waved amicably to each other. Their youngest son was named Ezra, but I wasn't sure how old he was. Their oldest, Elijah, was at least eighteen, a few years younger than Margo. The night of the storm, Dennis explained, Ilena Klein had thought Elijah was at his father's office, where he'd been all day. When the telephones had stopped working, she'd assumed that both men were stuck there. David Klein had arrived home alone the next morning; he hadn't seen Elijah since the previous afternoon. "I didn't want to tell you," said Dennis. "I knew you'd be upset."

I had a distant memory of Elijah jet-skiing down the canal in Bermuda shorts, chubby around the middle like his father. The image dissolved. I would find that my mind wouldn't focus on Elijah. Instead, he teetered on the edge of my awareness like a slowing top.

We took long drives in the evenings, luxuriating in the car's air-conditioning and gawking at the devastation: homes stripped of walls and ceilings, lots stripped of homes. But Dennis's car — the junkier of our two — was running low on gas. We didn't want to harm mine by driving it through debris-filled streets, and lines at gas stations were a mile long, so we decided to siphon gasoline from my car into his. I stood shading my eyes from the sunlight while Dennis inserted one end of a garden hose into the fuel tank of my car, then took the other end between his lips. He drew a breath and made a face, then moved the hose to his car. A splash of fuel hit the ground. He spat and I handed him a glass of water. "Disgusting," he said, smiling.

Just then, a harsh and forgotten sound came from inside the house: The telephone! Civilization! The sight of land through desperate binoculars. We ran inside. Margo had the phone to her ear and was writing on the palm of her hand. She said good-bye and hung up.

"Who was it?" said Dennis.

"Penny Morales," said Margo.

"Who?" said Dennis.

"The woman selling that house in Coconut Grove." Margo and Stuart had decided to save money by not using an agent — his work paid well enough, but he was just starting out — and this had slowed the house-hunting process considerably, even before the hurricane. They'd called half a dozen home owners before the hurricane had brought down the phone lines. "She's going to open up for us on Friday," said Margo.

"We'll go with you," said Dennis, who was concerned about Margo's poker face. He wanted to knock on walls and declare them sound.

Margo yelled upstairs for Stuart. "What?" Stuart called.

"There's a house!"

"What?"

Oh, just go up there, I thought.

"A house!" she called again.

Stuart's steps on the stairs rattled through the kitchen, and he appeared. "Was that the phone?" he said.

"It was that woman from Battersea Road," said Margo.

He took her in his arms. "Which one was that?"

"The two-bedroom we saw in the paper."

He swiveled her and she dipped. I looked away. "Excellent," said Stuart. To Dennis, he said, "No offense, but we're ready for some solo time."

"So are we," I said. I hadn't intended to say it. Margo and Stuart righted themselves and stepped away from each other. I turned to the sink and opened the faucet, then busied myself washing dishes. Margo and Stuart left the room, and Dennis put his hands on my shoulders. He reached over me to turn off the faucet.

"All right," he said. "You have to be nicer."

"She's my daughter," I said, thinking: I want someone different for her. Someone taller, smarter, richer, more handsome. Things I never would ask for myself, I want for her.

Dennis turned me to face him. "This isn't

like you," he said. "You're generous."

"I feel stingy."

"None of it will matter. They'll stay together or they won't."

"You think they'll break up?"

"Who knows? Either way, you'll want to know you were fair."

Dennis was so reasonable, so conscientious. "I'm trying," I said.

"No, you aren't," he said. "You are not trying."

We set out on foot — this was Stuart's idea — to meet Penny Morales at her home. We carried mosquito repellent and bottles of water, and upon arrival received a delightful surprise: electricity, that elusive and munificent commodity, had returned to a several-block radius in Coconut Grove, including 4044 Battersea Road. We stood in the living room as the sweat dried on our skin, grinning. Dennis had given Margo and Stuart a little lecture about keeping their opinions to themselves in the presence of the seller, so we did not speak, but I'm sure our faces gave us away: the place was great. An oasis.

It was not, beyond the chill in the air, a remarkable house. The kitchen lacked counter space, there was no room for entertaining, and the closets were small — but the bedrooms were large and the ceilings high. Margo and I walked through the back den, which was flanked on two sides by sliding glass doors, and I saw a shadow of anxiety cross her face — surely she could not choose a house without evaluating its safety, even in a good neighborhood like this one. But then the look was replaced by determination, and she led me away, toward the dining room. There, our attention went immediately to the floor: glossy dark green tiles patterned randomly with dime-size black shapes. Margo checked over her shoulder for Penny Morales. "I love this floor," she whispered.

I nodded. I loved it, too.

Stuart came in. "What in heaven's name?" he said, staring down.

"You don't like it?" whispered Margo.

"It looks like squashed bugs."

"I think it's elegant," she said, and he looked down, reassessing.

Dennis joined us. "She's out front," he said in a low voice. It was great fun, this conspiring. "We have a few minutes."

"How did you get her to leave us alone?" said Margo.

"I asked her to," said Dennis.

In the kitchen, Margo opened all the cupboards and I watched her, imagining the dinners they would prepare there, stir-fries and omelets and shish kebob: newlywed food, no recipes required. Before we'd added an addition, our first house had looked much like this one, with its particleboard cabinets and cheap windows. We'd supplied charm in small doses, with area rugs and fresh paint.

Stuart opened the sink faucet and out ran a steady stream. He'd told Dennis he knew a lot about commercial real estate, but next to nothing about residential. "What should we be looking for?" he said.

"Well," said Dennis. He walked to the refrigerator, opened and closed it, then spoke in a hushed voice. "It's no bigger than the houses around it — in fact, it's a little smaller. That's a good thing. You see why?"

"Resale," said Stuart.

"Right," said Dennis. "The wiring's been updated. The water pressure's good. We'll check the water heater and hire an inspector. I'd like to see what happens after a heavy rain."

"What about a hurricane?" I said.

"Good point." He lowered his voice. "Otherwise," he said to Stuart, "there's no telling what will happen until you move in."

"Honey?" said Stuart. Margo looked at him and they seemed to communicate:

What do you think? I like it. Do you? I like it, too.

"I think this is our new house!" said Margo loudly, and Stuart rushed over to cover her mouth with his hand.

We were bystanders, Dennis and I. Within the year, Stuart would help Dennis plant our new rose garden and fix the flashing on the roof and — this took my breath away — drive the boat, navigate the bay. They would camp in the Everglades, something we hadn't done since Margo was a child, and boat down to the Keys to go fishing. I wonder now if Dennis looked forward to the relationship he would form with this boy, this new incarnation of fatherhood. And I wonder if he was relieved to welcome another man into our lives, someone to whom he might entrust responsibilities. In many ways, they were alike, he and Stuart. They were both curious and unselfconscious and sometimes serious; they both itched with activity. But of the four of us, Dennis and I were the romantic ones. Despite the hasty wedding, Margo and Stuart were more sensible than we'd ever been. One wishes a million things for one's child, and many wishes are not realized. For Margo, I wished for a man who made magic from ordinary life. Maybe Stuart could have been that man, but Margo — my own daughter, unlike me in as many ways as she was my twin — preferred hard reality to magic.

Dennis and Stuart walked out of the kitchen toward the garage — and as they went, it seemed to me that Dennis's left foot dragged for a step or two. But in the next moment, the next step, I thought I must have imagined it. Margo was at the oven, turning on each burner to test the flame. "We'll have an alarm installed," she said, nodding to herself. "We'll get the best one there is."

"It's a good neighborhood," I said, but I could see that this was not reassuring. The Williamsburg Village Apartments had been in a good neighborhood. I knew that she believed that in our home she was safe, and really nowhere else.

"Mom?" she said.

"Yes?" I went to the window, where I could watch the men walk to the garage.

"I'm happy."

I turned toward her. What she wanted to say — I knew it even then — was that she was sorry for keeping her romance with Stuart a secret, for shutting me out of her life and wrenching me back into it, for always doing everything her own way. A flame of irritation rose inside me, and I knew it was Margo — not Stuart — I resented for the secrecy and the bombshell, for rushing me into accepting this next stage of her life. "Then I am, too," I said.

I excused myself and left the house, and the heat hit me like a cobweb in the face. I wanted to return to the air-conditioning, but I'd been spotted by Penny Morales, who stood on the lawn in a jogging suit, smoking a cigarette. She wore a heavy gold-twist necklace and several rings. She had a sharp patrician nose and high cheekbones and smooth tan skin, and though I thought she wore too much eye makeup, her face was beautiful. She spoke with a heavy Cuban accent. "What do you think?" she said. "Good enough for your daughter?"

"Maybe."

"I hate to leave it. Divorce."

"I'm sorry."

She motioned inside with her cigarette. "They're newlyweds," she said. "I can tell. Something is wrong with me — I see a happy couple and I want to tell them to enjoy it while it lasts." She looked at me. "You probably think I'm a monster."

"Not at all." Actually, I'd been wondering what she must have thought of us. I'd met several Cuban ladies at the YMCA, and in their presence I always felt mild-mannered and drab. Miami was more than half Cuban at this point, and yet I could count the Cuban couples in our social circle on one hand.

Dennis emerged from the garage and Stuart and Margo followed. We told Penny Morales we would be in touch, then started walking. Soon the blue dim of evening settled. We followed a winding trail through piled debris. There was citronella in the air, which reminded me that inside the dark houses, whole families lived and breathed, impatient for a time when they could close their windows against the heat. We approached our neighborhood from the south side of the canal, intending to cross the bridge and circle back to the house, but then a ways off we saw that a house on the street behind ours was brightly lighted. When we got closer, we saw that it was the Kleins'. Light spilled from every window onto the lawn, just short of the sidewalk. The sight was as striking in the darkness as a lighthouse seen from the sea. A rapid-cycling motor rumbled from the side yard: generators. They must have spent a fortune.

Through the windows we could see a number of people — detectives, probably, plus some family and friends — milling about in what appeared to be the Kleins' living room. Ilena Klein sat in an armchair, staring up at a man in a suit who had his hands in his pockets. I couldn't see his face, but I could tell he was speaking. She lifted a hand to touch her hair, then returned it to her lap. Whatever the man said — an update on the search, perhaps — appeared not to make much difference. The man walked out of the room and Ilena Klein turned to the window. I feared she would see us standing there, but we were cloaked by the night.

"Frances?" Stuart's voice came out of the darkness behind me. I turned. Stuart stood with his hand under Dennis's arm as Dennis crouched on the sidewalk on one knee.

"Did you fall?" I said. "Are you OK?"

Dennis opened his mouth. He looked at me but didn't speak. His eyes were bright and fearful, but his face was blank.

"Oh, my God," I said.

"Something is wrong," he said.

"What is it?" I said, but he just stared at me, his blue eyes. "OK," I said. I helped him stand. "We'll get a doctor. You'll be fine."

"Should I call an ambulance?" said Margo.

"No," said Dennis.

"It'll be quicker if we drive ourselves," said

397

Stuart. I nodded, thinking: ambulance? hospital?

We clustered around Dennis and started to walk, and before we turned the corner I looked over my shoulder at the Kleins', and I understood that my life was going to change. It was terrifying, that knowledge. I have wondered, in rare, metaphysically inclined moments, if misfortune might be contagious. Perhaps the Kleins' misfortune overwhelmed their house and spilled out with the light. Perhaps it stole across the canal to my doorstep.

Stuart knocked on our bedroom door a few mornings later. Dennis and I were awake but still in bed. Sunlight saturated the room. Dennis's hand was on my stomach, his thumb stroking my skin. I find that the lens of memory focuses on him, regardless of what held my attention at the time, the heat or hot flashes or miscellany. "Swimsuits and towels!" called Stuart through the door. "Sunscreen and snorkels!"

The state of Florida had notified us by mail that it would send a demolition crew to raze the stilt house remains — at our expense, of course. We could have fought the decision, but we didn't. We were adjusting our bearings. It was Stuart's idea to have a last look around. "You need closure, Frannie," he'd said to me. He was the only one who had ever called me Frannie, and I'd found I didn't much mind it. "We'll just throw anchor and say toodle-oo, old house."

Again we coasted past the herons on the retaining walls, and Dennis steered through the bay to our spot of land. Stuart stepped over the boat railing and clambered onto the flat top of a piling. He sat there, balancing. "You brought the camera?" he said to me. I nodded. To Dennis, he said, "Back up a bit, would you? I want to see how it feels."

Dennis shifted into reverse and we drifted away, leaving Stuart to perch over the water. I snapped photos as Stuart posed, arms and legs spread. Dennis cut the engines and stood beside me. He leaned close. "Should we leave him?" he said.

"Yes," I whispered, but the bile was gone.

Stuart tried to stand but lost his balance and sat down again. "Don't fall," called Margo, and Stuart blew her a kiss.

Dennis started the engines and put the boat into gear. When we reached the pilings, Stuart gestured to Dennis. "Your turn," he said, stepping onto the boat. "It's surreal."

"Take the wheel," said Dennis. Dennis stepped onto the gunwale, using the rail for balance, and my heart seized. I wanted to stop him — what if he fell again? — but I did not. He climbed awkwardly onto the piling and shifted until he was facing us, then sat still with his hands on his knees, his shoulders slumped. I saw the shadow of the boy he'd once been flash across his features, then disappear. Stuart put the engines into reverse, and Dennis, unmoving, grew small.

"What did it feel like?" I said to Stuart.

"Scary," he said. "Lonely."

The doctor at the emergency room had referred Dennis to an internist, who'd referred him to a neurologist. We'd scheduled an appointment but it was weeks away. I now think of this period as stolen time, time to which we were not entitled and which we did not appreciate: an interlude. In the interlude, Elijah Klein's body was found. He'd gone out on the bay with friends, and they'd run out of gas and capsized when the storm hit. The entire crew had drowned. Elijah had been invited at the last minute, apparently, and initially hadn't been counted among the fatalities. I could not conceive how Ilena Klein would survive, how she would not simply stop breathing.

Also in the interlude, the National Guard

left south Florida, the electricity returned, and Margo and Stuart secured a mortgage to buy the house on Battersea Road. They used money my father had left Margo as a down payment, and on the day they closed we brought over champagne and cleaning supplies.

I searched through old photographs to show Stuart the stilt house — but in our photos, there is only a dock under Margo's feet, a railing behind Dennis's arm, a doorway framing my face. There was no photo of the house the way I remember it: from a distance, wholly intact. I did not understand, taking those pictures, that history must be collected while the subject exists. If not, what goes unrecorded can fill an ocean.

I do remember, though, the night of hurricane Andrew. Margo and Stuart stayed upstairs in her bedroom and I sat in the living room, watching the local weatherman's updates on a battery-operated television. It was late and the house was dark. Dennis stood at the French doors, staring out at the backyard and the boat bobbing on the canal. I wasn't concerned about the boat — if it was damaged in the storm, we would have it fixed; if it tore loose, we would find it, or we would figure out a way to buy another one. I was concerned, though, that debris would strike the glass door and it would shatter, with Dennis standing close enough to see his breath on the glass. "Dennis, please," I said. "We should be near walls." Still, I went to stand with him. Between flashes of lightning, the sky was purple-black and inky, more substantive than air and water and wind, as if the storm were its own form of matter. The melaleucas in the backyard bowed, nearing the ground and lifting, bending again. Leaves and twigs swept across the lawn, licking the surface of the swimming pool. A tree branch raced by, and there was a sudden, throaty crack of lightning. I saw the jagged light to the south, but the target — tree or house or other object — was concealed. In quieter moments, the wind relented and the trees righted themselves and the canal stilled. I hoped in these moments that the storm would ease, but then the water rose and lapped the pier again, the wavelets like little soldiers approaching battle on their bellies, and the wind returned, more furious than before.

One moment was quieter and lasted longer than the others. Dennis loosened his grip on me and went to check the news report. The eye of the hurricane — a black center on the radar screen, encircled by speedy strokes of red storm — had found our house. The yard and canal were still; not the stillness of a clear day, but that of a room with no windows, that of a bubble of air trapped underwater.

I knew that when the storm started again, it would be instantaneous, a dropped curtain. Dennis stood several feet away, his eyes on the television, and the promise that he would return to my side tethered us like a mooring line. I felt a calm anticipation, a sensation I recalled from when Margo was an infant, from late nights when she finally fell asleep. The storm would return, but for now the world was quiet. Dennis was not beside me but he was nearby, and this fact filled me with relief so intense that, as the wind started again in the trees, it welled inside me and spilled over, and I cried out for him.

1993

On the afternoon of my fiftieth birthday, I thought I saw my sister-in-law under the bougainvillea behind the back deck of our house. I was standing at the kitchen sink, watching the canal — the water reflected the sunlight in spots, as if revealing coins scattered just under the surface — and there Bette appeared on the edge of my vision, near the fence that separated our yard from Mr. Costakis's, wearing a lavender caftan I'd seen her wear a hundred times. I dropped the bowl I was washing — it cracked open against the porcelain sink — and ran to the kitchen door, which was locked from the inside. I turned the key, but it was rusted and stubborn. I jiggled it and cursed. Finally I was able to open the door and step onto the deck, but by the time I reached the railing — I believe I was going to leap over it the way someone half my age would — she was gone. Good Lord, I thought. My throat tightened. Oh, Bette, we need you back here.

I heard steps on the deck and turned, expecting Margo, home from the grocery store — but instead it was Marse, carrying two champagne flutes and wearing a satiny taupe pants suit with an ALS pin on the lapel. She'd worn the pin, as far as I could tell, every day since she'd acquired it at a benefit we'd both attended. Mine was in a drawer. She handed me a flute, saying, "I busted out the bubbly."

"Margo and Stuart went out for cream cheese. I couldn't finish the cake without it. I don't know what happened — I thought —" And then I stopped talking, because without meaning to I'd turned and faced the spot along the fence line where I'd thought I saw Bette. I knew what had happened: I'd been at the sink thinking, for no reason that I could fathom, about one afternoon in 1987 when I'd visited Bette at her old house in Coconut Grove, shortly after she'd bought it. I'd brought a painting her mother had given me to deliver, of a girl in a yellow pinafore holding a dog on her lap — the painting was of Bette, and Gloria thought Bette would treasure it, though when I handed it to her she held it at arm's length for a moment before sliding it into a hallway closet. "Did I really look like that?" she'd said, wrinkling her nose. She'd led me to the overgrown backyard, where we stood on the creaky deck and listened to the bufo toads as they skulked among the roots of the wart ferns. The backyard was a small plot of overgrown alamandas and firecracker ferns, fertile-smelling and closed in, and even from the porch I could not see through the thick branches of a mango tree to the neighbors' house. "I'm living in the wild," she'd said. "I'm an aborigine." She was the happiest I'd ever seen her, standing on that rotting porch in her lavender housedress. And in my kitchen, two years after she'd sold that house and moved across the country, my memory and my vision had crossed over, and there she had been again, in the backyard of the house where she'd grown up. "Fifty years old," I said to Marse. "Is that even possible?"

She put an arm around me. "We will be strong," she said. I noted that she wasn't making fun of me. This was remarkable for my friend, in whom my sentimentality usually inspired well-meaning jabs about self-pity. "You're going to love my gift," she said.

Together we walked inside and into the living room, where Dennis sat in his wheelchair, facing the makeshift entertainment system we'd assembled when he could no longer stand for long periods. On the marble living room floor, scattered around Dennis's wheelchair, were a dozen cases, some closed and some open with the CDs visible. Dennis said, "I'm almost done here." In the eight months since he had been diagnosed, he'd lost much of his ability to enunciate. His words ran together, elongating the vowels.

"OK," I said, looking down at the mess.

"Don't worry, I'll clean," he said. He laughed his watery, thick-tongued laugh.

The doorbell rang. Marse went to get it and came back with Gloria and Grady, who in the past months had taken to knocking. This habit — knocking before entering — was something I had wanted them to do for twenty years, but only when it was inconvenient (the physical therapist, whose name was Lola, was often working with Dennis when they rang, and I wasn't always home) did they adopt the habit. "Frances, the house looks lovely," said Gloria as she stepped down the ramp that led from the hallway to the living room — when we'd installed them, Dennis had compared the house to an Escher drawing, saying that all the ramps went in both directions, which of course wasn't true but seemed true: it was as if our two-story home, with all its steps down and up, had been suddenly transformed into one tilting story. We hardly used the upstairs anymore. Gloria had brought a casserole, which Marse shuttled to the kitchen. When I'd met her, Gloria had made large, colorful salads and tender pot roasts and pans full of stuffed shells. But since they'd moved to the condo, she had abandoned all culinary efforts, which I thought was her right. Still, she appeared to think it was inexcusable to arrive anywhere empty-handed, which made for creative offerings — this casserole, I guessed, had probably been in the freezer for months, since Grady's gallbladder surgery.

Gloria was wearing a pink bouclé suit and an ALS pin like Marse's, acquired on the same day at the same place. I thought maybe I saw my lack of a pin register in her eyes, but she was too smooth to be caught in judgment. He was my husband, after all — what did I need a pin for?

Grady passed us to greet Dennis. He bent at the waist and embraced Dennis's shoulders, and Dennis's right arm came up, the fingers crooked into a half-grip, and lay across his father's back. "My boy," said Grady, and then Dennis said something I didn't catch, and Grady laughed. They started to collect the CD cases and put them back on their low shelf.

"What can I do?" said Gloria.

"Margo and Stuart went for cream cheese, for the cake," I said.

"You baked your own cake?"

"I did," I said. I hadn't realized that I wanted one until that afternoon, so I'd run out for the ingredients before showering, but I'd forgotten the cream cheese. "It's carrot cake. It collapsed a little, but I don't care."

"Did you get candles?" said Grady.

"Fifty candles?" I said. "No, I didn't."

"We've got to have candles," he said, then left for the kitchen, touching Dennis's back as he went.

Marse told me to take Dennis outside. "It's your party," she said. "Have a drink."

But Dennis wanted to change his shirt, so I wheeled him up the ramp into the hallway, then down the hall into the guest room, where we had both taken to sleeping at night, he in a low cot and me in a single bed. (Yes, I missed having my husband in bed with me, and every night I curled up against him for an hour or so before moving to my own bed, because I knew neither of us would be comfortable all night in the tiny cot. And he needed his rest, now more than ever.) I held up three shirts for him; he pointed to the one on my far left. I knelt to help him pull his T-shirt over his head, and though I kept my hand at the cuff, it was really he who did the lifting and pulling. When it was off, he dropped it on the floor, and I kicked it toward the hamper. I handed him the fresh shirt — a white linen button-down — and knelt to help him free his hands from the sleeves and button the buttons. "You," he said. The sound he made was much like the speech of a deaf person, but also had a tone to it that was exactly the same as it always had been. It was this similarity I clung to. "You," he said again, softly. I sat at his feet, my hands in his lap. I could smell the soapy smell of his skin — he was still bathing himself, albeit with some help into and out of the tub, though before long he would need someone there the whole time, and surprisingly, more often than not that person would be Stuart. "You are fifty," he said.

I smiled and brought his hand to my lips. "Isn't it ridiculous?" I said. "It's not what I thought it would be."

He made a jerking gesture with his head. "Under the bed," he said, and I crawled awkwardly in my skirt until I could reach under his cot, where there was a small box wrapped in red paper, encircled by a white ribbon.

"Can I open it?" I said, and he nodded.

At Christmas, before the wheelchair, Dennis and I had gone to Italy. We'd spent three days in Rome, two days in Venice, a week in Florence, and two days in Milan, where we'd seen Pavarotti sing in *Aida* at La Scala. (Marse's firm had acquired tickets somehow, and she'd given them to us.) Near the end of the first act, during the "triumph" scene, I'd looked over at Dennis and was startled to find him staring straight ahead and sobbing quietly, tears rolling slowly down his cheeks. He saw me watching him and wiped his face. After another moment, he'd stopped, and we didn't speak of it. Later that month, we'd gone to Grady and Gloria's church to see her sing in the choir, and during one of the hymns Dennis again started to cry. We didn't know, then, that his disease and these uncharacteristic displays were connected. Dennis was moved by *Aida,* but he wouldn't usually be brought to tears by it. For that, we had the disease to thank. Shortly afterward, Dennis's doctor prescribed antidepressants for a condition called *pseudobulbar affect* — which until the moment the doctor said it was a term I'd never heard.

In the guest room, when I tore open the red wrapping paper, I found a three-CD set of Pavarotti singing Radames, and it was my turn to cry. I knew why Dennis had chosen this gift. The night we'd come home from La Scala, we'd lain in bed in the hotel room discussing the opera — his voice was just starting to weaken then — and he'd said that his favorite piece was "Celeste Aida," because it reminded him of me.

"So 'Celeste Aida' is for me?" I'd said to him.

He'd looked at me. "All the songs are for you," he'd said. And on the card that came with my birthday gift, there was only one shaky line: *All the songs are for you.*

The diagnosis had come after a series of tests, most of which were designed to rule out lesser, more treatable afflictions: ALS was left over after the MRI, the spinal tap, and the threading of Dennis's largest leg muscles with an electrode wire. His muscles had weakened; we'd known this going in, before we were even referred to the neurologist, Dr. Auerbach. We knew he'd lost weight — his spine was more prominent, his knees were bonier. We knew he'd had trouble every so often coordinating simple movements, like taking a step or standing up from a chair. I'd thought: Marcus Beck had Parkinson's. I can live with Parkinson's, no problem. We'll have a dozen years or more. We might have had only that long anyway. And I thought: if it's MS, that's OK, we can handle it, I can keep Dennis from becoming tired or overstressed.

But after each test, as the evidence for ALS mounted, my mind became blank. I'd never known anyone with this disease; I didn't know anything about it. Was it genetic or acquired? Was it curable or treatable? Would it kill him, and if so, when?

We liked Dr. Auerbach. He was a very tall man with curly white hair. He had pink, vein-lined cheeks and soft hands that were small for his frame. He referred to his nurses as Miss Diane and Miss Sara, which made me think he was southern, though he didn't speak with an accent. In his office were photographs he'd taken in Thailand, Tibet, and Vietnam, all framed with white matting and a little signature, his own name in sloppy cursive, in each bottom right-hand corner. When he gave us the prognosis — ALS moves steadily, either fast or slowly, depending on the person, but it doesn't speed up and it doesn't slow down, and Dennis's case was unfortunately moving fast — he sat on the edge of his desk and put his hand on Dennis's shoulder. He offered a referral in case we wanted a second opinion, but Dennis said no, he didn't need a second opinion, thank you. "Dennis," said Dr. Auerbach, "ALS attacks the muscles, the body. It usually doesn't take from the mind or the spirit."

In the car on the way home, I said, "I want a second opinion."

Dennis put his hand on mine, then took it away to change lanes. "If you think it's necessary," he said.

"What if —" I said, but then I stopped. I didn't doubt the diagnosis, really. What I doubted was the prognosis: two to four years at the most, Dr. Auerbach had said. This stunned me. Three years before, Bette had still lived in Miami, Margo hadn't been married, the stilt house hadn't been destroyed. In the doctor's office, when this news had been delivered, Dennis had said, "We'll shoot for five, then, won't we, baby?" and when he turned toward me he looked almost eager, like he'd found a great big project he was itching to tackle.

I washed my face and applied lipstick while Margo finished the frosting, and when we went outside, Marse was there with a video camera, recording us as I rolled Dennis onto the porch. "Where did you get that?" I said to her. I'm afraid I sounded a little irritable. I touched my hair. I felt about having video cameras around the way I felt about having strangers around — self-conscious and defensive.

"This?" Marse said, then without answering turned it on Margo and Stuart, who were standing together against the deck's railing, her in his arms. It was always a little surprising to notice that she was taller than he, though only by a touch. They waved at the camera and Stuart kissed Margo's cheek.

The food was already set out, so I wheeled Dennis into place and sat next to him. Marse sat on his other side, and Grady and Gloria sat next to her. Stuart sat beside me and passed the sweet potato casserole I'd made early that morning, before sunrise. It had been quiet and still in the kitchen. I'd put the casserole in the oven just as a sliver of sunlight had started to spread across the canal, like a door opening onto a darkened room. I loved living in the big house. I loved the thicket of bougainvillea between us and our neighbors, and the gentle slope of the lawn leading down to the canal, and the ferns along the gravel driveway that Grady and Gloria had never bothered to pave. I loved the memories — ones I had and ones I couldn't possibly have, of what had come before us, when Grady and Gloria slept in our bedroom. I loved the telephone nook in the den and the breakfast nook in the kitchen and the sun-bleached wooden deck, where Dennis and I spent an hour almost every evening.

Grady was talking about the time he and the family had run across a corpse in Biscayne Bay. It was an old story, but Stuart had never heard it, so Grady was animated and bug-eyed as he spoke. "Mercy!" he was saying. "We thought it was just a bit of detritus, something that had snagged a piece of fabric."

"It was clearly fabric," said Gloria. "It had that shine of fabric in water."

"Exactly," said Grady. "So we idled up to it and I cut the engine, and when our wake hit it, it turned a bit in the water" — he made a gesture with both hands, like rolling a log — "and there was his eye looking straight up out of the water, this blue face."

"Blue?" said Stuart.

"Black and blue," said Gloria. She waved her hand around her face. "Beaten. It was horrible."

Grady said, "Gloria covered the kids' eyes, but they saw — we all saw."

"I lost my cool, you might say," said Gloria. "Here you are, in your boat, with your family, on a Sunday afternoon —"

"And suddenly —" said Grady.

"And suddenly you're faced with this gruesome thing, this *news story*." She shook her head. "We're used to it now, but Miami was still just a small town then. The drugs were small potatoes, and the mob was a country away, in New York."

"Obviously not," said Stuart.

"No, that's right, obviously not. It was like the end of innocence, that day. That was the year that both these lots were built up." She pointed on either side of the house. "And that was the year they built the expressway."

"My grandparents left Florida," said Stuart. "Then my parents left."

"Everyone left," said Grady.

"You didn't," said Stuart.

Grady shook his head. "This is my home. This is where I was raised. This is where I raised my family."

I didn't know I was going to speak before I spoke. "Lots of people leave their homes," I said. "I left mine." It felt strange to put it that way, strange to recall that there had been a time when Georgia was my home, and Miami had been just another distant city where I'd never been. Over the years, every time my mother had visited, usually in the winter months for a week at a time, she'd commented on the transition I'd made. "Miami suits you," she would say. "Too harum-scarum for me, but it suits you."

Grady looked at me. "Sure, but where would I go? Where could I dock my boat behind my house year-round? Where could I fit in a round of golf after getting off work?"

"True," said Stuart.

We were quiet for a moment, and then Marse started talking about a man she'd met, a man who owned a chain of car washes, but I had trouble paying attention. Beside me, Dennis was taking long, slow bites, as carefully as a child who didn't want to spill.

After clearing the table, we opened gifts in the living room. I sat cross-legged at Dennis's feet. Dennis's family were gift-givers and always had been, no matter how trivial the occasion. Gloria had once brought me a ceramic garden toad when I'd been promoted at work. They kept the gifts simple, at least, and I suspected that Gloria had a place where she kept a stockpile of possibilities to pull from when events (or semi-events, like Valentine's Day, which Dennis and I had never celebrated) came up. This was a practical birthday, it seemed from the start. Margo and Stuart gave me a new Speedo swimsuit, a swim cap, and a pass to her health club, where I was signed up to take water aerobics once a week for two months. I wondered, meanly, if this was a hint about my weight — if I'd gained, I hadn't noticed — and I kept myself from mentioning that there was a pool in my backyard. (I'm glad I stayed quiet, because I realized later that Margo had become fond of her water aerobics classes, and meant for us to take the classes together, even though to me they seemed like an older person's exercise.) Gloria and Grady gave me a gardening service to come twice a week and water my roses. This was a generous and helpful gift, as watering the roses — Dennis had given them to me for our anniversary, to replace the ones we'd lost in Andrew — was a huge chore that Dennis and I had once shared. I was less and less available for chores that took me away from Dennis. I had been neglecting the roses — Gloria had noticed, surely — and so this was a small weight off my shoulders.

Marse saved her gift for last. She handed me a large pink envelope. "You can't take it back," she said. In the envelope was a gift card from a local catering service — I knew the name from weddings and other events, and knew that this caterer was not only good but considered the best in certain circles. Inside the card was a sheet of office paper with my gift typed in black lettering: two meals a day, six days a week (no delivery on Sundays), for six weeks. Marse patted Dennis's knee after I finished reading. "I told them soft food," she said. "They said that was no problem. Pumpkin ravioli, chicken casserole, things like that. It's all set up."

"How helpful," I said. I tried to sound appreciative, but I was suddenly sad about something I couldn't quite name, possibly the delegation of one of my principal wifely duties. I folded the paper and put it back in the envelope. "Does everyone want carrot cake?"

Marse followed me into the kitchen to help clean up. "You didn't say anything about Paul," she said.

"What?" I turned off the water and dried my hands. It was starting to rain. This was what happened in the summers in the subtropics: it was beautiful, clear, and sunny until mid-afternoon, then rained heavily for an hour, then the clouds cleared and the sun came out again. I loved this and always had.

"I thought maybe you'd have some words on the subject," she said.

She was standing with her hand on her hip, wearing one of my aprons, a red checkered one I'd had since moving to Miami. It was too short on her. I looked at her, trying to recall the conversation from earlier. Marse didn't often ask me to pay attention to her love life. Maybe I was out of practice. "Should I?" I said.

"He told me you might not think very highly of him," she said, and that was when I realized that she was speaking about Paul of years past, Dennis's old friend whom she'd briefly dated. Once again, Miami's close boundaries, its intimate circles, flared. In twenty-five years, I'd come to understand that people bounced around their social stratum like pinballs, knocking into one another.

"I thought he owned a nursery," I said.

"He did, but now he owns that car wash chain, with the big one on Dixie."

"With the purple sign?"

"Yep."

"Is there money in washing cars?"

"Apparently. He owns a condo on Fisher Island."

421

I often passed the car wash on my way downtown; there were always dozens of black and Latino boys in purple shirts and black pants dashing to and fro with chamois in their hands, each attending to one part of a hulking SUV. "You like him?" I said, but I said it nicely.

"Very much."

"Bring him over. We'll have a meal. It will be good to catch up." Since Dennis had started to lose his voice, we hadn't entertained anyone but family. But once upon a time Paul and Dennis had been good friends.

"We'll do that." She had a look in her eye I hadn't seen, or had seen only once: she was smitten. I'd been too wrapped up to notice.

"How long has it been?" I said.

"About two months."

"And?"

"And it's good."

"This," I said, "is wonderful news."

That night, Dennis read and I lay in my bed, fidgeting, unable to relax. We'd put his bed next to a wall and lined it with pillows so he could hoist himself up and turn on a lamp when he wanted to read. The light barely reached me on the other side of the room. "Dennis," I said. He put down his book. "Did you realize that the man Marse is seeing is Paul whatshisname?"

He made a sound like a snort and said, "Yep. I say good for her. Nice guy."

Years earlier, after its edges had dulled in my memory, I'd told Dennis what had happened between me and Paul. I'd gotten the feeling he didn't entirely believe me, or believe my interpretation — Dennis would have a hard time believing that a friend would ever make a pass at his wife — and I suppose his reaction had rubbed off on me, and I didn't entirely believe myself anymore. "Would it be awful to have them over?" I said.

"Why awful?"

"I don't know. Do you feel up to it?"

"Do you?"

"Good point."

"Paul is a grown-up. We all are, especially you."

I laughed at his joke. Dennis had teased me about my age on every birthday since we'd met. " 'Don't worry,' you say," I said. "It's like saying, 'Stop breathing.' "

"I know," he said softly, and the sounds slurred together. I missed his clear, strong voice. When I lay beside him that night after turning off the light, I put my ear to his chest and listened to the steady rhythm of his hard-beating heart. Then I pulled myself away from him, and went back to my own bed.

Before the wheelchair, there had been a walker. It was black with hand brakes and a leather shelf where Dennis could sit if he ended up stopping somewhere — in line at the grocery, or in the foyer when someone came by. Standing for long periods and sitting in a regular chair had become difficult, and so he was faster, really, with the walker than he was without it. It lasted almost six months, but then one afternoon I came into the kitchen to find him on the floor, using a kitchen cabinet to hoist himself up, his legs splayed out behind him on the tile. I helped him into a chair. When he was rested, he was able to stand with his right leg, and he used the walker to leave the room to go and lie down; but the following week at our appointment, Dr. Auerbach said it was time. "Better now than after you break a hip," he'd said. When the wheelchair was delivered, Dennis had watched from the front porch as the driver unloaded it. "Once I go in, I don't come out," he'd said to me. It sat unused in the foyer for another week, but after that it became indispensable. The walker went into the guest room closet.

Dennis surrendered to the wheelchair seven months after his diagnosis, and it was around the same time that he tendered his resignation from the firm where he'd practiced, happily, for a dozen years, and agreed to work on a for-hire basis. At first, he worked from home two or three full days per week, but as his voice weakened, he worked less, and then not at all, and then we were living off our savings and my meager salary from the medical practice where I worked, trying to stall retirement as long as we could. Out of kindness or loyalty, Dennis's firm kept him on the books and continued to pay his health insurance.

Before the wheelchair, when we knew that it was coming but didn't know when, Dennis decided I needed to learn to drive the boat. "It's for our sanity," he said. "I should have taught you years ago." When he was at the helm, he had to stand for long periods at the console, braced against the waves, while Margo and I sat at the stern in cushioned captain's chairs. I realized that he feared if I didn't learn to captain, if he didn't teach me immediately, he might never get out on the water again.

We went out one Sunday morning. We'd invited Marse but she had plans, so it was just me and Dennis. The lesson started as soon as we climbed into the boat. Everything he did was familiar, but I couldn't have replicated it alone, even after watching him do it a thousand times: he taught me to lower the engines into the water, to check the fuel level of the starboard and port tanks, then check the oil level. Then he walked me through starting the engine in neutral and dropping the lines and reversing out of the slip slowly, facing behind me so I could see any boats that were headed our way down the canal. Once I'd backed up, I put the engines into neutral before putting them into forward, and headed slowly down the canal, pushing tentatively against the heavy knob of the throttle.

It was a different view from the helm. Driving the boat gave me less leisure than usual to stare into the backyards of our neighbors. The Kleins had moved away a year earlier, and a former Argentine Olympic swimmer had bought the house and added a sprawling coral rock patio and an enormous swimming pool; sometimes when he swam, I watched him from my back deck, entranced by his powerful flip turns. As I drove — considerably slower than Dennis would have done, though any wake at all was not allowed in the canal — I sneaked sideways peeks out of habit, and near the mouth of the canal, in the backyard of an imposing Grecian-style house with two stone lion statues bookending the back steps, I saw a couple entwined on a blanket. As we passed, they stopped kissing long enough to look up at us, and I waved and they waved back. I looked again before increasing speed, and they had returned to kissing. Briefly, I wondered if they were the man and woman of the house, or if someone was cheating. Surely two married people don't make out half naked in the backyard of their own home?

Dennis stood briefly to point out the channel markers I should follow — we were headed to Key Biscayne, to stop at Sunday's on the Bay for a sandwich so I could practice docking in a tight spot (Sunday's was always crowded, and in my opinion a terrible place to practice, but Dennis was determined) — and then he sat down again. I stood alone at the helm, watching the span of the blue water, scanning the channel in front of me for other boats or the lighter color that indicated shallows. After ten minutes, I sped up, and Dennis yelled, "Yee-haw!" and my visor lifted off my head and flew into our wake.

When we arrived, I was able to idle while a family pulled away from the dock, and with little fuss fitted the boat into the space they left behind. Dennis affixed a line to the stern starboard cleat, but it was low tide and he couldn't lift himself onto the dock. I cut the engine and hurried to step onto the dock and fix the bowline, but when I stepped back onto the boat, Dennis was shaking his head at me. "You never leave the boat," he said. "You're the captain."

"I go down with the ship?" I said.

He pointed at the line I'd tied. "What if the line didn't hold? What if you dropped it? What if the current's too fast, and the boat drifts, and you're standing on the dock?"

He was irritated — not at my mistake, I knew, but at his inability to help with the docking. "Those things didn't happen," I said.

"But they might have, Frances. You're the captain, so you have to think of these things."

"All right," I said. "But you're here — you could just start the engine and turn around."

He looked at me, and his scowl softened. His shoulders slumped and he wiped his face with his right hand, his stronger hand. "But what if I'm not?"

And I suppose this was approximately

when I started to make plans. Nothing concrete, nothing deliberate — but I have always been a person who thinks of contingencies, and though I hated to do it, it came naturally. I thought of living alone in the big house, maybe traveling a little with Marse or Margo, but every mental picture of life in Miami without Dennis was so repulsive to me that I felt physically ill. If Bette had still been living in the area, it might have been different. But I realized that afternoon that when Dennis died I would leave Miami, and possibly never come back.

Lola, the physical therapist, came twice a week at first, to help Dennis with exercises that would slow the degeneration of his muscles. She laid mats on the back deck and they wore sunglasses while they worked. She was an elfin woman with short dark hair and small, bony hands, and she wore black stretch pants and button-down shirts that looked like they were made for men and made her seem dwarfed, almost neutered. I'd mentioned this to Dennis once — I'd said, "Why doesn't she wear clothes that show that she has breasts?" and he'd said, "Oh, she definitely has breasts." I'd raised my eyebrows at him. "Don't be jealous," he'd said. "When you help me exercise, I look down your shirt, too." Eventually, Lola came three times weekly, then four times, and then she was cleared by our insurance to come two hours a day, five days a week.

When Margo picked me up for our first water aerobics class, Stuart jumped out of the driver's seat as I stepped out to meet them. I shaded my eyes as he came toward me in that hyperactive way of his, scaling the stone steps in front of the house in one long leap. "Where's Dennis?" he said as he went past me, slowing briefly to kiss my cheek.

"Out back with the therapist," I said, and as he entered the dark house, I heard him singing *"Lola, L-O-L-A Lola . . ."*

Margo put the car into reverse before I'd even shut the passenger door. "What's the matter?" I said.

"Nothing." Her hair was in a ponytail, which was one of the ways I loved it best. She looked like a girl who was about to ride a horse — something she hadn't done in her lifetime, except once at summer camp when she was ten years old.

"Don't speed," I said as we pulled out of the driveway onto the street.

"I'm not. Do you have everything? Do you have your cap?"

I patted the bag I'd brought with me. "I'm a little nervous, I admit."

"Don't be. You're very coordinated."

At the health club, we rinsed off in the showers and changed into our swimsuits in the locker room, and when we got to the pool there was already a group formed in the shallow end. A few of the ladies — not all of them were older, as I'd suspected they would be — acknowledged Margo with a nod or a quick hello, but mostly they were busy stretching. When Margo was in the water, she pulled each knee to her chest and bounced on the balls of her feet. "You'll want to warm up," she said.

In tennis, when I wanted to warm up, I hit serves or rallied with myself against the backboard. Here, in a warm pool with barely four feet between me and several other women, I wasn't quite sure what she meant. But I followed her lead and started by bouncing on the balls of my feet, then bringing each knee to my chest, one and then the other, until I did feel a bit winded. The instructor, who arrived in a flurry just as the clock struck the hour, wore a yellow Speedo and tiny mesh slippers. She was a small, compact girl with crooked teeth and thin, straight hair. "Let's line up," she said authoritatively, and around me, the ladies began to swish into position, forming two lines. Margo pulled my elbow and we moved deeper, toward the back of the group. Already, my arms were tiring from the constant motion of maneuvering in the water.

Margo raised her hand. "Cynthia?" she said to the instructor, who stood above us on the pool deck. "This is my mother. She's new."

Cynthia looked over the crowd at me and squinted. "Welcome," she said. "Try to keep up, but if you can't, take a breather and start again." She clapped her hands once, then stooped at the edge of the pool and swung down into the water. "We'll start with some quick tummy tucks," she said, and the rest of the ninety-minute class played out like a manic version of follow the leader: Cynthia demonstrated with her strong, calculated movements, the women in the row in front of me followed with slightly less sharp motions, and I followed them, sloppily and quickly out of breath. Near the end — the class consisted of a circuit of quick exercises, each emphasizing one muscle group, none lasting more than five minutes or so — Cynthia's tone changed, and she went to the edge of the pool to change the music. She told us to close our eyes. The music sounded

Indian in flavor, a slow-running piccolo and some plucky instrument I couldn't name, like a fiddle but more refined. "Concentrate on your breathing," Cynthia said.

I opened my eyes shortly after closing them, realizing that I wasn't at all prepared for whatever was starting now, whether this was another exercise or simply an ending ritual. Cynthia looked at me as she spoke. "Feel your feet against the smooth cement of the pool," she said. "Feel your belly in the warm water. Feel your strong legs and arms being supported by the warm water as it surrounds you and lifts you up." She glanced around the group, then her eyes settled back on me. "You're unconcerned about the past, unconcerned about what is to come. All you feel is the warm water and the beat of your heart."

I closed my eyes for the final moments, wherein Cynthia instructed us to breathe deeply, five counts in and five counts out. Then she told us to hold our breath and submerge, which she said would steel us for the week to come, and when we came up again we would be rejuvenated.

On the ride home, I rolled down the window and felt the sunlight on my arm. Through the canopies of the banyans along Bird Road, the light scattered into dozens of warm spires. At the house, we found Dennis and Stuart on the back deck with Lola. Dennis's wheelchair was not with them. This was something I'd noticed about Lola's sessions with Dennis: she discouraged him from using the chair. For moving around, she helped him stand, supported him while he shuffled forward, then helped him sit again. It made me think I was allowing him to depend too much on the chair. If he could still walk, even slowly, even gracelessly, shouldn't he? But to me he seemed so much more comfortable in the chair, so much less helpless.

They were laughing at something as we stepped onto the deck, and Stuart stopped in mid-sentence and looked behind me at Margo. I realized from his slightly spooked expression that they'd had an argument earlier that morning. "Does anyone want to go for a swim?" I said. I was thinking, really, that I'd had enough of swimming for the day and there were half a dozen things that needed to be done: laundry to be folded, prescriptions to be filled, groceries to be bought. But the sunlight was warm on the wood of the deck and the day was bright and clear, and the morning's exercise had given me a free, relaxed feeling.

Lola told Dennis she could show him

exercises he could do in the water, and asked me if I had a spare suit she could borrow. Margo said she had one, then gestured for Lola to follow her inside. By the time I'd helped Dennis change and rolled him outside again — we came around the front, because we hadn't yet gotten around to installing a ramp off the back deck — Stuart was doing handstands in the shallow end and the women were watching him. Lola supported Dennis while he went down the pool steps, but once the water was up to his chest, she let go and stood a few yards away. "Swim to me," she said. It reminded me of being at Stiltsville when Margo was a little girl, when Dennis taught her to swim at low tide. He would back up, let her swim to him, then back up again, until she was red-faced and sputtering and begging to be held.

Dennis was a good student. I don't know if it was Lola, or the humility that came with the disease, or both, but he did as he was told. "Swim to me," she repeated, and he did. They made it all the way to the deep end, and then she let him hold on to the side for a few minutes while he caught his breath. After they crossed the pool again, Lola led Dennis to the steps and he sat in the shallow water, squinting in the sun. I sat next to him. "What did you think of that?" I said.

He nodded. "Hard," he said. "Feels good."

Lola asked me if we had any bottles of water. "The big kind, half gallons."

I nodded and stood up to get them, but Stuart beat me to it. He hoisted himself over the side of the pool and went inside — without using a towel, I noticed, but I didn't say anything — then emerged with two gallon bottles of water. Lola took them and motioned for Dennis to stand again, which he did, shakily. She put one bottle in his left hand and one in his right. The second one dropped and she dove under and fished it out, then handed it to him again. She put her small hand around his to help him grip. When he had them both tightly in hand, she led him to deeper water, then said, "Do what I do." She raised both hands above her head, slowly, then lowered them until they were beside her ears. He mimicked her, equally slowly, and I noticed the water in the bottles shaking. This is why we have a therapist, I thought. Because if I were to help Dennis with these exercises, I would have stopped the first time his arms shook. I would not have been able to stand the sight of my husband wobbling in the water. As it was, I had to look away.

As if she knew what I was thinking, Lola called out to me. "You see this? He should do this every other day. On land or in water, but water is best. More stable."

"I thought I wasn't supposed to tire him out," I said, and Dennis looked over at me. It was my tone, I suppose: snappish.

"He's not too tired," she said. "Are you too tired?"

"No." He smiled at me. "Not tired." He lifted the bottles over his head.

Early the next morning, Stuart showed up at our doorstep. This was his new thing: early morning runs from their house to ours. When I opened the door, he said, "Is the captain awake?"

"He's in the kitchen," I said, and Stuart bounded past me down the hallway. From the living room, where I was straightening up, I could hear Stuart's horsey laugh and Dennis's brief pauseless sentences, but I couldn't make out what they were saying. The phone rang, and it was Marse, confirming dinner plans for that Friday night, with Paul, and even as I was saying I looked forward to it, my stomach tightened. I could not imagine a situation in which Dennis could socialize normally, or even close to normally, with an old friend. After I hung up, the doorbell rang again. Stuart went past me up the stairs — getting a swimsuit, he said — as I went to answer it. It was Gloria. "I bought a pie," she said, and handed me a white box with a cellophane lid. "It's lemon chiffon. Very soft."

I thanked her and invited her in. We stood in the foyer.

"I don't know why I'm here," she said. "I was doing the shopping, and then I just bought this pie and drove over." She looked around as she spoke. The cutout in the entranceway, where she'd once kept a marble bust that she'd inherited from her parents, was littered with mail and keys.

"You're welcome anytime," I said, and because she looked so lost and out of place, standing in the foyer of what used to be her home, I meant it.

"I don't want to intrude," she said.

"No, no. Stuart's here. I think he and Dennis are going to swim."

"I could make lemonade," she said. "I bought lemons." She put up a finger and slipped back out the door. Her car trunk slammed, and then she appeared again with a bag of lemons. "Grady likes them in his water," she said.

"I have to get to work in a little bit," I said.

Gloria looked disappointed. "It's Saturday."

"It's only until one, and then I'll be home." This was a four-hour shift that I took twice a month, at time-and-a-half pay. It was a sleepy shift with only one doctor working. The few patients were worried mothers and their toddlers, or the occasional case of chicken pox or spontaneous diarrhea. It had occurred to me that I might have to give up working altogether, but then, as Stuart rushed down the stairs wearing swim trunks, waving hello to Gloria as he passed, I realized that this might not be necessary. For better or worse, our lives, Dennis's and mine, had opened up in a way they never had before. From this point forward, our door would never really be closed. It was not even eight in the morning, and already we had guests. Lola was due at eleven. Grady would stop by at some point, I knew, to watch a home building show with Dennis or to check on the boat engines. Marse would rush by on her way somewhere and end up canceling her plans and staying for dinner, which we would fashion from the delivery food that had already started to arrive in tightly packed boxes. My privacy wasn't a priority anymore. I knew, even before the tide was under way, that I had no choice but to ride it out.

That Friday night, Marse arrived with Paul while I was in the kitchen, arranging a plate of vegetables and hummus, and Dennis was in the guest room getting dressed. I had decided to cook, not because the delivery food wasn't good — it was — but because it wasn't special. It was green beans and manicotti and mushroom lasagna and steamed spinach, and no matter what I did to arrange it prettily on a plate, it always looked to me like it had come from a box. Instead, I'd grilled salmon and asparagus outside while Dennis looked on, giving me directions, and we'd argued over whether the salmon was overcooked. He'd told me I was incapable of taking directions, and I'd told him I couldn't read his mind, and he'd said it would be a hell of a lot easier if I could. We'd ended up laughing.

Paul was wearing a white guayabera and tan slacks, and Marse was wearing a lime-green tank dress that accentuated her smooth tan neckline and thin arms. I was running behind schedule, and still needed to change out of the black cover-up and shorts I'd been wearing all day, so after pleasantries at the door — Paul handed over

440

a bottle of wine, which he said he'd bought on his last trip to Spain — I led them onto the back deck and filled their glasses and put out the hummus plate, then excused myself and went to change. Paul looked to me a tad paunchier and maybe a little less cocksure than the young man I'd known more than two decades earlier, but essentially he was simply an older version of himself, with thinner hair. Dennis rolled out of the guest room as I headed up the stairs. He'd washed his hair and it was still damp. "They're on the back porch," I said. "I'm just going to put on a dress."

"I'll see you out there," he said. "Relax, please."

I changed into a sleeveless navy dress that I had worn only once, and that I thought showed off my legs, which were, at this point in my life, my best feature. When I came out onto the deck, Paul was talking and Dennis was laughing. "What did you do?" Dennis said, and Paul — to his credit — understood his slurred speech, and answered. "I fired his butt, and hers."

Marse said to me, "Paul found his accountants having sex with each other in the break room."

"You're kidding," I said, wondering how the topic of sex had been broached so early in the evening, with so little wine.

Paul said, "It was like something out of a movie. They're both these mousy types. No one I'd suspect."

"And you fired them," I said.

"On the spot. But you know, it was only me who saw — we were closed, everyone was gone — and after, I thought that might have been rash. I mean, they were just having some fun."

"Maybe you should let them come back."

"That's what I told him," said Marse.

"I agree," said Dennis.

"Maybe I should," said Paul. He stood at the deck railing and looked out at the lawn and the water. "You've got quite a place here."

The house was not, certainly, the fanciest or most well appointed of our friends' (surely Paul's Fisher Island bachelor pad was grand, and Marse's condo downtown was virtually a palace, almost as large as our home), but living on the canal was a rare gift. The waning sunlight on the water was golden and rich.

"I don't know if you remember," said Dennis as clearly as he could, "but I grew up in this house."

This time Paul didn't understand. Marse spoke up before I could. "He said he grew

442

up in this house."

Paul nodded. "I've been here before. We stopped by once, before you were married. We picked up your father to go fishing. I didn't come inside. I didn't get to see this view."

"We caught two marlins that day," said Dennis, and Paul understood.

"This big," said Paul, his arms wide, and we all laughed politely.

"It's been too long," said Dennis. "When was it? The air show? Margo was just a little kid." I was surprised at how much he was talking. I could see the toll it took on him. He stopped after every sentence to swallow, then continued. "I remember being eaten alive in the Everglades."

"We caught nothing that trip."

"Who was that with us? Marcus?"

"Yep, Marcus Beck."

"Good guy."

Paul shook his head. "You know he died last year. I didn't go to the funeral, I just heard through the grapevine."

"We went," said Dennis. "Nice service. His girls spoke."

"Should I get the grub?" I said, and Marse nodded and offered to help.

In the kitchen, she said, "What do you think? I think it's going well."

"Sure."

"You're not reassuring." She said it off-handedly, like it was a statement more on my character than on the moment.

"I'm sorry. I was so nervous."

"You were nervous? I was nervous! I made Paul change his shirt twice."

I found myself slightly shaky all of a sudden, as if I hadn't eaten in a long time. I leaned against the counter with both hands. "I didn't know what to expect. I don't give Dennis enough credit, I guess. There's no reason he can't have friends, even now."

"Especially now."

"Something's changing," I said. My voice trembled. "People are here all the time. Gloria and Grady. And my goddamn son-in-law."

"But isn't that good? Don't you need a break?"

"I miss my husband," I said, but just then, I could see Dennis through the window, and I remembered standing in the same kitchen so many years before, watching Dennis and his father make their way toward the house from the dock, knowing that he was telling his father that he was going to propose to me. And now, he was more the same than he was different. His hair was lighter and thinner, but he had the same charming smile and the same way of moving his hands when he spoke. Of course there was the wheelchair, but it was easy, in that moment, to think that he was just sitting down, that we were just having some friends to dinner, and that instead of focusing on him, I should be focusing on my friend, who was in love. "I'm sorry," I said, and I turned toward her and wrapped my arms around her shoulders. She hugged me back. She wasn't much of a hugger, and let go early, but she tried. I said, "I've been so wrapped up. Paul seems very nice. And he's obviously smitten." This was true. While he'd been speaking, he'd glanced sideways at Marse every so often, as if for approval. He seemed robust and shining, like a person newly in love. I was envious of them, of course. I pushed down the envy — there was no room for it.

"He told me he loved me."

"That's wonderful."

"I know you're skeptical."

I shook my head. "I'm not skeptical." The decision was like a flipping switch: I would no longer be skeptical. Marse arranged the salmon and asparagus on a platter and sliced some lemons. I gathered plates and ice water on a tray, and together we stepped back into the evening, still warm but without the bite of the afternoon heat. The sunset was reddening. We sat down around the table, passing plates and filling them, and when we all had food in front of us, Paul did something I never would have expected. He brought his hands together and said, "I'd like to give a blessing."

I looked at Marse. "I forgot to mention," she said. "Paul's a Christian. But he promises not to drag me to church."

"Of course," said Dennis. He bowed his head.

In a hushed tone, Paul said, "Lord, we give thanks for this abundant food, for this glorious day, and for old friends. Guide us and keep us. Amen."

"Amen," said Dennis.

"Amen," said Marse.

"Let's eat," I said, and stood up to pour more wine.

The evening settled into a languor of the sort that happens only with old friends — it was this, more than anything else, that convinced me that the whole thing had been a good idea. Paul and Dennis made plans to go fishing, and after the meal I brought out a key lime pie and Paul assumed, incorrectly, that it was homemade, and we all talked about how the key lime pie from Publix was the best and there was never any sense in making your own because it wouldn't measure up. Then we talked about a new development going up down south, replacing a shoddy batch of mini mansions that had been leveled by Andrew, and how Paul knew one of the contractors and was thinking of buying there. His condo on Fisher Island was overpriced, he said, and the ferry was a pain.

"An awful lot of room for one," said Dennis, and Paul said, "Aye," and looked over at Marse, who was beaming. In all the years I'd known her, she had never lived with a man. The man she'd known best and longest was Dennis, and after I'd come along her friendship with him had channeled its way through me.

Paul offered to build us a ramp from the back deck to the patio. "It would take an hour — two, tops," he said, and, as an example of how much our lives were changing, how unfitting our usual preferences had become, Dennis accepted the offer and said he would appreciate it.

It was dark now, and the water lapped quietly in the waterway and gurgled in the swimming pool. The mosquitoes were out. I lit the citronella candles that sat on the deck railing, and the light shone on our profiles. Paul's face was round and fleshy in the

447

torchlight, and hair showed at the neckline of his shirt. I could tell that he and Marse were holding hands under the table. Dennis's face was sharp by contrast. He coughed a little and smoothed down his shirt. "I haven't laughed this much in a while," he said, and Paul leaned forward, as if to get him to repeat the comment, but Marse repeated it for him. She was another wife to Dennis. I'd thought this before, but it was truer now, with her running his errands (just that week she'd picked up his prescriptions for him, then stayed for dinner), and making meal provisions and repeating his sentences when guests couldn't hear. She was almost as at home in the role as I was. I had shared him, a little, all those years, but I didn't mind. Paul's blessing came back to me. It wouldn't hurt, I thought, to give thanks a little more often. But I knew that if I tried to institute a mealtime ritual, Dennis would scoff. It was fine for company, but for us alone, no ritual was needed.

One Saturday later that month, Paul came over to build the ramp, and while he worked, Marse and Dennis and I lolled in the pool. Marse had brought water weights — they were dumbbell-shaped floats that filled with water — and led Dennis through the exercises he'd learned from Lola. Margo and I had been to water aerobics that morning, and now she was taking a nap in her old bedroom, and Stuart was in the front yard, trimming the alamanda bushes, which he'd noticed were growing unruly. I'd let go of the gardener. The expense had seemed unnecessary in this time of tightening our belts. It was as if — as Marse led Dennis in his exercises and Paul hammered away on the ramp and Stuart gardened — we'd acquired a whole new staff.

Lola's pool exercises were working. Dennis had regained a little strength in his hands and legs. He'd been walking more — just from room to room, that sort of thing — and seemed always to be gripping something — a racquetball, a water bottle — even when we were watching a movie or reading. He was sleeping less fitfully; Lola said his muscles had been too weak to make the basic adjustments needed for a comfortable night of sleep. His voice, however, was still deteriorating. It occurred to me that we were marking time, unit by unit, and those loyal compatriots who were with us now would be with us until the end. And distantly I wondered, as I did almost continuously, when that would be. It was nearing but not yet urgent, like a hurricane that's only just started to form in a far-off place. There was a part of me that believed this was how it was meant to go: we had met, we had married, we had raised Margo. Still, I was barbed with envy of any couple fortunate enough to spend their golden years together, Grady and Gloria included.

I went around filling glasses. Paul was finishing the ramp and Marse and Dennis's exercising had deteriorated and they were lightly splashing each other, teasing about something. If Marse weren't an almost daily visitor, I wondered, would she still understand his slurred speech? I went through the house to see if Stuart needed anything but came on him in the front hallway, under the stairs, with Lola. I saw them before they saw me: Stuart had a hand on Lola's waist, and his head was cocked and they were standing a bit too close to each other — his posture looked as if he meant to persuade her of something, but I didn't hear what he'd said. When he realized I was behind him he took a step back and turned. He said, "Frannie, we think the captain might want a ride. Want to go for a ride?" He met my eyes as he spoke. I wasn't sure what I had seen.

"You go ahead," I said.

"Aye, aye," said Stuart, and took large strides down the hall toward the back door, leaving Lola and me standing on the hallway carpet. She was not the actor Stuart was, and I could tell by her inability to meet my eyes that she was embarrassed.

"Lola," I said, and she looked up at me. She was such a little person, so elfin and doe-eyed. I almost felt bad for her. "Why don't you take the afternoon off? We'll see you Tuesday."

She nodded. Her large green duffel bag was at her feet, and she picked it up and walked to the door with it. "Tuesday?" she said.

"Yes," I said. After I'd heard her little red coupe start up and drive away, I yelled up the stairs to Margo. "Wake up, sleepyhead," I called. I willed my voice not to shake.

"What?" she called down. We had always been a family that shouted from room to room.

"Time to get up. Stuart's taking you for a ride."

She might have balked, told me to tell him to go without her, but maybe there was something in my voice, because I heard her feet hit the floor and she said, "Tell him I'll be right down."

Outside, Marse and Dennis were beside

the pool, drying off. He sat on one of the teak chaise lounges, toweling his hair, while she wrapped herself in a beach towel. When she saw me, she said, "What's this I hear about an activity?"

"I was thinking we might grab lunch instead, let them go without us."

"Fine with me," she said. "Paul keeps asking me to fetch things for him. It's like because he's working, his legs are broken."

"You're not coming?" said Dennis, and then he swallowed hard. He was tired.

"Go ahead. Let Stuart drive. Don't wear yourself out."

Paul came over from the deck. "Let's test my handiwork," he said. "I want to make sure you're not going to roll right through this thing."

Margo came outside, blinking in the sunlight, adjusting the straps on her red one-piece, and she and Stuart went down to the canal to get the boat engines started. Paul helped Dennis into his wheelchair, and then they rolled down the ramp right away, without the hesitation I might have shown, especially for a ramp that was not professionally installed. But they made it down, and I didn't notice the ramp give at all, even in the middle. Paul had made it long, so the slope was gentle, and the base abutted the limestone patio that surrounded the pool, so when Dennis reached the patio, he turned right around and drove the chair up again, then back down.

"Thank you so much, Paul," I said.

"It's fantastic," said Dennis, and put his hand out to shake Paul's, and then Paul reached down and gave Dennis an awkward half hug, and this time it was Paul who welled up, red-faced, and had to wipe his eyes with the back of his hand. "Glad I could help," he said.

"Sissies," said Marse to me. She rolled her eyes.

I packed a cooler of beers and sodas and Marse and I walked down to the pier to see everyone off. Margo was practicing reversing out of the slip, and Stuart kept reaching over to correct the steering wheel until she snapped at him and he stepped away. Paul waved to Marse and blew her a kiss, and Dennis waved to me. When Marse and I turned back toward the house, there was a figure standing on the deck in a yellow shirt-dress, holding a brown leather purse. It was Gloria. She waved, and we waved, and in a moment we were beside her. "What's this?" she said, pointing with one sandaled foot at the ramp. "This is not pretty," she said.

"Marse's boyfriend installed it this morning," I said. "For Dennis."

"Of course it's for Dennis," said Gloria. She sighed. "Grady is on my last nerve."

"I think it's going around," said Marse.

We drove in Gloria's sedan to a café on Miracle Mile. We sat outside in wrought iron chairs and ordered salads and iced teas, then Gloria spotted Eleanor Everest, and went off to say hello. Marse took off her floppy pink hat and tilted back to show her face to the sunlight. "I'm beat," she said. "I don't know how you do it."

"Do what?"

"All this being together all the time. I need a break."

For a moment I thought she meant a break from Dennis. I said, "Marse, you aren't obligated to —" but then I realized she meant a break from Paul. "You get used to it," I said. "It becomes like being alone."

"Sometimes it's a little like work," she said. "I shouldn't complain. I'm really very happy."

"I know you are. Growing pains."

Our salads arrived. Marse said, "I wanted to ask. Tell me if it's too early — but have you thought about what happens next?"

"Next?"

She spoke tentatively. "As Dennis declines."

I speared some greens, then put down the fork without taking a bite. We were in the heart of Coral Gables, and half a block away cars buzzed down Le Jeune Road in a loud, colorful blur. At the table next to us a family of four spoke Spanish, and the mother wore a ring with a diamond the size of a corn kernel. It sparkled in the sunlight. "You're asking if I'll stay? In the house? In Miami?"

"I'm afraid you're going to leave," she said.

Gloria reappeared at the table. "Leave where?" She sat down and put her napkin on her lap.

"Nowhere," I said.

She looked from me to Marse. Marse said, "I asked Frances if she was planning to make any changes . . . once Dennis's condition worsens."

"I'm not planning any changes," I said.

For a long moment, Gloria seemed frozen. She had ordered a salad, but I knew she wouldn't eat it, and at the end of the meal would have it boxed to take home. She pushed her tortoiseshell sunglasses up on her head. "It's a good question."

"It's not a good question. It's not time yet," I said. "We'll discuss it in six months."

Gloria touched her neck. "Six months,"

she said. She patted my hand. "That's what we'll do."

"All right," I said.

"All right," said Marse. "Let's talk about sex, then."

And over the course of the meal, we did discuss sex — apparently Paul wanted a little more than Marse, and Gloria said that she thought sex in her seventies might be the best she'd ever had. "There's no pressure," she said. "It's just fun. I guess I'm looser." She shrugged her birdlike shoulders.

Marse laughed. "I've never thought of you as loose."

Gloria blushed. "I didn't mean it like that."

It seemed to be my turn to divulge. Both women looked at me expectantly, but when I didn't say anything, they looked away. We don't sleep in the same bed, I wanted to say — though in fact we'd had sex the evening before, on the living room couch. Dennis had been taking longer and longer to orgasm, and afterward his muscles were sore from the exertion. Soon, I knew, it would be too much of a chore for him. I didn't mind terribly, except sometimes.

The boaters were still out when we arrived home. Gloria got into her car and left, but

Marse followed me inside to wait for Paul. The house was quiet and still. We slouched on the sofas in the living room, our purses in our laps. "You should take a nap," said Marse.

"What have I done to deserve a nap? I made iced tea and went to water aerobics. I'm fine."

"You're a little overwhelmed, I think."

"Do you think I'm handling things badly?"

She paused. "I think these days it's easier to be me than you. I've never thought that before." The afternoon light swept the room through the gauzy curtains, creating a smoky shadow around her. She placed her long, thin hands on her face, rubbing her skin like she was sleepy. She said, "You never told me that Paul came on to you way back when, at the stilt house."

I sat still. We stared at each other. "I'm sorry," I said. "After how I'd met Dennis . . . I didn't want you to hate me. I was selfish."

"You could have told me," she said, without a hint of resentment. "I don't think at the time I would have cared all that much. I would care now, of course."

"He's so different. I almost don't believe it ever happened."

"He was surprised I didn't know. I felt a little foolish, to tell the truth."

"I'm so sorry," I said again.

She waved a hand. "It doesn't matter."

"You're my oldest friend. What if I'd lost you? Where would I be now?"

"Over a man?" She shook her head. "Frances, give me a break."

I knew if I choked up she would be embarrassed, so I took a deep breath and fiddled with the tassels on a pillow. I said, "I think Stuart might be having an affair with Lola."

"Good Lord!"

"I'm not certain. But I saw them together, touching. It was awkward. He smiled right through it."

"That boy," she said, shaking her head. I'd always appreciated that Marse's instincts about people were similar to mine. She'd matched my mistrust of, and reluctant affection for, Stuart ounce for ounce.

"I don't know what to think," I said.

"It might be nothing. Don't tell Margo until you're sure they've sealed the deal."

"I'll never tell Margo. Poor Margo." I kicked off my sandals and lay down on the sofa. I closed my eyes. I heard Marse rustling, and when I opened my eyes again, she had lain down as well. It was quiet. I felt for a moment I could shut out the cacophony of the last weeks and months, the confusion of this nonsense with Stuart, the pain of all of it, and just drift off. But then I heard voices and heavy footsteps on the ramp out back, and the kitchen door opened and slammed shut, and though I kept my eyes closed for another long moment, I knew I had to wake up.

Paul and Dennis went fishing every weekend in June, July, and August, sometimes twice in a weekend. Dennis's alarm would go off in the darkness of early morning and I would wake up and make a thermos of coffee, and then Paul would arrive at the back door, loaded down in shorts with half a dozen filled pockets, and knock lightly on the glass for me to let him in. We would make quiet small talk. "Will you go back to sleep?" he might say, and I would say, "No, I'm up." He'd say, "You should really put your suit on and join us — it's going to be a beautiful day," and I'd say, "You go right ahead without me." Once, while we stood looking out the back windows, sipping coffee and waiting for Dennis to roll into the kitchen, he said, "I bet you never thought I'd be standing here drinking coffee with you."

"I confess I didn't," I said.

"Not so bad, is it? I used to be kind of an ass."

This made me laugh. Dennis came in and said, "What's so funny?"

Paul answered, "Your wife has forgiven me."

One evening in July, after a day of fishing with Paul, Dennis and I sat on the back deck with our feet up on the railing. He said, "I think I would have" — I didn't understand the middle part of the sentence — "with Paul."

"You think you would have *what* with Paul?" I said. This was something Lola had taught me: to repeat the part of the sentence I'd understood, so he wouldn't have to work so hard to make me understand. He repeated it, but I still didn't understand. He made a choppy, effortful gesture, hands together swinging an imaginary golf club, and then I understood. "You don't really enjoy golf that much," I said. Over the years, he'd played sporadically, without the passion he brought to running or fishing.

He took quick breaths inside his sentences. "I think I would have . . . liked it with him. Dad's so . . . comp-et-it-ive." He stumbled on the longer word, taking a breath in the middle. He took a sip of his beer. At a recent visit, Dr. Auerbach had recommended giving up alcohol, and I'd briefly rallied in favor of this idea. But Dennis didn't ever drink much in one sitting, and I'd remembered how good a cold beer tasted during an afternoon on the boat, or how good wine tasted when we were sitting together on the back deck in the evening. We hadn't spoken of it again.

On Saturdays, they might be gone on the boat until noon or later, but on Sundays Paul had to be back for church. Early on, Paul had brought over a wooden workbench and they'd set it up near the water, and that's where they gutted the fish. Paul hosed down the blood and they spilled the guts into the canal, and then packed the fish tightly in plastic wrap and divided the catch. When Dennis got home, he would shower and rest, and then Lola or Stuart might arrive for exercises, and by the afternoon the house would be full again. Several times when Gloria and Grady had been over, we'd run out of the prepared meals Marse had ordered for us, so Gloria had called the catering company and increased the spread: now the refrigerator was always full, and every time I opened it I felt a wave of relief and gratitude.

After the incident with Stuart and Lola, weeks passed without any hint of impropriety, and I started to doubt what I'd seen. Stuart remained his usual outspoken, grating, charming self, and he continued to visit almost every day. Margo was teaching summer classes — she was unavailable during much of the week — and so Stuart started to schedule his work hours around mine as much as possible, so he could be at the house when I wasn't. This was not something I'd asked him to do. One afternoon, Stuart and Margo and Gloria and Grady and I were in the kitchen at the same time, jogging around each other, while Lola and Dennis were out back. Margo and Stuart were making lunch, Gloria was making lemonade, and Grady was looking for an old washcloth to wipe down the steering column on the boat, where he'd accidentally applied too much WD-40. While I was bustling around, getting a washcloth for Grady and sugar for Gloria, Stuart was dicing tomatoes, and he asked me — it was bad timing, but he'd never been one to wait for an opportunity to speak — what shifts I was working for the rest of the week. I paused in front of the open refrigerator. "Is today Tuesday?" I said to Stuart. I handed Grady the washcloth, and he went out the back door.

Stuart sighed. "Frannie, you need to put up a schedule." He pointed to the refrigerator door, where there were four prescriptions and two wedding invitations — this was, as Stuart had noticed, the place where my reminders went.

"A schedule?"

"Write it down, and I'll print it out on my computer."

"I can print it out," I said. We didn't have a computer at home, but I used one at work; I was perfectly capable of making a calendar. "Is that necessary?"

"It is for us," said Stuart. "We show up here, but we don't know your work schedule or when we're needed. You need to start delegating."

"Delegating what?"

Stuart put down the knife. Apparently, he was finding me trying, and I wasn't quite in the mood to humor him. Margo said, "Let's not —" but Stuart put up his hand. He took a deep breath. "I'm just saying, if you posted your schedule, maybe we wouldn't all end up in your kitchen at the same time, fighting for space."

"Young man," said Gloria. She continued to section lemons as she spoke. "I'm not sure that tone is necessary."

He turned back to the cutting board. "I apologize."

"You don't have to be here," I said to him. "Why don't you go home?"

"Mother!" said Margo.

"I didn't ask for a full house. I did not ask for —" I stopped. My voice was shaking.

"I'm just saying, a schedule would make things easier," said Stuart.

"Goddamn it," I said.

Gloria stepped toward me and, in an uncharacteristic gesture, put both arms around my shoulders. I shook inside the circle of her thin arms. "I'll make a goddamn schedule," I said. I realized even then, even while on the verge of throwing my son-in-law out of my house, that this was a practical idea.

"All right," said Gloria.

Stuart left the room. Margo went after him, patting my back as she went. When I'd composed myself, Gloria let me go. We stood at the counter, looking out toward where Dennis stood in the swimming pool with Lola, lifting the water-filled weights above his head one at a time. I saw him struggling with each movement. I saw his muscles trembling. "I would have thought I'd be stronger," I said.

"You're plenty strong," she said.

"I'll stop feeling sorry for myself now." And as if something had jarred loose inside me, I felt suddenly that I could do it. I could stop mourning what I'd thought I would have.

"No one blames you," she said. "Except the boy, of course."

I laughed a little and she joined me. Then she picked up the pitcher of lemonade and headed outside. When she reached the door, she paused. "It would be a shame if you left," she said.

In August, almost a year after Dennis's diagnosis, Dr. Auerbach's nurse fitted him for a palatal lift, which made speaking easier by keeping air from escaping from his nose while he talked. We also bought a voice box, which Dennis held up to his mouth when speaking, to amplify and save his voice. The palatal lift was covered by insurance, but the amplifier was not; it cost $350. That same week, my car engine started knocking. I took the car in and was told in no uncertain terms that I needed either a new car or a new engine. Dennis and I debated — we would get nothing for the car if we sold it without a new engine, but there was no reason to keep both cars at that point. At the end of that week, Paul took Dennis's car to a friend's lot and sold it for $3,500, and we used the money to buy a new engine for my car. Then, the following week, Paul and Marse stopped by for dinner, and during dessert, Paul said to Dennis, "I hate to be the one to tell you, buddy, but I think you have termites."

Dennis brought his voice box to his mouth. "Where?"

"I saw some loose wood on your garage door, then more in the baseboards in the living room. I did some digging — you're infested."

I could see Dennis tensing up. "No problem," I said. "We'll tent the house. We'll vacation at the Biltmore for a few days. You and Lola can exercise in that gorgeous pool." I tried to keep my voice light, but I was thinking: How much does a termite treatment cost? Was it hundreds or thousands? Was it ten thousand? There was the possibility of getting a line of credit against the house, but that presented a new problem, one to which I'd scarcely given any thought: When Dennis died, would I sell the house? The house that had been given to us? Would I ever feel right profiting from Dennis's parents' investment? But if I didn't sell, what then? No home loan could ever be repaid, so no loan could ever be taken. By accepting the house, we'd put ourselves in this position: no real equity, no real assets. If our positions were reversed, Dennis could certainly sell the house — it was his birthright. But it wasn't mine.

"You'll stay at my condo," said Marse. "I'll stay at Paul's."

"There's a guy at my church who can cut you a deal," said Paul.

That week, I volunteered for more weekend shifts at work, and from then on Stuart and Margo came almost every weekend day, and when I arrived home in mid-afternoon, I found them — and usually Gloria and Grady or Marse and Paul — either on the back deck, or in the pool, or in the living room playing a board game. Or I'd find the house empty and a note stuck to the refrigerator: OUT FOR A RIDE (BOAT), or OUT FOR A RIDE (CAR). I had taken up the habit of posting a calendar of my schedule on the refrigerator. Dennis had rolled into the kitchen after I'd posted it the first time. I'd seen him take it in, then turn away.

One Sunday, Grady approached me in the kitchen while I made a pitcher of iced tea. "I come as an emissary," he said, "for Gloria and myself." He covered my hand with his. "We want to give you some money."

I sat down at the kitchen table and sipped from my water glass. "I can't, I'm sorry."

"This is not something one prepares for," he said. He sat down across from me.

467

"Marse told us about the termites — we should have had the place tented years ago. I knew it when we left. We did it once — let's see, it was 'seventy-five — but honestly, you have to do it every decade with these old houses. It's my responsibility."

"You're very kind."

"I mean to be convincing." He pulled a checkbook from his back pocket. "Do you have a pen?" he said. And this was the most humiliating part — not the weakness of my protest, not the relief that must have been obvious on my face, but the act of getting up and crossing the room to fish a pen out of the junk drawer, and walking back to him and handing it over. He gave me the check and I folded it without looking.

"I don't think I know how to thank you. I wish we'd —" I stopped. "I wish we didn't have to accept this."

"This is what you do for your children. You'll do it for Margo."

We left unsaid the fact that, given the present situation, I would probably not be able to do it for Margo. I hugged him before we left the kitchen. "Thank you very much," I said.

"Dennis is my *son*," he said, as if this were all the explanation required. He added, "And you are my daughter. If you need more, you tell me."

That evening, Marse and Dennis sat in the living room with magazines, and I told them I had forgotten to fill one of Dennis's prescriptions, and needed to run out. I went to the bank and used the drive-through machine to deposit Grady's check. I didn't look at it until I filled out the deposit envelope: it was for $20,000. I cried out when I saw it. I covered my mouth with my hand as relief pulsed through me. Even after we paid for the tenting — the estimate we'd gotten from Paul's friend was $1,500 — this would last for months. If we were frugal, it might last a year. From time to time, even now, I think about Grady's words — *This is not something one prepares for* — and about how we might have better anticipated this wrinkle in our lives. We had not saved enough, I suppose. We'd planned for retirement, of course, but not for emergencies. We'd figured we had the house for collateral if we needed it — but this eventuality, Dennis's early demise, made our retirement funds seem insignificant. Selling the house or even taking a loan seemed suddenly impossible. Looking back, I think that I should have started drawing against our retirement accounts. There would have been penalties, of course, and the money would

469

have needed to last much longer than we'd planned; but after all, it would have had to be only enough for one.

Looking back, too, I realized that this money from Grady and Gloria was probably not difficult for them to give — not only because, unlike my mother, they had it to give, but also because they were advancing in age and thinking about what they would leave behind, and realizing there would be one less person to whom to leave it. This had not been in their plans, either. Dennis's illness was sabotage, for all of us.

It was not until September that I saw again what I'd seen at the start of the summer, between Lola and Stuart. I was in the backyard watering the gardenias, and Lola and Dennis and Stuart were in the pool, not really exercising but just goofing around. Then Dennis pulled himself out and I helped him inside to take a bath, and when I came out again to roll up the hose, I saw Stuart dive under to pull Lola down by her legs. When they came up again, she had her arm around his shoulders and they were laughing, and though they pulled apart immediately, without even having seen me, I knew something more than harmless flirtation was under way. Whether the relationship had advanced behind closed doors, I didn't know, but I had the feeling it had not yet. If it had, I thought, wouldn't they avoid being together at the house? Wouldn't they look even more guilty?

"Stuart," I called. "Lola's going home." Stuart didn't look surprised. I dare you, I thought, to ask me why. He shrugged and swam to the steps. Lola followed, but didn't meet my eye.

That evening, Gloria and Grady came for dinner, and afterward, Gloria and I cleaned up while Dennis and Grady went into the living room to set up a game of poker. Gloria washed and dried the dishes while I cleared the table. "The boy rushed out of here earlier," she said.

"Hmm," I said.

"He was red as a beet. Problems?"

"No problems."

She turned off the water and faced me. "Is it the girl?"

"What girl?"

"You know what girl."

I hesitated. "How did you know?"

"Just a hunch," she said.

"Have you seen anything? I mean, anything — substantial?"

"Of course not. I would have told you."

"What do I do? Do I fire her? Do I

confront him?"

She dried the last dish and wiped her hands on a dish towel. "You do nothing. I doubt anything has even happened yet, knowing that boy. These things work themselves out."

I nodded. "We could be wrong."

"We're not," she said. "We are lucky, you and me," she said, and though I hadn't been feeling particularly lucky, I knew she was right.

The following Saturday, at water aerobics, I struggled through the cycles until we reached the ending ritual, in which I'd learned to close my eyes and lose myself in the shorthand meditation. I always wished that this part lasted longer, but this time, instead of letting Cynthia's calming voice lull me into that feeling of peace I'd come to cherish, I opened my eyes partway through and looked over at my daughter. She did not look peaceful. Her eyes were closed, but they were closed as if she were shutting them against something she didn't want to see, and her face was tight. I nudged her, and she looked over at me. "What?" she whispered, and I said, "Are you OK?" I felt Cynthia giving us a look. Margo started to cry. I held her in the water while the ladies dispersed, and before she left, Cynthia patted Margo on the back and said, "It's cathartic, exercise. It will heal what ails you."

Not this, I thought.

It was around this time that we had a lift installed on the downstairs toilet, along with grab bars on the wall and in the shower. I asked Dennis if we might want to ask Paul to build a railing on the pier — I lived in fear that Dennis might lost control of his wheelchair and plummet into the water — but he just smiled and said, sloppily, "Silly goose."

The summer had ended, but I hadn't really noticed. In November, Dr. Auerbach told us that Dennis's progression was faster than he'd hoped it would be. This came as a surprise — I'd had nothing to compare it with. Then one afternoon in December I came home from work to find Stuart sitting on the raised toilet in the guest room bath. Dennis was in the tub. The water had drained.

"We're waiting," said Stuart when he saw me in the doorway.

"For what? Are you OK?" I said to Dennis.

"We tried to get out, but it didn't quite work," said Stuart. "We're resting."

"I'm fine," said Dennis. The word *fine* was one elongated vowel, with hardly a hint of a consonant.

"I brought this," said Stuart, holding up a dry-erase board the size of a placemat. There was a blue marker affixed to its side with Velcro. This was something I'd asked him to pick up after Lola and Dr. Auerbach had recommended it. Dennis's speech had been getting worse. Within a month, he would be writing more often than speaking.

"Hate . . . writing," said Dennis. Long hard *a,* long hard *i,* short soft *i.*

"I know, baby. But I like reading." To Stuart, I said, "You can go. I'll help him out."

"No," said Dennis.

"It's difficult," said Stuart. "I think I should stay."

"I have to be able to do it," I said, looking back and forth between them. I'd been helping Dennis into and out of the tub when Lola and Stuart were not around; the last time I'd done it, however, had been weeks before, and I admit it had hurt my back. I figured there was a trick I was missing, a stronger posture. Lola was such a little thing — surely she wasn't more capable of lifting my husband than I was?

"Trust me," said Stuart. To Dennis, he said, "Try again?"

Dennis nodded and Stuart braced himself against the tub, then reached down and put

474

both arms under Dennis's armpits and stepped into the tub between Dennis's legs. He was confident and sturdy, and I knew that even if this attempt failed, he would be able to put Dennis down gracefully. I trusted him. This was, I suppose, as good a reason as any for not somehow forcing his flirtation with the therapist to end: what would I do without him? It was shameful.

When Dennis was standing, he could help a bit by getting his legs under himself, and Stuart reached down to bend Dennis's leg from behind and help him step over the side of the tub. He wrapped a towel around Dennis's shoulders and supported his weight while they walked to the guest bedroom. Dennis's spine had never looked more prominent, his knees never so knobby. But once he was dressed — Stuart helped, but as long as he was sitting down in a chair with arms, Dennis was still able to pull on his own clothes — that malnourished figure disappeared, and he was himself again. Skinny and weakened, yes, but himself.

I took Dennis and Margo — Stuart had a meeting — out on the boat that night, and we anchored in the spot where the stilt house had stood and ate stone crabs at the stern. I'd cracked all the claws into bite-size pieces before we'd left, and Dennis was able to dip each morsel in the mayonnaise sauce and eat it without too much trouble. Margo and I ate the same way. When we finished, I cut a piece of key lime pie into little squares and put the plate on Dennis's lap. We all ate from it. The downtown skyline, which had doubled in height in the thirty years since I'd come to Miami, resembled a foggy lineup of many-sized blue bottles. The buildings gave off faint stars of light. "From here," Dennis said very slowly into his voice box, taking a deep breath, "it looks like nothing changes."

The first time I'd been on Biscayne Bay, the only tall downtown building was Freedom Tower, where immigrants were processed when they first reached the country. It had changed slowly, yes, but it had changed.

"I miss Stiltsville," said Margo.

"Me too," I said, though I had the thought that with Dennis so sick, we wouldn't have used the stilt house much even if it still existed. It had collapsed before becoming a sad, abandoned treasure.

"Me too," Dennis said. The antidepressants were working: he didn't cry, and neither did I.

That second year after the diagnosis went

by in a bright, blinding flash, blanketing us in doctor's appointments, symptoms, and steady decline. Dennis woke almost every night coughing violently to rid his throat of phlegm, which he was no longer able to do naturally. We finally got around to having the house tented in January, during which time Dennis and I stayed at Marse's condo, as she'd offered. We spent evenings drinking wine in the chaise lounges on her balcony, watching the lights of the cruise ships making their way up Government Cut. "We could go on a cruise," I said one night to Dennis, thinking that surely cruise ships had handicap access.

"Why?" he said softly.

"Because it would be relaxing and fun. People would cook for us."

"People — already — cook — for us," he said.

It was a cool night and I'd spread a blanket over our legs and moved our lounges next to each other so I could hold his hand. Being at Marse's was a little like a vacation in itself. She had good crystal wineglasses and a big-screen television with more cable channels than I knew existed, and her bed was as high and wide as a boat, with a view of the bay. We used an ottoman to help Dennis climb into it. Lola had the week off, and every morning Dennis and I used the pool at Marse's condo for his exercises, but more often than not we ended up floating around with foam noodles laced under our arms, talking idly. "That's true," I said. "I guess we don't really need to get away."

"I — don't," he said. "My life is — vacation."

I looked over at him. His hair was disheveled from the breeze. I'd taken to cutting it myself, on the back deck with a sheet tied around his neck like an apron. In the moonlight, I could see the lines around his eyes and his sweet, soft half smile. He was happy. He was deteriorating and wheelchair-bound, and with anyone besides me he was more comfortable writing than speaking, and we were short on cash (a cruise was out of the question financially, anyway) — but still, in these and other moments, I saw his happiness. The illness takes the body, not the mind or the spirit.

In February, Dr. Auerbach offered us a twig of hope: a clinical trial. He mentioned it offhandedly, as an afterthought at the end of a checkup, saying that it was unlikely to work but he didn't think it would hurt. Dennis shrugged and wrote on his board, LET'S GO FOR IT. Later that week, we went to a clinic at the University of Miami and picked up a box full of needles and vials, a chart to mark each time the shots were given, and a list of dates when we had to check in at the clinic for tests. A nurse at the clinic showed me how to administer the shots on a grapefruit, then drew a bull's-eye on Dennis's hip with a permanent marker. The drug was called brain-derived neurotrophic factor, or BDNF, though in the weeks of the trial, after mixing up the letters a dozen times, Dennis and I would come to refer to it as BFD — Big Fucking Deal. There were almost two thousand patients enrolled at forty sites. We started the injections the night we received the drugs, and for a month the scheduling and checkups were like another job in our lives, but then the study was halted. No patients had reported progress. It was a bust.

In March, at his appointment with Dr. Auerbach, we learned that Dennis had lost a total of forty-five pounds. He hadn't been eating very much — this I had noticed. At first I'd thought he just wasn't hungry, but then I'd watched as he fought to swallow a piece of lasagna, and I realized that the struggle simply wasn't worth it. The doctor suggested a feeding tube — this was something we'd anticipated distantly, and now the time had rolled up on us in a tidal wave

— and at the end of that week Dennis spent the night in the hospital to have the tube inserted into his stomach. I was taught how to attach the feeding bag to the tube, how to add a can of Ensure to the bag, how to clean it before and after each use. Dennis could still eat — thank God, he could still taste food — but he could not get enough to sustain him, and from then on I, or Margo or Lola or Stuart, gave him a bag of Ensure three times a day.

And then one night I realized, after Dennis grunted his thanks when I handed him a pair of pajamas from the dresser, that he hadn't said a word to me in a week. His voice had trickled away like a stream in winter. This is actually what I thought of — the stream behind the home in Decatur where I'd grown up, which flowed modestly but steadily in summer and then in the fall slowed to a trickle, then stopped entirely after the first freeze.

Since inventing her image in the backyard on my birthday almost a year earlier, I'd thought of Bette every day and called her every week. We had long conversations, but they weren't the same as being together. When the doctor gave us some bit of bad news, as he seemed to do at almost every one of our monthly visits, I thought about what she would have said if she'd been around, what irreverent quip she might have added. When she flew in at Christmas, we spent an evening on the back deck together drinking wine, and in a weak moment I told her that I didn't think I could keep it together anymore without her. I said, "I feel like you chose her over us."

She wore turquoise earrings and a large silver ring on one index finger. "I wish you didn't think of it that way," she said.

"We could really use you around here."

She stared out at the waterway. "I used to sleep out here when I was a kid, did you know that?"

"Dennis mentioned it once."

"My father would try to make me come inside, and my mother would say to him, 'Dear, it's Florida — what's the worst that could happen?' It was different then." Her hair in the moonlight looked like the feathers of a white bird. Her sharp face was free of lines, free of worry. She said, "Once I thought I saw a ghost in those bushes over there, but it was just my eyes playing tricks on me. And once Dennis spent the night out here with me, and that night I found that with him there I was more afraid, not less. I lost all my gumption."

"I don't understand."

She shrugged. "What about when it's my turn? Dennis has you. If I left Suzanne, who would take care of me?"

"We all would."

She shook her head and changed the subject. Santa Fe, she said, had excellent museums.

Time passed in great swaths, and very little other than Dennis's condition seemed to change. I still posted a schedule every week, and everyone still signed up for days, using a pen that dangled from the fridge. Margo was promoted in her department to a coordinator position, which meant she taught a little less but worked more, and Stuart lost a big contracting job suddenly, but then found a new one building more or less the same thing, as far as I could tell. Lola went to Ecuador to visit her parents, and while she was gone a curt but capable male therapist named Mitch came to the house. Nothing monumental happened — except the one monumental thing that was happening, slowly and swiftly at the same time, all the time.

And yet I was surprised when, one afternoon when we were alone in the backyard, sitting in lounge chairs I'd dragged from the deck to the edge of the canal, Dennis handed me his writing board. It read: BEEN THINKING ABOUT MY FUNERAL.

It was the afternoon of the yacht club's annual chowder party, an event we hadn't skipped in more than fifteen years, since we'd first become members. I imagined that Grady and Gloria were there at this moment, drinking beer from colorful plastic cups, eating Gloria's deviled eggs with caviar, being served chowder by the senior members of the club. I didn't miss it. I didn't ask Dennis if he did — I knew the answer. Dennis had always enjoyed that particular event.

"OK," I said.

Dennis wrote carefully, with difficulty, I WANT TO BE CREMATED.

I closed my eyes. "I know, baby."

WE HAVE TO TALK, he wrote.

"OK," I said again.

SCATTER MY ASHES IN THE BAY, he wrote.

I nodded.

MY FATHER TOLD ME TO TELL YOU — he made sure I'd read, then erased with a cloth he kept in his lap, and started again. THEY DON'T WANT THE HOUSE. SELL IT. I shook my head. He erased again, nodding fervently. GIVE 1/2 TO MARGO. SHE WILL NEED IT.

"Is she having money problems? Do you know something?"

He hesitated, then shook his head and wrote, MONEY ALWAYS A PROBLEM.

I laughed a little, and laughing made me cry a little.

He wrote, THE BOAT — DON'T GIVE TO STUART. GIVE TO PAUL.

I hadn't given a thought to what would happen to the boat. It was worth eight thousand, maybe ten thousand at the most, but I knew boats didn't hold their value, and I supposed giving it to someone who would appreciate it was worth more than trying to make a little money. "Why?"

He wrote, FOR FISHING. He erased, then wrote again. HE'S BEEN HUNTING ONE JUST LIKE IT.

"Fine," I said.

UNLESS YOU WANT IT.

For a moment I thought about this. Maybe I would keep the house, and maybe I would take the boat out on my own and — what? "No," I said.

GIVE MY FATHER'S WATCH TO STUART.

"Fine," I said.

AND KEEP MY CUFF LINKS AND ROD — He made sure I'd read, then erased and started again. FOR HER NEXT HUSBAND.

I laughed and he laughed, and out of habit

I glanced around to make sure no one had seen, and gestured for him to erase. This was not something we'd allowed ourselves to mention before, but in that moment it seemed as though this possibility — a divorce for Margo, a second husband — was not all that awful, not any kind of tragedy. When we were quiet again, he wrote, WILL YOU — but then he stopped and erased.

"What?"

He shook his head.

"Will I what? Ask me."

He studied my face in the way he did sometimes. He paused with the marker in his fist, deciding what to write.

"Are you asking if I'll stay in Miami?" I said.

He put the marker down and nodded, swallowing.

I thought for a moment, and then said, "Of course I'll stay. This is my home."

And I justify saying it, because Dennis was alive and sitting beside me, and as long as he existed in this world I would have stayed. How could I answer him except this way? As long as he was flesh and blood and had the ability to ask the question, that was my answer, and in this moment I even partly believed it myself. And I think my answer gave him peace.

■ ■ ■ ■

We'd graduated from so many gadgets by this time: the cane, the walker, the voice box, one electric wheelchair, and then a better one. By April, when the mangoes started to ripen on the trees and the frangipani trees started to drop their pinwheel blossoms, he wasn't speaking or walking at all, and could barely make it down the swimming pool steps to exercise with Lola. Instead, they lay on the back deck and she pushed his muscles around for him, bending his knees to his chest or stretching his arms above his head. By May, by the time of my fifty-first birthday, he had no more use for the dry-erase board; it was too difficult for him to write. By June he was eating almost exclusively from the tube, and staying almost exclusively in the living room, because it was too difficult to move him back and forth. Marse bought him some expensive ergonomic footrest pillows, and I bought soft flannel sheets for the living room sofa. People still came by all day, every day, flowing into and out of the house, but instead of congregating on the back deck or in the kitchen, we hung around in the living room, mostly, and once or twice a day someone

helped Dennis into his wheelchair, fitted a
blanket over his legs, and took him for a
walk around the block. We played a lot of
board games — Dennis was still good at
them, though they tired him out. For
Scrabble, I sat next to him and he pushed
the tiles he wanted to use toward me, then
gestured to the spot on the board where he
wanted the word to go. I kept the windows
open all the time, and changed the sofa
sheets every time Lola or Stuart took Dennis for a bath. I bought him several pairs of
pajamas — he was usually chilly, even in
the heat of the day.

In July, Paul and Marse picked us up and
we went in Paul's truck to a drive-in movie
in Fort Lauderdale. We sat in camp chairs
and ate marshmallows — a treat that had
become one of Dennis's favorites — and
drank very cold beers. Paul had become a
deacon at his church. He explained what
this entailed, but I wasn't listening. I was
watching a foursome about our age at the
site next to ours, sitting in camp chairs and
eating sandwiches out of plastic baggies.
They laughed a lot, loudly, and I felt that I
truly hated them. I was relieved when the
movie was over and we could get back into
the cool car and drive silently back down
the crowded expressway. Paul and Dennis

continued to go fishing almost every weekend, but they returned early, usually without
fish, and Dennis slept for hours afterward.

In August, Paul and Marse sold their
condos and bought a house on the Biltmore
golf course, a mile north of ours. After they
moved in, I dressed Dennis in a sport coat
and put on a dress and invited Margo and
Stuart to come with us to the new house
for dinner. He wore a tie and she wore a
black dress and red heels. Stuart helped
Dennis into the passenger seat of our car,
then folded the wheelchair and lifted it into
the trunk — this was something I could not
do on my own — then put out his hand.
"Do you mind if I drive?" he said.

His blue eyes flashed with something I
couldn't quite define — anger, possibly, or
frustration. We hadn't exchanged two words
since they'd arrived at the house, fifteen
minutes late, so I surmised that whatever it
was, it had nothing to do with me. "I'd
rather drive," I said.

"Suit yourself." He stepped into the backseat, forcing Margo to shift over.

In the rearview mirror, I tried to catch my
daughter's eye. It had been months since
I'd stopped hunting for clues about Stuart
and Margo's relationship — were they
happy? — or, for that matter, about Stuart's

relationship to Lola, who was still an almost daily presence in my home. Nothing had been revealed to me since the day when I'd seen them in the pool, and Margo and Stuart were the same as ever: affectionate in bursts, independent of each other. But as I drove, I found myself wishing they would fight. A fight, in my presence, would at least shed some light on what transpired in the private space between them.

Margo kept her hands in her lap as we drove. We came to the bridge where she'd crashed Dennis's car when she was sixteen, and as we passed, Dennis raised one hand and made a grunting sound. "My bridge," said Margo in response, and she reached into the front seat and put an arm on her father's shoulder. "I think I see the Buick's fender in that bush over there," she said. "There's one of the headlights in the gutter."

Marse and Paul came outside while Stuart was still helping Dennis into his chair. Paul's aftershave hit me before he reached the driveway. Marse was stunning in a pink halter dress. It was a crisp, warm early summer evening, and the light streaming through the oak trees was the color of watery tea. The house, which I had seen the day they'd moved in, was a hacienda-style ranch with a gated driveway and long, wide carport. We went inside, Paul driving Dennis even though he was still capable of maneuvering the electric steering. There was a board leading from the brick walk up two steps to the front door; Paul had secured it with sandbags at each corner, and though it buckled a bit when Dennis's chair rolled onto it, it didn't shift or drop.

We entered a wide, open kitchen with new appliances and marble countertops, then continued through a family room onto a sunporch, then outside onto a back patio that overlooked a swimming pool. Beyond the fence was the Biltmore golf course, where Paul boasted he'd shot two under par in a round that very morning. Dennis touched Paul's arm and gestured around the yard, then forced his right hand into a thumbs-up. "Nice, eh?" said Paul, putting his hand on Dennis's shoulder. "OK if we eat outside?"

Dennis nodded.

"Can I get you a beverage?" said Paul.

Dennis nodded again.

Marse and Margo and I went to the kitchen. Marse handed me a bottle of red wine to open while Margo admired the house. "I'd like a big kitchen," she said. "Next house, I want a really big kitchen. It doesn't even matter that I don't cook very much. I just love a big kitchen."

"I don't cook much," said Marse.

"I don't remember the last time I cooked," I said.

"The benefit of having a spouse with a feeding tube," said Marse. She was the only one who could say things like that to me. "Paul expects dinner at the table every night. He's had my chicken carbonara a dozen times."

"And the rest of the time?" I said.

"Takeout."

Marse collected beers from the fridge and poured one into a plastic cup for Dennis — it would fit perfectly in an attachment that swiveled up from the side of his wheelchair — and in the cup she placed a long, aqua-blue straw. It touched me, the efforts they'd gone to. She left the kitchen to deliver Dennis's beer, then returned and started arranging a plate of cheese with strawberries. Margo said to Marse, "Are you going to marry Paul?" and we both looked at Marse expectantly.

She looked mischievous. "Do you think I should?"

"Oh, my Lord," I said. I put my hand to my throat. "Are you engaged?"

Marse held out her hand — I was ashamed

that I hadn't noticed — and on it was a beautiful (and elegant, and not at all showy) diamond ring. I grabbed her and shrieked. Margo came around the counter and hugged Marse, saying, "Congratulations!" and for a moment I just stood there, my hand over my mouth, watching my friend. She was as happy as I'd ever seen her.

Paul and Stuart and Dennis came into the kitchen. "I guess you heard," said Paul.

Margo hugged Paul, and said to her father, "Did you know?"

He nodded.

"You knew?" I swatted his arm.

He nodded again, smiling.

"We'll toast," I said, handing everyone a glass. "To our friends. May your life together be long and happy."

Dennis grunted and we all looked at him. He gestured to me, then to himself, then back to me.

"As happy as yours," said Paul quietly. Dennis again gave his awkward thumbs-up.

"Hear, hear," said Marse, and when I looked over at Margo, I saw that she had started to cry. Seeing this, Stuart threw up his hands and left for the backyard. Marse recovered for all of us. "We'll eat," she said, pulling a lasagna out of the oven. I put my arm around Margo and, seeing that the lasagna was in a carry-out container, said to Marse, "So sweet — you slaved!"

"Shush," she said. "I'm going to be a wife."

We carried water glasses to the back patio, where a table was set. I looked around for Stuart but didn't see him. Margo said, "He'll probably walk home."

"That young man is temperamental," said Paul "Am I right?" He looked at Dennis and Dennis nodded.

"I remember another temperamental young man," I said to Paul.

He looked up to see if I was smiling — I was. "Guilty as charged."

"Don't defend him, Mother," said Margo.

"She's not defending him," said Marse. "She's equivocating."

"Don't equivocate," said Margo.

Dennis laughed and a bit of his beer spilled. Paul wiped it up and said, "Better an interesting marriage than a perfect one, I say. Am I right?"

"Absolutely," said Marse.

"Just you wait," I said.

Margo was looking at me. "I know you suspect him."

"Sweetheart, I'm not sure this is the time —"

"Dad and I talked about it," she said.

I looked at Dennis. I saw something like contrition in his eyes. If times had been normal, if Dennis had been well, I would have told Margo we'd discuss this in private. But these weren't normal times, and it was rare that Margo wanted to talk, so I put my napkin in my lap and leaned back in my chair. There was a warm breeze off the golf course. It was almost eight o'clock, and still men drove carts this way and that, their deep voices carrying in the breeze. "OK," I said. "What is it I suspect him of?"

Dennis made a sound to get Margo's attention, then shook his head.

"You didn't tell her?" she said to him. She sounded touched. To me, she said, "It was months ago. Dad told me that Stuart and the therapist — well, they're a little too close for comfort." She put her fork down on her plate. "That pixie bitch."

"Oh, my," said Marse.

Paul said, "Sweetie, he's a flirt. A lot of men are. It doesn't mean —"

"He thinks he's in love," she said.

Paul looked at Dennis and Dennis shrugged, agreeing. I scooted my chair until I was beside Margo. It made scraping noises on the cement patio. I put my arm around her, but she wasn't crying anymore. She looked relieved. "People make mistakes," I said. "They get caught up. They go overboard." I could scarcely believe I had said it.

"They do, people do," said Marse. She was on Margo's other side, holding her hand.

"It's been a year," said Margo.

"Has anything *happened?*" said Marse.

"He says no," said Margo. "He swears. And now he wants to take this contracting job, and move, and he expects me to go with him, even after this."

"Move where?" I said.

She wouldn't meet my eye. "Seattle."

"You can't possibly move to Seattle," said Marse. "It rains every day there."

Paul nodded. "Seattle is out of the question."

"Well, he's going," Margo said. And — it shames me to remember — my first response was panic. I couldn't have Margo so far away, and — this was possibly even more imperative to me at the time — Stuart could not leave, not yet. We needed him. He was the only one who could lift Dennis out of the bathtub when Lola wasn't around. He was the only one who liked to do yard work and play poker past midnight when everyone else but Dennis wanted to sleep. He could drive the boat and load the wheelchair into the car, and, most important, he was distracting. If he'd been with us at the table, I might have told him so. As it was, I said to my daughter, "Then you'll just have to let him go." I'm glad I said it. It was the right thing to say, I thought, and when Margo looked at me — my daughter, searching my face for guidance — I was sure of it.

That night, I lay next to Dennis in his little cot, my head on his chest, and listened to his raspy breathing. "I didn't know you were suspicious," I said to him. "Did you know I was?"

He shook his head. I wanted him to talk to me. I wanted so badly to talk.

"Did you not tell me because you didn't want to upset me?"

He shrugged.

"Did you not tell me because I depend too much on Stuart?"

He was still.

"I guess I do," I said. "Some mother I am."

He made his sweet, throaty laugh sound.

"Should I have told her?"

He made a noise, a definitive sound that meant no.

"Why is it that you can break her heart but I can't?"

He shrugged again. It was true — if I had told her, she would have argued with me and been angry. Dennis, though, had leeway. It wasn't meddling when it was her father. She trusted him never to hurt her intentionally. This wasn't rational, and I didn't think it was based on historical evidence, but it was how things were.

I stopped by Margo's house later that week, when I knew she would be at work. Stuart was in the backyard, mowing the lawn. It seemed that anytime I stopped by, he was outside, keeping busy. I stood at the sliding glass doors in the living room until he noticed me and turned off the mower.

"I let myself in," I said when he was standing in front of me, sweating through his shirt.

"That's fine."

"I just want to know when you're moving. I'm not mad."

He wiped his face with one hand. "I appreciate it. No one likes it when you're mad."

"Don't joke."

His face fell. I saw that he was sorry he'd let me down. I'm sure that was doubly true for letting Dennis down. I remembered them together on the boat when Stuart was still learning, glancing up at Dennis expectantly, absorbing every direction, every mild criticism or bit of praise. "I told them I have some work to finish in Miami first," he said. "I'm not leaving yet."

I searched his face. "Margo's not going with you."

"I wish she would."

"Tough." I started toward the front door, then stopped. I half-turned back to him, but I didn't meet his eye. I said, "A couple of years ago, I met a man." I didn't know what I meant to say, or why I was saying it. "We became close. Nothing happened. In the end it didn't matter, I guess. There's a larger picture. You might not know this yet." It was a betrayal of Margo, I thought, to talk to Stuart this way. "I'm just saying that marriages go through phases," I said limply.

"I guess they do," he said. Then, "I'll be over by noon. Tell Dennis to get his poker face ready." I left the house without saying anything else, and as I got back into my car and fastened my seat belt, relief flooded through me. This was not entirely rational, but it was very real.

Later that month, we ordered and received a BiPAP machine that Dennis wore during sleep to help him breathe. At first, the low roar it made kept me awake all night but after a week we'd both gotten used to it. One night around this time I woke spontaneously, for no reason I could name, and when I looked out into the room, I saw a figure standing at the French doors that led out to the swimming pool, and a cry caught in my throat. I looked at Dennis's bed, thinking all at once that I needed him to protect me and I needed to protect him, but his little low cot was empty and his blanket was on the floor. Then I looked back at the dark figure and realized that it was my husband — standing on his own legs, having walked several paces without assistance. I held my breath. Dr. Auerbach had told us that once a patient is bedridden, the time left is measurable in months, not years. Dennis had been bedridden, more or less, for six months. He was still helped out of bed every few days for a roll or a boat ride, but otherwise he had only enough energy to move his arms a little, play a little bit of a game, maybe smile or laugh a bit, or take a few bites of frozen yogurt. Still, here he was, standing at least six feet from his bed, staring out at the canal. I got up quietly and walked until I was next to him. I had to will myself — it took all my strength — not to touch him, not to so much as take his elbow. He looked over at me when he sensed me beside him, and he smiled. Then he looked out through the glass again.

Outside, moonlight washed the blue-black lawn and cast a sheen on the water in the canal. The gumbo-limbo tree at the back corner of our property bent in the wind. In the dark, Dennis's profile was a mask of contentment and peace. I'd loved him for half my life. I'd loved him beyond the limits of how much love I'd thought I could generate. I missed him less in that moment, as we stood side by side watching the backyard in the moonlight, than I had in a year, maybe two. Then I took his hand, and when I did — it hurts me to remember — he lost his footing, and he fell.

Dennis died almost two months later, and we scattered his ashes in the bay and spent a long evening on the boat in the windless night, watching the lights of Miami in the distance. Margo slept over for a week, at which point I convinced her that I could be left alone. When she was gone, I missed her. In the next year, Stuart left Miami for the job in Seattle, then returned after six weeks so that he and Margo could try again to be together. Grady had a mild stroke that left the right side of his face a bit lazy, but he was otherwise his old self; he and Gloria invited me for dinner every Sunday night. Margo stopped by every other day or so, and we continued to take water aerobics classes together, though Cynthia was replaced by another instructor, who was not as good. Margo returned to sailing on the weekends. She said being on the water reminded her of him. She started a program teaching jazz dance to street kids in Liberty City, and this quickly became her full-time job, and she left the college altogether. Marse and Paul got a dog and named it Bennett. Marse wanted a big wedding but Paul said he'd already done all that, so she told him she didn't need reminding that this wedding wasn't special to him, then stormed out and spent the night at my house. They made up in the morning. They were married at the Barnacle, on the water, she in a green dress and he in a guayabera. They honeymooned in Peru and brought me a small cement bust, an infant head, which I perched on the windowsill in the kitchen. I played a lot of tennis, and at night I sat in the living room and looked around at the items that had populated my life — our life — for so long, and instead of getting easier this became unendurably painful, and I knew I had to go.

I moved to Asheville, North Carolina, where decades before, Dennis and I had spent a long autumn weekend at a bed-and-breakfast. We'd hiked and admired the foliage and watched street musicians in Pritchard Park. With the profit from the sale of the big house, I gave Stuart and Margo a nest egg and bought myself a two-bedroom brick townhouse on a quiet street. Gloria drove up with me and helped me arrange my kitchen, then flew back to Miami. Before she left she told me she envied me a little, retiring to a quieter life, but I think she was only trying to lessen my guilt over leaving them, over leaving Margo. I took a part-time office job and joined the local tennis club, where I play doubles with a woman who also has been widowed. My mother lives a three-hour drive away, and almost every weekend I visit her or she visits me. During my first summer, Bette and Suzanne flew out and we shopped for antiques. Margo and Stuart came for my first Christmas, and it snowed.

I've returned three times: once to stay with Marse while Paul was in the hospital for bypass surgery, once to spend Mother's Day with Margo, and once after Grady's second stroke, for his funeral. Bette and Marse and I started a tradition of going away together each year — so far we've been to San Francisco, the Outer Banks, and Guadalajara. Margo drives up for a long weekend every couple of months. She talks about moving to be closer to me, but though I am lonely for her, I don't encourage it — she needs to become steadier in her own life. I hope that one day she will have a baby. If this happens, though, I'll have to consider moving back, which is right now unfathomable to me. When I think about Miami, it is as if all I loved about the place no longer exists. It is as if every regret I've ever had lives there. But I miss my daughter, and I would like our family to continue.

The mountains and changing seasons here remind me of my childhood. I miss the ocean, of course, but I do not care to live near it again.

The night Dennis fell in the guest room, his hip snapped, and he lay moaning while I called 911. Before he was able to come home from the hospital, he developed pneumonia, and Dr. Auerbach — who I could tell didn't really believe me when I told him Dennis had crossed the room on his own — told us it was time for hospice care. He said he was sorry the disease had moved so fast. There are people, I know now, who live a dozen years or more with ALS — but here we were only two and a half years after the diagnosis, being shown the door.

I ordered a hospital bed for the living room. I probably should have done this months before, to make Dennis more comfortable and give him more space for visitors, but I was always a step behind the disease. In the hospital after his fall, Dennis had been on a continuous regimen of morphine and muscle relaxants, but at home he turned away when I tried to give him his pills. Only Lola could get him to take them, and her days were numbered — once hospice started, she would no longer be needed. Instead, we would have a head nurse who checked in three times a week, plus two rotating shift nurses who spent an hour at the house in the mornings and evenings, every day. The first night home from the hospital, after refusing to take any pain medication, Dennis was restless. His voice returned in the form of ghoulish cries, unintelligible and unfocused, and he was soothed only by my lying next to him in the little hospital bed and singing softly in his ear. At first I sang the lullabies I remembered from when Margo was a baby, but then I sang songs I knew he liked, by Neil Young and Jimmy Buffett and Dolly Parton. He didn't sleep, but he lay still; if I fell asleep, he would stir and cry out again, and

I would be jarred awake, and resume my soft singing.

After a week of this — Dennis no longer seemed to need real sleep; he was in a stupor most of the day, and the line between awake and asleep had blurred — Lola told me I would need to ask the hospice nurse for liquid morphine to add to Dennis's feeding tube. This was Lola's last shift before the arrival of the hospice nurse the next day. Forcing painkillers on Dennis was not a job I felt I could pursue, so to change the subject, I asked Lola about her plans. She said she was going back to Ecuador.

"So soon?" I said. "Do you have a beau there?" I didn't normally pry, but I was rattled in the face of losing her.

She didn't answer right away. Then she said, "My father is dying. It's been coming for a while."

"I had no idea," I said.

"It's fine," she said. She looked at me. "You will need to get some sleep." She knew what was ahead of me though I still didn't — the empty hours, the helplessness, the boredom. She went into the living room to say good-bye to Dennis. She stroked his hand, and he turned and made an expression that I took for a smile. She murmured quietly for a minute or two, and he grunted

505

in response, and then she stood and bent to kiss him on the forehead. She passed me as she left. "Take care of yourself," she said, and I said, "Thank you for everything."

The next day, while Stuart gave Dennis a bath, I called Lola's agency and left a message for her supervisor, saying that she had been a lifesaver and offering to be a reference should she ever need one. I never heard from her again. If Stuart acknowledged the end of her tenure at all, I didn't see it.

The head hospice nurse's name was Olivia. She was our constant during the weeks of rotating nurses and shifting medication schedules. She told us that Dennis's listlessness, his swollen legs, his disorientation, the heavy snoring that substituted for breathing all came from lack of oxygen and the buildup of carbon dioxide in his blood. She brought in an oxygen tank, and from then on, he wore a clear tube under his nostrils, hooked around his ears. Every so often I was shocked by the sight of him. Olivia started him on liquid morphine. He was barely able to focus on my face when I stood above him, so I lay next to him for hours at a time, day and night.

One night, three weeks after hospice started, when we were alone — Bette had flown in from New Mexico, and Gloria and Grady were at the house most of each day, so we were rarely alone — I was bleary from sleeplessness and from remembering song lyrics and thinking of what to say to fill the silence. In desperation, I went to the bookshelf and took down the book of Wallace Stevens's poems that Dennis had given me on our wedding day, and read to him until he fell asleep. When he woke, moaning, I read some more. I told him I remembered reading poetry with him when we were first married. I told him I remembered everything.

We fell asleep together after that, and he woke crying out and I fed him and read some more, and we fell asleep again. I woke as the sunlight began to worm across the floor, and I was shocked that it was morning. The next time I fell asleep, I woke with a startle not to Dennis's moaning, but to a terrible silence. And before I looked over at him, I knew. I knew by the stillness of his body next to mine. A sob rose inside me, but then it stopped. This wasn't a time for crying — that would come. This was a blessed pocket of time, a time without activity or mourning. I held my husband in my arms and pressed my face to his face. I kissed his lips. I told him I loved him. I told

him, Thank you, over and over. I told him,
Thank you for my life.

AUTHOR'S NOTE

Though I've attempted to portray from memory and research certain historical events that took place in Florida during the years 1969–2004, this is a work of fiction. I've taken a few liberties with dates — most notably, in real life the incident with Arthur McDuffie and the subsequent trial took place in December 1979 and March–May 1980, respectively. I hope that my alteration of the dates causes no reader to feel that I've disrespected Mr. McDuffie's memory or the events that followed the trial. Also, Christo's *Surrounded Islands* were completed in May 1983.

Additionally, I've tried to portray as accurately as possible the flora and fauna of the area, but I'm no ecologist. Ultimately, my hope is that I've conveyed a general sense of life in South Florida during the years covered in the novel.

ACKNOWLEDGMENTS

This is my first novel, and as such it owes a debt not only to its editors but also to the people who inspired me to become a lifelong reader and writer, and who stubbornly and enthusiastically supported my efforts along the way. This book is a direct result of the generous love and support I've received from my father, Bill Daniel, who shared his passion for the ocean; and from my late mother, Sue Collier Daniel, who shared her passion for words and books.

For telling me what I was doing wrong and how to fix it, I thank my teachers at the Iowa Writers' Workshop: Joy Williams, Chris Offutt, Elizabeth McCracken, Ethan Canin, and the late Frank Conroy, whose advice on life and writing I refer to regularly. I also thank Connie Brothers, who called me in the spring of 1999 and told me I'd earned a place at the Workshop, then guided me through my years there.

511

For giving me the time to write the first half of this novel, I thank the Wisconsin Institute for Creative Writing, with special thanks to Jesse Lee Kercheval, who rented me a quiet and happy apartment and introduced me late in life to babysitting (and quite possibly gave me the courage to start a family of my own).

Many thanks to my excellent readers, who no doubt improved the book immeasurably: my talented friend Miriam Gershow; my father-in-law, John Stewart, Sr.; and my friends Kathy Ezell and David Wahlstad, who fixed numerous inaccuracies with regard to regional flora and fauna, and more. For taking the time to lend me their medical expertise, I thank Dr. Marvin Forland and Dr. Ellie Golestanian. Also, thanks to my friend Marse Dare, who lent me her name.

I'm grateful to my agent, Emily Forland, and my editor, Jennifer Barth, for taking on the book — and for telling me that they cried at the end.

To my dear friend Curtis Sittenfeld, who for a decade has generously shared with me her steady encouragement, tough love, and excellent guidance, and without whom I would still be spinning my literary wheels — I cannot thank you enough.

Finally, I thank my husband, John Stewart, who inspires me every day to write love stories — then goads me into actually doing it. No better feet under which to spread my dreams.

ABOUT THE AUTHOR

Susanna Daniel was born and raised in Miami, Florida, where she spent much of her childhood at her family's stilt house in Biscayne Bay. She is a graduate of Columbia University and the Iowa Writers' Workshop, and was a Fiction Fellow at the University of Wisconsin Institute for Creative Writing. She has taught writing at the University of Iowa and the University of Wisconsin-Madison. She currently lives in Madison, Wisconsin, with her husband and son, where during the long winter she dreams of the sun and the sea, and of jumping off the stilt house porch at high tide.